The
WOMAN *Who*
BREATHED
Two WORLDS

The
WOMAN *Who*
BREATHED
Two WORLDS

SELINA SIAK CHIN YOKE

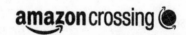

Material pertaining to Ipoh's founding has been used with the permission of Dr. Ho Tak Ming, author of *Ipoh: When Tin was King*.

Published by AmazonCrossing, Seattle

www.apub.com

Amazon, the Amazon logo, and AmazonCrossing are trademarks of Amazon.com, Inc., or its affiliates.

ISBN-13: 9781503939349
ISBN-10: 1503939340

Cover design by David Drummond

Printed in the United States of America

Dedicated to the memory of my Nyonya great-grandmother Chua Paik Choo

NOTES ON LANGUAGE

Languages and Dialects

The main characters speak a mix of the most common Chinese dialects in Malaysia (Hokkien, Hakka and Cantonese), which they intersperse with English or Malay.

Dialogue

Dialogue is used in this novel as an instrument to heighten the sense of place. Characters who have not gone to school speak in the way Malaysians normally speak (even in English); there is thus a reordering of words. A sentence such as 'I'll give it to you if you find me something I want' will become 'You find something I want, I give you'. However, as soon as a character attends school, his or her dialogue evolves into standard English.

Traditional Forms of Address

Family Relationships

In the novel, younger characters address older characters in traditional fashion, using titles which indicate the older person's rank and familial relationship. For example, you would address your father's second brother as 'Second Paternal Uncle', or your mother's youngest sister as 'Smallest Maternal Aunt'. Older characters, however, address younger characters by name.

Aunt and Uncle

The titles 'Aunt' and 'Uncle' denote respect. Even today, they are commonly used in Malaysia to politely address people who are not blood aunts or uncles.

Chinese Names

In Chinese names, the family names or surnames come before the name. Thus the protagonist's husband is called Wong Peng Choon, where Wong is his surname and Peng Choon his name.

Old Malay Spelling

Where Malay words occur, their spelling follows that which would have been used during the colonial era.

Malaysian Exclamations

In addition to the ubiquitous suffix 'lah', which all Malaysians sprinkle liberally in their sentences, characters in this novel use the exclamation 'ai-yahh' as a form of catharsis or to denote relief or surprise, as well as exclamations of Chinese origin when asking questions ('ah', 'mah' and 'moh').

Miscellaneous

In keeping with the spirit of the era in which they lived, characters occasionally use language which today would be considered politically incorrect.

PROLOGUE 1938

'In the days when genies roamed this valley of tin and tears, a warrior arose from among our people. His name was Hang Tuah, and he carried a magic sword.'

When I told my granddaughter the story of this fearsome warrior, it was a sultry Malayan afternoon, so hot that even the neighbourhood dogs would not settle. Through the open window came a baying chorus, eerie like sounds of the jungle, instead of the calming breezes I so loved, sublime breath of the gods that usually blew in from the limestone hills beyond.

The heat made me drowsy, though I could not sleep. I sat at the teak dressing table Mother had given me, now darkened by the years, counting what I had accumulated from a lifetime of toil: the silver and bronze coins with their raised heads of a white man, and the wads of bills, which I enjoyed tying and retying into thick bundles. By the time my granddaughter appeared, the tips of my fingers smelt of well-thumbed metal and greasy paper.

The heat had little effect on Lai Hin, who came in search of her afternoon tales with customary vigour. When she heard about Hang Tuah, she jumped down from her chair, placed both hands on her hips the way she had seen adults do and demanded, 'Ah Ma, he where get that sword?' (Paternal Grandma, from where did he get this sword?)

I had to smile. Lai Hin, then only three years old, was already displaying the verve for which I was famous. She unnerved the world with her intense almond-shaped eyes the way I had once done. My fire and fearless tongue were known throughout Ipoh, the Malayan mining town where I had lived most of my life.

This reputation had nearly been my downfall. Temper in a woman is only tolerated, never celebrated. Neighbours had hissed about the potent mix of blood in my veins, lethal for any girl. How would I ever find a husband?

Yet my spirit had served me well. In moments of despair I imagined myself a warrior with a golden sarong around my waist and metal glinting in my hands. Like the warrior Hang Tuah, I too was given a sword, but I had not recognised its powers until much later.

I told my son's daughter that Hang Tuah lived many moons ago. He had served the Sultan of Malacca, a town south of ours, which was once rich. Because of Hang Tuah's courage, the Sultan had sent him to visit a kingdom in Indonesia. There, Hang Tuah was challenged to a duel by a local warrior. The local man always carried the same sword – a magic sword, some said – and had never lost a fight.

Hang Tuah faced his opponent unafraid; he did not know what he was fighting. Only as the hours wore on did he realise he had an unusual adversary. The men were evenly matched. Neither would give in, and the hours turned into days. When seven days passed, the people knew they were witnessing the battle of their generation.

Weak with thirst, Hang Tuah fell to the ground. Before him was the Indonesian warrior, holding the curved blade which had killed so many. In those moments Hang Tuah thought of his home and the Sultan who had sent him. He remembered his family, his friends and the people who had kept faith. He could not die defeated in a foreign land.

Heaving himself off the ground, Hang Tuah leapt into the air so high that he stunned the local warrior. With desperate effort, Hang Tuah kicked the magic sword from his opponent's hand. No one had ever before relieved the Indonesian warrior of his sword, and the blade came alive, making a swooshing noise as it twirled as if flung, swirling, whipping the air, cutting through wind, then swinging around like an echo and coming straight back for its owner's heart.

The people, astonished, murmured Hang Tuah's name with reverence. The kingdom's ruler went down on his knees as he handed Hang Tuah the victim's magic sword. 'You have proven yourself worthy. This sword will now follow your command.'

My granddaughter's eyes were wide open by then. 'Ah Ma, this sword look like what?'

I told her the magic sword was a *keris*, a dagger carved in the Malay style, its blade curved into thirteen waves to better kill a man. Like others, this *keris* had been hammered, ground on stone, smoothed with beeswax, beaten with boiled rice, soaked in coconut water and rubbed with lime juice. But the *keris* had also been anointed in a secret substance that gave it magical powers.

'Ah Ma,' my granddaughter cried, her mouth agape, 'I also want a magic sword!'

I looked at Lai Hin's thick eyebrows, knotted in a frown, at those dark brown eyes drinking in my stories. Her ancestors would fight for her spirit, but so too would the white devils who had come to rule. They had taken first our land and then our souls. The battles my granddaughter faced would be fierce, and I had little faith our ancestors would win. Many of us did not even know what we were fighting.

It was my best friend, Siew Lan, who first put the idea into my head. 'One day maybe . . . no more Nyonya,' she had whispered, referring to our heritage. Siew Lan's face, etched with deep lines, looked even sadder then, as if by saying the words she would hasten the end. She sipped tea as she said this, cradling in both her palms the Nyonya cup with pink borders and green dragons she loved. I only half listened, never imagining that our age-old practices would ever be forgotten.

Yet as I savoured the smells from our kitchen that afternoon, of ginger being sliced and coconut milk being steamed, as I listened to the scraping, pounding and grinding and saw in my mind's eye the vivid blue of butterfly pea flowers smashed against black stone, I knew that what my friend had said was coming to pass. My eldest son, Weng Yu, Lai Hin's father, had become lost. His dreams took him away. My hopes rested less with my son than with his daughter and the other little ones, who still clamoured to hear our stories.

'Lai Hin,' I said, 'you must listen to Ah Ma. Then like Ah Ma you one day also will find your sword. This you must never lose.'

Stroking my grandchild's hair, thick like mine, I resolved to pass on to her the wisdom of our ancestors. At this late hour the time had come for me to open up, to tell my stories to a scribe and speak my heart.

PART I:
MY EARLY YEARS
1878–1898

1

I was always in trouble. I never went out of my way to look for trouble; it found me.

The first time Mother took me to the village temple with Elder Sister, when I was given a lit joss-stick I wondered how hard I could shake my stick. Not hard at all, it turned out, as the stick flew straight out of my hands and on to Kuan Yin's marble forehead. On striking the Goddess of Mercy, its burning embers left traces of ash dribbling down her flawless white nose. Kuan Yin was smudged grey, while Mother's face turned the shade of her curries. Amidst disapproving stares, she hurried towards the village priest and breathed furiously into his ears. Afterwards Mother grabbed my right hand and dragged me away. Once we were home, she smacked both my hands and kept me inside the house for what seemed a long time. Elder Sister told me later it was just a week, but it felt like a whole year.

'Your daughter is small Tiger – what you expect?' the other women said to Mother. They spoke in soft voices, but their glances were furtive. Mother's friends called me wild and ill-tempered, traits they attributed to the time of my birth: the 4,575th year of the lunar cycle – the year of the Earth Tiger. Girl Tigers were said to bring bad luck and trouble, a reputation to which I lived up.

As soon as I had served my punishment, I rushed outside to see my friends. We village children spent our time terrorising little creatures, chasing whatever we could see, even butterflies. Like typhoon winds, we would tear along the fields with a discarded net a fisherman's wife had given us. Its wire mesh was fractured on one side. The butterflies would flit in panic, and we had to pounce like mad dogs to make sure our beautiful targets didn't squirm away.

Once, we managed to catch the stray village cat. Father had told me that cats could swim, but I had never seen a cat swim. I thought that if we threw the stray into the pond near our field, we would know whether Father had told the truth. To our amazement the cat stayed afloat. When it crawled out of the water, its blue eyes were frozen and its black head had turned white from the bath. The cat's pale yellow fur clung to its stiff body, as if it had been singed. Fortunately Mother never found out about the cat.

But when I fought with my brother Chong Jin, who was a year younger, Mother learnt everything. Chong Jin was the only boy in our family and Mother's favourite. For him she saved rice and choice pieces of meat. He received new clothes before any of us, even before Elder Sister, though she was three years older. Mother always worried about my brother. 'Chong Jin, you must eat more,' she would say, or 'Chong Jin, you today so pale. Go out, take fresh air,' as if he were a sickly child who needed special attention. Elder Sister accepted this state of affairs, but I chafed at the bedroom my brother was given as his own and the chicken drumsticks Mother piled on his banana leaf. 'Don't take what not yours!' Mother yelled when she caught me trying to steal a juicy lump from Chong Jin's leaf. I looked up at Father, but his handsome face was staring out of the window. Father remained studiously silent, his large Adam's apple unmoving. The house was Mother's domain; she ran it as she wished, and Father would never have interfered in something so trivial. It took far more for him to step in.

An opportunity came the day I discovered that my favourite butterfly, a rare species it had taken us months to catch, was missing. The butterfly had khaki-brown wings dotted with a beautiful turquoise. It was my most treasured possession, sheltered inside its own box, unlike the other game chips that were stuffed roughly into the wooden box Mother had given me. Each game we played had a winner, who was entitled to a chip. None of us had much, so we collected colour and life: sweet wrappers and cigarette packets with bright pictures, as well as little creatures, including butterflies. Those were my favourites because of their delicate wings.

Among us children I was known for my skill at picking up game chips. I did not always win them, but I had an eye for finding new things no one else had thought of, which I would then trade for what the others had won in our games. It was I who introduced butterflies. It was also I who led my friends towards the sea and its treasures. I have always had an uncanny feel for what others would like. This knack for spotting opportunity came naturally, which is just as well considering the twists and turns my life has taken.

To get my hands on that rare butterfly, I had traded in a set of seashells from the beach near Songkhla, my parents' village. The shells were shiny and smooth against my skin, and I had had to walk barefoot for many afternoons, pressing my soles into sand as hot as a steam iron, to find them. I loved rubbing my shells, but I coveted the rare butterfly even more. My brother, Chong Jin, did too. He always asked to stroke it, but when I saw how roughly he handled its wings, I stopped letting him hold it. My brother demanded that I give him the butterfly. 'You find something I want, I give you,' I retorted. I thought the transaction unlikely. Chong Jin simply didn't have the patience for finding treasure, nor did he like work.

When the butterfly went missing from its box, I thought immediately of Chong Jin. I ran into his room and grabbed him by the shoulders.

'You put where?' I shrieked.

My brother's eyeballs darted shiftily. 'I not know you talk what,' he replied, as if he didn't care.

'Tell me! Tell me!' I cried, pummelling Chong Jin's chest with both fists. His screams brought Mother into the room just in time to see me pull my brother's hair.

She smacked my hands. 'Stop it!'

Because I thought Mother would understand, I told her the whole story, even showing her what I had hoarded in the wooden box that had been her gift. There was a hushed silence, the first time I saw Mother speechless. Instead of the hairpins and combs she had expected, Mother found stringy spiders, lizards with tails still intact and shrivelled butterflies. When her fingers dug deeper, they clutched the cards and smooth-edged pebbles I had been hoping to trade for another butterfly.

'You win this all from the other children?' Mother asked with a questioning stare.

I nodded. 'Also exchange some,' I said, my voice suddenly feeble.

'You not take things that not yours?'

I shook my head.

'When I speak to you, you answer properly!' Mother shouted. Her thin lips pursed dangerously close together and a flame rose up – the one that would become a large fire if untamed. Mother's nostrils were flaring.

'No, Mother, all mine,' I replied hurriedly.

Satisfied, Mother turned to Chong Jin. 'You, you take Second Sister's butterfly or not?' she asked in a tone that brooked no lies.

Hanging his head, my brother murmured 'Yes' as softly as a cat pawing. From beneath his mattress he brought out my butterfly, its beautiful wings badly creased on one side and split on the other. Crying, I snatched my turquoise treasure from him.

'Ai-yahh, Chye Hoon, don't cry. Only a butterfly,' Mother said, folding me into her sarong. 'You, Chong Jin,' Mother spat, her face dark. 'What kind of son I bring up? Tell me, what kind? A thief? Father get home that time you wait.'

'Yes, thief!' I repeated. But Mother was quick to swivel round.

'Who tell you to laugh? Next time you no hit your brother.' With that, Mother disappeared, leaving Chong Jin and me with a sick feeling in our stomachs.

When Father returned, Mother shepherded him into their bedroom. The agitated rise and fall of her voice could be felt on the outside verandah, where Chong Jin and I huddled, not daring to speak. Father came looking for us, his face like a thunderous monsoon cloud. He called my brother inside. While I remained on the verandah, I heard the swishing of air and Chong Jin's screams. With a pounding heart I stood beneath the shade of Mother's mango trees, awaiting my turn.

It never came. I was spared because I was a girl and I had not stolen. My brother, on the other hand, ended up with a bottom streaked red where the skin was bruised, and palms flushed from the ruler Father had also used.

Chong Jin sobbed through the meal. 'You all, stealing not just naughty . . . stealing is bad. Father always cane,' Mother announced. Though her eyes were full of sorrow, she gave Chong Jin extra fish. Father ate in silence. Elder Sister and I kept our heads down.

That sombre dinner marked the first time the cane had been used in our house and the only time I was not in trouble. In fact, I overheard Mother telling Father, 'Pity Chye Hoon ours a girl – maybe she will be good in business.' It was a remark Mother would remember years later.

In those days Songkhla was a sleepy village where everyone knew every-one else. In my mind, much about Songkhla is shrouded in a film of light golden dust, yellowed like an old photograph. I have forgotten many things, but I remember the stars dotting the night sky like ants and the stories Mother told us each afternoon.

Mother spoke of wondrous things. In her world suns travelled on golden carriages, causing the earth to burn, and men turned into tigers. She had said this to stop us from wandering into the jungle near our house. 'You three, jungle very dangerous, got wild animals. Don't run here there by yourselves-ah!'

One day I asked Mother where we came from. She, Father and everyone in their families – had we all been born in Songkhla? Sitting as still as a lake on a calm night, Mother began to tell us about our ancestors. We heard that Father's great-grandfather many times over had been a trader from Amoy in southern China. He arrived a long time ago in a boat with a huge eye painted on its prow. 'Like wooden junks that we sometimes see off the coast,' Mother said with a faraway look, which told me she was picturing the scene in her mind.

I had seen how rough the South China Sea could become, had smelt the salt in its air and the fish from its depths. I marvelled at the courage of Father's ancestor. He had set sail with the monsoon winds, staying only a few months; when the winds changed, he had boarded his boat and returned to China. He continued this for several seasons, sailing to and fro. After a while he settled in Siam. There were others like him, Chinese men who chose new lives. They married local women and became Siamese.

The first time Mother told our ancestral story, she paused when I was least expecting it.

'Our ancestors,' Mother whispered, 'were different.'

I waited, watching for any change of expression in Mother's eyes. Mother had eyes I wanted for myself: brown and clear with dark seeds in the middle. The seeds in her eyes sparkled when she was animated.

Mother's upper eyelids had deep-set creases, considered attractive in our part of the world – unlike my poor Chinese eyes. Mother winked at me, and her tone led me to expect treasure.

'They married Siamese Malay women and became Babas and Nyonyas,' Mother said, almost to herself.

'What mean that?' I asked.

Mother answered that she was a Nyonya and that I too would grow up to be one. She said I would dress in Malay clothes but worship Chinese gods, wear my hair in a chignon and become known for spicy cooking. She told me Father was a Baba, equally at home in Mandarin-collared jackets or with sarongs around his waist, comfortable speaking many languages – Hokkien, Malay and Siamese – and, with the arrival of the white devils, even English.

I clung to Mother's every word. Her story gave a name to what was already familiar to me – Nyonya – and for my Father, Baba. By then I was accustomed to the languages in our house, each with its own set of sounds and intonations: to Hokkien, spoken often and always loudly by people who opened their mouths wide, as if the words had to be spat out; Malay, soft and even in its tone; and Siamese, with its nasal high-pitched torrent of words. I was used to seeing Mother go about her routine. She pounded chillies for aromatic dishes during the day and did needlework in the evening, stringing colourful beads by the light of the kerosene lamp. These activities, part of being a Nyonya, seemed as natural as the monsoon rains.

Unlike Mother, Father said little. He preferred singing to talking. When Father opened and closed his mouth, out would float a rich voice that lulled you into calmness. Even more amazing was his Adam's apple, a prominent sac which wobbled like the red bags below our rooster's throat. Once, while Father was going through his repertoire of Chinese and Siamese tunes, I reached out to feel his Adam's apple. Father merely smiled. He let my fingers touch the hard knob before putting me down so that he could continue with his song.

Though Father had eyes like mine – almond-shaped Chinese eyes with no double creases over the eyelids – I thought him handsome. Father's hair was the black of coals and his skin smooth, unlike that of other men, whose faces resembled Songkhla's streets – full of unfilled holes. Father's teeth, white and even, had no gaps between them. He was taller too and better dressed, his Mandarin jackets and tunics made by Songkhla's tailor.

Father was the village teacher. We lived near the schoolhouse in a wooden building with the thatched attap roof so prevalent in those days. Every morning Father would leave our house while the air outside was cool, and he would return in the afternoon when the sun was already high in the sky. After lunch he would sit at the dining table with stacks of books, two bottles of ink and a set of quill pens, and begin scrawling on his papers.

'Teach me write, teach me write!' I pleaded as I climbed on to a chair to watch Father work.

From their bedroom, Mother's stern voice would reach my ears. 'Come here. No disturb Father.' To keep us amused, Mother began her stories. But she always fell asleep. I would sneak back to Father then, to be indulged in ways Mother would never have dreamt of. Father was content to let me watch him dip his quill pen into ink; I would sit riveted by the grand strokes over sheets of paper.

I begged Father to teach me to write, but no matter what I did he refused. 'Writing is not for girls,' he would say in his deep voice. When I picked up a quill and tried to copy what he did, Father's jaw tensed. His Adam's apple stopped moving, a sure sign of displeasure.

The more Father refused to teach me to write, the more determined I was to learn. Somehow I preferred to start by writing rather than reading. I had no quill pen or ink, but I had sticks and sand. In between climbing trees and chasing live creatures, I would pretend to write in the sand. In order to write properly, I had to see from close up what Father's fingers were doing. I decided to climb on to the table.

Father's hands ceased their rhythmic movement. 'You should not be on the table, Chye Hoon,' he said. Nothing happened, though, that first time, or the second or even the third. Soon Father was happy to let me perch near his right hand, from where I stared in awe at his squiggles. The next day I would reproduce the same squiggles in the sand, without any idea what they meant.

One day Father wrote complicated characters I had never seen before. I waited until he had left the table to find a book before putting my head so close to his sheet of paper that my breath brushed every curve. Too soon I heard Father's footsteps, and I scrambled into my original position. On stretching a leg out, I promptly overturned Father's inkpot.

'Chye Hoon!' he bellowed. Father never raised his voice; when he did, we knew we were in trouble.

Mother came rushing in, eyes still powdered with sleep. 'Is your fault!' Mother said accusingly. 'You let her sit there.' Father clamped his jaw without saying anything, but the look he gave me was full of disappointment. When I felt Father's anguish, I was sorry for the trouble I had caused. I still wanted to write but thereafter could only watch from afar. I would look longingly at Father's lone figure, with only an ugly black stain on the dining table for company.

At the time there were changes taking place in the world beyond which even we children were aware of. We'd had a handful of visitors in Songkhla who looked as white as the ghosts that were said to roam our jungles. My friends had gone up to pinch their skins to see whether they were real, before laughing and running away.

From village chatter I knew that the white visitors were not well regarded. This singling out of a group in Songkhla was unusual, because our village was a melting pot into which all could be thrown. Anyone was welcome, provided the person respected local customs. Everyone married everyone else, and no one paid attention to race or religion.

It was different with this new breed of foreigners. They did not settle among us. When they first appeared, they were a curiosity. By the time I came along, their aloof presence was already resented. Never outwardly, of course, though it wasn't hard to peel away the veneer of politeness. They were casually referred to as 'white devils' in Chinese, occasionally as 'red-haired devils', and in Malay more politely as 'white people', but always in such a way as to imply undesirability.

As time went by, hushed conversations took place between the adults. Sometimes I caught snatches about happenings in the other Malay states south of us, where the white devils had arrived years previously. I once overheard Father say that there were many more of them now, and they had even started to rule in some areas. It was then that he began his English lessons. Father bought books with mysterious writing, a script very different to the signs around us. On his one rest day he would go to a friend's house for English lessons. When he returned in the afternoon, Father would sit in his bamboo chair on the verandah.

The verandah was his refuge. Like the rest of our house, it was raised above the ground on solid wooden poles and remained cool through the day. Father often sang in his chair, but after the arrival of the white devils he became preoccupied. He would sit like Lord Buddha, absorbed within his own thoughts.

One day we were visited by a man who dressed like Father. He wore a Chinese jacket and skirt but spoke in a strange accent and didn't understand Siamese. Mother told me to call the man Cousin-Uncle Lim. She said he was a distant cousin of Father's and that he came from a place called Penang. He must have been a very distant relative, because I could not tell how he was related to us. When Cousin-Uncle Lim was there, Father and Mother spent a long time talking to him.

After he left, my parents spoke in whispers. I tried to eavesdrop from behind the kitchen wall, but they kept their voices low, and I could not hear much. Change was in the air – I could smell it.

I grew nervous. I woke up talking in my sleep. Then one morning before daybreak I went walking around our house. Mother followed me; she said my eyes were closed, but I navigated without bumping into furniture. My sleepwalking set off warning bells for Mother.

That night she and Father gathered us children together and informed us matter-of-factly that we would soon be leaving Songkhla. With his Adam's apple bobbing, Father told us there would be a better future for us in Penang, where Cousin-Uncle Lim lived. Father explained where Penang was – 'Far south of here. It's controlled by the British.'

'Oh, white devils?' I asked, adopting the same sneer I had observed among the adults.

Father smiled, showing off his even teeth. 'You mustn't call them that, Chye Hoon,' he said.

I couldn't see why. After all, he and Mother had always used the term in the past, but there was a change in Father's tone that night, a deference that had not been there before. He talked enthusiastically about the 'British' and the development they had brought. 'They are opening tin mines and rubber plantations. There are new schools and hospitals and plenty of jobs for men like me who speak English.'

I looked at Elder Sister and Chong Jin. Like me, they sat dazed. I thought about never again seeing the field where we played each day and began to sob. 'Chye Hoon, don't cry,' Father said, his rich voice enveloping me in its cloak of safety. 'This is for your own good. We are moving to Penang for you, children.'

But when Father stopped speaking, I remembered my friends and my butterflies. 'I no want to go!' I wailed, until Elder Sister and Chong Jin also cried.

It was Mother who put us out of our misery. 'Ai-yahh! You three, stop it! You ride elephant.'

'Elephant?' I asked, tears instantly drying, taken over by rising excitement. Elephants walked our village streets, but seeing how they trampled on everything in their path, we kept out of their way. Now we were told we would soon be riding our own elephants. Mother encouraged this new-found fervour; she didn't want us dwelling on what we would leave behind. She kept saying we were off to a distant land to seek our fortune, just like our ancestors had done.

Just before we left Songkhla, a water buffalo fight took place. It divided our neighbours. Such fights were big events; in the weeks preceding, villagers would speculate about what would happen once the bulls were released inside the makeshift pen that was the fighting ring.

The buffalo owners, two of Songkhla's wealthiest farmers, shrewdly called the impending fight 'the battle of our lifetime'. Each bull was said to be a ferocious fighter, inclined to charge at the slightest opportunity. For weeks beforehand, while rice was being harvested from the paddy fields, the villagers spoke of little else. Father grumbled that the discussions seemed more heated than usual, and some men lost their heads. Our closest neighbour across the field, an easy-going man who loved to whistle, bet several months' wages on one of the bulls. He was a hired hand in Songkhla's general store, but he dreamt of being rich. In the fevered atmosphere he was sure he would win.

On the afternoon of the big day, when the fishermen had long been home, the whole village gathered in anticipation. It being my first water buffalo fight, I was eager for a good place at the enclosure. Mother, unfortunately, never liked getting anywhere early. 'Waste of time!' she would exclaim. 'Just longer to wait!' By the time we arrived, the ring was already crowded. We fought our way through, my younger brother

Chong Jin on Father's shoulders, Elder Sister and I holding tightly on to Mother's hands. We found our neighbours in a far corner, leaning against the wooden fence and talking loudly. He – the man from the general store – was red-faced, as if he had been drinking, while his wife, pregnant again, was slumped, so that the fence posts bent under her weight. Their children stood further along, where the barrier remained sturdy. As soon as Mother released my hand, I ran to join them, latching on to the first of the three rungs for a better view.

I could hardly believe that the creatures tied up inside the ring were the fighters everyone had talked so much about. I saw two black beasts with little funnels dangling down, like the one my brother Chong Jin had. The bulls stood placidly inside the pen. Though huge, neither looked fierce; each twitched its ears and blinked gentle brown eyes, first at me, then at each other, in a friendly sign of greeting.

When the bulls were finally untied and let loose, neither knew what to do. Even shouts of 'Rao, rao!' couldn't arouse them. They stood staring dumbly into the air and at the people shouting. One of the beasts started to sniff the other's rear end but quickly backed away. When it dug its right hind hoof into the earth, I noticed how dirty its hooves were from digging all day in mud and earth.

The bulls could not be encouraged to approach one another. When they eventually did, it was not to fight but to smell the ground beneath a tree. By then the crowd had grown impatient. Their screams were loud; even Father, normally a serene man, joined in, his deep bass voice echoing across the enclosure.

Without warning, one buffalo took its fellow buffalo by surprise. The attacking buffalo locked its black horns with the other's and tried to lift the gentler bull off its feet, driving everyone wild.

Next minute the bull which had been attacked raised its head, took one look at its opponent and decided to come straight towards me, staring with terror in its eyes. I screamed, jumping off my place on the fence. It turned out I need not have worried, because the running buffalo veered in another direction. The two ran around the ring until they found a hole through which they were able to squeeze. The bulls were chased in every direction by villagers carrying coir ropes, led by a tall paddy farmer with burnished skin who was the fastest runner in Songkhla.

Our neighbour was not among them. With his head buried in both hands, the man from the general store sat crumpled on the grass. In between terrifying silences he emitted growls and inhuman cries, like the noises we heard from the jungle – the sound of a hundred elephants dying, according to Mother. I stared at our neighbour, fearing the worst. But when Mother went to put her arms around his wife, the man lifted a hand, and I saw that he would live. He was only crying, the first grown man I had seen with tears on his cheeks. His children – my friends – looked away.

When we reached home, the air was brittle. The knob on Father's throat tensed as he declared, 'It's best to work instead of gambling and dreaming of easy money.'

Mother nodded. 'Yes, Husband, I know . . .' But when she saw that Father was unmoved, Mother's glare turned icy. Her thin lips tightened, curving decidedly downwards. I held my breath. 'Have heart, Husband,' Mother finally erupted. 'They have children!' In the distance cicadas screeched.

That night Mother and Father had their biggest argument ever. The floorboards of our wooden house shook under the weight of their words, and Elder Sister and I had to draw blankets over our heads. It was morning before calm returned. When our neighbour's wife next came to our house, Mother handed her some rice and a portion of the chicken curry Kapitan she had made, rich with chillies and coconut. Mother had won; we shared what we could with our neighbours, but it wasn't much, and my friends grew skinnier. Sometimes their stomachs rumbled when we played. It was the first time I had known anyone hungry.

◆ ◆ ◆

Our last days in Songkhla were a blur. One minute I was happily collecting butterflies, the next I was gathering my belongings together. In no time at all we were in dense jungle, rocked by lumbering beasts and bitten by leeches. My elephant was called Thongkum and he was bald, like the monks in Songkhla. The journey took such a long time that by the end the leeches no longer bothered me. When we finally arrived at Province Wellesley in the Straits Settlements, I bid farewell to Thongkum and faced, across a narrow strip of water, the island that was to be our new home.

It loomed out of the sea, its hills curved like the back of a pig: Pulau Pinang, which in Malay means 'the island of the betel nut palm'.

At our first glimpse of Penang, we children jumped up and down, pointing repeatedly. 'Look, look! Over there!' Father and Mother, though, were silent. They stood staring at the island across the water. The decision to leave Songkhla had been theirs, but at the moment when a new life beckoned they became wary of taking the last step.

Eventually Father hired two sampans, small wooden ferries, to row us across. Each had a large eye painted on its prow – just like the boat his ancestor had sailed in. Our sampans were steered by Chinese men, two in each boat – one at the front, the other at the rear. The men wore conical hats, inverted like bowls. On their scalps hung pieces of rough cloth, stained brown from years of faithful use, which shielded their necks from the sun.

It was late afternoon when we set off, but our rowers began wiping their sweat after just minutes. For us passengers, though, the ride was magical. We sat low in our boats, lulled by the soft, rhythmic flapping of oars, which made me feel a kinship with the ancestors who had once crossed waters.

When we came close to shore, the strong smell of mud from mangrove swamps tickled my nose. And then I saw them – the betel nut trees which gave the island its name. They emerged like a dream, fringing every bay and cove. Their trunks swayed lazily, slowly left, then slowly right, as their long leaves were swished by the gusts blowing in from faraway seas.

By the time we rowed into George Town, the waters had turned blue-black, but the jetty, made of stone, was still teeming with life. The Chinese labourers whom we referred to as 'coolies' scurried about, moving gunny sacks and crates that filled the air with the familiar aroma of cloves, pepper and drying coconut. Indian men sat forward on bullock carts, touting for business. Everywhere there was yelling and jostling and bartering, yet a strange order prevailed, as if the goods and people and animals moved to unspoken rules.

A sheltered waiting area stood near the water. It was a large room flanked by brick arches and an attap-thatched roof, where Father's relatives stood waiting. Distant aunts and uncles who smelt of fresh soap and powder came to greet us. My younger brother, Chong Jin, and I stumbled out of our sampan, so tired we had to be given piggyback rides to the home of a friend of Father's, where we would remain until we found a house of our own. Through a haze I saw that the broad streets of the town were lined with betel nut palms and rain trees. In the distance an imposing square mansion with many windows stood apart – the town hall I learnt later. Until my arrival in Penang, I had never seen anything so grand. It even had its own grounds, on which the grass was neatly trimmed, like a green rug.

I have only one clear memory of that first night – the bath Mother gave me. I was exhausted. In my mind Mother's shadow, cast by the single kerosene lamp in that strange kitchen, has mingled with soapy water. I can still picture the bright moon visible through the open air well, hear the clack-clacking of lizards scuttling about dark walls. In the rooms beyond chattering voices reverberated, while around me, stacked neatly on the floor and on wooden cabinets, were the utensils that would one day be my weapons.

2

Shortly after our arrival in Penang, I met the ting-ting man.

Then as now, travelling vendors would battle heat, rain and tropical thunderstorms to ply their wares. Every hawker had a signature call which told us exactly who had arrived. The poetic cry 'Walk faster-lah, wei!' meant we would see a devil with thick eyebrows curving into bushes at the sides who touted Penang's famous prawn noodles. The sound of Chinese castanets – of wood beating against hollow bamboo pole – heralded wonton dumplings. The simple clanging of a porcelain spoon on a bowl announced that soft-boiled bean curd was at hand, always doused in sugar cane syrup by the thin hunchback who sold it.

The ting-ting man brought with him a new sound, a metallic banging I had never heard before.

We were living on Ah Kwee Street, in one of those old brick shophouses with an open verandah – called a five-foot way – in front and a door which opened on to a street at the rear. The five-foot ways were corridors running down entire streets of shophouses, five feet in width, which became a life unto themselves. Five-foot ways were used by everyone for everything: by the nosy for gossip, by children for their games, by hawkers to sell their wares and by vagrants for shelter.

The windows at the front of our house looked out on to the five-foot way. Our windows were mere holes in the walls but beautifully finished, with wooden burglar bars running vertically downwards and outside shutters painted in light blue. The shutters were carved with the motif of a bird, its wings outstretched – free, like my younger brother and the neighbourhood boys. I, in contrast, was imprisoned once we reached Penang. I had to content myself with peering out on tiptoe, which I did so frequently that Mother would yell, 'Stand there some more, you get stuck to the window. Come inside-lah!'

The evening the ting-ting man came, I grabbed the window bars as usual for balance. I must have appeared strange from the outside . . . half of a little black head bobbing unsteadily, a pair of almond-shaped eyes beneath, the dark seeds in their middle darting from side to side, observing everything. Those eyes were what I was known for along Ah Kwee Street; it was said they could pierce a person when focused. 'Your daughter-ah! So small yet so big courage. Not scared to look,' the neighbours would tell Mother. This, I knew, was no compliment. More than once Mother had scolded me, but my curiosity proved impossible to curb.

The ting-ting man, with the enormous tray over his head and a metal hammer and chisel in his hands, was a tantalising sight. Children and their mothers trailed behind him like cows behind a cowherd. The man shuffled to the five-foot way on the other side of our street, where he perched on a stool. It became difficult to see much else, though we still heard his jangling. By then everyone had joined me at the window, including Father.

'Mother, that person selling what?' I asked.

It was Father who replied. 'I think it must be some kind of sweets,' he said in his deep voice, looking not at me but at the ting-ting man. 'Not good for children.' With those words Father turned, and his tall figure disappeared back inside our house. This was typical – Father had made his opinion known and saw no reason to discuss the matter further. The buying of sweets was neither important nor interesting to him; it was a 'woman's thing', best left to Mother while he took a second look at his newspaper. That's what Father did in the evenings: reread part of the paper while there was enough natural light. Papers then were just a handful of sheets. Father told me he read the *Penang Gazette*, and on the few occasions when I walked with him to buy the paper, I realised he was one of a handful of locals – mainly Baba men – who read it to improve their English.

After Father had gone, I noticed Mother glancing at me. I only had a fleeting glimpse of her face, but I sensed we would soon be going outside. She looked relaxed: her thin lips were loose, hinting at a smile. 'Go look only, maybe no harm' was all she said.

It was a lovely evening. We were still at that magical hour just before darkness falls in Malaya when the skies are a pale blue but the heat of the day has already subsided. The streets buzzed with people out on gentle strolls, all relaxing, or 'eating wind' as we liked to call it. As we approached the group opposite, Hean Lee, a tall boy my age who lived a few houses away, was already heading home. Like his mother and siblings, he held a brown paper packet in his hand. Hean Lee gave me a wide grin. There was a glint in his eyes, and his face seemed more puffed up than usual. He was red from ear to ear, as if he had just seen something special, like stars dancing.

I squeezed my way to the front of the crowd. There in the middle sat a man with a wrinkled face, chipping away at a layer of hardened brown sugar on a tray. Its colour reminded me of *gula melaka* – a deliciously sweet, viscous ingredient I often saw in our kitchen and into which I would dip my fingers when no one was looking. With his metal tools, the wrinkled man broke off small natural rocks of roughly equal size. *Ting-ting . . . Ting-ting.* The sound of his tools was what we had heard in our house. It was a slow, laborious process. My eyes remained glued to the man's hands. Down went his hammer, the chisel hacking into layer after horizontal layer, pieces shearing off as his fingers moved down, down, down, then up again, his rhythm unchanging, the pace uncompromising. I was amazed at how he used just a hammer and simple chisel to carve off sugary rock, each piece small enough to fit into a child's mouth and each more or less of the same size.

Every time he finished preparing an order, the man would place the freshly cut candy into a brown paper packet. He was happy to sell however much you wanted – even a half cent's worth, which in those days bought enough for a child.

I turned around, looking for Mother. She was standing near the back chatting with a neighbour. I was desperate for a taste, but I knew that Mother did not approve of other people's sweets. I spent a few minutes studying her.

At the time I was growing up fast. I knew I was the only child who dared ask for things; Elder Sister was less spirited and Chong Jin still young, so they relied on me to take the lead. With Mother I understood I had to choose my moments. That evening my timing could not have been better, because Mother was in a good mood. She had made Father's favourite dish of Siamese laksa: noodles served in a rich spicy broth, tangy and full of pungent chillies, garnished with leeks and cucumbers that had been pickled in white vinegar for two days. Father had been delighted, so Mother too was happy. But she was pregnant again; with Mother being more temperamental, it was difficult to predict her reactions. Still, I thought I would try. I wiggled my way to where she was.

'Mother,' I said in the nicest tone I could manage while pulling gently at her sarong. I glanced up obliquely, not wanting to meet her eyes. 'Mother . . . those sweets, we can try or not?'

'Ai-yahh, Chye Hoon!' she replied, looking at the man's tray and at the children sucking noisily on their candy. 'Eat so many sweet things, your teeth all will rot.'

'Mother, just small piece-lah?' I persisted. I felt Mother's hand on my head, stroking my hair.

'Chye Hoon-ah, you listen to me. Maybe next week, okay?'

'Maybe next week' was one of Mother's choice phrases. I think she hoped I would have forgotten by the time next week came along, though I never did. The initial no made me even more determined to get what I wanted. That evening I didn't have to try too hard after all. Flushed from her day's triumph, Mother soon relented. 'Okay-lah, Chye Hoon, this week you all good, so you can share one packet. One packet only-ah!'

It was when Mother started speaking to the ting-ting man that I noticed how ugly he was. He had a terrifying black mole just below his lower lip on the left side, from which three straggly hairs grew, one longer than the other two. With his withered skin and teeth blackened by decay, the ting-ting man was even more fascinating than the devil who sold prawn noodles. He looked old, yet his body seemed strong – which it must have been, given the distances he walked each day.

When the ting-ting man handed me a packet, I did not take it. I could not stop staring at the hairs on his mole and the pockmarks on his face, large indentations where the skin was no longer smooth but had become grainy like sand. 'Take-lah,' he said.

If truth be told, the ting-ting candy itself was disappointing, but the man never failed to draw us. The speed of his fingers combined with the horror of his face proved addictive.

Over the years we got to know the ting-ting man. His name was Ah Boey and he came from Fukien province, just like our Chinese ancestors. Ah Boey told Mother he had also been transported to Malaya in a wooden boat, but the journey sounded less romantic when I heard it from him. On his boat the men had to take turns standing during the nights, because not everyone had space to lie down. After just a day at sea he began to vomit from the stench. All they had for a toilet was a single bucket they took turns emptying. When they ran out of water, they relied on the South China Sea for their daily cups of tea. Disease took many lives; Ah Boey himself barely survived. When he arrived in Penang, he crawled off the boat a walking skeleton.

Even when we knew him, Ah Boey remained skinny. He often walked naked from the waist up, so that his ribs were visible. I once asked him why he did not wear clothes, to Mother's horror – 'Chye Hoon, if you no learn better manners, you not find husband!' Turning to Ah Boey, Mother apologised profusely on my behalf, but Ah Boey only grinned, waving his hand to indicate he had not been offended.

Ah Boey told us one of his uncles had made and sold ting-ting candy in China. That, he said, was how he had learnt the trade. It had not been his intended business when he set sail for Malaya. He worked at the dock first, loading and unloading steam ships, but he had been a virtual slave, unable to save even a cent, as all his wages went on food. Somehow – Ah Boey did not provide details – he managed to gain release from his boss after a year, and the idea of making ting-ting candy came to him. Ah Boey claimed that his sugar concoction was based on a secret family recipe. I didn't believe him. Ah Boey was full of far-fetched stories, and it was hard to know how much one could trust him.

Then Ah Boey stopped coming to our street. There was no warning, no goodbye, nothing to indicate he was going away – he simply disappeared. In time another man took over the sale of ting-ting candy on the island. We found out that Ah Boey had left Penang to try his luck at tin mining. In those days there was a rush to develop tin mines on the mainland. A mass of Chinese men went off to seek their fortunes, Ah Boey among them. I didn't know then what working in a tin mine meant. In my mind Ah Boey would soon become rich. I pictured him, ugly as ever, in a shiny blue silk suit with a smart Mandarin collar just like the one Father wore to school.

3

By the time I was eight, my three younger sisters had all been born. It was thought unnecessary to send any of us girls to school. What was the point, since we would only get married and have children? In our close-knit Nyonya community the emphasis was on us girls becoming skilled in women's work: cooking, sewing and homemaking.

One day Mother took me aside and in a firm voice told me, 'Chye Hoon, you want to be a Nyonya, you have to cook like Nyonya.' I was still too young to wield a cleaver knife or to light wood fires, but ripe enough for cooking lessons. As Father had turned his hand to small-scale trading, we could afford a maid by then, and Mother wanted me to watch while she and the maid worked so that I could learn to fan fires and practise simple chores. There were many catties of ingredients, all plump and awaiting attention, strewn on the kitchen surfaces to be turned into a feast for our household of nine.

I hated cooking. I loathed the kitchen, the part of the house where I broke into perspiration as soon as I entered. Its array of mills and grinding stones were hulking monsters fashioned from granite I couldn't move, let alone lift.

On that memorable day my apprenticeship began with a mortar and pestle: a deep round bowl in black stone with a matching, equally heavy cylindrical pounder that had a rounded end, tapered to make it easier to hold. The pestles and mortars were Mother's favourite instruments of torture, used daily to pulverise dried shrimp or garlic or whatever took her fancy.

I stood in one corner, grumpily watching our maid, Ah Lai. Ah Lai had toasted dried shrimp paste and was transferring it into the round mortar bowl, ready for mixing with the chillies she had already chopped. There was a pungent aroma in the air. 'Come closer-lah, Chye Hoon,' the maid beckoned, wagging her finger. 'If not, you can't see.'

I dragged my feet into the kitchen. My younger brother, Chong Jin, was about to start school, and I wished I could be outside with him instead of being cooped up in a stuffy room full of smells that made my eyes water. When the billowing smoke choked me, it all became too much.

'I not like to cook!' I burst out, running off to the room I shared with Elder Sister. I resolved never to step inside our kitchen again. Within minutes Mother stormed up and yanked me roughly by the hand. 'You do as you're told!' she screamed, her voice trembling.

With my heart thumping, I tried to pull away. A scuffle followed. I shouted, 'No, no, no! I no want!' and Mother grabbed both my arms while hoping to coax sense into me. We were far from evenly matched, though I must have been the more vigorous, because the sleeves of Mother's baju panjang, the calf-length long-sleeved tunic she wore, were pulled high up on her arms, exposing naked flesh. It was too tempting. Like a person possessed I bit into Mother's lower arm, sinking my teeth near her wrist. I still don't know what came over me.

When I lifted my head, the kitchen was silent. Both Elder Sister's and Ah Lai's eyes were round from shock. My teeth had been on Mother's arm only for a split second, but there were marks where my jaw had clamped down. Without warning Mother's hand swept swiftly and hard across my left cheek. Whack! It was the first time she had slapped me in the face. I cried, shaking in humiliation.

That evening I ate dinner on my own, after even Ah Lai, and was made to do all the washing-up. I worked my way through the countless plates, the heavy wok, the bulky pots and the cumbersome stone implements the maid helped me lift – the pestle and mortar and roller which had been used against the flat grinding stone.

Afterwards, Father asked to see me alone. Remembering how the cane had been used on Chong Jin, I stood expecting the worst. Father was quiet for many moments.

'Chye Hoon,' he said when he finally spoke in his sing-song voice, 'why so stubborn?' His eyes looked kind, but underneath I saw a steely edge.

'I want to go to school, Father.'

'Chye Hoon, you're a girl.' He said this as if it needed no elaboration.

'But Chong Jin go to school. I older than he.'

'Chong Jin is a boy.'

'Why so different, Father? Girls why also cannot go to school?'

'Chye Hoon, in a few years you will have to get married. No man will want you unless you know how to cook and sew.'

'I no want to marry.'

A guttural laugh escaped from within Father's throat. His Adam's apple vibrated wildly. 'Don't be silly. All girls must marry. How will you look after yourself? Now, do as you're told, and for heaven's sake don't bite your mother again.'

I walked to my room, forced to stare defeat in the face. I hated being a girl. I hated life within the towering walls of our house: a prison of endless chores and chattering. Most of all I hated our steamy kitchen.

At that moment I hated Chong Jin too. Tears clouded my eyes. I stood quivering at the thought of him at school, because I knew I was as smart as he was. When Father was teaching Chong Jin the abacus, I had joined them at the table, and Father had playfully shown me how to move the beads up and down along the wooden rods. Chong Jin needed several attempts, but I understood how to count after only one lesson, to Father's astonishment.

That night I cried myself to sleep. In my dreams I became as powerful as the warrior Hang Tuah. I turned into a boy with a magic sword who roamed the earth, slaying dragons and anything in my path. I vowed I would not lose another battle. I continued to dream the same dream long after accepting the fate destiny had bestowed on me.

One soggy monsoon afternoon when the rains beat down on Ah Kwee Street, I discovered yet another strand to our roots. Mother told us her own grandmother had been a Menangkabau from western Sumatra. I asked where that was, and Mother, with one finger pointing at the window, replied dreamily, 'Indonesia. Very far from here.'

Mother said Menangkabau women were warriors, as good at fighting as men. She might even have used the word 'fierce', but I think I heard that subsequently – as a description of me. When Mother told me about our Menangkabau bloodline, I was too young to understand what inheritance meant. Eventually I learnt that the Menangkabaus passed land and property from one generation to the next via their womenfolk – a very sensible principle, I thought.

A dispute arose between Mother's people and the prince of a neighbouring province. To settle the argument, both sides agreed to a water buffalo fight. The prince sent a large, aggressive water buffalo, while Mother's people shrewdly chose a baby water buffalo, but one whose horns had been sharpened over many days. For twenty-four hours before the fight, the baby buffalo was starved. As soon as it was released into the fighting ring, the baby buffalo ran towards the large buffalo. In the process of trying to suckle, it spiked the large buffalo to death.

Thereafter, Mother's ancestors were known as 'the people of the victorious bull', or Menangkabau in Malay.

Mother had told this famous legend to illustrate the patient cunning of her ancestors, but it disturbed me. Recalling the fight in Songkhla and the terror in the losing buffalo's eyes, I felt sorry for the horrible death of the large Menangkabau bull. 'Ai-yahh!' Mother said. 'Don't cry-lah. Long time ago that happen.'

To distract me, she said her grandmother's family had intended to go to Phuket but had set sail in the wrong month and been blown by the wind towards Songkhla, where they ended up living.

'You mean . . . you in Songkhla accident only, Mother?' I asked. Imagine being blown by monsoon winds to the wrong place. How could anyone have made such a mistake?

But Mother remained composed. 'Yes,' she replied, her eyes on the rain, which had turned into a fine drizzle. Mother's lack of concern could mean one of two things: either she had accepted the fate decreed by higher powers, or the entire story had been made up to stop my crying. I never found out which it was.

My best friend during those years was a girl named Hooi Peng. Her mother, also a Nyonya, befriended Mother soon after we arrived in Penang. Hooi Peng's family lived on a street about ten minutes' walk away, and our mothers visited each other at least once a week.

Before Penang, I had assumed all Nyonyas and Babas were the same; meeting Hooi Peng taught me otherwise. She spoke mainly Hokkien, while we spoke more Siamese and Malay. She ate with her hands like we did, but several of our dishes surprised her, as did our penchant for drowning vegetable salads in lime juice.

When I met her, Hooi Peng was a slip of a girl, so tiny and frail she seemed at risk of disappearing. Her hair, like the rest of her, was thin and fine – long black strands that behaved themselves, unlike mine, which refused to lie flat when combed. Hooi Peng's eyes were just that bit too far apart and, combined with a flat nose, gave her an impish look, as if she were always up to mischief.

Once we were older, Hooi Peng and I trained together in Nyonya cooking traditions. We spent years in the same kitchen and, like many before us, did not stop to wonder how things came to be the way they were. Our days were long: there was much chopping and pounding, scraping and grinding. We learnt how to slice vegetables so thinly they looked as if they had been shredded, to dry spices in the sun, to extract flavours and colours from a bewildering variety of leaves and flowers. There was the sword-like pandanus leaf we tied into knots for perfuming pots of rice. There was also the butterfly pea flower, whose petals were pounded, mixed with water and strained for their blue dye. We even used the heart of the banana tree blossom, boiling it until tender for our salads.

Our work was physically demanding: we had to mince and pulverise and blend, all by hand. I found grinding the most difficult. Though we were taught to position ourselves over the large slab so that we used the weight of our bodies and the strength of our shoulders, crushing rice or green peas was still hard work. I tried shortcuts, until it became clear that sloth made a difference to the taste of what I cooked. Mother could tell at once which of her instructions had not been followed. In shame I stopped cheating.

Over time Hooi Peng and I stamped our personalities on our cooking styles. My laksas and sambals tended to be fiery, bursting into flavour on the first mouthful, while hers were understated, requiring patience for their brilliance to show.

It was in our speciality of *kueh* that I really came into my own as a Nyonya cook. Everyone told me how wonderful my *kueh* were – 'The best we've ever had.' My nine-layered *kueh*, from which the individual pink and white slices could be separately peeled, became legendary throughout Penang. Nothing made me happier than making *kueh*.

Fortunately we had many varieties, and Hooi Peng and I could make two types every day without boring anyone.

Kueh is Malay for 'cakes', but Nyonya cakes are different from Western cakes, Chinese cakes or any other type. Our cakes assault the senses with their colours and their textures. We use no wheat flour, only rice or tapioca or green pea flour, and no milk other than the milk of the coconut, which we squeeze by hand from the flesh of grated fruit. Not all our *kueh* are sweet; there are savoury radish and taro cakes, and even spicy rolls of glutinous rice. Most *kueh* are eaten cold, but some, like our yam cakes, are best warm. The result, after centuries of trial and error, is a riot of blues, greens and reds that stop people in their tracks, and contrasts which delight the tongue.

Hooi Peng and I were already proficient cooks when I made a chance remark to her. 'We so lucky,' I said. 'We cook Chinese style, Malay style. We make pork dishes, spicy dishes. We use wok to fry, hands to eat. We are really *champor-champor*, a mixture of things. I very much like.'

My friend stopped what she was doing. After a minute she murmured, 'Yes.' Then Hooi Peng asked, 'You think you more Malay or more Chinese-ah?'

'I am both,' I replied uncertainly. 'How can more one than the other?'

Hooi Peng had started to fill out her clothes by then. Her face had grown more angular, altering that look of childish mischief I had become so familiar with. When pensive, Hooi Peng could appear deadly serious, as she did that moment. She confessed to feeling more Chinese than Malay, musing that perhaps it was because she spoke only Hokkien at home. 'We worship Chinese gods,' she persisted. 'So we more Chinese, isn't it?'

I cast my mind back to my Menangkabau great-grandmother, who had been a Moslem before marrying my great-grandfather. She had converted to Taoism upon her marriage. Had worshipping a new god made her less Menangkabau and more Chinese? I didn't think so.

'A god is a god,' I said. 'You worship which one, also no difference. Just fate our great-grandmothers took their husbands' religion. So we now with Chinese gods pray-lah. But we also follow Malay customs. I think to which god I pray also makes no difference.'

Still, I was troubled by Hooi Peng's question. Everyone talked about what Nyonyas did, not who we were. We were recognised by our clothes, our cooking and our tableware. But what did these outward signs really say about our heritage?

Our family stories told us that our community had grown at the crossroads between cultures. I thought back to my great-grandfather many times over, the one who set sail from Amoy, to the Malay woman he had married, and their children and their children's children. Our ancestors had mixed up their customs and traditions, borrowing from each as they melded them together. After hundreds of years we were no longer either Malay or Chinese – we couldn't be. My roots could not be split.

On a cool Malayan night I began to shape an answer to the question I had once asked Mother: 'Nyonya, what does it mean?' A Nyonya, I told myself, is a woman who breathes two worlds – not just one or the other, not more one than the other, but both equally. My two worlds were alive: Chinese and Malay rolled into one, blended by the centuries that had passed.

4

As soon as we were old enough, we girls were taken on trips to the market by our mothers. We would leave when the skies were barely light and arrive home before the heat of day became overpowering.

Chowrasta Market was a rough-and-ready place then: hygiene was unheard of and the odours intense, but it was colourful – anything went. I took immediately to its lively and bustling atmosphere. I liked the noise, the yelling and the stallholders – men and women – who competed for our attention with live animals.

Before long I developed a reputation in the market for a fearsome temper, which then spread through the island. This began one especially torrid morning.

We left early as usual. I was already a young lady then, a smaller replica of Mother, with a basket in one hand and a long-sleeved tunic – the baju panjang – flowing down to my calves. I wore a sarong around my waist and clogs on my feet. We always put on our clogs for Chowrasta Market, because of the fish. The fish, after being brought in from the sea, would be placed on thick slabs of ice; when the ice melted, pools of water formed on the cement floor, which mixed with discarded scales and blood to make walking hazardous. I would never have dreamt of putting my beautiful beaded shoes on that dreaded floor.

We would go to the dry section first, to look at the vegetables and fruit; only after that would we visit the fishmongers and meat sellers. Vegetables freshly transported from farms in the hinterland were set out on low wooden planks on the floor. I selected brinjals that day, two fat marrows and a large bagful of my favourite vegetable, *petai* – the stinking bean. In the fruit section I looked at bananas in different shades and sizes, some long and green, others small and yellow, yet others with light red skin – the favourites of our gods and goddesses.

When I first accompanied Mother to the market, I shuffled from stall to stall, struggling in my sarong and baju panjang. The sarong and calf-length tunic were a trial until I found ways to fasten both loosely, the former through clever folding, the latter by using brooches in just the right places. Such ruses are important if a girl is to walk with any degree of comfort.

As a market novice I spent time observing the interactions that took place. I learnt to watch the vegetable sellers carefully in case they exchanged the tomatoes you had chosen with others less succulent. I realised that negotiating with the fishmongers paid off, because they could lop a tenth off their prices with ease, and that you were wise to be wary of the pork sellers, keening your eyes while their snake-like fingers slid counterweights up and down along their incomprehensible Chinese scales.

Soon I was able to argue with the stallholders over their prices. When it became clear I was good at bargaining, I began to make the purchases for anyone who came with us to the market. Most often that happened to be Hooi Peng and her mother, who would select what they wanted, after which I would speak on their behalf. It was an activity I enjoyed, this exchange of friendly banter with the vendors where each party understood the give and take.

Some stallholders appreciated the nature of these interactions better than others. Ah Ying, the chicken seller, was one. A dark-skinned woman with a red scarf on her head, Ah Ying was someone I liked doing business with, even though the smell in her corner was particularly pungent. There, live chickens pecked noisily at the sides of their cages. The less fortunate lay in groups on the floor, their feet bound together by string. There would invariably be loose feathers around Ah Ying's stall, some drifting in the air as they floated towards the floor.

'Ai-yahh, how come so expensive-ah?' I exclaimed at Ah Ying, until this became our ritual. She would respond by grabbing the poor bird in question, lifting it to show me its glories and pointing out how well it had been fed and how beautifully smooth its flesh was. 'Yes-lah, exactly what we need,' I would say. 'But, Ah Ying, we are good customers. One cent less, can-ah?' Ah Ying would consider it before either acquiescing or offering another price. *'Kamsia, kamsia.'* Ah Ying always concluded by thanking us in Hokkien. Through the years I felt she acted fairly, giving us a lower price whenever she could.

Other stallholders were not quite so amenable, but we were forced to give them our custom all the same. When you visit a market regularly, the best source of any item becomes part of the information you store in your head. We knew, for example, that Ah Lin sold the sweetest *chikus* in the market. I bought these sapodilla fruits from her even though she was a grumpy old devil who never once smiled at me.

The vendors, while not exactly friends, became fixtures in our lives. So much so that when a stallholder went missing – from illness, for example – we would notice. Each corner of the market became associated in our minds with a particular person, a set of sights and smells and voices we grew to expect, the absence of which altered our shopping experience.

It must be said that I never found my footing with the pork sellers. They were men with shifty looks and a deliberately slow manner, as if they heard you but what you said was too silly to deserve a reply.

They drew out their answers in long-winded sentences that tested my patience.

On that morning we went to a vendor who was new to the market. He had recently taken over a stall from which we had bought pork for years. The newcomer, a rotund man with a shiny pate and a tree trunk of a waist, looked like the slabs on display at his counter: smooth white skin glistening with grease, the odd strand of hair here and there.

We were looking for our usual pork belly that morning. When the new seller placed the piece of meat I had chosen on the metallic plate of his scale, he slid the counterweight along his calibrated wooden rod. His hands were faster than his predecessor's, faster in fact than anyone else's I had ever seen. But before he removed the meat, my eye told me the weight wasn't in its usual position.

'You no count wrong-ah?' I asked the large man. 'Maybe better to weigh again.'

Unperturbed, the man put the piece of pork on his chopping board and prepared it for dicing.

'Ten years already I sell pork,' he said gruffly. 'I know how to count.'

'Uncle, I know you know how to count,' I responded. 'But easy to count wrong.'

He ignored me, continuing to chop, his back a silent wall. When he started to wrap the chunks of pork belly in brown paper, I asked to see them.

With his back still facing me, he mumbled to himself, thinking he was out of earshot.

But I heard his every word. Heat rushed up to my face; my nostrils began to choke, and my eyes watered.

Impotence made me pick up the only weapon I had at hand: my clogs. I removed the left clog. Standing on my right foot, hand clasping the stall counter for balance, I hurled the free clog as I had once thrown a joss-stick – straight towards the back of the fat man's head. 'How dare you disrespect my mother! How dare you, you dying person's head!' I screamed at the top of my lungs.

It happened in a split second. The shocked pork seller turned around and my clog hit him high up against his right temple, where the baldness of his skull looked especially inviting. There was a loud clunking noise, which stopped all trade in Chowrasta Market. The man clutched his temple. He carried a bruise for weeks afterwards, so I was told. It took minutes before the other vendors turned back to their customers.

When the neighbouring pork seller returned my clog, I walked away, shivering but quietly satisfied. Mother hurried us off as quickly as possible. She didn't say anything while we walked, as if deep in thought. Her silence disturbed me; I had a fear, an inkling of what was on her mind.

Later that evening she and Father took me aside. My siblings were sent to their rooms and the three of us were alone. Mother clasped her hands nervously as she sat in a chair, her lips pursed into a downward curve. Father paced up and down before clearing his throat. Uncharacteristically it was he who began the conversation.

'Chye Hoon,' he said, 'you must learn to control your temper.'

'Father, but—'

'Listen to me,' Father said. His baritone voice that night was like deep-fried *tau foo*: creamy on the inside, but with decidedly hard edges. His Adam's apple throbbed. 'We aren't rich, and you will need to get married soon. If you become known for your temper, it will be hard to find a husband for you.' As I listened to Father, I fretted about the future and my actions of the morning.

Father, in turn, looked at Mother. Her hands had stopped fidgeting, but she wasn't her usual bundle of energy. Instead, a gaunt, tired woman looked at me with shoulders hunched and eyes tinged with sadness. Mother sat still for what seemed a long time.

'I not know what to do with you, Chye Hoon,' she finally said, letting out a sigh. 'I know you good girl, but so impetuous! You have to be calmer.'

'Mother, I hear that man say what,' I pointed out. 'He . . .' I stopped, unsure I should repeat his phrases in the presence of my parents.

'I no hear, but I can imagine,' she replied quietly. 'So what? Let him say what he want.' Mother paused for a minute, adding in a low voice, 'Don't forget, you now a woman, Chye Hoon.'

She was alluding to the recent moment when, on discovering a damp red patch on my sarong, I had run to her in panic. Ever since, knowing looks had been exchanged between Mother and the other Nyonyas who visited our house. I was given to understand that I had come of age – although I had done nothing – and their glances made me proud yet uncomfortable at the same time. 'Not long now you will marry,' Mother continued. 'You not watch your tongue, man also not want you.'

'Chye Hoon,' Father said, screwing in the final nail with his voice, 'you're not as pretty as Elder Sister, but you are a better cook. Also your sewing isn't bad. We should have no problem finding you a husband – provided you don't become known as a dragon.'

I swallowed. I knew I wasn't the best-looking in our family, having inherited Mother's dark skin and Father's coarse hair, strong like a man's. After my eyes, my hair was the next most popular topic along Ah Kwee Street, because it was as unruly as a labourer's. Even when swept over my crown like Mother's and held by five outsized pins, stray strands inevitably escaped. 'Look, look!' people would whisper, pointing their fingers. 'Pins so big, hair also fall. Stubborn, just like the owner.'

When I walked beside Elder Sister, the whispers became vicious. Some found it hard to believe we were sisters. Elder Sister's hair was fine and smooth, her complexion fair – a quirk of nature, aided by her preference for feminine pursuits and staying indoors. To make things worse, she was demure and petite. I, in contrast, am sturdily built; slim in those days, but definitely solid. I had known for many years that Elder Sister was considered beautiful while I was not, but Father was the first to say so to my face. A lump made its way to my throat.

Before the lump could settle, Mother spoke. 'Elder Sister already got fourteen years. We look for husband for her soon. What you do also affect her future. You no want to be selfish, is it?'

I didn't want to be selfish, of course.

But I also knew I couldn't live the life that Elder Sister would. I had to remain true to myself. Except I didn't know what that meant, or how to do it. Yet what was there to say in the midst of this onslaught?

I went to my room, numb from the shock of hearing the truth spoken so baldly, numb too from the imminence of marriage in my life. In my innocence I had no idea what actually took place between a man and a woman. 'Your husband, he know what to do' was all that Mother would whisper. There were times, while chewing betel nut leaves with her friends, when I could hear Mother and the other women giggling. From the little I could deduce, marriage was both a thing to be desired and a burden to be borne – and I didn't want it.

Yet the time was at hand for Elder Sister to make a match. I knew that my turn would eventually come. It seemed as inevitable as night following day.

5

When I look back, it feels as if my life has flown by at the speed of Penang's waterfall, as if it were only last week when a rickshaw arrived outside our house on Ah Kwee Street, bringing with it a short woman with narrow eyes whom I recognised as a matchmaker.

By then seven years had passed from the time of Elder Sister's marriage. As a child I had not wished to be married, but when the matchmakers did not call at our house for years after Elder Sister's wedding, I began to be afraid. The fate of a spinster is pitiful, possibly worse than death, and I didn't relish becoming one. It was a fear which worsened over time as first my third sister, Chye Phaik, was chosen and then my fourth sister, Chye Lian. Being spurned was painful. I sometimes woke up in a sweat, imagining myself at fifty with both my parents dead and me alone in a world where my siblings were scattered far from Penang.

When the matchmaker arrived, only two of us remained within the family home: my youngest sister, Chye Keat, and me. Being already accustomed to disappointment, I assumed she had come to make enquiries about Chye Keat.

On receiving the visitor, Mother called for coffee and her *sireh*, or betel nut–chewing set. With Father's increasing success and fewer mouths to feed, we had become wealthier, and Mother had acquired a betel box with silver inlays. This was no simple box but a box within a box. Snugly tucked inside was a removable container divided into four compartments, each with its own lid, which could be lifted out and placed on a table. The betel box felt heavy in my hands. While carrying it, I admired the curves on its surfaces. They intertwined gloriously, ending in two circles in the middle that looked like a pair of knowing eyes.

I took the box into the hall, where Mother sat chatting amiably with the matchmaker. When I entered, I noticed the woman's oval face and thick lips, heavily rouged. In turn the matchmaker gave me the once-over with her inquisitive eyes. For a minute I wondered whether she could have come to enquire about me, but I quickly dismissed the idea. After the incident of the clog, my reputation on the island had gone from bad to worse. Words like 'uncontrollable' and 'dragon' were used. Outwardly, I shrugged them off; inwardly, I could not help thinking that if my brother Chong Jin had done the same, he would have been lauded as a hero for defending his mother's honour.

As a result I remained unmarried at the age of twenty. In my era girls were married by sixteen, and those still single at eighteen were called old maids. Spinsterhood was a fate everyone assumed would befall me.

I thought the same. I knew it would require an exceptional man to contemplate marrying me.

The matchmaker spent a long time with Mother in the hall, chewing betel nut leaves and sipping coffee. After she left, Mother continued chewing on her own. That was unusual, because despite her beautiful *sireh* set, Mother had never fully taken to this Malay custom. She didn't indulge unless she had company.

I spied at Mother from a secret peeping hole behind the partition separating the inner and outer halls. She looked deep in thought. She picked up a betel leaf absent-mindedly with her tweezers, opened the lidded container, which held the white lime, and spread the chalky substance on her leaf. All the while there was a distant look in Mother's eyes, as if she were dreaming. She took a piece of dried gambier cake from another lidded container and then sat still, not doing anything. After a few minutes, remembering where she was, Mother crumbled the brown powder between her forefinger and her thumb. I could tell she wasn't paying attention, because she started to peel and cut up betel nuts with the guillotine knife, before noticing the pile of nuts already prepared and laid aside. Selecting several, Mother placed them on her leaf. She then wrapped the leaf carefully and put the package into her mouth.

I watched as Mother chewed. She was oddly nervous, rubbing her hands constantly. She looked beautiful in a distracted way, her cheek-bones made more prominent by the rotation of her jaw. When she could no longer contain the juices inside her mouth, Mother spat into a brass jar, exposing red, blood-coloured gums. Afterwards her eyelids drooped while she moved the cud inside her mouth.

I wondered what was worrying her. Perhaps the matchmaker had come on a mission from a towkay, one of the wealthy bosses, with an express interest in Chye Keat for his son. I thought it unlikely Mother would consider such a proposal, since her opinions about the sons of the wealthy were well known.

On the other hand, could it possibly be that a towkay had become interested in me? I chuckled. The more I mused, the more I realised my parents would be in a difficult position. I wondered how they would react. If, on the one hand, they had me, their problematic single daughter, and on the other they had a rich towkay proposing marriage, what would they do? I reminded myself not to be silly. No towkay would want his son to become entangled with a woman known to speak her mind and who threw clogs at stallholders.

I watched Mother for a long time, sorry I was no longer able to go and hold her the way I used to as a child. We were close then, Mother and I. I remembered how she would lift me on to her lap. I adored her smells, that slight whiff of Javanese face powder mixed with the fragrances of garlic and lemongrass, which were always on her clothes. Those times seemed an age ago; whenever I felt lost, I longed to be four again, despite the friction I had caused in my headstrong childhood.

After Father came home, he and Mother conferred late into the night. I heard them even when I was preparing for bed. Over the following days neither gave anything away – nothing was said and nothing happened. Mother went out as usual – to the market, to visit her friends, to play her card game, *chiki*. She made a trip somewhere out of the ordinary one afternoon, disappearing for several hours. When she came back, she looked more satisfied than usual. Once again she and Father had a long conversation after he returned from work.

A week later the matchmaker returned. This time it was our servant, Ah Lai, who served them coffee, along with Mother's *sireh* box. The matchmaker's second visit was brief, lasting barely fifteen minutes. After she left, Mother did not remain in the hall chewing betel nut leaves. Instead, she bustled about with renewed vigour and then went out without saying where she was going.

As soon as Mother left, I cornered Ah Lai. 'That matchmaker twice come here already. My mother, she tell you something-ah?'

The maid smiled wryly, shrugging her shoulders. 'Young miss, you really think Mistress tell me anything?'

Beneath Ah Lai's dark eyes there was the hint of a twinkle. 'Ah Lai, you really nothing know-ah?' I asked a second time. 'You must tell me-lah.'

'Young miss, believe me, I really not know. But if you marry next, no surprise to me. Matchmaker come to same house two times, must be reason.'

'Chye Keat not yet married,' I countered. 'Who want me anyway?'

'Ah, that I can't say,' Ah Lai replied, eyes now sparkling. 'I tell you,' she whispered. 'I take coffee in that time, I hear them say your name.

Sure one.' At that my cheeks burned and my heart beat faster. I wondered if it could possibly be true and who the man could be. Hadn't he heard about my reputation?

For the next while my parents seemed on edge. I walked around in suspense, watching them closely yet not daring to ask what I was dying to know. One day Father enquired out of the blue, 'Are you all right, Chye Hoon?' He tried to sound casual but could not conceal his simmering excitement. Something was about to happen, and he knew I suspected as much.

My parents eventually called me into the hall, and every second of what took place remains ingrained in my mind.

Father and Mother were seated when I entered. Their eyes followed me as I walked, and they would have noticed how nervously I clasped and unclasped my hands. Clearing his throat, Father spoke. 'You're a smart girl, Chye Hoon,' he began. I stared at that familiar wobble of his Adam's apple. 'I'm sure you've guessed that we have news for you.'

I nodded.

Father went straight to the point. 'A recently arrived Chinese worker, a Hakka man by the name of Wong Peng Choon, has been asking about you . . . It seems he's heard of your Nyonya cooking.'

Father paused to let this pronouncement sink in. I, meanwhile, asked myself a thousand questions. Who was this Wong Peng Choon? What was he looking for?

'The man wants a healthy, good-looking girl, a wife skilled in cooking, homemaking and sewing,' Father continued.

'You already see the matchmaker, of course,' Mother interrupted.

'Yes, Mother.'

'Hah!' Mother said airily. 'You know what they like. She sing Peng Choon's praises . . . so good-looking . . . got smooth skin-lah and fine teeth and look like a prince! But me, I must go see for myself.'

Mother paused to catch her breath. 'Well, Chye Hoon, no joke-ah – he is really handsome. And tall – taller even than Husband,' she continued, beaming proudly at Father.

My heart thumped. So, a good-looking man wanted to marry me. I tried to picture his face but failed.

'And he's well educated,' Father said. 'He's fluent in Hakka as well as Hokkien and has taught himself English since arriving in Malaya.'

'Now, normally we no tell you now, so early on,' Mother added quickly. 'Like your sisters, everything done only, they know about their marriages.'

I waited. What was about to come?

Mother looked me directly in the eye. 'Wong Peng Choon already got wife and son in China . . .'

Her words hung in the air. 'This good of course,' she continued, voice lilting to emphasise her point. 'Means he already know what to do.' I blushed, embarrassed at having the delicate matter of my wedding night referred to.

When I recovered, I asked, 'He want to live in Malaya?'

'Yes, Wong Peng Choon is doing well here and wants to make Malaya his home.' It was Father who replied. 'Do you understand?'

I nodded. At the time few Chinese women were allowed to leave China. If this man wanted to settle, I knew it was unlikely his wife and child could follow.

'Chye Hoon, you very lucky girl!' Mother interjected, her mouth curving into a crescent-like smile. 'You have man who want to marry you . . . good-looking, have education, successful. What more any woman want, hah? I ask you?'

Thus on a moonless Malayan night my destiny was sealed.

The news brought relief. Yet marriage worried me too. It wasn't being a second wife which was the problem – this was common enough, and China seemed a long way off. But what if my husband hadn't yet seen me and was disappointed on our wedding night? What if he drank?

Or gambled? Or was a wife beater? What if he turned out to be a womaniser? In looking to marry again, he undoubtedly wanted a new son. What if I failed to bear him one?

Those were the thoughts which plagued me. I would soon enter a new world, one I knew little about, a world spoken of in whispers here and there in what appeared to be equal degrees of embarrassment and thrill. I was curious too about the man who was to be my husband. Why was he undaunted, treading where other men feared to come? I decided that this Wong Peng Choon must be very unusual. I was excited and nervous at the prospect. It made me feel young again, like a child waiting for the ting-ting man.

6

A traditional Nyonya-Baba wedding is no straightforward affair, as my husband Wong Peng Choon was to discover. First, our horoscopes had to be checked to ensure there was no clash. If our horoscopes were incompatible, any hopes for marriage would have been dashed. Fortunately, the temple priest who was the expert in geomancy settled the matter easily.

What followed next was a snag which could have led to a different outcome. For months Mother parried my questions – 'Chye Hoon, we only talk about details. No need for you to worry.'

But I grew anxious. 'He changed his mind-ah?' I wondered aloud.

'Ai-yahh! Don't be silly-lah,' Mother would reply. 'Of course not. What for change his mind?' I in my nervous state could think of a hundred reasons. Perhaps, having set eyes on me, the man wanted to call things off. 'But you not bad-looking girl,' Mother assured me. 'Anyway, more important to him is you know how to cook. Your health also, because he wants sons.'

As it turned out, the truth was more complex. Knowing what I do now, I'm sure my bridegroom would have acted more decisively if the argument had been about a purely trivial matter. Unfortunately what he wanted was to take me away immediately after marriage – to Ipoh, a town at the heart of the tin-mining region in the Kinta Valley. Ipoh was 180 miles south-east of Penang, in a state called Perak, part of the Federated Malay States. In Mother's mind this was so remote he might as well have suggested taking me to China. Ipoh, a town I had never even heard of before, presented an obstacle which nearly derailed our marriage plans. The town remained a sticking point with Mother for weeks, because she did not want me to move so far away. In today's world, where people move hither and thither and there are large steamships and even flying machines, her reaction may seem strange, but back then we moved about only on elephants and in rickshaws and gharries, horse-drawn cabs.

The compromise between my parents and Peng Choon, when it was finally struck, would also appear exceptional today. Peng Choon agreed to a *chin-chuoh* marriage: he would move in to our house immediately after our wedding and live there with me for six months before we went to Ipoh. This was a Nyonya-Baba custom, and it eased my parents' minds considerably.

Peng Choon's willingness to accede to a *chin-chuoh* wedding spoke volumes. It showed he was prepared to brave the raised eyebrows of his fellow countrymen out of consideration for Mother. In his mind, living side by side for six months would allow us to spend time together while Mother got used to the idea of our leaving.

Of course, there was another side to the whole question, and I'm sure that Peng Choon, being no fool, understood at once. He was a Hakka man alone in Malaya, contracted into a traditional wedding in a culture that wasn't his. By agreeing to a wedding in *chin-chuoh* style, he at once handed all responsibility for the wedding arrangements to my family. The compromise was ideal.

But it came at a price. You can imagine what was said behind Peng Choon's back – 'There goes the henpecked husband, poor fellow'

– which is why, even in the Nyonya-Baba community, where *chin-chuoh* marriages were known, they became uncommon.

Once the solution had been agreed, a ring of fiery gold, set with a heavy sparkling diamond, arrived at our house. In return, my parents sent over a silver ring on which a large stone of pure green jade sat. These gifts sealed our contract, after which Mother took charge, as she had always done. Things became a blur. I would wake up every morning to be given instructions for the day and would then set about my tasks as if they were all unreal. I sewed and embroidered; made artificial roses for decoration; shaped petals from coloured crêpe paper, thin wires and silk; did beadwork for the tops of slippers; stitched dragons and phoenixes; and helped with my own trousseau, putting together the bajus, sarongs and petticoats I would wear.

In those days time stood still. Life was suspended between two worlds: one I hadn't yet left, the other I hadn't quite entered. I was anxious about the things to come and constantly wondered what would take place on my wedding night. How would I know what to do? It occurred to me to ask Mother again, but for once I felt too shy. I so wished I could have talked then to my childhood friend Hooi Peng. If only she had married closer to home.

Throughout, Mother ran in and out like a mare untethered. She swirled in different directions, one minute looking at my bridal chamber, the next shrieking that we hadn't enough tableware and she would have to go to the shops again. Mother went shopping every day. She never came back empty-handed; there was always something: a brand-new bed she had ordered, or materials for bedspreads, bedcovers and pillowcases, or beautiful pieces of jewellery meant for my husband and me.

One day Mother brought home a familiar-looking woman whom I had noticed around Penang but had never spoken to. Introducing her as See Nee Ee, Mother announced that she would be the mistress of ceremonies at my wedding.

On the few occasions when I had seen See Nee Ee, I was struck by her poise. She didn't have a beautiful face, but she was elegant and carried herself with grace. Her neck, long and fair, was like a swan's. See Nee Ee dressed simply the day she first visited our house: in a light blue baju, and beneath that a patterned black sarong. Lines showed on her forehead, yet when she walked in I looked up, my attention caught by her confident tone.

See Nee Ee didn't say much after we were introduced. She just looked at me with kindness in her eyes. Taking my hands in hers, she told me not to worry. 'I will be here to guide you,' she said. I put down my portable embroidery frame. Engrossed in stitching peacocks at the time, I did not pay See Nee Ee the attention I should have. I only had a vague idea then about the role of the mistress of ceremonies. There had been mistresses of ceremonies at my sisters' weddings, but I was needed in the kitchen and did not know how much these women were involved in determining what would and would not happen.

In the following weeks See Nee Ee visited our house many times to confer with Mother. They would chat over coffee, chewing betel nut leaves and laughing. With the date of my wedding already settled, I could not imagine what more there would be to discuss. I pestered Mother with questions – 'Mother, you two talk about what? How come still so much to talk?' – until Mother pushed me away, telling me to leave such matters to those with experience.

Three days before the wedding, red cloth was put up over the front doorway of our house. I stood on the five-foot way outside, staring at the cloth and tapestry just above it. The tapestry was one I had seen many times suspended over other doorways, and yet as I looked up it held new meaning. The silk tassels which dangled from its borders waved in the breeze. I can still see the characters, beautifully embroidered in golden thread: the symbols for prosperity, wealth and longevity that Father had pointed out to me. As I looked up, my heart was full, because I knew that the gods and the world around us were being exhorted on my behalf. Finally it was my wedding those symbols proclaimed. They made the doorway on Ah Kwee Street look both familiar and strangely foreign, as if, with the tapestry hanging overhead, the house had ceased to be part of my life.

Soon after, Mother's friends arrived. They congregated in the kitchen, where they cackled uproariously; sounds of chop, chop, chopping and frying could be heard, and wonderful aromas filled the air. Large earthen pots of tempting pickles called *achar* appeared; there were *achar awak* and *achar* fish and *achar* prawn, all cooked under Mother's supreme direction and sprinkled with sesame seeds to finish.

While the cooking was being done, See Nee Ee came to our house. This time she asked to see me alone. She looked as elegant as ever, walking slowly in her pristine cotton baju, her back straight and head held high. We went into my room, and she calmly told me she wanted to talk about what would happen on the wedding eve and day itself. She said all this with a knowing look in her eyes. I realised at once that I had found my answer. See Nee Ee, who knew everything there was to know about weddings and marriage, would reveal to me the mysteries of the night.

On the day before my wedding, See Nee Ee came to our house at noon to help me dress. The guests, who could turn up any time after three, had not arrived, but already I was feeling spent and weary. Having tossed and turned through the night, I had slept only fitfully. Like a sampan caught in a storm, I was overwhelmed; excited, because I would soon be leading a household, but apprehensive also, wondering how much independence I would have. Would this Wong Peng Choon let me run the house, as was the tradition among Nyonyas? Or would he expect me to be a subservient Chinese wife? I knew my husband-to-be wanted a son. What if I failed in that regard? Would he take a mistress in Malaya?

As soon as See Nee Ee entered, she saw the unease in my eyes and sensed the trembling in my bones. She asked gently, 'Chye Hoon, have you had anything to eat?' I shook my head. The hired chefs for the day had been making a cacophony in the kitchen since early that morning, and our house smelt of spices and steaming soups, but I had not been able to swallow a thing. See Nee Ee fed me a bowl of soup before helping with my toilette. If it hadn't been for her, I would have been overwhelmed during those anxious hours.

By the time we began welcoming guests, no one could have imagined what I had looked like just two hours before. I was wearing a bright new baju I loved. Fastened with diamond-studded brooches at the front, my tunic matched the green Pekalongan sarong Mother had ordered specially from Indonesia, with its hand-drawn motifs of butterflies in yellow and turquoise. I knew I was looking my best, and happily addressed everyone as they entered our house. 'Sah Koo, Sah Kim,' I called out to my third maternal uncle and aunt, who were the first to arrive. A few minutes later my eldest paternal uncle and aunt came in. 'Toa Pek, Toa Mm,' I said, smiling. The trickle of people soon turned into a stream, and I was continuously occupied. I could tell that our guests were impressed, as much by my dress as by the five gold pins in my hair, studded with pinpricks of stone that glinted in the sunlight.

The feast followed. It passed quickly and my mind was far away . . . on what would happen later in the night. Shouts intruded into my thoughts and I would glance at my parents, both busy playing host. Sometimes, when someone made a remark to me I mumbled in response. See Nee Ee remained by my side throughout, a tower of authority and silent reassurance.

After our guests left, the moment I both longed for and dreaded approached.

At midnight a Chinese oboe sounded, its solemn notes announcing the start of the hair-combing ceremony. The night was quiet. The music floated eerily through the air, making me shiver. I had changed by then and was dressed in a simple loose coat and trousers of cotton, completely in white.

While the oboe played, I was led by See Nee Ee to the makeshift altar in the main hall. I did everything I was told as if in a trance. She helped me to stand on a rice measure that had been turned upside down. I was given lit incense sticks, which I held in my hands. I bowed many times, first to Thi-Kong, the god of heaven, then to the gods of our family and finally to my ancestors.

A young boy appeared beside See Nee Ee, who helped sit me down on the rice measure and, with a comb in one hand, began to part my hair. Guided by See Nee Ee, the boy moved the comb in slow, smooth strokes. I felt it as it travelled down one side of my scalp all the way to the tips. At the same time, See Nee Ee uttered a blessing, something about being loved by my husband. For a second time the comb moved downwards while See Nee Ee uttered another incantation. In this way my hair was combed stroke by stroke, blessing after blessing, with See Nee Ee's voice echoing into the stillness around us.

Next I was on the red velvet rug, kneeling before my parents, with my hands in front of me in an attitude of worship.

'Now, worship your father,' See Nee Ee was saying. 'With sweat and toil he has brought you up and fed you. Show your love and gratitude.'

And I did, with tears swilling in my eyes. My forehead touched the softness of the velvet repeatedly as I bowed. I thought of how hard Father had worked for all of us, and for me especially. I remembered his acts of kindness, the resignation in his voice that told me he had not enjoyed scolding me. Memories came flooding back: the images of Father's Adam's apple merging with shadows across the field I used to play in as a child.

See Nee Ee held me. She led me slowly to a chair on my right, where Mother was sitting. 'Now worship your mother, who gave birth to you,' she told me. At those words tears streamed down my face. I regretted the temper tantrums I had thrown, the acts of waywardness I had forced upon her. I was sorry for biting her arm, sorry we had drifted apart. I longed to apologise but found I could not say a word. I just kept bowing and crying, until See Nee Ee held me up and whispered gently, 'Enough, enough. You have been a filial daughter. That's enough now.'

◆ ◆ ◆

The next day – the day of my wedding – I woke before dawn. Mother, my sisters and friends of Mother's who were staying in our house were already up. I could hear the familiar early-morning noises as they went about making breakfast, their quiet laughter just audible.

I lay in bed, drained. My head was heavy, as if I had been intoxicated the night before. It reminded me of how I had felt once after drinking a cup of Maotai, a popular Chinese liquor, whose potency had put me to sleep. The last thing I wanted was to get married.

There came a knock on the door. Before I could answer, See Nee Ee strode in. 'Chye Hoon, how are you?' she asked. Her tone was brusque, but the kindness was clearly there. I looked at her silently, bleary-eyed. 'I'm afraid you need to get up,' she told me. 'We don't have much time. We have to feed you and then get you ready.'

She pulled the covers off my bed and dragged me gently by the hand.

I followed her downstairs. A dish had been made with the leftovers of yesterday evening's dinner, and I swallowed a few spoonfuls of the soup. Mother came to my side, looking anxious. She squeezed my hand and, on coming closer, stroked my hair, whispering, 'This is big day for you, Chye Hoon. Make sure you eat, so you have enough strength.' Thinking about this later, I realised it was Mother's way of acknowledging the love I had demonstrated the night before.

Afterwards, See Nee Ee led me to the bridal chamber. My hair was longer in those days; when it was let down, halfway to my waist, I felt its weight. See Nee Ee anointed my hair with a scented oil, which she combed through in long, deft strokes with a brush. She told me I had wonderful hair – 'Black as a starless night, strong, but easy to roll.' It was the first time anyone had given me a compliment, and it made my heart tingle.

See Nee Ee coiled the last foot of my hair expertly into a chignon at the top of my head, using the diamond-embedded gold pins of the evening before to hold the bun in place. She then twisted and turned the rest of my hair. Not being able to see, I had no idea what she was doing. I smelt wax and felt See Nee Ee's hands fashioning a shape. When she held a looking glass up for me, I gasped. At the back of my head the mistress of ceremonies had created a spectacular sitting duck – with its tail standing up.

'See Nee Ee, so beautiful,' I said, wide-eyed.

'Yes, I think so too. That's all yours – all your hair.'

'The tail won't fall-ah?' I asked, worried about spoiling the effect.

See Nee Ee looked at me and smiled. 'It's held up by hair wax. Should stay in place, but you must follow instructions!' Then with a twinkle in her eye she winked. 'Wait till you see what's next! No danger of you running around today, Chye Hoon.'

And she was not joking. After applying vermillion paper to my lips and charcoal pencil to my eyebrows, See Nee Ee placed ceremonial robes over my body, robes I imagined the empresses of China wore but which I had never dreamt I would put on. There was a richly embroidered red silk skirt, which hung all the way down to my ankles, held up by tapes tied together at the waist. On my top she placed a heavily brocaded jacket with long, loose sleeves. As I put it on, I could see multicoloured threads in gold and silver, red and yellow, outlining fantastic pictures of birds all the way down to my knees. Over my shoulders See Nee Ee draped a cape; leaf-shaped pieces that had been sewn together hung magnificently off it, glowing with the sheen of satin.

When I began to perspire, See Nee Ee called in a bridesmaid to fan me. She hadn't yet finished dressing me and asked for patience. 'You look pretty, Chye Hoon. But I need more time.'

She continued by placing an elaborate piece of headgear over my head. My head became even heavier, and I could barely see. Styled for Manchu princesses, it had a veil of tiny glass beads and imitation pearls, and the piece was finished with two silk tassels at the back.

Still See Nee Ee said I wasn't ready. She put socks and shoes on my feet and jewellery all over me – necklaces, rings, earrings, bracelets and anklets – all bearing down until I was laden as if pregnant with five babies at once.

It was a miracle I could sit upright at all. When See Nee Ee held a looking glass in front of me, I could not believe what I saw. For the next while I wandered about as if in a dream. I obeyed instructions but was strangely absent. I took small steps forwards and backwards, like a child walking for the first time.

Just before noon I heard the sound of the oboe, the clash of cymbals, and the beat of gongs. And then firecrackers were let off, the signal that my husband-to-be had arrived. My heart beat wildly.

See Nee Ee came into the bridal chamber. She went down on her knees, so that her face was directly in front of my veil. 'Are you ready?' she asked as she tried to peer into my eyes. I nodded, throat too dry to say a word. See Nee Ee told me to follow her, and I walked slowly down the long staircase. I clung tightly to the hand of the pageboy who had come to help, aware that all eyes were on me.

I kept my eyes glued to the floor, terrified of stumbling and making a complete fool of myself. I still had not seen my husband-to-be and did not know where he was standing in the hall. See Nee Ee led me to him. As we faced each other, I saw that he too wore traditional garments and had a heavily embellished skirt on, but those were the only details my veil allowed me to see.

We were led to the family altar, where we were told to kneel. All the while my heart thumped so loudly I was sure that other people, and certainly my bridegroom, could hear it. I was given a handful of incense sticks. On being instructed to worship the gods and our ancestors, I bowed reverently. My hands, holding the incense sticks, trembled. I was saved only because all I had to do was wave the sticks up and down.

And then we were sent up to the bridal chamber to spend a few minutes with each other. I heard the blood coursing through my head as we walked slowly up the stairs. See Nee Ee came with us. Once we were inside the room, she invited Wong Peng Choon to lift the veil off my face. 'I will leave you now for a few minutes,' she announced.

Through the mists of my veil, I glimpsed the outline of his hands. I could see that he had long, slim fingers. I stood absolutely still, barely breathing. Gently touching the beads at the bottom of my veil, Wong Peng Choon raised it, and for the first time I looked into the face of my husband.

PART II:
THE HAND OF FATE
1899–1910

7

In the days when there were genies, a sea captain from Sumatra crossed the Straits of Malacca. He steered his ship up the Perak River to an unknown spot. There, hearing sweet music, the captain stopped. He was at a waterfall, and he saw a flying lizard leap into the air across the water. The sea captain liked the music and told his crew, 'The name of this river shall be Kinta, because it flows like the sound of tinkling bells. The flying lizard told me so.'

Immediately afterwards the flying lizard disappeared. The sea captain interpreted this as a sign and said, 'The Genie of Kinta has transformed himself into a flying lizard. This is a fine place for a settlement.'

So it was that the Malays first made a settlement along the Kinta River, at a place known as Gunong Cheroh. They built attap huts along the river, planted orchards and earned their living by fishing, farming and panning the riverbed for tin. Before that only the Orang Asli, the indigenous native peoples of Malaya, had been there.

In a dream the Genie of Kinta told the sea captain that his sons would be the lords of Kinta. Thereafter the sea captain took an Orang Asli wife and began a lineage in which Orang Asli blood flowed.

By the time my husband and I arrived, the settlement – already known as Ipoh – had become a bustling town. The Kinta District was turning into the principal tin-producing region of Perak, and Ipoh, as the centre of all mining activity, was humming.

It was a clear morning when we descended on the town. What stands out in my memory are the hills surrounding Ipoh, which undulated in layer after layer. From afar they loomed like round fluffy creatures, the trees covering them thick as fur. I wanted to hug Ipoh's hills. As we went closer, I saw the violence nature had wrought: in the patches made bald by rain, where pinkish-white rock glistened; the jagged edges which rose to culminate in sharp peaks; and the protruding scars of badly cut faces. Amidst this havoc was also rugged beauty: in between the deep crevices, years of trickling water had left magnificent clefts, which flowed as if weeping.

Peng Choon said the hills were made of limestone. I loved looking at them even on that first day.

In the distance they turned from dark green to a hazy blue, like the waves over the South China Sea of my early years. Someone later told me that Ipoh's hills eventually become the Blue Mountains, which split Malaya into two. I could believe it. The highest summits stretched lazily towards the heavens, where clouds floated, casting a dreamlike veil over the range.

On the other hand, my impressions of the town were far from favourable. I found Ipoh chaotic after the orderliness of Penang. Coolies ran everywhere. In some parts attap-roofed houses stood higgledy-piggledy, as if they had sprung up overnight.

On top of all this was the smell, the 'Ipoh aroma' much discussed throughout the district. In the evenings, when vehicles roamed the streets collecting 'night soil', strolls were unpleasant affairs, but the stench was even worse during the day, as I discovered first-hand. It was close to noon when we entered the town. After starting our journey on foot, we had caught gharries and rickshaws the rest of the way and arrived in

Ipoh at a time when the Malayan heat aided the decomposition of dead animals – the dogs and gamey fish and pole cats – which lay on the sides of streets. Wafts of decaying life mingled with the odours from heaps of rubbish, also unattended.

'Why you bring me here?' I asked Peng Choon within minutes. The fire must have been apparent in my eyes, because my husband looked sheepish when he told me he thought Ipoh was going to be the future of Malaya. He would one day be proven right, but as I stood surveying the Kuala Kangsar Road, it hardly seemed possible. I had barely set foot in town and already I was desperately missing Penang. I longed for the sea.

Peng Choon was as handsome as Mother had described. He turned heads everywhere; he certainly turned mine. On our wedding night, as soon as he lifted the veil of my headgear, I saw his dimples, tiny depressions carved into the bottoms of both cheeks. They charmed others too, because even those who barely knew him talked about 'the man with the dimples'.

Peng Choon was older when he married me – thirty – but retained a copious head of hair, the strands so black they shone. His lips, thin and malleable, were like a woman's, while his cheekbones stood out as if they had been carved. He was tall, at nearly five feet eleven inches, with a muscular body he held straight when he walked – 'A carriage like a prince's,' as Mother had said.

I was pleased Peng Choon had chosen me for his wife, but there were many occasions when I worried he would be tempted elsewhere, especially during that first year. He travelled the length and breadth of the Kinta District, visiting estates all over, inspecting their books and preparing their accounts. Because transportation then was hardly what it is now, he was forced to spend many nights outstation – and I sometimes wondered how he coped. He never gave me cause to worry, but that didn't stop me from imagining and fretting and wanting to quickly bear him a son before he went about looking for a woman who could.

When we were first married, I asked Peng Choon why he had picked me. He laughed. He was a man who knew what he wanted: a family run by a strong hand – a healthy woman who could cook, bear him sons and look after the household. He expected to travel and needed an independent wife who would get things done without him.

So when the matchmaker mentioned me, he immediately became interested. 'You sure-ah?' she had asked. 'This girl has strong will and a temper.' She told him where we lived, and he had strolled along Ah Kwee Street in the evenings, spying on me now and again. He told me he noticed my lustrous hair, glistening in the light of dusk. He tried to imagine what it would look like hanging down. He said he liked how healthy I appeared as I strode about; I took strong steps yet it was clear I had been well brought up. One morning, when he followed me to the market, he noticed that the stallholders didn't try to cheat me, as they did other women. That was the day he decided he would marry me.

All this he told me, and more. In those first lonely months my husband also became my best friend.

Wong Peng Choon was a Ka-Yin-Chu Hakka from a village in Chiao-Ling County, in the north-east of Kwangtong Province. He came from a family of farmers who lived at the bottom of hills in the countryside. In their village, life had remained unchanged. The air was fresh, and people quenched their thirst by drawing water from wells – spring water that tasted sweet on the tongue. Peng Choon told me he had missed China badly during his early months in Penang. He would think about his village, about how tasty the rice was; he would picture the succulent vegetables, imagine the lusciousness of fruit as it ripened on trees and dream about home.

But then he remembered why he had left.

For years, whenever the *sui-hak*, the recruitment men, came to call, Peng Choon would listen to their tales. They spoke of fabulous lands beyond the South China Seas, places where money could literally be dug from beneath the ground. Peng Choon absorbed these stories and was tempted to follow the *sui-hak*, not because of what they said but because he yearned to see the world. He looked around his village and tried to imagine what lay over the hills.

Among the Hakka it is the women who work in the fields, while the men sit in the shade of trees playing the erhu and chatting. I was amazed; I would have hated being in a Hakka family. Fortunately, it wasn't a life that had appealed to Peng Choon either: as he grew older, he became increasingly restless.

Being the eldest boy in the family, Peng Choon alone was sent to the village school, where he learnt to read and write and memorise Confucian classics. He was also taught arithmetic, which he very much enjoyed. Peng Choon had a natural ability with figures, which was how he landed his job in Ipoh.

In all the time that my husband remained in his village, he was given only one task: to sell what the women in his village grew year in and year out at the best possible prices. It was hardly challenging work for an intelligent man, and Peng Choon spent hours reading Confucian classics in the shadows of the hills. At his father's insistence he married a Hakka girl from the next village, who bore him a son after a year.

Despite this seemingly idyllic life, Peng Choon became troubled as time passed. On the annual visits of the *sui-hak*, he saw men leaving, men from his village as well as the surrounding areas, each carrying a bundle under his arm. He watched as they marched towards a new life.

One night Peng Choon had a dream. A large bird appeared, hovering overhead, pointing its beak as if it were telling him to go forth. When the bird landed, it stood upright, and Peng Choon saw that it was a noble-looking creature with fiery reddish-orange feathers. In his slumber Peng Choon recognised the Vermillion Bird of the South, but when he woke he was engrossed again in his reading and forgot about the dream. The next night the Vermillion Bird of the South appeared once more. This time it spoke. 'Go to the Nanyang, the South Sea,' it told Peng Choon. On the second day, when Peng Choon woke up he remembered his dream, but he did nothing with it and told no one. Finally, when the Vermillion Bird of the South appeared for the third night in a row it said to him, 'You must go to the Nanyang, and do it soon.' This time Peng Choon revealed to his wife and family what had happened.

Over the next week much wailing could be heard in the Wong household. While Peng Choon's parents and wife agonised, offerings were made and the gods duly consulted. On that occasion the gods remained stubbornly silent. Convinced nonetheless by the strength of the apparition, Peng Choon stood firm, telling his family, 'I have dreamt the same dream for three nights in a row. It is an omen. I must obey.'

When the *sui-hak* next came to his village, Peng Choon made preparations to leave. His wife and son bid him a tearful farewell, while he was fearful and excited at the same time. Peng Choon set sail from Swatow in an old junk cramped full of men. It looked rugged on the outside, but once set on the seas the boat was tossed like a toy. Peng Choon thought it would capsize and they would all drown.

Because he could read and write and spoke Hakka as well as Hokkien, Peng Choon found work easily in Penang. Within days he was hired by a coconut- and copra-exporting company owned by the Khoo family – as a clerk, to look after its accounts. The Khoo company accounts were kept in both Chinese and English, but Peng Choon didn't speak English at the time and dealt only with the Chinese accounts. The English accounts, meanwhile, were managed by Baba men who spoke English. As a result Peng Choon became friends with many Baba men and started learning English from them. An impatient student, he read everything he could get his hands on, beginning first with primary school textbooks and thereafter progressing to other books and eventually to newspapers – to the *Penang Gazette*, just as Father had done.

His diligence was soon noticed by his boss. Peng Choon was given increasing responsibilities with the company's books and ledgers. The Khoo family also owned estates in the Federated Malay States. When an opportunity came up in the Kinta District, Peng Choon jumped at the chance.

At that point he was forced to consider his future. He had been in the Straits Settlements for three years by then; he knew there was no turning back. In deciding to put down roots, he had to find a wife. Not surprisingly, he chose to look for one from within the community most familiar to him in Penang.

When we met, Peng Choon had already been introduced to Nyonya-Baba culture. He had a natural affinity for the Malay customs we adopted. He adored the colourful baju panjang and sarongs I wore and the quaint phrases I spiced our conversations with, which I often had to spend time explaining. He relished the fiery dishes I put in front of him. Night after night, as we sat down to dinner – he with his chopsticks, and I with my bare hands – he would lick his bowl. I smiled, thrilled at my power to tickle his palate and satisfy his hunger.

Under my influence Peng Choon learnt to savour dishes he had never tried before. To my surprise he even developed a taste for *petai*, the stinking green bean unique to South East Asia. Normally stir-fried in a sambal paste, *petai* is best known for the pungent aroma it leaves in the room – and in latrines afterwards. I love its texture and smell, but *petai* is an acquired taste. I was amazed my recently arrived Chinese husband took to it.

Over time we wove ourselves into the fabric of each other's lives. Our mixed marriage never created difficulties; I could hardly have asked for a better husband. The fears I had before our marriage never came to pass: Peng Choon did not drink or gamble or smoke, and I'm confident he was faithful. Had he taken a woman on the side, I feel sure I would have known.

As was typical for a Nyonya woman, I was head of our household. Unusually for a Chinese man, Peng Choon had agreed to this arrangement at the outset of our marriage, while we were still living with my family in Penang. Every month, when my husband brought home his income he would hand me the money, and I would store it in a fireproof safe we kept securely locked in one corner of our bedroom. I realised early on that the way I managed our budget would decide what type of food we ate and where we could afford to live once we had our own home.

For his part my husband worked hard. He would leave our house at seven every morning and return only around six in the evening. The hours in between were painful; the change from our house on Ah Kwee Street came as a shock. There I had always had others for company: Mother or Ah Lai or my sisters. After moving to Ipoh I was alone inside a silent house for hours, and sometimes days, on end.

I know Peng Choon worried about this, because he often asked how I was. I always told a small lie. He had plenty to cope with in his new job and I didn't want to add to his list of burdens. In those early months I longed for the hour of his return.

8

It did not take long for me to get used to Ipoh. As I became familiar with the town, I understood what my husband meant: things were happening. Within weeks brick-and-mortar buildings had sprung up to replace wooden sheds; tracts of land were cleared where smallholdings of rubber trees and *lalang* weeds had previously been, and Chinese immigrants poured into town in a never-ending flow, so that the population grew before my very eyes.

We had not been there long when we ventured out for a good look around town. Heading out of the Chinese quarter, we went first towards the higher ground reserved for English buildings – the area around the Padang, the main playing field, where the white devils liked to congregate. Everything about the Padang looked tidy: the playing field was well tended, its lawn evenly trimmed and the grass a shiny green, as if watered several times each day. Peng Choon told me the Padang had only been created the year before, paid for by members of the Chinese community who wished to commemorate the sixtieth year of the reign of the English queen. There had been equally big celebrations in Penang, but I was engrossed then in wedding preparations and had paid little attention to the festivities. For the first time I heard the queen's name said in English. Peng Choon made a sound like 'Beek-toh-lia'; I remember it being difficult to pronounce and meaning little, as I had never seen a picture of her.

I was impressed by the English quarter, though, with its wide streets and open space. The weather that morning was nearly perfect for a long stroll. Rain had fallen hard the night before. The skies, though overcast, remained clear, and the sun was lurking and threatening to break out, but it was still cool. In the morning air everything smelt crisp and fresh. Water droplets visible on the leaves in the English quarter gave them a bright emerald hue. There were far more trees than buildings. The few buildings were shaded, built of brick and painted completely in white. They looked exalted and grand, even though they were not all public buildings.

My attention was diverted by a set of houses directly opposite the Padang which stretched across the entire width of the field. Peng Choon told me they formed the Ipoh Club, a place only whites were allowed to enter. He said this bluntly with an undercurrent of animosity that caught me by surprise. Till then I had absorbed Father's deference towards the British without giving it much thought. They were our rulers, a fact I accepted; we had after all left Siam because of the opportunities brought by the British to the Straits Settlements. But the tone in Peng Choon's voice stirred memories that must have lain buried inside, for I suddenly recalled the days of my childhood in Songkhla. I remembered things I had heard a long time ago – the sense of brooding resentment in how the whites were discussed: politely, yet not quite as others were talked about, their rule accepted because it was our fate; tolerated, but never fully welcome. After we arrived in Penang, Father's attitude had shifted to one of complete respect, and I forgot how it had been before.

Walking around the perimeter of the Padang, I recalled all this as I stared at the Ipoh Club. Its ambience was different from that in the parts of town in which I spent my time, and though everything was perfectly kept, I did not like it. Hardly anyone was around, unlike where we lived, and nothing seemed to be happening. I couldn't imagine what the whites did inside their sedate buildings.

Peng Choon told me they drank. He said that unlike everyone else, white devils were allowed to buy alcohol inside their club without paying in cash, so they went about drinking and owing money. Sometimes they would come out on to the field to play ball games. There was a game they especially liked, one Peng Choon had watched in Penang but of which he had been unable to make head or tail. He saw men around a field, one hurling a ball, another trying to hit it with a wooden bat. There was a spurt of running, but most of the time the men stood watching the ball or trying to retrieve it from some extreme corner. A Baba friend had tried to explain the rules, of which there were many, but Peng Choon had given up. It was too complicated and rather boring, as matches went on for days. Who else but whites could find so much time?

We continued walking. We went everywhere that morning, very much enjoying each other's company. I remember feeling young, light-headed – a feeling that hadn't touched me since my days in Songkhla. As we ambled along, I looked at Peng Choon many times and glowed. I was so proud of being seen with him. There were times in those early days when I still couldn't quite believe he was my husband.

That morning I was dressed in the delicate red baju panjang and Pekalongan sarong I had worn on the eve of my wedding, while Peng Choon had on a pair of baggy trousers and a white Mandarin jacket with wide, loose sleeves. Over his head he wore a dark Chinese cloth cap, but you could tell he didn't have the traditional queue – he told me he'd had it cut off once he made a decision to settle in Penang. It was a symbolic severance of ties. On this, as on other matters, my husband was ahead of time; it was still the fashion then among *sinkehs*, the recent Chinese immigrants, to wear their hair long, twisted into a braid at the back. I was glad Peng Choon didn't keep a queue. I thought they looked silly, though he would have been handsome regardless.

After our circuit around the Padang we turned on to Hugh Low Street. At my insistence we went towards the Kinta River, because I was curious to see what lay on the other side. In those days New Town had not yet been built and there was hardly anything on the other side, but I was not going to be satisfied until I had seen it. Peng Choon went along with the idea just to please me. By then the sun had broken through and the dark clouds had disappeared. My husband opened up the paper umbrella I had brought so that we could continue walking comfortably huddled under its shade.

After the lush greenness of the English quarter, the contrast in the Chinese part of town was stark. Here the richness of life was on full display. People sat inside coffee shops with legs stretched out on solid wooden chairs, some with knees lifted towards their chins, eating rice with roasted duck and noodles with dumplings, chatting, smoking, laughing and occasionally shouting raucously. Over the backstreets clothes were strung on bamboo poles suspended overhead, one end against the window ledge of a house, the other end resting on the ledge of the house opposite. Every type of garment could be seen: jacket, trousers, skirt, socks, underwear – all exposed to the world. On the ground was noise and merriment, because the theatre on Leech Street was in full swing; it always seemed in full swing whatever the time of night or day.

Despite the ruckus there were men fast asleep on the five-foot ways. They were many yards from us, yet the thick smell of unwashed bodies reached my nostrils. Piled next to one another, they were dead to the world, some with mouths wide open. In the shadows cast by the pillars and walls, I could see the tobacco stains on their thin singlets, and a few had tattered shirts which barely covered their bones, so that their ribs showed. All were blissfully unaware of anything around them.

'One day the white devils will pay for what they've done.'

Peng Choon said this sharply, almost hissing it out. I turned round to touch his arm, even though it was broad daylight and I knew that people would look.

I searched my husband's face, trying to understand what had made him so angry. Peng Choon was a passionate man, but unlike me he had an even temper and was not given to public displays of emotion. Yet when he uttered those words, his voice was tinged with a bitterness I had not heard before.

'You know an opium addict?' I asked. My husband was silent before turning to face me. I could not see his eyes properly because of the brightness of the sunlight and the shade from the umbrella, but he sounded sorrowful. His voice was shaky.

'There was a man from my village.'

With a preoccupied air he resumed walking. Peng Choon told me about the man from his village, a man called Tet Weng, who had left to seek his fortune in Swatow. They weren't close, but they had been playmates as boys. Nothing was heard from him for years. Then just before boarding his boat for Penang, Peng Choon saw Tet Weng sitting on a side street of Swatow, emaciated and weak. He was a shadow of his former self but was still well enough to turn away in shame, and Peng Choon regretted not having gone up to greet his fellow Hakka.

'Whatever he has become, it isn't all his own fault,' my husband said to me.

That was the first of many conversations we were to have about opium. Until then I had conveniently clung to Father's beliefs, one of which was that smoking opium was a habit the Chinese were born with. When we first arrived in Ipoh, I had been shocked by the number of addicts on the streets, but I had since grown used to them. Although I pitied the men, I assumed they were responsible for their own misery.

Peng Choon was the first to tell me that it was the British who encouraged opium addiction. The colonial administration sold opium indirectly – via opium farms, which were rented out as concessions.

Chinese businessmen were encouraged to bid for the farms and to run them; in turn, they plied the drug to the coolies who worked for them. It was the same with gambling. There were gambling concessions and farms into which Chinese coolies were enticed every payday. In fact, the only people allowed by law into gambling dens in Perak were the Chinese. Through these simple means the colonial administration raised money – while keeping its conscience clean and its Chinese workers in thrall.

My husband forced me to view British rule in a new light. Unlike Father, who was deferential, Peng Choon was critical. In China, he said, the British treated the Chinese like dogs; they behaved better in Malaya, but he was still angry about the way they sold opium. He thought their actions would come back to haunt them. Peng Choon was an advocate of the Anti-Opium Society years before its formation in the Federated Malay States. The seeds of disquiet he sowed in me turned over time into animosity. I could no longer have the rose-tinted view of white rule Father had had.

Such thoughts bore down on me as we stepped on to the Hugh Low Bridge to cross the Kinta River. The Hugh Low Bridge was still a wooden structure then, but the Kinta River looked very much the same as it does now, its waters brown and muddy. We rested on the bridge for a minute. I marvelled at the river, at its simple existence. It was just there – flowing placidly along, oblivious to the tumultuous world around it.

In the early days the Chinese called Ipoh 'Pa Lo'. The name comes from the Malay word *paloh*, which referred to the pools alongside the dams of the Kinta River. The fishing traps that were placed into these pools became famous, and a temple was built close to the riverbank. Dedicated to the founding spirit of the Chinese settlement, the Pa Lo

Old Temple was surrounded by trees when I first visited. The open space in front of it – the People's Park – came later.

Pa Lo Old Temple, the first temple ever built in Ipoh, was guarded by a pair of handsome stone lions. It had an ornate roof, with elaborate carvings of deities, dragons and phoenixes decorating its ridges.

But it was in atmosphere that Pa Lo Old Temple excelled. I felt at home at once. As soon as I stepped beyond the white fence which protected the verandah at the front, an inner peace descended. It was as if I had walked through a magical door. The abundance of trees helped, as did the tranquillising call of the turtle doves outside. Stopping on the verandah to listen, I was spellbound. Sometimes, when all was quiet, I could hear the water of the Kinta River as it trickled past.

Inside the Pa Lo Old Temple, while holding a handful of joss-sticks and thinking about the beauty in this world, I met Siew Lan. Because she was dressed in similar fashion to me, we noticed each other immediately. Unlike Penang, Ipoh did not have a ready-made Nyonya-Baba community, and whenever I saw someone whose clothes indicated she was a Nyonya or he a Baba, my interest was aroused. I could not help myself; my eyes would dart straight to the other person.

So it was with Siew Lan.

There are people whose lives are etched into their faces, and Siew Lan was one of these. She had the saddest face I've ever known: eyes stamped with the imprint of harsh words; a forehead creased by worry; and a smile so diffident I thought it would disappear, as if she dared not be happy even for a moment. Which is not to say that Siew Lan was unattractive; her lips were thick and sensuous, and when animated, she glowed with a beauty from within, unenhanced by jewel sets or rings, rouge paper or charcoal pencils.

Siew Lan was timid, but I liked her at once. I took instantly to that exquisitely innocent face which told a thousand stories of hardship. We started chatting at the temple and continued as we walked to my house.

I heard how, when Siew Lan was fifteen, her mother had been duped. Siew Lan was married to a man from Hainan who had been described by the matchmaker as a businessman in his thirties. The bridegroom turned out to be twenty years older than purported and a dishwasher at one of the Chinese coffee shops on Leech Street. He was dirty, infected with tuberculosis, and violent when drunk. Siew Lan endured a year of marital hell. After one beating too many, she left him while he was working at the restaurant.

Siew Lan fled Ipoh for Taiping, the capital of Perak, where she found work cooking and looking after children. That had been nine years ago. She had not dared to return, knowing that her husband had been looking for her all around town and even as far afield as Batu Gajah. It was only after consumption took his life that she returned to Ipoh, her dignity intact but with a deep regret, for in her absence she had missed her poor mother's funeral.

When we met, Siew Lan was looking for work. It took a while before she was hired, because she demanded seven dollars a month – a princely sum at the time. On top of that she was picky about her household. Siew Lan had managed to save a small amount, and because of her renowned culinary skills she could afford to be choosy. With free time on her hands, Siew Lan spent hours at my house chewing betel nut leaves and chatting. We talked about Ipoh, about the households and prospective employers she had seen. We discussed our favourite stallholders in the market and told stories from our past. We exchanged street gossip about the women who lived nearby, their husbands and what they did. There was no limit to what we talked about; sometimes we ended up rolling on the floor, cackling like children.

Besides my husband, Siew Lan became my first real friend in Ipoh. Peng Choon was happy I had a companion. He told me so himself as he gave me the warmest of smiles. But there were times, beneath the flash of his dimples, when I had a sneaking suspicion that he was just that little bit jealous.

One day I felt a sensation in my belly. It was only a mild tug, but the pull was sharp enough to make me look down. I stroked my stomach. My monthly bleeding was already several weeks late. It now seemed that the time had come.

I wanted to shout to my husband. He of course was at work, so I did the next best thing: I went to see Siew Lan. She held both my hands in hers as she told me, with tears in her eyes, 'Chye Hoon, I so happy for you.'

9

It was an agony like none I had known. Squatting with legs wide apart, I clung to Mother for dear life. The *bidan*, a Malay housewife in her fifties who had delivered babies for a quarter of a century, knelt beside me. She watched every contortion of my face. When the time was at hand, she moved behind my back.

Alongside Mother, the *bidan*, whose name was Soraiya, was with me continuously during the final twenty-four hours. They took turns wiping my brow, giving me water and massaging my stomach with herbal oils. Soraiya, who could feel the baby, assured me everything was fine. She told me its head and legs were in the right position and she expected a straightforward birth. Still, it was my first child. When the contractions began, I was unprepared. I lay on my back, sprawled out in shock.

The *bidan* dabbed at the perspiration on my forehead with a damp towel. When the spasms started, they were just pangs; later on they became more intense and frequent. At some point I began to scream. I cried, shouting at the top of my lungs. Soraiya murmured, 'Not long now, my dear,' as she rested her hands on my belly. She continued massaging me with herbal oil. During those last stages I felt a force under her expert hands as the life within me made desperate attempts to get out. Between contractions the *bidan* helped me sit up. Getting out of bed, I thought I would faint, but somehow, holding on to Mother, I made it on to the floor. My waters had broken earlier with just a pop, a sound so soft it could barely be heard. Then the fluid gushed out, wetting a large patch on the bed. As I squatted, more fluid continued flooding the floor. I had not been especially large during pregnancy, and I was amazed by the volume of water.

Soraiya's able kneading of my back soothed me. When the paroxysms returned, they came with explosive force, faster . . . and harder . . . then faster . . . and I heard the *bidan* say, 'Nearly there, my love. And now you must push.'

I know I was screaming then as I had never screamed before. Peng Choon, who had been sent outside, described my cries as heart-wrenching. Back in his village his first wife had barely shouted during the birth of their son, and he became worried when he heard me.

I was aware of little except the pain. I had to brace myself for each spasm; as soon as it gripped, the shock forced me to release my lungs, so that the pangs completely enveloped me. Sounds exploded in my head. I could not bear the slightest rustle or clink; even the scrape of a teacup against its saucer drove me mad, and I yelled at Mother to stop drinking. Somewhere in between Soraiya said, 'Relax. Now push, keep pushing.' I responded, doing the only thing I could: I relaxed, then pushed, relaxed, then pushed again in continuous rhythm. By the end the whole of my body was sore, every bone . . . every muscle . . . the whole of my back . . . a torment so excruciating all I wanted was for my baby to come out so that it could all be over.

When I first suspected I was pregnant, my excitement was mingled with anxiety. Peng Choon's reaction was similar; he became in turn ecstatic, laughing loudly ('Good, good!') and then worried ('You sure-ah?') and finally excited once more, grinning like a child. We stood facing one another for a long time, as if in disbelief, caressing the loose baju covering my belly. It was what he wanted – a Malayan-born son. We both hoped it would be for real, that we were indeed moving towards that world of his dreams.

After the initial tug, sickness interrupted my morning routine. I noticed new sensations early on. A strange taste lingered in my mouth, a bitter taste I associated with rusty nails. That was why I developed a craving for sour food. I would go into our kitchen looking for the Malay gooseberry pickles we kept in lidded bowls and sit stuffing them into my mouth. Other times I woke up dreaming of stir-fried cucumbers in vinegar and would long for the taste of them. I made *achar awak* so much that I added it to my culinary repertoire. Its assortment of cabbage, carrots, cucumbers and long beans, dried in the sun, then pickled in a wonderful lemongrass-infused paste and topped with nuts, kept the bitterness in my mouth at bay.

For many months I remained small. People who did not know me thought I was simply putting on weight. I'm the same height as Mother – five feet two inches – and I was a slim woman then, before my children came, so that my pregnancy was not obvious. I felt strangely alive. Every part of my body grew. My hair, which at the time already flowed down to the waist, suddenly reached the floor; my fingernails, all pink and rosy, demanded frequent attention.

One day I felt a gentle tickling inside my belly like the flicker of a butterfly against the skin. The sudden touch brought back memories of Songkhla and the butterflies I had once caught. Soon the tickling turned into a tumbling as my baby made itself comfortable deep inside me.

It was then that other worries came to the fore. I remembered how weak Mother had been after the birth of my younger sister, Chye Keat. When I had demanded to be allowed into her room, Mother had looked so limp as she lay in bed that I feared she would die. We knew women who had died giving birth and had heard stories of many others bleeding violently, their babies stillborn or strangled by their own cords. I longed to have Mother by my side when the time came, to have her wisdom with me.

I confided as much to Siew Lan. My friend often came to see me. We would sit chatting, she drinking coffee and chewing betel nut leaves, me sipping tea as we made plans for my pregnancy. It was Siew Lan who persuaded me to invite Mother to Ipoh. I was then worrying about anything and everything. Wild, random thoughts raced through my mind. What if my child was born dead or sickly? There seemed to be so much I did not know. How would I cope without help, as we could not afford a servant then, even though Peng Choon tried to persuade me otherwise? As for a *bidan*, if I were to locate one, how would I judge whether she was any good? These were things Mother would have at her fingertips. A wave of relief washed over me when she agreed to stay with us for six months.

Newborn babies look ugly, unless they happen to be your own.

Professionals, of course, know what to say, and Soraiya had a tender look as she handed me a bundle in soft cloth. 'You have a lovely baby,' she whispered. 'A girl, yes, but so pretty.'

Disappointment gripped me. Mother, though, fussed about with cooing noises, and when I saw my baby girl I understood why. She was beautiful, with her pink face, shock of black hair and the tiniest fingers, which lay unmoving. My baby was so placid I was not even sure she was alive, but then she started to cry.

Through a slit in the window, a slice of light showed up motes of dust. My husband charged through the mist, expecting the worst. When he saw the two of us lying peacefully together, he let out a palpable sigh.

'You have a sweet baby girl,' Mother announced proudly.

I looked hard at Peng Choon, knowing his desire for a boy. We'd talked months before about the Chinese custom of giving away girl babies as sacrifices to the gods in the hope that a boy would eventually come. It was a practice I found odious. I was pleasantly surprised by Peng Choon's assurance that he would never ask me to give away a child. 'Wife,' he said, 'I want a son, but giving away a child – no, I can't do that.'

Yet I wasn't sure I completely believed him. As I searched his face, I wondered what he was thinking. If my husband felt any disappointment that day, he masked it well. He told me later he had been convinced from my screams that I would die. While pacing outside, he swore he would accept whatever the gods granted. He just wanted us alive and well.

After entering the room, he stared at me as if he had seen a miracle. He ran to my side, asking repeatedly, 'You well? You all right?' And then he looked at our baby and for a while just stood smiling. Finally, he asked to hold his daughter.

'She's a healthy baby,' he said softly. 'We have time enough for a boy.'

We called our first daughter Hui Fang in the hope that she would grow up with the fragrance of kindness.

For seven days after Hui Fang's birth, Soraiya came to our house from her kampong to attend to my postnatal care. She took a long-handled piece of iron with an end shaped like an elongated bat, heated it over clumps of charcoal in the kitchen and then wrapped the bat in layers of cloth. Next would begin the slow massage, her wrapped-up bat carefully dabbing my exposed abdomen portion by portion to expel the airs that had aggregated in the course of pregnancy. How much excess air I had I did not know, but I savoured every minute of Soraiya's rhythmic circling.

In addition to this Malay tradition, I was kept inside the house for a month, because we also followed the Chinese practice of confinement. Mother coddled me endlessly, and there were times when I felt like a child once more. She sat watching me eat the dishes she had prepared, food smothered in plenty of sesame oil and sliced ginger to replenish lost energy. Every evening she gave me a cup of Chinese rice wine, and she kept me on a diet so strict I could hardly wait for the month to end, even though I was spoilt by not having to work.

During the day Mother took Hui Fang off my hands and carried her about so that I could rest. I would wake to see Mother in the chair opposite our bed, cradling my daughter in her arms. We did not talk then, as we were loath to wake the baby, but we would look at each other, Mother and I, exchanging smiles. The warmth in her eyes told me she enjoyed being with us.

Through Mother's diet I recovered my strength. Meanwhile I nursed my daughter, who grew bigger by the day.

To celebrate Hui Fang's first month and the end of my confinement, we made the traditional Nyonya meal of many colours. I was stronger by then and able to help in the kitchen, but Siew Lan also joined us, as there was much work to be done. We joked while stirring coconut milk into the yellow turmeric rice in a steamer, and I laughed so much I had to sit down. I watched Mother prepare the chicken curry, its rich sauce dripping red with chillies. The aroma of shallots and garlic frying – smells so familiar to me – drifted through the air. As I looked at Mother and Siew Lan, I was reminded of our boisterous kitchen in Ah Kwee Street, where women had congregated to gossip, giggle and make delicious food. A longing for times past hit me. I was suddenly proud of my kitchen, of what I could do inside it. *This*, I thought, *is what being a Nyonya means*. Deep within my bones I felt my culture stir – the calling of my ancestors.

Later that night we delivered peach-shaped *angkoo kueh* and pink-coloured eggs to our new friends in Ipoh. For Nyonyas and Babas, the gifts mark a baby's first full month in this life. We had been uncertain what to do with friends who were not Nyonyas and Babas. Under my direction Siew Lan made extra *angkoo kueh*, which were one of my favourites. When my husband returned from work, I persuaded him to carry the *angkoo* and pink eggs all around town in our *sia nah*, our black-lacquered containers. In total he visited thirty households. For some the *angkoo* were a novelty, for others a pleasure, and in some homes there was surprise that so much was done to greet the arrival of a girl.

10

Mother returned to Penang when Hui Fang was five months old. I was sorry to see her go. We had grown close again, and the house felt tomb-like after she left, its silence broken only by the sounds my baby made.

In those first few days I hated hearing the little one cry. I really missed Mother then. In between double boiling bird's nest soups and preparing herbed rice to dispel the winds of pregnancy, Mother had managed to calm my daughter. She made it look easy, at times rocking Hui Fang, at other times bringing her to me.

Then she was gone, and all I had were instructions. Among these I recalled the simple words 'Sometimes you must let her cry.'

But that was easier said than done. With Mother no longer there, I was awake at all hours of night, able to steal only a few moments' rest during the day.

As the weeks passed, my rage gathered. There were times when it became too much, when my head felt as if it would burst. I would scream unwittingly, and my poor terrified daughter would bawl. Remorse filled me then; I would pick my daughter up to hold her close – so close I could feel her breath on my skin – and be overcome by this tiny bundle in my arms who seemed to want me no matter what I did or didn't do.

Until I learnt to put Mother's strictures into practice, I walked in a fatigued haze, ground down by my daughter's push and pull. I wondered how Mother had done it, how she had ground spices into pastes, chopped and fried, braised and steamed, made lunch and dinner over and over while we three older ones had torn around, bruising her in our wake. Mother had toiled on her own, yet she had found the time to nurse mangoes and limes and papayas in her garden and pickle them in glazed jars. I felt sudden shame. I had not even thought to thank her.

It was also Mother who had brought Soraiya to us. Within days of her arrival Mother found her way to Kampong Laxamana across the Kinta River, where, on making discreet enquiries, she discovered this gem seemingly without effort. I hardly knew Soraiya, yet I trusted her instinctively. I had not seen her since the seventh day of Hui Fang's birth, but I knew I would call on her again.

Peng Choon missed Mother too, except he may not have realised it. I was livelier when she was with us. Without Mother I could barely stand by the time I saw my husband.

He did not help. In his head he knew life had changed, but in his heart he did not like sharing me. No longer could I wait breathlessly for his return or dine uninterrupted. Instead I would cast my eye in the direction of the little sling, a piece of soft cotton cloth hanging from a nail in the ceiling, where the little one was cradled while we had our meal. Peng Choon never said anything, but his dimples disappeared, which told me he missed being the centre of attention. There were moments when I had to rush to Hui Fang's sling. Those were the times Peng Choon looked at me with eyes full of reproach, as if to say, *What about me?* He was just like a boy sometimes.

To make it up to my husband, I took extra pains preparing his favourite dishes and sweeping and dusting, so that the house looked welcoming when he came home. I never knew whether he realised how much harder I had to work after Hui Fang's arrival. A word of acknowledgement now and again would have done wonders, but this never came.

Yet it thrilled me that my husband depended on me for his every need. I fed him, warmed his bed, gave him solace and provided order in the house while also seeing to our daughter. Between the two of them, my daughter and husband kept me on my feet, but at least Peng Choon had no reason to be tempted anywhere else.

Meanwhile Siew Lan found work in the house of a white devil, a Scottish planter who was a bachelor. She knew I didn't like the idea. 'The red-haired devils like to drink,' I said. 'Who knows what he might do?' But my friend brushed me off, pointing out that there were other servants – a gardener who lived in and a washerwoman who visited each morning to do his laundry. I told her this made it worse, as it meant she spent her nights with two unmarried men. Siew Lan merely smiled. 'That why the pay so good-lah!' Although she said this breezily, I could tell she was twitchy, because her thick lips trembled. 'Anyway this red-haired devil not so bad.' Peering closely at my friend, I asked, 'So, he pay how much?'

'Ten dollars a month' came the reply. It was a lavish sum; I only hoped he wasn't expecting additional services. As I said this, Siew Lan looked away hastily. She started talking about him, about how old he seemed, but then declared that it was hard to tell the ages of white devils because their skin wrinkled earlier than ours. Even the younger women who visited had lines on their faces and crinkles around their eyes.

Peng Choon never took an interest in these conversations, deriding them as 'women's talk', but when I told him about Siew Lan's new employment, my husband listened intently. His immediate reaction was that she was out to snare the white devil.

'Ay, this my friend,' I retorted indignantly. 'She not like that-lah.'

'You wait,' he replied.

Taking a deep breath, I bit my tongue. Siew Lan's refusal to meet my eye told me she liked the white devil. But who was I to know what she was hoping for? Given the life she'd had, I did not wish to stand in judgment. I only hoped my dear friend would have enough sense not to damage her reputation.

Not that I had time to worry, because I soon fell pregnant again. This time, when Peng Choon suggested that we hire a servant, I consented. He had just received a pay rise and money was less tight.

When I mentioned to Siew Lan that we were looking for a servant, her eyes lit up: she said she knew a Cantonese girl called Ah Hong who happened to be looking for work. Ah Hong came knocking one morning, and Siew Lan had liked her instantly. There are some people, she told me, who you just know will be dependable. Ah Hong was one of these.

Ah Hong was a slender seventeen-year-old when we met. Her hair, tied up into two dainty braids that hung down over her shoulders, made her look younger. She was painfully shy and would only smile in answer to questions. At the time I thought it was because she hadn't understood. Between us, with my Hokkien and Hakka and her Cantonese, we were like hen and duck and had to resort to sign language. Over time, when Ah Hong did not speak even when she could, I realised she preferred to smile, brightening up the whole room with her face.

After Ah Hong came to live with us, my second pregnancy passed in a flash. Ah Hong proved a rock, but I longed for Mother. I would have felt so much more secure if Mother had been by my side. That was not possible, since one of my sisters needed her. Despite Mother's absence I was more relaxed, as if knowing what to expect would make it less painful. In the end the second birth was difficult; if it hadn't been for Soraiya's wealth of experience, I would have died. I could feel every twist of Soraiya's fingers as she tugged and cajoled. The towels she dabbed me with were soaked red. I shrieked and screamed and ground my teeth hard. Outside, Peng Choon covered his ears. When he finally came in, his face was white and his hands shook.

The fears my husband harboured must have taken the edge off his disappointment, for we had another daughter, Hui Ying. Once again I worried, because whatever his outward demeanour, I knew that my husband would have preferred a boy.

Ah Hong, though, who was in the room when Hui Ying came into this world, took to our baby immediately. She would cradle Hui Ying for hours, blowing garlic breath on to her nose and tickling the little one's fingers.

In the weeks following Hui Ying's birth, Hui Fang demanded more attention than ever. Already able to walk, the child crawled on to every table and chair, lifting bowls and chopsticks and whatever she could grab before she was stopped. It was a battle of wills, the first of many I was to have with my children.

Thereafter, the days and nights merged into one. With Ah Hong's help I learnt that, except for the lurching of my heart, nothing terrible happened when I left the newborn to cry. My own recovery proved painful. Despite Ah Hong's heroic efforts at replicating Mother's recipes, weakness seeped into my bones. I did not lose weight this time. On the contrary, with my bajus tight and my waist generous, it was clear that my girlhood figure would remain a distant memory. As soon as I was able, I snipped at the rolls of fabric Siew Lan had brought to make the clothes more appropriate for a mother-of-two.

For Ah Hong, work multiplied. She was up for twelve hours every day scrubbing, shopping and cleaning. She never complained, even washing her three pairs of samfoos – the Chinese tunics and trousers she wore – twice a day, after they were soiled by baby Hui Ying's persistent dribbling. More than once I thanked Kuan Yin, the Goddess of Mercy, for the gift of Ah Hong, who supported me the way a column holds up the temple roof.

Peng Choon took the adjustments in his stride. Our nights were disturbed, my state dazed and fragile. Those months proved difficult for other reasons, because it was then out of the blue that my husband received news about his mother.

This was brought by a *sinkeh* from a neighbouring village, who told Peng Choon that his mother had fallen ill and become thinner. After the doctor in the nearest town had prescribed herbal concoctions, my mother-in-law stopped spending long hours in the fields. But with her upbringing, she was unable to cease completely and insisted on doing work.

For the first time since our marriage, there was a faraway look in Peng Choon's eyes. It would only flicker for a moment, but it was there long enough for me to glimpse. I knew at once that a longing was growing in him for his mother and his homeland. It was a feeling against which we could not compete. As I grappled with my failure to bear him a son, my husband's yearning for China cut through my heart.

Other children followed. When Weng Yu, our first son, arrived in 1902, I breathed a sigh of relief.

With his birth I understood how important it was for a woman to bring a boy into the world. As soon as Soraiya handed me my newly washed baby, she whispered, '*Sayang!* You have a beautiful child. A boy this time. Well done.' Even in my feeble condition I saw that her eyes shivered with a glimmer that hadn't been there at the births of my daughters. When Peng Choon stepped into the room, he was on fire. My husband glowed, barely able to stop looking at his son. 'My boy,' Peng Choon murmured, stroking Weng Yu's head. 'My Malayan-born son, you will continue the Wong family name here.'

My husband showed more understanding after Weng Yu's birth than after the arrival of our daughters. It was as if, having borne him a son, I could be forgiven anything. During my confinement he worried about keeping draughts out of the house and even started pestering Ah Hong about my food! 'More ginger,' he would tell her. This solicitude made me proud. I had been the woman to make his dream come true.

At the end of my confinement the celebration of Weng Yu's first month was a big event. Once again Siew Lan spent the day at our house, and, with Ah Hong helping, we prepared the celebratory meal. Finally, I was able to bring out the *angkoo* moulds I had purchased in anticipation of a son. The moulds were special: beautiful wooden blocks with the furrows of exquisitely carved tortoises.

Making *angkoo kueh* was an activity I had enjoyed since accepting my destiny as a Nyonya in Mother's scorching kitchen on Ah Kwee Street. The *angkoo* intended for the full moon of Weng Yu, my firstborn son, took on added significance. Nyonya *angkoo* had to be just the right shade of orange red, neither too orange nor too red, unlike the *angkoo* the Chinese women made, which looked like freshly squeezed blood. I took special care while adding water and colouring to the dough for the *angkoo* skins – tiny spoonfuls of red followed by orange. Rolling a small piece of dough on to my palm, I put it into a bamboo steamer for testing. When the colour came out perfect, we were ready to begin.

We flattened small pieces of dough, filled them with balls of the mushy mung bean we had prepared and then wrapped the skins up by creasing the edges with our fingers. Pressing the balls carefully into my tortoise-shaped moulds, we knocked the *angkoo* out. Siew Lan and I cackled at Ah Hong's initial attempts; instead of falling out naturally, her *angkoo* remained glued and emerged looking more like frogs than tortoises. She soon learnt. Together Ah Hong, Siew Lan and I spent hours making *angkoo*, laughing and all the while inhaling the ambrosial fragrance of pandanus which lingered. The spirit which pervaded my kitchen that afternoon has stayed in my mind. Life seemed so much less complicated then.

When Peng Choon carried the *angkoo* and pink eggs to our friends, congratulations poured in from every corner. We received messages of goodwill, fruit and *ang pow*, gifts of money wrapped in red envelopes. They came from all and sundry: neighbours, Peng Choon's colleagues, even acquaintances who were near-strangers. My family of course were truly delighted. Mother asked Father to write a short letter in which she said, 'Now breathe, Chye Hoon, you have a son.'

When I was well enough to go out, people on the streets rushed up to greet me. They would say, 'Peng Choon Sau, many congratulations! You had son, very good.' Or if we went for a stroll, with Peng Choon holding one of our daughters and me carrying Weng Yu, passers-by who stopped to ask about the baby would croon over him, 'Ah . . . a boy! Good, good!' Everywhere I went I was bathed in smiles and nods, the aura of approval for the mother of a newborn son.

Peng Choon was pleased with the attention showered on Weng Yu and me. Yet in a strange way his profound satisfaction also caused turmoil, because his loyalties remained split between Malaya and China. He had always sent money back to China via the *sui-hak*, but his mother's illness reminded him of his Chinese wife and son, making him feel a guilt he hadn't had before. He told me he had been selfish to leave them behind, seeking adventure and a life for himself at their expense. With the birth of a son in Malaya, the contrast between his two families was magnified, and Peng Choon was torn.

He toyed then with the idea of taking a trip back to his village, but the time didn't feel right. The Khoo family had reneged on a promise to promote him if he did well, and Peng Choon was certain they would replace him if he went away for months. His worries puzzled me. 'You can't get another job-ah?' I asked. Peng Choon explained that because he wanted to strike out on his own some day, he would remain with the Khoo family estates for as long as he could – they brought him a wide network of contacts. 'You never know what may be useful in the future,' he said.

So Peng Choon remained in the Kinta District with the Khoo family estates, savouring his Malayan-born son on the one hand, but with a mind half on China on the other.

Meanwhile we tried to save, but it proved impossible. Our expenses kept rising: we soon had a third daughter, Hui Lin, and what with another mouth to feed, new clothes to be made and yet more to be done, Peng Choon couldn't just leave for a few months. We simply did not have enough savings, and in those days it felt as if we never would.

11

Shortly after the birth of our second son, Weng Koon, the Khoo family estates brought in a young white man who had just stepped off a British steamship to be my husband's boss. Peng Choon, normally calm and controlled, was so furious he could hardly speak. 'There are plenty among our people who think the white man superior,' he told me in disgust.

Peng Choon resigned. Fate finally spurred him to start his own business. Peng Choon felt he had enough contacts in the Kinta District to make a go of it. Nonetheless, given our expanding family, it was a decision we pondered extensively. We discussed every aspect in minute detail, going over the pros and the cons back and forth, until Peng Choon was sick with worry. In the process I learnt what was required to run a business. I could not have foreseen how pivotal this information would one day become.

After much agonising Peng Choon set himself up as a roving accountant. He visited businesses to inspect their books and then produced accounts as often as these were required. His clients included many of the plantation and tin-mining companies in the district, which turned out to be both a bonus and a drawback: good because he was never short of customers; bad because his fortunes were inevitably tied to theirs. When rubber and tin were booming, my husband was handsomely rewarded; when prices fell, his clients were often unable to pay. That was how Peng Choon ended up with parcels of rubber estates, plots he accepted in lieu of cash.

Around the time that Peng Choon began his business, my fears for Siew Lan came to be realised. She hurried to our house one day, flustered and out of breath.

'I not know how to tell you,' she began.

'What-ah?'

Without preamble, Siew Lan blurted out, 'I pregnant.'

We sat looking at each other. 'Is his-kah?'

'Just happened,' Siew Lan replied rather defensively.

I longed to take my friend's hands in mine and say reassuring words but found I could not. Yet if I did not voice my concerns, who would? For it was clear she had such a blind spot for the white devil that she could no longer see the way the world worked.

'He want with you marry-ah?'

Siew Lan stayed mute.

'Good heart, open your eyes-lah,' I said. 'With white marry, how can-ah? I ask you.'

'In town have Eurasians,' Siew Lan declared, eyes momentarily flashing.

'Yes,' I said sadly, 'because before got so few of them they with us mix. Now they got so many, no need with us *champor*. Also you are his servant.'

'So?' Siew Lan's look was reproachful.

His friends, I imagined, would be horrified. 'You think they let you into their club-ah? Hah? Your Nyonya-Baba relatives, they how? You think they also happy-ah?'

At this my friend burst into tears. I stopped then; I had never intended to make her cry. I reached across to touch Siew Lan's arm, which only made her stiffen. My own muscles tensed, as if I had been the one to break her heart.

Siew Lan gave birth to a girl early in 1905. When I visited my friend days later, I was surprised by the thick black strands and crinkly skin, which reminded me of other Chinese babies. That was also when I met the white devil, who proved memorable for different reasons. He had thinning white hair like uncombed spiders' webs on his head, a face full of the red blotches seen on men who drank too much, and though it was only eight in the morning when I arrived, his eyes, crawling with red veins, were already bloodshot. Siew Lan claimed it was because he had been up all night, but I wasn't convinced. From that first impression I could not understand what she saw in him.

Siew Lan and I remained ensconced inside her quarters at the back of the house. Despite its tiny window, her room was surprisingly airy. It was sparsely furnished, with a pale yellow canvas bed, a bamboo mat on the floor and a small wooden box, in which Siew Lan kept her worldly possessions. Her boss came in regularly, hovering over her to make sure she didn't lack for anything. Each time he appeared he asked in bazaar Malay whether everything was good.

'See?' she said. 'He not so bad.'

I decided not to mention the clumps of hairs exposed by his short-sleeved shirt, thick curly tangles sprouting on both arms and pushing against his shirt buttons. It had taken all my will power not to stare. I asked, 'His name is what?'

'I no can say it-lah,' Siew Lan giggled. 'Have to learn. Sound like Se-Too-Wat-ah.'

I logged this at the back of my mind in case it came in handy. The man would not expect me to address him by name of course. They were all called Tuan, the Malay word for 'sir', and on entering the house I duly addressed him as that, a form of greeting he appeared satisfied with. I was only a friend of his servant's after all; Se-Too-Wat would remain Tuan, unless our circumstances changed. That was unlikely, since Siew Lan told me the Tuan wasn't intending to marry her.

An involuntary murmur escaped my lips. 'But then . . . you be his mistress-ah?'

Siew Lan refused to meet my gaze. Instead she dragged my name along her tongue. 'Ch-ye Ho-on,' she said, 'I happy. Yes, people going to talk-lah. So what? He to me better than my cursed husband!'

At that moment I recalled what Peng Choon had said about my friend having set out to ensnare the white devil. For a moment I wondered if it could be true. Siew Lan had put on weight with her pregnancy; her face was rounder, softer, her cheeks less gaunt and even the frown lines on her forehead had eased with the arrival of a child, as if someone had taken a steam iron to them.

In an attempt to ease the tension in the room, we started speaking at the same time.

'Siew Lan,' I began, only to hear her call my name too. We laughed. For the first time my friend looked up.

'You first,' she told me.

'Good. Tell me,' I said. 'He force you or not?'

'Of course not, Chye Hoon!' Siew Lan coloured. 'Why you think so bad about them . . . ? Why you so much hate red-haired devils?'

'I no hate them.'

'But you no like them.'

'No.'

'Why? They have done what to you?'

At that moment Siew Lan's baby girl burped. My friend thumped her daughter's back, causing white bubbles to dribble out of the little mouth. I watched the gurgles, comforted by Siew Lan's humming. I remembered Songkhla, how I had not wanted to leave – the walk I took around Ipoh with my husband – and how the white devils kept to themselves, away from everyone else. Yet, stronger than all the images was a feeling that something was wrong with the way things were, but what exactly was wrong I couldn't have said.

When Siew Lan reached across, I blurted out the first thing that came to mind. 'They look down on us.' My friend breathed out deeply. 'He no look down on me,' she insisted.

I gave her a quizzical stare. 'Of course he look down on you. You his servant.'

'But Chye Hoon, not so easy. He also with me sleep.'

I sighed. I knew I was right but I could not stand up to Siew Lan's arguments. Things weren't always clear; there was mingling, especially with the richer locals.

I mumbled, 'He with you sleep not mean he no look down on you.'

There was a triumphant look in Siew Lan's eyes. Amidst an exchange of diffident smiles, we reached a tacit agreement: we would avoid the subject of the Tuan and his people, at least until further notice. I departed, thoroughly annoyed with myself.

Siew Lan's daughter was given a Christian name, Flora, which sounded easy, yet neither of us could say it properly. In the weeks which followed a second servant was hired, and Siew Lan became one of a team of two. From what she told me, I knew she remained his mistress. Somehow they managed to work out an arrangement; over time I was to understand how. But until I knew the details I remained loyal to our unspoken agreement and never asked.

With each addition to our family my appreciation for Mother grew.

As I woke in the semidarkness of our bedroom, bleary eyed, I remembered how Mother had done the same things a long time ago. She hurried to our sides whenever we were ill. If we cut or bruised ourselves, Mother would tend to our wounds with a face full of anxiety. It was Mother who washed and dressed us, who combed our hair, fretted about our manners and whether we had shoes. Finally, I understood her heroic efforts and the toll we, her children, must have taken on her life. I felt close to her then, knowing that I was doing exactly what she had once done.

One night while feeding our second son, Weng Koon, Mother's lilting voice traversed the years, bringing with it the story of Nu Kua, the divine mother of all humans. Mother had said that Nu Kua came down a long time ago to repair the sky. She arrived after a terrible battle, in which the monster Kung Kung had wreaked havoc, when the earth had fallen into itself, mountains were flattened and the oceans overran land. Everywhere fires burnt night and day, raging out of control. The chaos caused the earth's points to be misaligned, and a large hole was ripped across the sky. The destruction saddened Nu Kua. She knew she would have to repair the damage for the sake of the earth's children. Holding five coloured stones in her hand, she calmed the waters, put out the fires and repaired the sky. Then she said, 'The sky will now be blue as an eternal symbol of hope for the children.'

I immediately shouted out, 'But the hole is where, Mother?'

'Hole no more. Nu Kua repair the sky.'

'But before she-repair-the-sky time, the hole is where? You show me, can-ah? Maybe we can see where the sky torn before,' I said in a voice full of hope. For weeks I remained fascinated by the idea of a hole in the heavens. With one hand shielding my eyes from the glare, I surveyed the Malayan skies, disappointed that all I could see were the fluffy white clouds floating freely above.

The news came on a clear day in 1905, shortly after our third son, Weng Fatt, was born. I was still in confinement, only able to walk slowly inside our house. Soraiya, the loyal *bidan* to all my children, had just stopped visiting for her massages. It was also the day on which I had finally given permission to our boisterous second daughter, Hui Ying, to play with the neighbourhood boys. She had perfected her puppy-dog look to such an extent that I could not say no. How to refuse eyes so forlorn?

I was nursing Weng Fatt in the privacy of our bedroom when our eldest daughter, Hui Fang, appeared and said that a strange man was at the front door asking for me. I told her he had to wait; my newborn son had only just begun to feed, and I did not wish to see precious milk wasted.

When I finally went to the door, I saw that the man brought bad news. His demeanour was grave, and he avoided my eyes. Introducing himself as a *sinkeh* from Chiao-Ling County, he told me in a soft tone how sorry he was that the mother of Wong Tsin-sang had passed away.

I immediately worried for my husband, then outstation on business. What would he do? After replacing the heavy wooden bolt across the back of our front door, I hurried into the kitchen. Grabbing a handful of oranges, I put them into a plain white bowl and, with heart beating fast, laid the bowl on the altar table in our inner hall. *Kuan Yin, give me your energy,* I repeated silently while lighting three joss-sticks.

In those days we did not have a statue of the Goddess in our house, only a colourful painting. The woman before me, with thin black lines for eyebrows and eyes which slanted powerfully upwards, soothed me. Through tendrils of smoke I stared at her demure mouth.

With Hui Ying playing outside, the house was quiet. I lost all sense of time. I whispered prayers for the soul of my mother-in-law, but my thoughts were on us, on our children. Whenever I opened my eyes, I glimpsed our eldest daughter, Hui Fang, watching me. She peeked from behind a wall, her tiny brows knitted into a frown. My heart went out to her, already the most obedient of our children. I had known she would be good early on when during our battle of wills I had easily won. Hui Fang was then five and pretty, having inherited her father's fair complexion and high cheekbones and my lustrous hair. She looked like the Kuan Yin at our altar table: calm, dependable, always smiling.

Hui Fang stood observing me. After an interval of silent contemplation, she came up and touched my hip tentatively. In a small voice she asked, 'You good, Mama?'

Just then there was loud banging on the front door, followed by screaming. Our second daughter, Hui Ying, had come into the outer hall with her brother Weng Yu. I turned around to see her grabbing a chunk of skin on the boy's arm. Rushing at her, I shouted, 'Hui Ying, stop that! You don't pinch your younger brother!' I slapped Hui Ying's hand, and tears oozed from her eyes.

I often marvelled at my two eldest daughters in the same way that others had once pointed their fingers at Elder Sister and me. I could not have given birth to more different children: our eldest, Hui Fang, was timid, our second, Hui Ying, bold. Hui Ying was the child who would not sit still, squirming and wriggling constantly, always with a hand or leg where it shouldn't have been. She had my temper and my eyes, hot unyielding tongs that burnt holes through a person. But the rest of her face was her father's – smooth, fair and dimpled – which meant she could be charming even at her most trying.

As if that weren't enough, I worried about our eldest boy, Weng Yu, who had only begun to speak shortly after his third birthday. Even then my little prince didn't say much. He was famous along our road for a pair of dimples the women loved to pinch and a broody silence. 'Wah, your eldest son so handsome. Skin like baby's . . . and so quiet,' they marvelled. Weng Yu was a dreamer, his head never quite where his body was. When asked what he was thinking about, he would remain speechless, as if he had been struck dumb.

The skin on Weng Yu's arm became redder after his sister's attack, but otherwise he appeared remarkably unconcerned. Nevertheless I did not like what I had seen. My attempts at instilling in my children the values dear to me – filial piety, respect for the gods and good manners – ran into trouble early on.

I had agreed to let Hui Ying play with the neighbourhood boys on condition that she took Weng Yu along. She was tasked with looking after her younger brother, an example I hoped would teach the older ones about responsibility. All had gone well until one of the neighbourhood boys pulled Hui Ying's pigtails. Weng Yu, who loved his sisters, was unable to watch Hui Ying being bullied. He had bravely shouted at the boy, despite being the youngest among the children, but when a scuffle broke out, Weng Yu withdrew. His sister, though, was not easily put off. She caught hold of the boy, dragged him to the ground and pinned him with the full might of her wiggly body. Round and round they rolled, until the boy yelped in pain. The violence was too much for Weng Yu, who asked to be taken home. 'Second Sister, I no like when you fight. I tell Mama,' he announced. An argument ensued. Hui Ying, who had felt my wrath many times previously, knew what would come and had pinched Weng Yu in a desperate bid to keep him quiet.

'If you fight, I no let you play with the boys again,' I said, breathing out fire through both nostrils.

'I no start the fight.'

'You hear me or not?'

'But you also say, Mama, we should not let someone bully us,' my intrepid daughter pointed out.

'Hui Ying, I no want you fight with boys – they more strong than you.'

'They not.'

'Don't argue, otherwise no more playing outside again. You hear?'

'But Mama—'

I sighed. Feeling a headache coming on, I walked away, leaving a bewildered Hui Ying mid-sentence. I feel guilty whenever I recall the scene – that and many others. Unfortunately that's how it was in those years: with so many things needing attention I had to find whatever means I could to conserve my energy.

12

After his mother passed away, my husband became sad and distant, a shadow of himself. He seemed to leave us – physically present but with mind and heart elsewhere. On his return in the evenings he would give monosyllabic answers. 'Good' when asked how he was, or 'Not much' to the question of what he'd been doing. Admittedly, these replies were accompanied by smiles, but it still meant that we barely spoke. Our family meals became grim affairs at which even the children were more subdued.

It wasn't just Peng Choon's fault; I was responsible too. I knew that my husband's mind lay north – towards China, to the family he had left behind – and I did not wish to think about them. What he and I dared not confront drove a wedge between us. I spent hours praying to Kuan Yin, pleading for courage. The Goddess of Mercy guided me once again, but her response, when it came, took a strange form: tin.

The price of tin rose to new records in 1906. The metal, having provided the foundation of Ipoh's wealth, had long been a source of conversation around town, though not in our household. Therefore it was with amazement that I listened to my husband talking about tin one night over dinner. He said the metal, which had cost only sixty dollars a picul, or shoulder-load, the previous year, was then selling at ninety dollars a picul and could easily reach a hundred dollars.

I knew nothing about tin at the time, but I was pleased by the sparkle in Peng Choon's eyes. I did my best to encourage this new liveliness, because it had been so long since I had seen him animated. The sound of such a lucrative enterprise intrigued me. Our children paid attention too, especially Hui Ying, whose ears pricked up. I watched her while she ate, struggling with her fingers.

Only the eldest three ate with us then; the younger ones were fed by Ah Hong in the kitchen. I was determined to have my children well brought up and forbade them from speaking during meals. Conversation affected their chewing and digestion. It also interfered with their ability to concentrate, already in short supply when all three were learning to eat with their hands Nyonya style. As usual it was Hui Ying who seemed unable to obey my simple rule. I saw her opening her mouth, but before I could say anything she had already blurted out, ' "Tin" mean what, Papa?'

I was about to remind her not to speak at the dinner table when Peng Choon answered, 'It's a metal.'

I glared at him, furious that he had undermined my authority in front of the children. Peng Choon looked away, hastily avoiding my glance.

He, like Father, enjoyed indulging his daughters. While he was proud of his sons, it was the girls whom he spoilt, especially Hui Ying. Peng Choon had been disappointed when she was born, but by the time she was four that had long been forgotten. Of all our children, I thought he secretly admired Hui Ying the most. Peng Choon's business was then growing, which meant he often had to bring work home. While he wrote at the table in the evenings, he would allow not only our eldest son, Weng Yu, to sit beside him but also Hui Ying. She watched while he dipped his Chinese quill pen into an inkpot. Sometimes she climbed all over his books, as I had once done, begging her papa to teach her how to count and write. Peng Choon said nothing but smiled fondly. I, afraid she would upset the inkpot, found myself echoing Mother . . . which only made the writing seem more mysterious to my daughter. Many a time an accident was only just avoided.

When my husband and daughter began their conversation about tin, our son Weng Yu joined in.

' "Metal" is what, Papa?' he asked.

'A hard, shiny material. Ask Mama to show you her jewel box – she has gold inside, which is a metal. Remember the bridge we saw the other day – Hugh Low Bridge? That's also metal.'

I sighed. 'Enough talking, you two,' I said. 'You can ask Papa later, but you know Mama say no talk at dinner table.'

Peng Choon and I resumed our conversation. I was excited by the light in his eyes, which did not come a moment too soon. He had been in a state of detachment since his mother passed away, and I knew that sooner or later we would have to give voice to the fears and the darker feelings that kept us apart. My biggest worry was that Peng Choon would suddenly walk out and set sail for Chiao-Ling County. Though he had chosen me himself, I was only his second wife, and second in priority by Chinese custom. Knowing my husband, I thought it unlikely he would simply abandon us, but as Mother had once told me, with men you can never be sure.

Tin gave us a topic to latch on to. We talked of how Ipoh had changed since our arrival, the extent this prosperity had been due to tin, and how the price of tin had become the talk of the entire town. Over the weeks Peng Choon and I too became gripped, because there seemed no end to tin's rise and rise. We moved from tin to rubber, which was then also enjoying a boom. We talked about how crowded Ipoh was becoming: with people flooding in, the town was bursting at the seams. Extended families had to cram into single houses. We were fortunate in having rented our own place a few years back, but not a day passed when we didn't hear the patter of feet running up and down the wooden staircases next door. As Peng Choon and I talked, I was reminded of something I had long wanted to do – find a larger space for us all. With China forever looming in our lives, though, the time never seemed right.

Gradually Peng Choon opened up, until there came a time when we spoke as freely as we once used to. I heard how raw he was from the loss of his mother. He thought often of her and deeply regretted not having seen her one last time.

The moment gave me a perfect opportunity. 'So, your wife and son, how-ah?' I asked, holding my breath while awaiting the answer.

Peng Choon looked at me long and hard before replying. When he did, his voice was gentle, if a touch sorrowful.

'You know I won't leave my Malayan family.'

My husband smiled and I smiled back. Strands of silver had found their way on to his head, but unlike some men, he wasn't balding at the crown. If anything, the touch of grey gave him an aura of dignity, making him more handsome than ever in his Mandarin-collared jacket and trousers.

'I have to go back some day,' he sighed, quickly adding, 'Only for a short visit of course.'

'You know when?'

Peng Choon hesitated. He finally said, 'No, I don't know when. I can't leave yet – too much business. I need to be better established. If I go now, they'll just hire someone else, and then it'll be hard to get the job back.'

Peng Choon was referring to the towkays of Ipoh, with whom he had only recently started working. Winning their business had been a slow process, and he was loath to put it at risk. When he had sought them out, it helped that he spoke their dialects and could prepare accounts in both Chinese and English, but with few connections, gaining their business still proved a challenge. Peng Choon's persistence and charm eventually paid off. He was tough without being rude, a man of few words – the sort who could earn a towkay's trust, because with him you knew exactly where things stood. Some of the best-known tin-mining companies were now clients, and Peng Choon worked alongside the leading entrepreneurs of the day.

The first time my husband visited a tin mine, he saw an enormous crater in the ground, a hole so deep that his head spun when he looked into it. Hundreds of coolies ran around, climbing down flimsy ladders into the pit and then up again with baskets on poles slung across their shoulders. When told by his client, the manager of the mine, that it was a hundred feet to the bottom, Peng Choon refused to descend. He remained at the top, his heart filled with admiration. He could not believe how the coolies scampered up and down like ants oblivious to danger.

My husband's eyes focused on one of the men, who wore only dark trousers, having taken his shirt off because of the heat. The coolie scurried down a ladder and disappeared. Peng Choon did not know what he did at the bottom, because you had to stand near the edge of the pit to see, and my husband had instinctively moved away from the precipice. Within minutes the coolie came up again, one hand balancing the pole over his shoulder, the other hanging on to a makeshift ladder, which swayed dangerously from side to side. Even as he watched, Peng Choon held his breath: one small slip could have spelt the end. He could not imagine how the men carried the baskets all day up those ladders, which were roughly hewn from the trunks of coconut trees and creaked under their weight, because when Peng Choon tried to lift one of the rattan baskets he lost his balance.

Peng Choon could see from the coolies' faces that they were Chinese *sinkehs*, or new immigrants – a fact confirmed by his client, who grinned at the question.

'Who else would do this kind of work?' he asked rhetorically. Peng Choon shrugged. 'Malays?' His client guffawed. 'Them? You must be joking!'

Then, remembering that Peng Choon had married a Nyonya, the manager's tone softened. 'They like an easy life . . . not work. Mark my words: we Chinese will build this country. The white devils couldn't do this either. And they know it. That's why they import all this labour' – at this the man swept his arm around, pointing to his group of coolies.

When my husband recounted the story, I was more at ease with his client's words than he had expected. With each new child life aggravated me less. I grew calmer, as if having to slow my impulses for the sake of the children doused my internal fire. The children still had the capacity to rouse my ire, but as for Peng Choon's clients, why should I care what they thought? What would the fools know anyway?

I was intrigued by the coolies. 'You speak to one of them-ah?' I asked Peng Choon. I wondered how they lived, what they did when not working, but my husband could not say. Instead he had examined mining machinery, looking at pumps and goodness knows what else.

In his line of business Peng Choon was inevitably closer to the towkays than to the coolies. Sometimes he told me stories about the towkays, but I couldn't distinguish one from another, though I had heard their names. I had even seen some of them, but they lived in another world, among other rich men.

The first time I saw a towkay must have been around 1902, when we had already been in town for several years. The man came thundering out of nowhere – inside a metal can with seats. It scared the life out of me, this huge contraption which appeared to drive itself . . . making a noise so loud you knew to get out of its way. When I asked what the thing was, I was told it was a motor car – the latest type of vehicle; one that didn't need a person or an animal to pull it. The towkay's was the first in Ipoh. Afterwards more and more of these cars appeared. At one point, before rules were introduced, we had to be careful when crossing the roads, because the cars, which competed with the rickshaws and gharries and bullock carts for space, bullied everyone else. They were invariably driven by towkays or white devils, who did as they wished and tooted for everyone else to get out of their way. From what I could see, the rich had little to do except rush off to unsavoury places, to their drinking holes or concubines' dens.

Peng Choon's stories hardened these opinions. My husband didn't always respect his clients, no matter how wealthy. He had to hold his tongue, though – which he did unless asked to cook the books. As soon as he had to compromise his integrity, Peng Choon would give up the business, resigning as their accountant on the spot. Ironically, this sealed his reputation for solidity among the towkays. He began to get more clients than he could deal with and had to consider hiring a second man to help him.

It was around then that Peng Choon began mentioning a fellow by the name of Foo Choo Choon. He told me he had recently begun working for this towkay, also a Hakka, whom he described as 'visionary'. It was rare for my husband to be so effusive. When he said that Foo Choo Choon was different, my ears naturally pricked up.

'How?' I asked.

'To begin with he doesn't have a concubine.'

On seeing my raised eyebrows, Peng Choon assured me his client was happily married with children.

'How you know he no have mistress?'

My husband laughed. 'Everyone knows. Not a secret whose concubines are whose on Panglima Street.'

'Hmm.' I thought for a moment. 'That all-ah? Why you say he so good?'

'Because of the money he gives to charity. He's just built a Chinese school. I hear he donated to that new missionary school on Lahat Road as well . . . and what's more, he has spoken out against the opium trade. He's a patron of the Perak Anti-Opium Society.'

That was how I came to hear about the Anti-Opium Society, which was then recently formed in our state of Perak. Its mission was to combat the rise of opium: to educate about its dangers, to treat addicts and to press for changes in law. More sceptical by nature, I was uncertain it could achieve anything unless it had white members too. Peng Choon assured me it did; in fact, the Perak branch had been started by a white doctor with a medical practice in town.

'Some of them are on our side. The doctors and missionaries – they can see what's happening. They want to help.'

There was to be an anti-opium conference soon, which made my husband very excited. He thought that if we were united, towkays could be persuaded not to bid for the British opium farms.

'Let them do their own dirty work,' my husband said.

I, on the other hand, remained convinced that success would come only if white members led the effort.

'They only listen to each other,' I said. 'Make sure you have them on your side.'

With his trip home to China deferred, we settled back into our lives. Peng Choon worked all hours of the day and occasionally the nights. Our children climbed trees, invented games, fell, hurt themselves, howled and learnt to get back up and to carry on. Ah Hong and I watched over everything and everyone – bathing, cleaning, feeding, visiting the market and cooking for the family. Despite this semblance of routine, my fears about my husband's first family in China never went away; they would rise to the surface when I least expected them.

Going to the moving pictures had been my husband's idea. With so many mouths to feed, I was frugal, not given to frittering away Peng Choon's hard-earned dollars and cents. Watching moving pictures seemed such a waste of money that I did not yield until the children pleaded. 'Mama, Mama, I want to see,' each had shouted. Hui Ying went one step further and asked what she could do to change my mind. 'You let us go, I no play outside today,' she offered in a voice so sweet, even I had to smile.

That was how I found myself, during the fifth month of my seventh pregnancy, ensconced inside a large tent one weekend evening. My second daughter, Hui Ying, sat on my lap, our eldest girl, Hui Fang, beside me, while my husband sat on the other side of her, holding our son Weng Yu in his lap. The cinematograph was managed by a Japanese man, Matsuo, who took his tent, his machine and films all around Malaya. We watched a comedy called *Troublesome Mother-in-Law*, a black-and-white film that caused raucous laughing and the children's jaws to drop open.

At the start Hui Ying whispered, 'Mama! The people, they really there-ah?'

'Where, Hui Ying?'

'There, in front of us.'

'No-o.'

'Then they where-ah?'

'See that machine over there?' I pointed to the middle of the tent, where a creaking monster stood. Peng Choon had told me beforehand it was called a projector. 'They on a reel of film in that machine.'

'Oh,' my daughter replied, unsure what to ask next.

She watched in silence after that, following every scene as the people in it stumbled and shouted, their actions grandiosely exaggerated to ensure their intentions were understood. Every now and again Hui Ying would glance at the projector, her eyes staring as if it were unreal.

I looked around, not at the movie machine, but at the audience, who from their attire seemed a very mixed bunch indeed. There were ordinary families like us, a few customers with large amounts of jewellery, and a sizeable number of men, who cheered and wolf-whistled. When displeased they booed loudly and stomped their feet. It wasn't behaviour I wished our children to witness, but the young ones seemed oblivious. Their eyes were fixed pointedly on the moving images in front or occasionally on the machine itself, which received reverent looks. I later discovered that they had thought the actors were inside, shrunken in size.

That night my husband seemed equally engrossed. He sat stroking the head of his Malayan-born son. When funny antics came up, he and Weng Yu would guffaw, but I could not concentrate. China unwittingly came into mind; only a boat ride away in Chiao-Ling County were people my husband would have to visit. A trip wasn't imminent, but one day I knew it would come.

13

Together with her daughter, Siew Lan visited our house regularly. In the distance Siew Lan's daughter, Flora, looked like a Chinese from the north, with skin the texture of marble. Porcelain skin, they called it. Once you looked closely, though, Flora's Eurasian features became obvious: greenish-brown eyes like a cat's, eyelids with those lovely deep-set creases, and black hair not straight and thick like ours but thin and wavy.

Siew Lan and I exchanged news about everything. Well, almost everything. We never talked about him directly, but she often referred to Flora's father. She told me the white devil doted on his daughter and was even attempting to teach Flora English.

'And you-lah?' I mused aloud. 'You going to teach your daughter Nyonya customs-ah?'

'Hmm . . . Some, yes,' she replied pensively.

'Only some?'

'Ai-yahh, Chye Hoon! Hard question-lah! How to know which customs to teach her? I have to see.'

At the time I had just given birth to our fourth son, Weng Yoon, and I was determined to teach our children all our customs. I had already begun telling my eldest children the stories Mother had once told us. The little ones were enraptured by the tales of our ancestors, as I had once been. Our eldest boy, Weng Yu, encouraged by his second sister, Hui Ying, even imagined braving the seas in boats with eyes painted on their prows. But I was disappointed, too, because the boats were what my children were most interested in, not what we believed in or practised.

'What to do-lah?' I would complain to my husband, who merely shrugged. And now it was my friend Siew Lan who seemed less concerned about passing on our traditions.

'But why not teach her all our customs?' I persisted. 'Some more important to you-ah?'

Siew Lan's face took on a pained look. Outside a rooster crowed. 'Flora' – she actually pronounced it as 'Flo-lah', because neither of us could master the child's name – 'they say she just *chapalang* – not white, not yellow. No one unkind, but they think she just *chapalang*.'

'But if she learn Nyonya customs, she have family,' I pointed out.

Siew Lan looked at me then, her eyes crossed by the shadows of sadness that had never fully left. A sliver of maroon juice dribbled out from the side of her mouth. 'World different already, Chye Hoon.'

As light flooded on the *barlay*, the wooden platform in our outer hall where I received guests, I poured us more coffee.

'I proud to be Nyonya,' my friend said, 'but *sinkehs* not like us. They now got power. Soon Nyonya and Baba may be no more. Then what is there left for my daughter?'

I paused. A world without Nyonyas or Babas? I couldn't imagine, though I knew what Siew Lan meant. The world was changing; life moved quickly, and people rushed more than they did when I had been a child in Songkhla. I didn't like how we had less time for one another, how we kept to ourselves instead of reaching out as our ancestors had done. Yet Siew Lan's words sounded overly sombre.

But if what she said came to pass, what would it mean to be a Nyonya? I no longer knew. I thought I had once found an answer in my family, but the world, like quicksand, had shifted. I would have to ask the question again and either find an answer I could live with or sink.

Whatever the future brought, I wanted our children to know the legacy their ancestors had left behind. I never wanted to hear anyone say that I hadn't brought them up properly. They would respect their elders, give offerings to our gods and become considerate, well-mannered people.

When our eldest son, Weng Yu, was five, I told him about an emperor who once ruled China, the land from where his father hailed. This Chinese emperor was exceptionally wise and had begun reigning when he was only fifteen. He was given the name Yao. Emperor Yao divided time into years, years into moons, the moons into days. He conquered floods, kept barbaric hordes at bay, and banished evildoers into the desert. When he died, the people mourned for three years. In that time no music was heard and no theatre performed, in remembrance of the great emperor.

For several exquisite seconds after I finished, my son's liquid pools stared directly into mine, before he trained his eyes dreamily into the distance. 'When I big, Mama . . . ,' he announced, 'I want to be a prince.'

I laughed, yet in a strange way I believed my son. He was already regal, like his papa. From that morning on our eldest son, Weng Yu, became my little prince.

He was an exact replica of his father: lanky, with a long, narrow nose and pointed face. His trademark lay grooved into both cheeks – the dimples everyone found irresistible, especially women, who had the urge to squeeze them. When he walked, my eldest son adopted his father's gait and kept his back straight just like a little prince.

But I worried about his reticence. As Weng Yu grew older, what had been broody quietness turned into pouting silences, full of the melancholy and clamped lips which even a *changkol*, a Chinese back-hoe, could not have prised open. The only people able to lift my eldest boy's moods were Hui Ying and my husband. Weng Yu adored his father; he was a different person in the evenings, after his papa returned. The boy would run to the door to greet Peng Choon, eager for every nugget which dropped out of my husband's mouth. Peng Choon too was a man of few words, but he bristled with energy, whereas Weng Yu was languid, never taking the lead, having instead to be pushed. In the fast-changing world we lived in, I feared Weng Yu lacked the drive to succeed. *If only he were more like his sister Hui Ying,* I often thought.

My little prince had a hidden talent I only noticed through surreptitious observation. When he thought no one else was listening, his voice, high-pitched like a girl's, would ring in melody around the house. As soon as another person came near, he would stop, but once alone again Weng Yu would resume, whistling and humming as Father used to. It appeared I had passed Father's love of music on to my son.

This was an unusual talent and one I did not wish to encourage. Even if Weng Yu was gifted, singers in the Federated Malay States didn't earn much, unlike businessmen or those in professions. I ignored my son's talent. It was the best I could do at the time.

Meanwhile Ipoh grew in the background. By then Old Town was full and there was nowhere else to build, except across the Kinta River. One of the towkays, Yau Tet Shin, courageously took up the challenge by announcing that he would build hundreds of new shophouses on virgin land.

Everyone thought him mad. The largest project the town had ever seen just when the price of tin had started to fall? Speculation was rife that construction would never take place. Yet happen it did: in due course jungle and *belukar* – formerly cleared land already starting to revert to jungle – were cleared, and building commenced in earnest.

Despite talk of a depression there was a buzz in the air. We were thrilled about a whole town taking shape in front of us, even more by the delicious prospect of fewer people on our side of the Kinta River. Some started calling the other side New Town to differentiate it from Old Town – our side of the river. The names have stuck to this day.

In the midst of such excitement our fifth son, Weng Onn, was born. I gave thanks to Kuan Yin for such blessings: five sons and three daughters. And on top of that, my husband's business was also beginning to take off! Life was going our way finally.

We could even afford to hire a Malay washerwoman to attend to the household laundry. Unlike Ah Hong, Siti didn't live in; she came at dawn six days a week to wash, scrub and iron and then returned to her kampong. But with eight children to look after, Ah Hong and I were rushed off our feet every minute of each day. We so badly needed an extra pair of hands that even Ah Hong, dear loyal Ah Hong, began to grumble. There were times she fell asleep in the evenings, totally exhausted, holding one of the children in her arms. Unfortunately, there was no room in the house for another servant.

When Peng Choon suggested we move, I began the project I had long harboured: to search for a larger house to rent. This took months; in between nursing the newborn Weng Onn, I had seven young ones in different modes of running, walking and crawling about. Besides, I was exacting in my requirements: I had Mother in me after all.

The delay turned out to be for the best, because there was a large flood in Ipoh in 1907. Thanks to the rising waters, Peng Choon and I decided to look for a house further from the river. We even considered moving across to New Town. Once completed, the houses would be wonderful, we thought, but most townspeople didn't believe New Town would be completed. 'Just wait! He'll abandon his project!' some scoffed. Or 'This is a hare-brained scheme, and Yau Tet Shin will have no money left.' The talk was that unfinished walls would be all that would remain of the New Town dream. With eight children depending on my search, I couldn't take such a risk and focused therefore on those parts of Ipoh we were already familiar with.

Peng Choon proved of little help in the house search. He was so busy that he couldn't even attend the anti-opium conference, which took place that year. The conference had apparently been a success, following on the heels of a petition to London. 'Hmm . . . ,' I said.

'Yes, Wife,' Peng Choon enthused, 'the petition was led by a white man, the Ipoh doctor.'

'We will see,' I replied, too busy worrying about where we would live to think about much else.

We eventually settled on a rented house on the Lahat Road, which was quiet in those days and not the busy thoroughfare it is now. With four bedrooms – two for the boys, one for the girls, one for Peng Choon and me, as well as two servants' rooms downstairs – the house was a palace compared to what we were living in before. A new school was to be built nearby – Yuk Choy School, which we earmarked for the boys – so the house met most of our needs in one stroke.

The problem which remained was a school for the girls. We could not think what to do, since there were hardly any Chinese schools for girls then. I worried about not sending them to school, but worried too that education would damage their ability to find husbands. Instinct told me that men didn't like wives cleverer than them. Even my beloved Peng Choon, wonderful husband that he was, liked to think of himself as the smarter of us two, which for the sake of peace I allowed. What he said told me all I needed to know – 'Ai-yahh! That is rubbish-lah! You talk just like a woman!', as if talking like a woman were such a terrible affliction.

We debated education for months, until Peng Choon threw up his arms. 'Wife, let's move first and then see what we do.' This left me prickly, but my husband assured me we would deal with finding a school for the girls at some point. 'One thing at a time,' he said. 'We have to think of the boys first. The girls will get married after all.'

Just before we moved, Siew Lan came on one of her visits. Unusually, she was without Flora that day, which pleased me, as it meant more time chewing betel nut leaves and chatting.

I had just placed a folded leaf on my tongue when my friend made her announcement out of the blue.

'Chye Hoon, I pregnant again.'

Next door, feet trampled down a set of wooden stairs while I thought about what to say. I knew I would have to ask about the white devil – I had no choice. I took my time. With the leaf already inside my mouth, I chewed slowly. Moving the cud round and round, I mixed it with saliva until I could no longer bear the sensation, at which point I hurled the bloody juice out with the full force of my breath straight into the brass spittoon.

'He know-ah?'

'No, not yet.' Siew Lan bit her lip, which looked paler than normal. She remained quiet, her face glum.

I called out to Ah Hong for more coffee and a refill of the betel nut box. We would need reinforcements.

'Siew Lan,' I said as tenderly as I could, 'I want to help you – you know that-lah – but you everything also must tell me. You can do that-moh?'

With eyes averted, my friend poured out her story: how she had tried to stop sleeping with her boss after Flora's birth but had eventually caved in – 'He so persistent' – until over time she became increasingly fond of him and didn't want to stop, even though she wasn't sure where it would lead. At first, the white devil had continued his life much as it had been without her: he went to his club in the mornings, saw his friends, had lunch, drank, and then came home late in the afternoons smelling of whisky and sleep. He would wake for dinner, during which he consumed even more alcohol. Under her influence he reduced his drinking, because she refused to sleep with him if he stank badly. 'Of course,' she said, 'I know he always must have a drink . . . He cut down good enough already-lah.'

As Flora grew older, her father started spending time at home on some mornings. The old devil loved his daughter. He gave her piggyback rides, happily took her for strolls and was teaching her to read.

When Siew Lan paused, I urged her to marry her boss, amazing myself in the process.

Siew Lan pounced on my words, sparkles of disbelief showing in the middle of her irises. 'Hah, then you change your mind-ah?' she asked. 'So, whites now different-ah?'

I shook my head. 'No, but like this now you cannot go on. How many more children you can have with no father? Not fair on them.'

'What, you say with white devil marry, hah? Must be you think they not so bad, then.'

I continued shaking my head. 'Look, I not sure I can explain better.'

The patter of little feet was once again heard next door. Spitting out more betel nut juice, I swallowed hard, the words weighing on my tongue.

'My friend, you wrong before that time,' I said. 'I no hate anyone – white skins people too, like us. But they put on airs here.'

Siew Lan muttered a protest, which I ignored. 'Yes, I tell you! They look at me, they not really look – like I not there at all. Like I just thin air in front of them, invisible.'

'Maybe you speak their language, Chye Hoon, things different.'

'What, you think they start not treating me like air-ah?'

'I only say may be good idea to learn a bit of English. I already pick up one or two words from Se-Too-Wat.'

'Ai-yahh, Siew Lan, got nothing to do with language-lah! I tell you, all about attitude. They act like masters here because they are masters. I no like how they treat us. Don't tell me they no look down on us – I feel it when I outside. You know they call us Chinamen-ah? That not a compliment, you know.'

'And we call them white devils. What so different-ah?'

'What is different,' I cried in exasperation, 'they rule over us. They make all laws. We say ten words also not so important than they say one word!'

When Siew Lan looked away, I reached across the table to touch her on the shoulder. 'Look, this not important – make no difference to our friendship. You always be good friend. Even if you marry him, we still friends. I think you should tell him to marry you for children's sake.'

Siew Lan smiled then, for the first time that day, a wide beaming smile which animated her face. Both our backs straightened in relief. My friend added timidly, 'I have favour to ask you, Chye Hoon.'

'What?'

'If I marry him, I want you stop calling them white devils in front of me. I know everyone do, so you no stop; just not in front of me or my children. Okay?'

I smiled sheepishly, promising to do my best. Over the years I curbed my tongue. Though I continued to think of them as white devils, I was careful not to mention this in the presence of Siew Lan or her children.

Thus it was that Siew Lan, erstwhile maid, sometime mistress of Stuart McPherson, the Scottish planter with the unpronounceable names, finally became his wife in 1908, several weeks after the birth of our sixth son, Weng Choon. I attended their wedding on my own, because Peng Choon remained unsure of the bridegroom and refused to go with me. He planned an outstation trip on the exact day. The marriage ceremony was held in a room called a registry office – a first for me. Siew Lan was beautiful in a gorgeous red baju, while Se-Too-Wat, wearing a suit so white it sparkled in the sun, looked better than I had ever seen him. But the ceremony itself was a dull affair, so different from any other wedding I had ever been to. It served to accentuate what I already knew – that these white devils came from another, duller world. Admittedly, I could not understand a word of the proceedings, but I doubt if knowing what was said would have made it any more colourful.

14

When the Emperor Kuang-hsu and the Empress Dowager passed away in 1908, Chinese shops in Ipoh closed as a mark of respect. Most of the *sinkehs* were staunch supporters of the monarchy. Nonetheless, everyone was stunned when a two-year-old – the dead emperor's nephew Pu Yi – was named emperor. This seemed so absurd it beggared belief. In those years it appeared that anyone with the means to leave China did so. From newly arrived *sinkehs*, Peng Choon found out that his father, by then elderly, was unwell, and his son, whom he hadn't seen since he was a toddler, was nearly a grown man.

Despite the torrent of bad news, Peng Choon remained reluctant to leave us. Something always held him back. In the early years, when we weren't financially secure, he couldn't have gone. Yet even after we had moved into our house on Lahat Road and employed two servants, Peng Choon continued to hesitate. It wasn't that he thought less about China; China remained on his mind, and feelings of guilt about his first wife and son haunted him. A powerful force must have kept him in Malaya. Somewhere in his heart my husband seemed to fear what would happen when he did go.

Finally, when even the *sui-hak*, who could be relied on to describe water as wine, told Peng Choon that things were getting bad in China, he was spurred to a decision. By then port cities like Swatow had deteriorated; lawlessness was rife and travel hazardous.

It was a balmy night when Peng Choon took me aside. I often looked at the stars; they reminded me of the births of my children. I was surveying pricks of light in the sky, recalling the exact hour, day and month each child had arrived in this world, when Peng Choon touched my right shoulder. 'It's now or never,' he said very softly. The words shook me out of my reverie. 'I'd better go before things get worse.'

I heard the emotion in my husband's voice and turned to face him, but he moved away quickly. When he had regained his composure, I saw that his eyes were moist. 'I promise to come back,' he whispered. 'I promise.'

The moment I had been dreading, when it came, was worse than I had imagined. I could not sleep that night and for many nights afterwards. The worries that had brewed in Matsuo's tent while we sat watching moving pictures boiled inside my head, forming vicious bubbles. What if he did not return? *Silly,* I told myself. *Your husband is not like that.*

But then I thought about his father, his first wife, his firstborn son, the village he loved and the pull that had always been there. My husband's split loyalties dangled before my eyes like strings of birthday noodles, with China on one end and Malaya on the other. *He loves his Malayan-born children too.* I had to remind myself of this and of how much Peng Choon would miss them, especially his daughter Hui Ying and his son Weng Yu.

Nonetheless I woke with bags under my eyes. They stayed with me until my husband left.

Peng Choon was to be away for four months, and though we did not discuss it, thoughts of his other wife stabbed me. No matter how my husband tried to reassure me, I could not erase her from my mind.

He reminded me that he had chosen me himself, whereas his first marriage had taken place out of deference to his father's wishes. None of that mattered, because she would still be there with him, ready to do as he desired.

Above all I feared for our little ones. Peng Choon, too, worried about how the children would react. In this my husband was exceptional; most men would have left the burden of communication to me.

In the end we gathered seven of our children together – our three daughters and the four sons who were aged three and above at the time – and without fanfare broke the news of their papa's impending trip. The children remained remarkably composed. In my anguish I had forgotten that stage of innocence, when all life seemed straightforward, its dangers unimaginable. Only our eldest daughter, Hui Fang, sat as still as Kuan Yin, while the others started talking all at once, so that no one could be heard. When calm was restored by a clap of Peng Choon's hands, my little prince Weng Yu remembered the stories I had told him and asked which part of China his papa would be visiting. He was shouted down by his second sister, Hui Ying, who true to form asked without a second's hesitation to go with her papa. This brought howls of protest from the boys, who all wanted to sail in a boat. The loudest among them was Weng Yoon, our fourth son, then only three but already fierce. He would make a face if anyone tried to bully him, clenching his snub nose until his nostrils were tight and his eyes narrow, so that he looked like a pugnacious bulldog. I admonished Weng Yoon every time I saw the face he pulled, but it made little difference, because my scolding merely gave the boy the absurd idea that he was brave.

We had many more family discussions about their papa's trip, none as long as the first. Over the weeks our eldest child, Hui Fang, guessed my mood and continued looking wistfully at me. Alas, my husband didn't make it easy: he dragged the process out, forever extending his departure date further into the future, until the younger ones stopped believing he would actually go.

On the one hand, the delay was understandable: Peng Choon wanted to make sure we were well provided for, but the flurry of activity included projects that seemed of dubious value at the time. First he acquired seven plots of land deep in the heart of New Town, which by then had been completed. Peng Choon bought land away from the river, because he thought that was where the greatest profit would lie. The lands, being undeveloped, were covered in jungle and *belukar* and went cheaply – the area didn't even have a name. Six of the plots were intended for the six sons we had then – one plot each – and the seventh Peng Choon bought simply for good luck. Next he acquired three shophouses on Hale Street in the Old Town. The three lots, in good condition, were rented to tenants on long leases. 'The income may turn out helpful,' he said, 'in case I'm delayed in China.'

When the acquisitions had been made, Peng Choon came home with a brown cloth bundle, the small sack in which he always carried his income. There was urgency in his step that evening, but his breath was soft. He ushered me into our bedroom and emptied the contents of his bundle on to my dressing table. Silver and copper coins crashed on to the wood, alongside five- and ten-dollar notes.

'The last payments from my clients,' Peng Choon said.

Finally a thick roll of yellow paper fell out, beautifully tied with pink ribbon. When Peng Choon unfurled the ribbon, the roll of paper turned into ten sheets, each scrawled with Chinese writing.

'A deed for each plot of land, and one for each shophouse,' my husband added in an even voice.

He rolled the deeds up, tied them once more with the pink ribbon and put the scroll into his cloth bundle. Back, too, went the coins, followed by the dollar notes, with their pictures of white kings and queens. Holding the cloth bundle with both his hands as if bestowing a gift, Peng Choon handed me the pack. His eyes were dewy.

'Wife,' he said, 'you have always been the head of our household. These are for you. I hope they keep you all safe while I'm gone.'

I accepted the bundle from Peng Choon with a bursting heart. *This is what it means to be a Nyonya,* I thought. A dream I once had came back to me: I imagined myself as a sword-wielding warrior who slayed dragons in my path. At last I had found my sword: it was what I ran our household with. I knew then that I would always be a Nyonya, and I wanted the same for our children, especially the girls.

Before setting sail, Peng Choon asked my permission to donate one of our plots of land to the Malay community. To cement his relationship with his adopted country, he wanted the land to be used for the building of a mosque. I know he did this for me, in recognition of my Malay ancestry. It was a farewell gesture that, like the midwife's tongs of iron, warmed my soul.

My husband took so long to leave that I was pregnant again by the time he set sail. Peng Choon wanted to stay for the birth, but I discouraged this. I needed to get the farewell over with so that we could look forward to his return. 'You go-lah,' I told him. 'Then I-give-birth time you at home already.'

When the moment arrived, my mind turned blank. I did not have the strength to accompany my husband to the port and contented myself with seeing him off at our front door. Peng Choon, who could have hired a rickshaw, chose to walk to the railway station, carrying in his hands the single cloth bundle in which his belongings had been wrapped. 'I'll be back,' he said cheerfully, flashing his dimples as he set off with a Hakka friend. 'Then we can talk about the girls' education.'

I stood on our five-foot way staring at his straight back as he descended the hill on Lahat Road. For a long time afterwards, even when my husband and his friend had disappeared, I remained outdoors, thinking of the quiet moments he and I had shared. Then, wiping away a tear, I went in to prepare lunch for our children.

15

In Peng Choon's absence our house became a lonelier place. His return from work was a ritual ingrained into our days, except we did not know it until he had left. At six every evening I would imagine the sound of his footsteps. The children did the same; for a whole week they gathered as they always did in the hallway in anticipation of greeting their papa. Our eldest son, Weng Yu, who had been the child most excited by my husband's homecoming, was especially morose. He spoke even less and could be coaxed out of his shell only by his second sister, Hui Ying.

The sole cheer in the house was brought by a new and young servant, Li-Fei, who joined us when we moved to the Lahat Road. Barely sixteen, Li-Fei, like Ah Hong, had been introduced by Siew Lan. Of Hakka descent, Li-Fei was blessed with the stout physique of one used to working in fields, with skin permanently tanned and hands calloused from hard labour. When we met, I noticed her large feet, untouched by the odious practice of foot-binding. With her big-boned frame, she was able to lift and carry the loads that defeated Ah Hong. Our servants were both good workers, and loyal too. My heart grew warm whenever I saw them together: fair, slender Ah Hong, who never said more than a few words, beside dark-skinned, muscular Li-Fei, the more vivacious of the two, who would chatter endlessly to the children.

With Peng Choon gone, I asked Ah Hong and Li-Fei to eat with us, bringing the younger ones in tow. The children brightened every meal, but I missed my husband's dinner-time stories about the world beyond the Lahat Road. In his absence a gaping hole was left which no one and no amount of stargazing were able to fill.

The children were a solace, especially our eldest daughter, Hui Fang. When her father sailed for China, Hui Fang was already nine – old enough to understand that I was troubled. Sometimes, while helping Ah Hong and me with the preparation of meals she would announce 'I myself can do this now, Mama' in a grown-up tone, which made me proud.

Hui Fang was tall for her age. She stood five feet tall then, nearly my height, and having matured early, she was already delicately curved. A robust build was all she had inherited from me; everything else seemed to be from someone else. Where her placid nature came from was a mystery. Whenever I looked at her, I thought of the Goddess of Mercy, though I doubt if the men eyeing her had piety in mind. The lecherous glances my daughter received on the streets from stallholders and office workers alike told me we would have difficulty keeping predators at bay.

Hui Ying was also growing up fast. While Peng Choon was away, her carefree days came to an end. I set her to work in the kitchen, to begin her Nyonya training. Like me, my second daughter put up a fight, though thankfully this had not stretched to biting my arm. With Hui Ying no longer shooting marbles or climbing trees, I had it in mind to make a new baju panjang for her, a dress she could now wear with less risk of its being torn. I knew just the right colours – green and a rich brown – which, together with five-pronged hairpins, would show off the piercing glint in her large almond eyes.

A few weeks after Peng Choon's departure, our eldest son, Weng Yu, went to school for the first time. He looked smart in his brand-new clothes – a Mandarin-collared navy-blue jacket matched with loose brown Chinese trousers. A pair of sparklingly white shoes and socks covered his feet. On his shoulder he carried a brown cloth satchel containing an exercise book, its pages so new they still smelt fresh, a set of pens, whose quills were as yet untainted by ink, as well as his lunch, since school did not finish until three in the afternoon. We had gone on a special shopping trip the previous fortnight, searching for shoes, books, pens, a bag and material for new clothes. The expedition, led by Siew Lan, was an education for me. I had never until then bought books and pens, nor shoes that had not been handmade by a cobbler on the street. I dragged Siew Lan and Weng Yu into one shop after another, checking the prices and quality of goods. With nine children to think about and another on the way, I had to count our coins, despite being well provided for by Peng Choon. Three hours and a dozen shops later, I was finally satisfied and we completed our purchases. Weng Yu was silent but grumpy; he had found the afternoon trying.

Yet when I gazed at the result, I thought it had all been worthwhile, especially his homemade clothes, the fruit of my own labour. Having obtained the pattern from Siew Lan, I spent days cutting and stitching the long-sleeved jacket and trousers. Even the vest he wore beneath was tailored by me. I was surprised how well the clothes hung on Weng Yu's lean body: starched and pressed, they seemed a natural fit.

We walked the half mile to Yuk Choy School, which was then located along Lahat Road. As we marched forward, Weng Yu in a small voice asked me when his papa would be back. 'Soon,' I mumbled before turning to stroke my little prince's hair. If Peng Choon had been around, he would have accompanied our eldest son to school, and Weng Yu knew it.

When we arrived, I was ashamed at not being able to understand a word written anywhere. The building, situated in the middle of a huge compound, was large and divided into many rooms. I had to ask someone to tell us the way when we got lost. My son, meanwhile, dragged his heels. 'Come on, Weng Yu!' I prodded. 'This your first day. You cannot be late-lah!'

We were directed to a room at one corner, where a number of boys were already seated, each on a wooden chair behind its own desk. All faced the teacher at the front, a short man with a Chinese cloth cap on his head and a trimmed moustache over thin lips. The teacher looked surprised to see me.

'Ngi ho,' he greeted me in booming Hakka, giving a quick bow of his head at the same time. 'I am Lee Tsin-sang.' His voice, which bounced off the bare walls of the room, struck me as extraordinarily loud for a man so small. I introduced myself before giving the teacher Weng Yu's name and age. Lee Tsin-sang noted the details.

'Do you have the fees with you?' he asked casually. 'It's two dollars per month.' I nodded, handing him the money. It seemed a wholly reasonable rate, but I wondered about the boys whose families could not pay. I supposed they were sent home. I was glad we could afford school for Weng Yu and all our children, even the girls.

After these formalities I turned towards my son, whose face resembled that of a trapped animal. Stroking Weng Yu's head, I whispered, 'I stay outside, Son.'

'Peng Choon Sau, you want a chair to sit on?' Lee Tsin-sang had taken his cap off and was looking solicitously at me. I saw that he was bald. Despite the gloom of the early-morning light, the teacher's crown shone as if recently oiled. I was visibly pregnant by then and grateful for his kind offer. 'Thank you,' I replied.

I placed my chair at a spot where Weng Yu could see me. There was one other parent present, a young woman whose face was heavy with make-up. With her thick layer of powder and black lines of charcoal pencil, she looked like an actress who had just come off the stage. We smiled politely at one another. Then we waited.

The boys in Weng Yu's class looked like a mixed bunch. They were all Chinese, Yuk Choy being a Chinese school, but a handful, whose shirts and shoes already looked worn despite it being the first day of school, clearly came from less well-off families. In contrast, there were also boys who apparently had everything, whose lunches sat on the floor beside their desks in beautifully lacquered containers.

Not much was taught that morning, and I had to remind myself that the boys had only just arrived. First they had to say their names, and Weng Yu mumbled his so badly that he had to repeat himself more than once. Afterwards the teacher went through simple counting, something my son had already learnt from his papa. I watched proudly as Weng Yu completed his counting tasks without needing help.

Then the teacher asked whether someone would sing the whole class a song. To my surprise my son raised his hand.

'Weng Yu, you want to sing?' Lee Tsin-sang asked in his loud voice. Weng Yu nodded.

'Ho, ho,' the teacher said. 'Stand up.' Turning to the rest of the class, he asked the boys to clap.

I watched in astonishment as my son stood up, pulled his shoulders back and opened his mouth wide, as if he were about to eat a whole Nyonya dumpling. Out floated a voice as sweet as the *gula melaka* we cooked with, and everyone's ears pricked up. When Weng Yu finished, his classmates clapped spontaneously. A few even asked for a second song, bringing a grin to Weng Yu's sharp face.

In those days Siew Lan came often to see me. After her marriage to the white devil, she became the mistress of a wealthy household. Now, with two servants working for her, she had time on her hands.

Despite her newly elevated status she did not put on airs. We sat as we had always done, a pot of strong coffee brewing beside us, a tray with a betel nut box and chewing implements laid out in front. Of all the Nyonya women I knew, Siew Lan was the one who enjoyed betel nut chewing the most. Her gums and teeth, stained blackish red by betel nut juice, were testament to her favourite pastime.

It was inevitable that my friend's new-found affluence would be reflected in the clothes she wore. Shortly after her wedding I saw for the first time a sumptuous sarong of the Pekalongan variety in pale purple with Javanese motifs of flowers and leaves intricately stitched. Shades of black, red and green swept its folds, criss-crossed by golden threads. It was a sarong I was to see on her many times over the years, a piece which would become much loved. That first afternoon when she wore it, Siew Lan stepped gingerly up on to our *barlay*.

'You all right, Chye Hoon?' she asked as she moved the maroon cud inside her mouth. 'You lost weight-lah! Eat properly-ah?'

I turned away, unable to respond. For many weeks sleep had eluded me. I was weighed down by a mysterious foreboding, a dreamlike heaviness which even hours of chanting before Kuan Yin could not lift. I had spent so long staring at the ceiling above our altar table that I knew every patch of brown which had been singed by the rising smoke. New wrinkles had appeared around my eyes and even slivers of grey on my hairbrush – the first signs I was ageing with worry.

Siew Lan interrupted my thoughts. 'You worried about her-ah?'

I shook my head.

My friend raised an eyebrow. Under the gaze of her doleful eyes, I gave voice to the apprehension I had felt even before my husband's departure. 'I have bad feeling,' I said nervously.

It was a dread I had not dared acknowledge to myself. I certainly hadn't mentioned it to my husband, not wanting to burden him with silly fears, unwilling, I suspect, to also be laughed at. But the premonition had not dissipated; if anything, it had grown stronger. Almost daily I braced myself for bad news.

'Only natural,' Siew Lan assured me. 'There a lot to think about.'

Spitting out a mouthful of pungent betel nut juice, I wondered whether to tell her everything. When I married Peng Choon, I never for one minute imagined I would one day be fretting about a land which had seemed so remote on our wedding night that it might as well not have existed.

'Your husband sure to come back,' Siew Lan pronounced. 'He not the type to just leave.'

On hearing such kindness, I burst into tears.

When I finally looked up, I was grateful for the woman across the table, who had been my best friend since our arrival in Ipoh. She was as solid as the Pa Lo Old Temple. Even her husband, the red-haired devil, had grown on me. Whenever I visited their home, he was neatly dressed, his shirts and trousers always white and free of creases. His cheeks, though still pink, were much less ruddy than when we first met, and the hairs on his arms less disagreeable without the accompanying stench of alcohol. Siew Lan told me that after the birth of their second child – a son – her husband consumed even less drink. He still held his own at any banquet, but she was delighted by the new restraint. I could tell how much Se-Too-Wat loved his children; he played incessantly with Flora and made a fuss of their lovely baby boy, Don, who was a smaller version of his mother, with flat cheekbones and thick black hair.

Siew Lan said people always looked at them on the streets; not for long or with malicious intent, but everyone took a second glance. The curiosity of Ipoh's townfolk did not bother my friend any more, as she and her children were left alone for the most part. It seemed that Eurasians were taken as living proof of our acceptance by our white rulers. 'Look, they can't think we're that inferior,' went the whispers.

None of this street gossip was important to me. What mattered was that Siew Lan looked happier than I had ever seen her. We smiled at one another across the table.

'For baby's sake you must eat properly,' she told me a little sternly. 'I bring bird's nest soup next time I come.'

16

The night after Siew Lan's visit I had a nightmare.

In my dream I fell or was chased or both – I could not tell. It was pitch-black, so dark there was not one glimmer of light. Nothing could be seen anywhere, not even the faintest outline. *This is what it must be like being blind,* I thought.

I moved quickly, floating through a tunnel. I was hounded by a presence, a thing that seemed to come for me. I was scared, and my heart beat faster. My throat felt dry – parched, as if I had been shouting. Perhaps I had been shouting . . .

. . . and then I saw him – my husband's handsome face staring straight through me, grinning broadly, his dimples leaving shadows on both cheeks. I saw him clearly, but only his face and the top half of his body. He was dressed in a black Chinese top with a Mandarin collar, the type he always wore to work. He winked at me with his left eye. Then he was gone.

Next there was a buzzing sound – *bzzz-bzzz, bzzz-bzzz* – that seemed close by, almost next to my ear. Further away someone tapped on the door.

I woke up drenched in sweat. My hand had unwittingly swatted a mosquito, which was still alive. I could hear it hovering just over my face. A figure had opened the door to my bedroom and was standing near the entrance with a lamp. As my eyes adjusted, I saw that it was Ah Hong, who asked in a soft voice, 'Ah Soh, Ah Soh, you all right?'

I sat upright. 'Yes,' I replied. 'Just a bad dream-lah.' Then, looking at Ah Hong, I worried about what else I might have done in my sleep. 'You hear me-ah? I wake up the children?'

Ah Hong shook her head, stepping closer with the lamp, and in whispers assured me that all was well. 'So hot I no sleep, so I go to the kitchen to sit under the air well. I hear noise so check on the children-lah. You soft, Ah Soh, no one wake up.'

When Ah Hong had gone, I could not settle. I walked around in a daze the next day, tired and tense, the bags growing under my eyes.

For several nights I was wary of sleep, fearing a nightmare in which I ended up screaming. I did not want the children to know how worried I was that their father would not return.

Siew Lan pulled up the week after in a rickshaw, carrying a small lacquered box in her hands.

'The soup I promised you,' she announced. 'In dry form-lah! Ah Hong can put in a pot of water. I show her how much cane sugar must add.'

The rickshaw puller, who had just set the vehicle down, was panting and puffing from the incline on the Lahat Road which led up to our house. Most rickshaw pullers managed it without fuss; this one, though, made such a noise that I gave him a glance. A jolt came over me, for I would have recognised that face anywhere – ugly as ever, full of pock-marks, with its hair-infested mole below the left side of his lower lip.

It was the ting-ting man of Penang.

His clothes were as sparing as in my memories: that day he wore a sleeveless singlet, generously stained with tobacco, so unwashed its whiteness had turned a creamy yellow. He was even skinnier than I remembered, all bones and no fat, and I wondered how he managed to drag his rickshaw at all. I stood staring, struggling to recall his name.

And then it hit me. 'Ah Boey,' I called out. But Ah Boey did not recognise me.

'Ahh . . . long time no see,' he said in Hokkien.

'You remember me?' I asked.

'Of course, of course,' he replied rather doubtfully.

'This gentleman was ting-ting man when I lived in Penang,' I explained to Siew Lan. 'His name is Ah Boey. But Ah Boey got so many customers, I sure he can't remember me. Now I am called Peng Choon Sau,' I said.

The words jogged my own memory. Images of our house on Ah Kwee Street came back, and with them I remembered that Ah Boey had gone to seek his fortune in the tin mines. Of course he would have ended up somewhere in the Kinta District.

Turning back to Ah Boey, I told him, 'We lived on Ah Kwee Street, you remember-moh? My mother is a fierce Nyonya woman, Cheng Tee Soh.'

'Yes, yes, I remember now,' Ah Boey insisted. 'You got one brother and many sisters. I how can forget you and your mother? She always scold me.' He laughed loudly, as if he found the recollection amusing.

This chance encounter was a surprise. I had forgotten all about Ah Boey, the last person I would ever have expected to see again. Remembering Peng Choon's story about the tin mine he visited, I wondered whether Ah Boey had been one of the coolies running up and down those unsteady ladders. I was curious to know why he was pulling a rickshaw now. Had he left the mines?

'Ah . . . Peng Choon Sau, long story-lah,' he replied. He looked away, asking Siew Lan for his fare instead. Surveying him, I surmised that things must have gone badly and didn't press Ah Boey for an answer. With Siew Lan waiting to go into our house, it wasn't the right time.

Over the next months I kept a lookout for the former ting-ting man. My eyes searched for a skeleton in rags, face heavily pockmarked, who dragged a rickshaw around town.

With each passing day my sense of foreboding increased. We expected Peng Choon back after four months, five at most. When six months had passed, I gave birth to our tenth child. Siew Lan was in the room when our youngest slid into this world; she smiled as she took the baby from Soraiya, washing it gently before placing the infant in my arms.

'A boy, Chye Hoon,' Siew Lan whispered.

I called our seventh son Weng Foo, a name we had chosen before Peng Choon's departure.

The arrival of the little one distracted me from my preoccupations. For a whole week Soraiya called to give me a daily massage with her steaming-hot iron, always coming late in the morning when the sun was already high in the sky. It was the part of day I most looked forward to, the slow rubbing of hot metal in circular motion on my skin, bringing relief from everything I had been through.

When at the end of her last visit Soraiya announced she was retiring as a midwife, I was choked by a lump in my throat. She told me she had already stopped working but had made a special allowance in my case, because she had known our family for so many years.

We bade each other farewell, our eyes moist with tears. As we held one another's hands for the last time, I promised to have *angkoos* sent to her kampong when our son turned one month old.

The weeks passed with no sign of Peng Choon.

Siew Lan fed me news from China whenever she could, things her husband had read in the papers. Her titbits did little to calm me, since what she related was generally disturbing. With trade controlled by the foreigners who lived in concessions that the weak and barely functioning Manchu dynasty had been forced to sign away, there was much unrest. We heard stories of revolts, of riots, even the burning of schools. Amid clashes between uniformed factions and foreign patrols fighting the local warlords, the environment was volatile, and I had to trust that Peng Choon, who had his wits about him, would know how to keep safe.

Every day that brought no sign of him caused new wrinkles on my face. Yet there was little for me to do except wait.

One day a stray dog appeared. It was black except for the tips of its paws, which were white, and a small spot above the muzzle, also white. Black dogs brought bad luck, which explained my instant dislike of this vagrant.

The dog parked itself directly outside our house in the corner of a wall along the five-foot way. It was Hui Ying who first noticed the creature. She came running up to say that a dirty-looking dog had arrived out of nowhere. When I went to investigate, we stared at one another, the dog and I, our eyes locked in mortal combat.

The creature's eyes were yellowish brown and intelligent. Before long it lowered its head and lifted a hind leg while sticking out a long pink tongue, which it used to lick itself. I could see then that the dog was male, its balls lying flaccidly on the floor like loose pouches. Although it had short hairs on its body, the animal must have been beset with fleas, for it scratched itself vigorously.

Taking a broom, I shooed the dog away. 'Get lost, you ugly beast!' It scampered off with a start but stopped within a few paces of the house, apparently intent on returning to its chosen spot. Sure enough, when I came out that afternoon the dog was back where I had found it earlier, sleeping peacefully in the shade of the five-foot way.

I chased it away again, this time forcing the creature to run further than it had done previously. Li-Fei, our junior servant, was tasked with coming out every hour to ensure a dog-free corridor outside our house.

The animal had a persistence that matched my own, however, because when night fell it was still there. No matter what we did, the black vagrant came back, always parking itself in the exact same spot. By the time the sun set in the sky, I had resigned myself to having the dog outside our house for the night.

When morning came, my head was pounding. The dog had disappeared from our five-foot way but I had not slept a wink, because the creature had howled continuously through the hours of night. My hands shook while I prepared my joss-sticks for praying. I knew I would spend much time in front of our altar table that day. As I laid out oranges on plates and lit fresh candles, I whispered silently to Kuan Yin, asking for her mercy.

What followed remains clear in my mind even today. It was a Friday afternoon and the rain had already stopped. Looking out on to the Lahat Road, I spied the *sinkeh* who had been Peng Choon's travelling companion walking towards our front door.

I saw him alone, and I knew.

The man's pace was painfully slow, but my eyes were transfixed. This view of a man, head resolutely down, taking one small step at a time up a long incline is forever etched into my memory.

When the man finally reached our door, he said softly, 'Peng Choon Sau,' his head still bowed. '*Ngai tui imcher.* I so sorry have to tell you.' He paused. 'Your husband, Wong Peng Choon, passed away in his village in China.'

I put my hand to my mouth as a gasp escaped. Although I had been expecting bad news, hearing the words still came as a shock. I stumbled, faint from distress.

The man held my arm to steady me. 'Peng Choon Sau, we may go inside-moh? Then you can sit down?' he asked quietly.

I nodded. We walked slowly, stepping gingerly over the raised entrance of our front door, which kept away the evil spirits. I led the *sinkeh* into the second hall.

Ah Hong stood nearby awaiting instructions, as if she had known what would come. I told her to bring a pot of tea and to make sure the children were out of earshot. Then I let the man speak. We sat together for an hour as I listened to what had happened.

He told me how everything had gone well at first. He and Peng Choon arrived in Chiao-Ling County without a hitch. Although there were problems in China and he thought the Manchu government likely to fall, things were not as bad as the newspapers portrayed. He and Peng Choon even took a trip to Soochow, which they had thoroughly enjoyed: they saw silk being produced and breathed fresh air in Soochow's many gardens.

'Peng Choon Sau, your husband often talked about you and your children,' the man interjected, at which point I felt the colour rise in my cheeks. He stumbled at my embarrassment. 'Only . . . I think . . . I think . . . you want to know.' I forced a smile to save him from further squirming.

And then, the man said, trouble had begun. It was after their return from Soochow that Peng Choon fell ill. He complained first of drowsiness and ate less than usual. A few days later my husband was laid down with fever. He stayed in bed for days but continued to be unwell. Unable to hold food down, he lost weight, but there was no doctor in his village. By the time the villagers panicked and sent to the nearest town for a doctor, Peng Choon was beyond help.

When he heard how ill Peng Choon was, the *sinkeh* told me he had walked across the hill to see my husband. During those last days Peng Choon was shivering with fever and would often hallucinate, mouthing my name or the names of our children. Those who heard him knew he was trying to communicate, but Peng Choon had become incoherent and his words, mumbled amidst trickles of sweat, could barely be deciphered. During moments of lucidity, when he regained his previous clarity, he told his father he needed to write a letter. His family eventually succeeded in getting hold of pen and paper, and the man handed me several crumpled sheets from inside his cloth bag. I would ask Father to read them later, in the desolate weeks following my husband's death.

They would tell a sad story, one I would not connect to my own future until it was too late.

Immediately after handing me the letter, the *sinkeh* took out a small brown urn. It was then that I froze.

For the first time in my life I felt nothing except emptiness. It would be many months before I shed a single tear. From then on the days swirled around me. Time stood still, with the minutes stretching into hours, the hours into the next day, then the day after that, and still I remained numb. I was aware of furious activity, of people coming and going: Siew Lan visiting, telling me my parents would soon arrive; neighbours popping in and people asking questions, so many questions I thought my head would explode; questions to which I could give no answers, and so they were left dangling in the air, like the wind chimes we hung up to keep bad luck away.

Despite the noise I slept whenever I could. I dozed constantly. I woke only to feed the children, to bathe and dress them. While I slept, I dreamt. I saw the *sinkeh* walking towards our house, dressed completely in black: a dark cloth cap on his head, the black Chinese suit with Mandarin collar on his body, his feet in dark cloth shoes. Even his face was a black mass, its features indistinguishable; it was a face I could not see, yet I knew it was him. In my dreams I had a deep longing to wake up in a different world, one in which the *sinkeh*'s appearance had been nothing but a bad dream.

Yet whenever I rose and went downstairs I would see the urn in the middle of our altar table, its shape unmistakable – this clay vessel in plain brown. For two whole days I could not bring myself to touch it.

Then Monday morning came. When I went downstairs, the first thing I noticed was the urn sitting squat in its usual place. As I gazed at it, I recalled the *sinkeh*'s question. He had asked what he could do to help. 'Maybe you like me to contact the temple. Arrange a place for your husband.'

A place for my husband . . .

For the first time I reflected on the arrangements that needed to be made. With a jolt I realised how many there were, all awaiting my attention – mine and no one else's – now that Peng Choon was gone. It was a sobering thought; in the stillness of the morning air, it seemed more than a little daunting. Before I could even light the joss-sticks in my hands, the quiet was broken by a shriek. 'Mama, Mama, Papa is where?' I turned to see Weng Yoon, our fourth son, barely four years old but already a little tiger, running towards me with tears on his cheeks. As I folded the boy into my arms, I was gripped by traces of my husband on his face: lips that could twist into a hundred shapes, his double-creased eyes and fair skin.

Looking into my son's face, I knew that it was then or never. I took a deep breath, stood up and walked to the altar table. Picking up the urn for the first time, I ran my fingers around it, feeling the grainy hardness. Cupped within both my hands, the vessel left no doubt as to its solidity. I caressed it gently for several minutes before putting it down where I had found it.

Then, taking my son's hand, I led him towards the kitchen, leaving my husband behind on the altar table.

PART III:
STRUGGLE
1910–AUGUST 1921

17

It was nearly noon when Ah Boey turned up. The coolie lifted the cover from the highest rung of bamboo baskets to reveal row upon row of the delicate *kueh* we had spent hours preparing. They lay untouched, sweating in the heat. The pandanus-infused topping of the *seri muka* remained a lovely olive green and the glutinous rice beneath a creamy white, but their previously perfect diamond shapes were no longer pristine; they had begun to flop inside Ah Boey's containers. Yet their promise of sweetness oozed into the air, making my mouth water. I stared at Ah Boey's pointed fingers. How could it be that no one wanted our *kueh*?

'Peng Choon Sau, sorry-lah, I try,' Ah Boey said weakly. With his face shaded by the broad conical hat he wore on his head, it was easy for Ah Boey to avoid my eyes. I merely nodded before brusquely handing him his wage for the day.

As I walked towards the altar table, a feeling of desolation swept over me. The thought of feeding my children Nyonya *kueh* for the fourth time in a week filled me with dread. If our fortunes didn't turn soon, I would have to sell one of the shophouses my husband had left us, and that would further reduce our safety net.

I lit three joss-sticks. In front of the altar table I chanted while gazing absent-mindedly at the tendrils of smoke rising vertically through the still air. Whenever I closed my eyes, I imagined Peng Choon's last moments as he lay with fever on a sickbed. Pity for my dead husband usually engulfed me when I did this, but not on that day. On that day other thoughts took over. 'Yes, you had a terrible time,' I mumbled under my breath, 'but now you've moved on into the next world, while we are the ones left to suffer.'

That terrible scene – the one in which a *sinkeh*, dressed all in black, slowly approached our house up the hill – kept playing in my head. 'Your husband,' he had said, 'has passed away in his village in China.' I tasted bitterness in my throat and for the first time felt anger. If my husband had not visited China, he would have been alive and our children would have a father. The thoughts swarmed in my head, alongside imagined visions of China and his first wife, even his village in the hills. The more I thought about them, the more enraged I became. Why did he have to go then, with our children still so young? Could he not have waited?

With every passing moment my anguish became greater. At some point I began to shiver. 'Why, why, why?' I lashed out – at him, at the world and everyone in it. Standing there, all I could do was shake. I hoped he could hear and see my agony from beyond.

The pictures came into my head from nowhere: our children begging; my daughters in tattered clothes on a street corner, their little hands held out to the pity of strangers. I closed my eyes more tightly, but the images convulsed me no matter what I did, whether I placed my hands against both temples or shook my head from side to side. Nothing worked, not even removing the five-pronged pins which held my chignon up. Eventually my little prince, Weng Yu, came into view, rain-soaked and hungry, and my dammed heart could bear it no longer. The tears, which for weeks had refused to flow, came streaming down.

I sobbed before Kuan Yin as pain sliced my soul in two. I knew I would do anything for my children, absolutely anything. Lying on the floor, curled up like a baby with my head buried in both hands, I lay shuddering, until a gentle touch roused me.

I looked up to see my eldest daughter, Hui Fang, gazing at me, eyes wide with fright. 'You good-moh, Mama?'

'Yes,' I said in between sniffles. 'Mama just sad.' My daughter nodded like a sage who could see the ache in my soul.

'I know,' she said timidly. 'Don't worry, Mama, everything good in the end.'

On hearing that, I folded Hui Fang into my arms and wept.

Selling Nyonya *kueh* to earn money had been my idea.

Siew Lan helped me to come up with it after my parents' arrival, when I was no longer in a stupor. We spent hours in the inner hall of my house discussing what to do. Peng Choon had left us with what had once been a substantial amount of cash, and with my frugal nature a portion remained unused, but it would run out in due course. What then? Should I sell a shophouse or perhaps a piece of land to raise cash? Cash from any sale would eventually be depleted, and with only three shophouses and six plots of land in New Town, it would never be enough for our future. What we had to decide was how I would earn money while still looking after our children. It had to be an activity I could continue until the girls were married and the boys able to fend for themselves.

'Food!' Siew Lan had exclaimed enthusiastically. 'You know how to cook, and people always need to eat.'

Mother nodded in her corner of the second hall. 'Good idea, Siew Lan,' she chimed. 'And Chye Hoon from here can do it. But so much work-lah!'

Undeterred, Siew Lan suggested that we take a night tour of Leech Street. Over the years the street had remained the heart of the Chinese quarter. With the old theatre still there and plenty of opium dens and brothels to boot, human traffic was guaranteed. Where the Chinese congregated, there were eating places – dozens of them. At night I heard that hawkers set up makeshift food stalls on the road itself, and the whole street became very lively, with crowds and seductive smells.

The night we set off to learn about Leech Street for ourselves, Siew Lan's husband did not join us – few white devils ever ventured into the Chinese quarter. It was seven o'clock when we turned into Leech Street from Cross Street. The sun had already disappeared; as we approached, the entire street seemed aflame, with a necklace of lights stretching all the way down. When we got closer, we saw the line of portable stalls set up on wooden wheels. The stalls nestled against one another, barely an inch between them. Their trestles were attached with vertical poles, ingenious contraptions crossed by additional planks overhead from which awnings and kerosene oil lamps were suspended. The lamps cast their warm, yellowish glow everywhere.

Wending our way through the crowd was a challenge; there were so many people that a snail would have been faster. I had expected only coolies and mine workers and was surprised to see so many women at the fruit stalls, which were piled high with local favourites: lovely bananas, plump purple mangosteens and the durians, with their unmistakable fragrance. It was a fruit Peng Choon had been unable to abide, likening its smell to unwashed feet. I had missed durians during our marriage. We ate them in Songkhla and Penang, but Peng Choon loathed them so much that I had refrained, unable to find a way of disguising their powerful smell.

Besides fruits, hawkers plied every imaginable dish. We passed stalls where whole chickens, freshly steamed, were laid out on chopping boards, ready for hacking into bite-sized pieces. We saw men standing behind gigantic woks, braving flames from the open fires that rose high into the air. They worked furiously, a ladle in each hand, deftly tossing and turning noodles with both hands at the same time. Drinks stalls were marked by their transparent blocks of ice and the water dripping into bowls as it melted. Alongside piles of freshly shaven ice there stood tall jars of beans, coloured water and jelly.

The whole of Leech Street was pervaded by delicious aromas. The smells made us hungry even though we'd had dinner. Succumbing to temptation, we ended up perched on wooden stools around one of the many circular tables dotting the place. Under the warm Malayan night sky, we consumed fried *kuay-teow*, our signature noodle dish, and also seafood Cantonese noodles, which we washed down with ice *kachang*.

As I listened to the loud clanking of chopsticks around me, I realised that Siew Lan was right. People would always eat. The only question was what I should cook, and how to go about selling it.

Days later the idea came to me. It was simple really once I had thought about it. The work would be hard, so it had to be something I enjoyed making. I realised it could only be the passion I'd had from girlhood: Nyonya *kueh*. I saw also that our *kueh* was not then available in Ipoh – on Leech Street or anywhere else.

Father, ever the sceptic, doubted my ability to eke out a living from *kueh*. 'Do you know any other woman doing this?' he scoffed.

Mother, on the other hand, liked the idea. 'But the *kueh* Chye Hoon make so delicious!' she told me with an animated face.

It was only when I heard Mother's encouraging words that I began to truly take in her presence. She looked youthful despite the passage of time; few lines graced her face, and her hair retained its jet blackness, thanks to her ingrained habit of regular dyeing. Mother's lively mind, undiminished, invariably led our conversation down an interesting path. 'Remember when you small that time, the things you collect?' she asked. I scratched my head, not understanding what she was referring to. Mother started talking about the leaves I used to pick up, the brightly coloured cigarette packs, shiny pebbles and wings of butterflies – things from childhood which I had forgotten.

'How is that important?' Father asked with a sneer in his melodic voice. But Mother would not be put off.

'Chye Hoon, she all the time know what the other children like. Remember? I said then she good at business,' Mother continued triumphantly.

I had forgotten, but I saw Mother's point. Whenever Peng Choon had spoken to me about his business, I had listened avidly, and my reaction had sometimes surprised my husband. For example, after the surge in the price of tin in 1906 a deep slump set in. The next two years were terrible. We noticed the change in town: coolies who had lost their jobs in the mines flooded in. Many had no choice but to turn their hands to pulling rickshaws; some became vagrants, seeking shelter below Ipoh's many bridges. Piecing the things my husband had told me with what my own eyes could see, I told my husband that I thought this whole mining enterprise rather risky. Peng Choon had looked at me in surprise. 'That's why it's lucrative,' he had replied. 'Ai-yahh! Good heart,' I said. 'You spend so much on machinery, and the thing most important – the price of tin – you cannot even control.' I told him I much preferred his type of business, with no machinery, no huge spending and plenty of clients. He fell back into his chair, laughing.

Sadness filled me as I recalled this conversation. Yet once I knew I would start a business I tried to remember as much of it as I could – that and others like it. Make sure you can generate a profit, my husband had mentioned early on. Sales cannot be controlled, but costs can, so businesses should keep their costs low. When I reflected on this, it had seemed obvious: why would you not keep your costs down? Other pronouncements included one on the importance of pricing correctly: businesses which didn't sell at the right prices would get into trouble. My husband was thinking about a client, one of the first mechanics in Ipoh, who at the outset had been able to charge anything he liked.

Over time competitors arrived on the scene, men who to win business began charging a fraction of the price of Ipoh's first mechanic. But Peng Choon's client refused to reduce his prices. Even during the slump he claimed he provided better service and had no need to change. By the time he opened his eyes, his customers had gone elsewhere, and winning them back proved hard. The town's pioneer mechanic never regained his early standing.

I recalled all this as I asked myself how I should best sell Nyonya *kueh*. I was in the enviable position of having no competitors and felt confident despite Father's cool response. Father tried one last time to make me see sense. 'Chye Hoon, why are you so stubborn? You know nothing about business. How will you make money? Find someone to employ you. Even a cleaning job would be better – you would get guaranteed income.'

Seeing my pursed lips and smouldering eyes, Father reluctantly conceded defeat. Our first challenge was to find the best way of getting *kueh* to likely customers. We looked at setting up a stall on Leech Street and discovered that each stallholder had to pay a licence fee, which would drive costs up. I would also have to hire a helper, since a mother-of-ten could hardly stand at a stall night after night. For a new business, the costs of Leech Street were intimidating. Then there was the small problem that I didn't like the place itself. Its popularity meant I would attract customers, but I wasn't sure they were the type of customers I wanted. Not that I had an exact picture of what my customers would look like. I only knew there would be many women; I would somehow have to find a way of reaching them.

While I was mulling this over, Ah Boey unexpectedly came back into my life. I was walking to the market one morning with Mother when we heard a shout behind us. 'Peng Choon Sau, Peng Choon Sau!'

Turning around, I saw a sticklike man waving. His other hand held a rickshaw that he dragged along the road. I knew at once who it was and said excitedly to Mother, 'Remember the ting-ting man? That one is him.'

I have never seen Mother as astonished as she was then. She stood at a loss for words until Ah Boey came closer and she could see him clearly, at which point Mother said breathlessly, 'So it is!'

We were both dressed in the black clothes of mourning, which Ah Boey must have noticed from afar. Huffing even more than before, he grinned. 'You both good?' he asked. 'Sorry you have mourning clothes.'

'We good,' I replied. 'Only my husband passed away recently.'

'Oh no!' Ah Boey responded with genuine feeling. 'So sorry, so sorry.'

'You remember Mother?' I said, lifting my hand towards Mother.

Ah Boey had given no indication of recognising her, but he proceeded to make a good show of it, telling her, 'You look so young, I no think can be you!' Mother's face flushed with pleasure.

We ended up having coffee at one of the eating shops on Leech Street, where Ah Boey sat in a pose typical of the rickshaw puller: sandals off, one leg stretched out on a stool and the other leg folded, with the right knee up against his chin. Ah Boey mixed three spoonfuls of sugar into his coffee. Then, lifting his cup, he slurped its contents noisily.

He was reluctant to tell us much about himself. 'Nothing to say-lah!' he replied diffidently.

Having waited months to bump into him again, I was not going to let him get away that easily. 'Cannot be, Ah Boey. Mother not seen tin mine, I also not seen tin mine. Of course must have things to tell. Exciting, no, working there? Was where, your mine?'

And in that way, by peppering Ah Boey with questions, I began to find out little by little just what the reality of tin mining was. Ah Boey told us he had worked in two places. The first, located a short distance outside Ipoh, was a piece of land flooded with water, where men like him were given no implements other than *changkols*, the ubiquitous

Chinese backhoe, and nothing more than two baskets and a yoke pole each to carry their treasure. They would lift their *changkols* high in the air and then fling them into the ground, until they had dug up enough to fill two baskets. After that they had to wash what they dug up, and they did this with bare hands, sifting carefully for the ore. Once they had filled their two baskets with ore, they would place a basket on each end of their poles. Then, slinging the pole over their shoulders, they would carry the baskets a short distance to a large box.

The men did this for six hours a day in two shifts of three hours each, with a three-hour break in between. I was overwhelmed with pity as I listened to Ah Boey talk about such hard back-breaking work, but I could feel burning excitement at the same time. In the midst of thinking how best to sell my Nyonya *kueh*, a solution presented itself before my very eyes.

I peered closely at Ah Boey. Would anyone buy *kueh* from him? He looked as unprepossessing as ever, with his pockmarks, his missing teeth and that hair-infested mole beneath the lower lip, which still drew my eyes. Recalling the first time we met, I realised that his appearance had never stopped us from buying his ting-ting sweets. Of course, if there had been another ting-ting man, things might have been different. For as long as I remained the only Nyonya *kueh* maker in Ipoh, Ah Boey would suffice. If we placed the *kueh* into two sets of baskets suspended from the ends of a bamboo pole, Ah Boey could carry the pole on his shoulder, much as he had done in the tin mine, except that the *kueh* would be lighter than tin ore, and he wouldn't have to work as hard. He could take them for sale from one neighbourhood to another, and we would all benefit.

I didn't immediately tell Ah Boey what I was thinking, because doubts remained in my mind. I baulked every time I set eyes on him, this man with fingernails patched in black who spat out heavy glob-ules every now and again. Ah Boey's teeth – the few he had left – were prominent inside his mouth, yellowed and crooked. I would have to tell him to clean up and fit him into a new Chinese suit. I tried to imagine what he would look like spruced up and neat. Somehow my mind couldn't get there.

As I sat weaving a solution to my *kueh*-selling problem, Ah Boey continued with his story. He hated the work, he told us, and the life that went with it. There were many times when he would have gladly returned to selling ting-ting sweets in Penang; only he couldn't have left, because like most coolies he had fallen into debt. If he had escaped, 'they' would have come for him. 'Who?' I asked quickly. I had only been half listening, but my ears pricked up at the first mention of trouble. 'The contractors, the towkay's men, many people,' Ah Boey replied absent-mindedly.

'How you become rickshaw puller?' I asked.

Ah Boey told us the first mine he worked at ran into trouble. He couldn't remember the exact year, but it had happened probably fifteen years ago, around 1895. People who must have been the owners – white devils – appeared one day and he lost his job, as did many other miners. There was little he could do, so he ended up pulling a rickshaw until he found another job in a mine. The new mine sounded similar to the one Peng Choon had visited, with its deep pit and men running up and down ladders all day. It was clear Ah Boey had once been strong, and a troubling question came into my mind. I went straight to the point, while Mother squirmed in her seat.

'Ah Boey,' I said, 'you smoke opium-ah?'

Mother shot me a telling glare, which I ignored. Ah Boey struggled to answer. His face took on a foolish expression; he tried to look away, then laughed in embarrassment before finally nodding. 'You must not think bad of me, Peng Choon Sau.'

Ah Boey told us everyone at the mines smoked. Smoking opium helped him feel part of the group. It was easy, he said, as natural as breathing. He made it sound as if the men were encouraged to smoke – which was what Peng Choon had told me – and I remembered how angry my husband had been when he spoke of it. Ah Boey was even advanced money for both food and opium. His wages were so meagre that those daily advances swallowed up almost all that he would receive; by the time payday came he was left with little. Nonetheless he and men like him visited the gambling halls on paydays.

'But, Ah Boey, you no need to go.'

'Peng Choon Sau . . . ai-yahh, have pity-lah. Coolie life very hard,' Ah Boey muttered. He described how the gambling halls, brightly lit and festive, provided a contrast to their dismal living quarters; it was hard to resist the lure, if for nothing other than the solace of being somewhere cheerful for a few hours. The place he frequented had a band and beautiful singers, all women. Besides, the halls always smelt of delicious food – whole roasted ducks and chickens hanging up, so different to their normal bowl of white rice and a few miserable vegetables, if they were lucky. Gambling proved to be Ah Boey's undoing. He fell into debt and was unable to extricate himself until the second mine, too, fell upon hard times. At that point he lost his job and turned once more to pulling a rickshaw to survive.

'I no gamble since,' he said almost proudly. 'Good,' I replied. 'You must stop smoking opium too, Ah Boey. Now got places can help you,' I told him, repeating something Peng Choon had once said to me.

Ah Boey looked out doubtfully at the street. As Mother and I rose to take our leave, I requested that Ah Boey call at our house the following week. We fixed a day and time. 'You want go somewhere-ah?' he asked. I nodded. I would have to discuss my idea first with Siew Lan and my parents.

'Hmm,' Mother said, her eyebrows knitted into a frown. Siew Lan too looked at me as if she had not heard correctly. 'Right idea, wrong person,' she pronounced.

'You don't want an opium addict taking *kueh* around,' Father said with finality. I studied him, surprised by how little his views had changed through the years. Outwardly Father had aged, and he walked with a stoop he'd never previously had; inwardly, though, he was the same man I had known as a child, ironclad beliefs intact.

At the end of the day I took the risk because I was impatient to start. Desperation had seeped into my bones, and Ah Boey happened to be conveniently there. I didn't even know whether he would agree, though I suspected there was a good chance he would. At the time part of me naively wanted to help a man who had hit a streak of bad luck.

When Ah Boey turned up at our house, I invited him inside. The coolie seemed surprised, as did my eldest son, Weng Yu, who was returning from school just then. The boy, unable to take in the sight of a rickshaw puller entering our house as a guest, stopped in mid stride, his deep-set eyes becoming rounder with each passing second. He stared like an owl, and his whole face curved into a smirk. My little prince had become silent after his father passed away, withholding words as if to punish me, but on that afternoon I had little time to worry about this, because Ah Boey gratefully accepted my offer.

I can never forget the morning we made our first batch of *kueh*. It was only four when we woke, but our excitement was palpable. Hui Fang and Hui Ying stood alongside Siew Lan and Mother and me. With a heavy heart I had roused them from sleep, because we sorely needed the extra pairs of hands. I decided we would make two types of *kueh* every day, one savoury and one sweet. For our debut we prepared savoury yam cakes and *pulut tai-tai*. The latter was to be accompanied by the coconut and egg jam we call *kaya*, which meant plenty of coconut milk was needed. Within minutes of waking, Ah Hong was in full flow, squeezing milk from the grated coconut out of a muslin cloth she had wrapped into the shape of a bag, while her younger compatriot Li-Fei busied herself grating the fruit.

Siew Lan had insisted on coming. She stood at a kitchen counter chopping garlic, chillies, spring onions and dried shrimp. Mother too had wanted to help, but I had firmly refused. Nyonya cooking was too strenuous, too taxing, so Mother was forced to sit in a corner, rising now and then to check on the steaming baskets of glutinous rice and yam.

As I pounded butterfly pea flowers in a heavy mortar bowl, my heart was filled with lightness. I loved the hard work, had loved it ever since I stopped fighting with Mother over whether I would learn to cook. On that first day of *kueh* making, I was so glad I had embraced tradition. I breathed in those familiar smells and gave thanks to my Nyonya heritage, convinced it would save my family.

When at last the *kueh* were ready, I surveyed the room. Our *pulut tai-tai* looked truly delicious. Their grains of shiny glutinous rice were streaked blue by the dye we had mixed in from the violet petals of butterfly pea flowers. They sat beautifully layered on slices of banana leaves, almost too heartbreakingly pretty to cut. Siew Lan spooned some of the *kaya*, the thick coconut egg jam, on to a small piece of *kueh* and nodded in approval. 'Very good to eat!' she exclaimed.

And it truly was. The yam cake too turned out exquisitely – garnished with Siew Lan's handiwork of bright red chillies, spring onions and finely chopped toasted peanuts. My mouth began to water as I looked at our *kueh* in their baskets, ready for Ah Boey.

When he turned up, I could not recognise him. Wearing the new suit I had purchased, Ah Boey brought with him a bamboo pole and two lengths of rope, which he proceeded to knot tightly around the ends of his pole. My Nyonya *kueh* business had commenced.

All went well at first. I was then the only Nyonya *kueh* maker in Ipoh, so it's hardly a surprise that our *kueh* sold easily. Which is not to belittle our efforts, because even after other Nyonya women began to compete with us, everyone said the Wong family *kueh* were the best in town. In the early days Ah Boey told us that the people who came to take a peek inside his tiffin carriers were invariably awed by the colours they saw. 'Wahh! So blue-ah!' they would say about our *pulut tai-tai*. Many were converted when they saw the subtle olive green of our *seri muka* and the telltale orange-red tint of our *angkoo* skins – 'Very different,' they said, 'from Chinese *angkoo*!' Most of Ipoh's townsfolk bought our *kueh* without knowing what to expect, but at the rate they devoured what Ah Boey carried around, I was convinced there was a future for Nyonya *kueh* in Ipoh.

My heart leapt the first time Ah Boey handed me back the brown pouch I had given him. It was nothing more than a small bag of coarse cotton, yet I held it close against my breast as if cradling a child and carried the pouch gingerly into my bedroom to study its contents. When Father offered to help, I refused, knowing instinctively that I would need to go through this ritual myself. As soon as I was installed inside my bedroom, I poured the coins eagerly on to the teak dressing table that had been among Mother's many gifts when I married Peng Choon. It was the same table on to which my dead husband had, not many months previously, poured out the last payments from his clients and our property deeds. The table, golden yellow when new, had once been a prized possession, but with its colour darkening over the years, I was no longer so cautious with it. I allowed the first coins we earned from *kueh* to tumble roughly on to its exposed surface. I felt like a child again. The coins made loud clanging noises that sounded like music to my ears; a few rolled about and dropped over the edge of the table on to the wooden floorboards below.

In the moments which followed I was thankful for having run the household Peng Choon and I had shared. It meant I was familiar with money. I knew how to handle it and had little trouble counting how much we had made.

I separated the coins, as Peng Choon had taught me, first the light bronze coins, then the heavier silver ones. In those days all our coins were round and came in varying sizes. The larger and heavier they were, the higher their value, and silver coins were worth more than the bronze ones. Naturally I cared most about the silver circles; they glinted in the morning light, those piles of five-, ten-, twenty-, even fifty-cent coins, which brought me such a thrill.

Once I had arranged the coins carefully into piles, I began counting each pile. I grabbed hold of the tiny five-cent coins first and counted aloud: five, ten, fifteen cents and so on . . . slowly, laboriously. Keeping the numbers in my head was a challenge; I had always examined Peng Choon's earnings in his presence, and he was a man who could hold ten numbers in his head all at once and still retrieve each and every number at will. When I finished with the silver coins, I started on the bronzes: the quarter-cent, half-cent and one-cent piles. And then I repeated the whole exercise a second time to be sure I hadn't made a mistake. If the numbers did not match, I would do the whole count again. Sometimes I was forced into a third count before I was satisfied. There were days when counting what we made took a whole hour.

On that first morning counting was easy. In fact, everything seemed straightforward and exciting, if somewhat unreal. We made eight dollars in total, a sum which delighted me. Unable to believe how much we had sold in a single morning, I sat in my room for a long time, caressing the pieces of silver until my hands smelt of dirty metal. I ran my fingers along their patterned rims. I turned the coins round and felt the raised head carved on their backs, the head of a white man with a crown on his head and a beard on his face. This, Peng Choon had once told me, was the king of the white devils.

Staring at that strange head, I felt a surge of hope. A long-forgotten dream came floating back in which a warrior stood with a magical sword in his hand, its blade curved for deadly thrust. At last I had found my sword. It lay in Mother's gift – the culture that had given me a way to survive. I vowed to guard Mother's legacy with every breath I took and with my soul.

In the following months our cakes continued to be popular. Ah Boey returned at the end of each morning, his load lighter, with only the odd cake left inside his carriers. I altered the menu daily so that the coolie was constantly supplied with fresh varieties of *kueh*, a device I hoped would prevent our customers from becoming bored.

Then a decline crept in. It happened so slowly that for a time I didn't notice anything amiss. The number of coins Ah Boey handed me dwindled, but I put this down to the vagaries of business. When sales fell, I took less pleasure in money counting; what had once filled me with nervous energy turned into a chore I put off till the evenings, after we had finished dinner. Inevitably the day came when almost no *kueh* had been sold, and Ah Boey returned with his carriers still full.

Something inside me crumbled then. I had a sense that all was not what it seemed, a hunch I could not possibly have explained to anyone else. I wanted someone to follow Ah Boey on his rounds. Knowing that the person could not be me, I turned to Siew Lan for help, and she suggested her junior servant.

Thus it was that Rokiah, a Malay woman who had worked in Siew Lan's household for many years, was let loose to track Ah Boey as he left our house one morning. Pretending to be a washerwoman, she tailed him for a week. She told us that he went first to Leech Street, where she saw him entering a shop she thought was an opium den, carrying his pole and baskets inside. He remained there for hours, forcing her to loiter in the market and at different eating stalls until he staggered out with a hazy look on his face.

At the end of each morning, when I questioned Ah Boey he looked at me shiftily. The downward, guilty cast of those slanted eyes was unmistakable, and though I gave the wretched man every opportunity to confess, he never did.

After a week Father and I walked to Leech Street. It was a wide street with sturdy double-storey shophouses lining both sides, each fronted by a common corridor, the ubiquitous five-foot way, running along the entire line of shops. Being at the heart of the Chinese quarter, Leech Street and its five-foot ways bustled at all hours of the day or night, and it was no different that morning. The usual assortment of characters crowded our way: women in Chinese tunics and trousers returning from the market with woven baskets filled to the brim; men in Mandarin-collared jackets rushing by; and hawkers, so many hawkers everywhere, squatting on the five-foot way or on the sides of the street itself. Customers squatted alongside, their faces stuck behind ceramic bowls. The wonderful aroma of freshly cooked food filled the air, smells my sharp nose told me came from Chinese delicacies: dumplings being steamed and rice flour cakes roasted, *tau foo* being deep-fried and eggs prepared the double-beaten way. It was noisy too. Apart from the hawkers yelling to the world what they sold, loud conversation drifted out from the coffee shops, spiced by the odd raucous shout.

It didn't take long to spot Rokiah, because not many Malays ventured into town, and few were ever seen on Leech Street. Rokiah, with the beautiful double-creased eyes of her ancestors and lashes that flicked naturally upwards, waved to us from across the street as she pointed towards the shop Ah Boey had entered. I thanked Rokiah, telling her she was at liberty to return home.

As Father and I approached the door of the shop to which she had pointed, the clanking of mah-jong tiles could be heard. The sounds came from a shop nearby, one which had its doors and windows thrown wide open despite being a gambling parlour. Before long choice words spoken in the Hakka dialect reached our ears. 'Ayy! Fuck your mother's stinking cunt!' I felt the heat rise in my cheeks. Two men stumbled out, pushing and shoving one another, leaving behind the din of tables crashing and cups being broken. The terrifying clatter shook me, as did the sight of coolies in tattered rags pummelling each other with their fists. My heart beat faster, even though the brawl had nothing to do with us. The men were soon separated and led away, and normal brisk activity resumed in that corner of Leech Street.

With my heart still pounding, I walked into Ah Boey's opium den with Father. As soon as we entered, I began to understand the attraction of the drug. There was a cloying odour in the room, sweet and sickly. When it invaded my body, my head felt faint. In such a cloud I could see why people imagined their troubles disappearing.

When I asked for Ah Boey, we were told there was no such person there. It was only when I raised my voice that the man relented, agreeing finally to show us into a room, where Ah Boey lay in a stupor. The rooms weren't dark and dingy as I had supposed but bright and remarkably inviting. I hauled Ah Boey up by both shoulders and shook him.

'This is how you repay me-ah? Hah?' I shouted. 'So this is why no one buys our *kueh*!'

The miserable coolie woke up in an instant, as if he had risen from a bad dream.

'Pe-ng Choon Sau, Pe-ng Choon Sau,' he spluttered.

Though Father didn't say anything, it was reassuring to have him there. He looked like an ancient sage, an impression accentuated by the dignified silence that accompanied his slight stoop and completely white head. No one would dare lift a finger so long as his figure, which still towered over most men's, stood beside me. Not that I felt afraid; when it came to defending my children, the flame in me rose up, unabated.

'You no need to come back, you lousy person's head!' I told Ah Boey in no uncertain terms. 'You owe me money, but I know that you one cent not even got. Today your wage also I no give. You die even better-lah.'

With that I lifted the pole Ah Boey had cast to one side. Father and I strode out with our baskets of *kueh*, leaving astonished whispers behind.

18

Shortly after I fired Ah Boey, Siew Lan and her family travelled to Singapore for a short visit.

'Ai-yahh! Sorry about what happened-lah,' she told me with sympathy in her sad brown eyes. 'You sure to find someone else.'

But I had decided that no one else would sell my *kueh*: I would do the work myself. A sharp shrill noise escaped from Siew Lan's mouth, a sound in between a horrified whisper and a gasp. 'You no need to do that!'

'I know,' I replied. 'But more easy. If not, must find someone, pay him, then still worry he do what.'

Siew Lan thought me mad, as did Mother. Women worked then as servants and as *dulang* washers, standing in cold riverbeds to sift for tin, but few walked around town bearing bamboo poles on their shoulders; that was only to become commonplace later. None of this deterred me, and the look on my face must have warned my friend.

Siew Lan's attention then turned elsewhere – because I'd had another idea. As soon as she mentioned her family's planned trip to Singapore, I recalled the dresses and trinkets the white devil had bought her during his trips away, in the days before their marriage. Many of his trinkets had looked cheap, but the dresses he brought were outstanding.

They were made of beautiful material in vivid colours – reds, blues and browns – and their motifs of animals and flowers were intricately embroidered. The name Singapore was linked in my mind with lovely dresses.

While looking at one of Siew Lan's dresses, I thought it a pity that the cloth from which it was made could not be found in Ipoh, because if it could there were surely women like me who would rush out to buy it.

And with Siew Lan headed to Singapore in a motor car, I knew what I had to do. 'I need a favour,' I said.

'What?' she asked quizzically.

I explained about her dresses and how I thought there would be willing buyers if the materials from which they were made were available. 'If you see cloth you like, something you want to use to make your own clothes, buy it. You buy first, later I sell. We share the profits.'

Siew Lan looked at me in astonishment. 'Chye Hoon,' she laughed, 'you always full of surprises! How you know you can sell them here?'

I didn't know, I replied. But hadn't other women complimented her on her dresses? After talking it through, my idea no longer sounded silly to my friend. 'I get six rolls this time,' she said. 'My husband sure to go to Singapore again. If we sell, he can get more.' I must have looked sceptical, because Siew Lan immediately asked, 'What's the matter? He choose the materials first, no-ah?' Yes, I told her, but he wouldn't know how to bargain. I wouldn't make money if we paid their prices. The words 'white devil' had nearly slipped out of my mouth, and she had known it too. We both laughed.

'Ai-yahh! Don't worry-lah. I train him. I tell him what highest price he can pay.'

By the time I asked Siew Lan to purchase fabric for dressmaking, our circumstances were desperate. With our takings from *kueh* reduced, we were forced to live off income from the shophouses Peng Choon had acquired at the last minute; this in turn proved insufficient for the number of mouths I had to feed. Having little choice, I'd had to tap extensively into the savings Peng Choon had left me and had run it down to our last fifty dollars. Mother and Father contributed what they could, but I was filled with dread. That was why the idea of selling rolls of cloth came to me. Even if successful, the profit would have fed my family for no more than a week, but given where we were I had to try everything.

On the morning when I first set off with a bamboo pole across my shoulders, Mother stood on the five-foot way in front of our house. She watched me with red eyes. Though I did not turn around, I could feel her gaze against my back, willing me forward.

During the first hour the carrying was easy. When I left, there was already enough light to see the roads, but the day was still cool. The baskets of *kueh* were also surprisingly light. I barely felt them as I ambled along, shouting, 'Nyonya *kueh*! Nyonya *kueh*!'

Siew Lan and I had chosen my route carefully. We decided that I would first traverse the whole of the Lahat Road, making my presence felt among the residents in the large houses, with their monumental gardens, before heading into town. I walked a few paces, yelling loudly that Nyonya *kueh* were available for sale, and then waited to give customers time to come outside. The good townspeople were just waking when I started out. There were signs of life inside the houses – of lamps being lit and lights coming on in those which had been electrified. The hum of servants chattering and babies screaming surrounded me. When they heard my shouts, the women poked their heads out of the windows to look at me curiously. Some recognised me as the woman recently widowed on the Lahat Road, while many were faces I did not know. Among the women who came out that morning, there were a few who bought *kueh* purely out of pity. I didn't care. I needed them to buy my *kueh*, and if sympathy helped me sell a few, so be it. Besides,

I was convinced they would like the Wong family *kueh* once they had tasted them.

That turned out to be the case. One of my most loyal customers over the years was Hong Seng Soh, a Nyonya woman who lived in one of thirteen houses along a stretch of Lahat Road known simply as Thirteenth Street. She came out that morning to tell me how sorry she was; although we did not know each other, she had heard about my husband and wanted to buy *kueh* from me. There were other women like her, so that by the time I wound my way up Belfield Street, my baskets were considerably lighter.

But I had not bargained on the strength of the Malayan sun, how it comes out blazing once it breaks through the clouds. Its rays penetrated the hat I wore, a conical hat with a wide brim just like the one I had laughed at when we first arrived in Penang. Underneath the hat I wore a white cloth to protect my face, but the heat pierced through the cloth and into my skull, which quickly became hot. That was when I began to feel the load on my shoulders. Even though I had sold many *kueh*, my bones grew weary.

At the top of the town I forced myself to cross the Birch Bridge, determined to walk until I had sold everything in the baskets. I ventured into Kampong Jawa, where I succeeded in persuading the ladies to purchase the last of the *pulut tai-tai*. By conversing for just a few minutes, I learnt which *kueh* they liked. Despite my physical discomfort it occurred to me that the various communities in town had different tastes and would have their own favourites from amongst our *kueh*.

Over the next months I discovered the tastes of the families in each neighbourhood. I tailored my routes according to which *kueh* I was carrying. If we had *rempah udang* or *ondeh-ondeh*, I made sure to include the Malay kampongs along the way. When we made savoury yam cakes or *angkoo*, I would cover the Chinese quarters. I tried everything I could to empty my baskets, but there were days when, despite walking until my legs could carry me no further, I still took *kueh* home. Those were the toughest times. I would cry silently, with head burning, blisters swelling and my spirit broken.

Through sheer necessity I persisted. Within six months my back became accustomed to carrying the load, and our *kueh* found a loyal following. The following year I received our first large order from one of the towkays when he gave a banquet in the compound of his mansion. That was in 1912, which coincided with another tin boom. The boom came at a fortuitous time for us: demand for catering soared and requests poured in for *kueh* and special Nyonya dishes at festivities. We created a different menu for each customer and were able to command prices which gratified me. I had to hire extra help to cope with that first banquet, because we would never have delivered our *kueh* and Siamese laksa otherwise.

Looking back now, I find it hard to remember how tough the early days were. When I muse that I could even have started a second business importing fine cloths for dressmaking, I forget the hand-to-mouth existence we led then. It's true that I sold all six rolls of cloth Siew Lan brought over from Singapore on that first occasion. My success surprised even my friend; knowing our struggles, she refused to keep her share of the profit. Thereafter, whenever her husband went to Singapore he was instructed to purchase a few rolls of cloth for me. I must say the white devil had a good eye for patterns, though his bargaining power could have been improved. Had I continued pursuing that as a business line, we might well have made it work. Who knows? We might even have become wealthy. But I did whatever was thrown our way just to survive and had no time to think about another business.

We could not have lived through that terrible period if my daughters Hui Fang and Hui Ying had not always been in our kitchen, bleary-eyed but willing. For this they paid a price: my eldest, Hui Fang, never went to school, and my second daughter, Hui Ying, didn't learn to read until she was older.

Within months of my husband passing away, Hui Fang asked me why people had to die. Looking into my daughter's demure eyes, I took her hands in mine. 'Daughter, we all die at some point. But we return too. We come back as what, depends what we do now in this life. That's why must be good.' Hui Fang remained silent but continued looking wistfully at me, as if unsure what my answer said about us or her papa.

Our second daughter, Hui Ying, meanwhile, suffered from nightmares. She would wake up screaming in the middle of the night. She could never tell me what her dreams were about, only that she was frightened. She slept in my bed while her grandparents were with us. After their departure, Hui Ying refused to return to the room she shared with her sisters. Ignoring her pleas, I ordered her back into her own room. One morning Hui Ying ran to me, sobbing. 'Mama! If you die too, what happen to us then?'

My throat turned dry. I stroked my daughter's head and put on a brave face, though my heart was breaking. 'Don't be silly, Hui Ying,' I said. 'Mama is here with you.'

She looked up, scrunching her nose. 'How you know? Maybe you die too. Then we like the orphans outside.'

I sighed. 'Hui Ying-ah, your *kong-kong* and *po-po* are still alive. They look after you.'

'But they old already, maybe they die too,' my daughter objected. I was forced to discuss our entire family, going through the relatives one by one, beginning with her *kong-kong* and *po-po*, my parents, whom I knew would care for them if need be. I reminded Hui Ying of her aunts and her uncle Chong Jin, as well as distant cousins in Penang. When my daughter finally calmed down, we went to work in the kitchen, cutting banana leaves into pieces and pounding mixtures of coriander seeds, ginger root and garlic for our daily *kueh*.

As I set out that morning with my baskets, my daughter's small voice haunted me. Hui Ying's question shook me, but I could do little except work harder for my children. It was the only way I knew how.

19

One evening three years after Peng Choon passed away, my eldest son, Weng Yu, surprised the family with a story.

Hundreds of years ago, when the Ming Dynasty ruled China, a Chinese princess was sent to marry the Sultan of Malacca. In those days China was a powerful country, its protection sought by many rulers. Fearing attacks on his kingdom by unfriendly neighbours, the Sultan of Malacca sent a representative to the Ming court to ask for help. Good relations were already established between China and Malacca, as Chinese traders had settled on these shores centuries before. Listening to the Sultan's pleas, the Chinese emperor gave the hand of his daughter Hang Li Po in marriage to the Sultan. When Princess Hang Li Po arrived in Malacca, she brought five hundred courtiers with her, dressed in magnificent silk robes which flowed to the ground. Their jade, rubies and other precious stones glinted in the sun, blinding the people of Malacca. The princess's courtiers were given an entire hill – Bukit China – just outside the town on which to live. Over the years they became an important part of the local community. With their thirst for adventure, famous warriors emerged from among them, and Malacca was spared from attack for many years.

Weng Yu's story came at a time when I was already able to relax in the evenings – 'to shake my legs', as we like to say – because the Nyonya *kueh* business was thriving. The cakes had become sought-after delicacies, while the catering sideline was also growing fast. In the beginning catering augmented our income just once or twice a year, but then we received a full-moon celebration order – for two hundred *angkoo* and *mi-koo* to celebrate a baby's first month. Thereafter, word of the Wong family *kueh* spread through the Kinta District. We were flooded with orders for baby celebrations, and I'd had to hire two girls permanently to help in the kitchen.

In the evenings I began to gather the children around once more, to enjoy the storytelling we'd had as a family before Peng Choon's departure. I held my youngest son, Weng Foo, on my lap while the others sat on the floor, their eyes fixed on me as they listened to tales of fighting buffalo and holes being torn in the sky. Weng Yu had scoffed at this idea. 'There can't be holes in the sky!' he exclaimed in contempt.

'It's a story, Weng Yu,' I told him. 'You don't like to hear my stories, I no tell them.' The threat had made my fourth son, Weng Yoon, scowl with a look that could have bored holes through his brother's cheeks. Though only seven, Weng Yoon held his gaze, until his older brother backed down. Casually my little prince asked whether I had heard of Princess Hang Li Po.

'No,' I said. 'She is who?' With that, my eldest son commenced his tale, in the process revealing a side of his character none of us had seen till then. Not once did he pause for breath; it was as if he could imagine the princess and her entire court in front of us. I thought about the report cards my little prince brought home every term, which contained snippets that had to be read out to me by a man who used to work with Peng Choon. They confirmed what I already suspected: that my son was bright but exceptionally quiet. 'Weng Yu is a good student. Needs to speak more' were two sentences I knew like the palm of my hand.

Afterwards Weng Yu asked whether I liked the story. 'Very much,' I replied. I had heard of Malacca, where many Nyonyas and Babas lived, but the story of Princess Hang Li Po was new to me. 'You learn in school-ah?' I asked, to which my son proudly nodded.

I was pleased to discover yet another side of my little prince, but I thought it a pity he would never make money as a singer or a storyteller. Not in Ipoh at least.

In those years the town continued to grow. New brick buildings shot up, English was heard more often and local men started putting on Western clothes for daily wear – not many, but enough to be noticeable. I accepted these creeping changes without thinking about them; I had too much else to do building my livelihood.

One Monday morning Siew Lan arrived at our house with her son, Don – 'Tong' to me – in tow. I was in a good mood. I had been reflecting on our labours and was pleased with what we had achieved. I sat brimming with ideas too; a new mechanism for delivering *kueh* had just occurred to me when I caught sight of Siew Lan.

She came trotting in holding Don's hand. He was the same age as my fifth son, Weng Choon, but because of his European father, Don stood much taller. With thick pouting lips like his mother's and skin as tanned as a coconut husk, I would have thought him completely Chinese if it hadn't been for the incongruous tuft of brown hair on his head. Don's hair always made me look twice. I could not imagine what would become of him when he grew up, how such wispily thin hair the wrong colour could fit on such a face. Siew Lan and I sent him off to play with my boys before sitting cross-legged on the *barlay*, with our customary coffee pot and betel-chewing tray laid down before us.

The look of steely determination in Siew Lan's eyes told me she had come on a mission. I wondered what it was. She had chosen her time well; Monday was my day off, which meant I had both the freedom and the energy to listen.

'Your boys, how many now in school?' Siew Lan asked, evidently about to get straight to the point.

'Four,' I replied, dragging out the answer as I wondered where the conversation was heading. 'Why?'

'I think they should go to English school.'

The scrape of my guillotine knife against the husk of a betel nut could be heard; in one swift move I sliced neatly into its core. 'English school?' I repeated mechanically, not quite able to take in my friend's question.

Siew Lan's large brown eyes looked straight into mine. With both hands she raised a bright porcelain cup etched with Nyonya motifs in flamboyant greens and pinks. 'Yes-lah!' she said emphatically. 'I hear people say . . . the one down the road is good.'

Siew Lan watched as I spread white lime over a large betel leaf. 'You know the world now change,' she prodded. 'You want them have the best opportunities, isn't it?'

Wrapping the leaf around my chopped-up betel nut, I placed the fat bundle on to my tongue. I didn't like the idea of an English school; I couldn't have said why – I just didn't like it – but I could see that my friend wasn't going to be put off. She and I behaved similarly when we believed in something. I chewed on Siew Lan's question until the juice made my brain drowsy and I had to spit out a mouthful of blood-red liquid.

'Siew Lan-ah, I really not know,' I said cautiously. 'I no want them to forget their roots.' I recounted how Weng Yu had surprised me with his story of Princess Hang Li Po. 'I happy they learn their own history. In English school they teach what sort of history?'

'Ai-yahh, Chye Hoon,' Siew Lan said with a deadly serious expression. She had her own juicy bundle inside her mouth and was moving the cud around. In between sucking she spoke. 'Those stories not important,' she mumbled, exposing red-black teeth. 'You work so hard for your children. But some things we cannot control.' With those words Siew Lan swept her arms up in a dramatic gesture to indicate the world beyond our windows. 'Learn about China, what for? China is going down. We not like, but true.'

That set us on a long discussion about matters we did not normally touch. Our lives revolved around marketing and children; we busied ourselves with the supervision of servants, with the childhood illnesses, which seemed to come without pause, with schools, and for me, with my *kueh* business. In the midst of such unceasing activity, I had stopped following developments in China. I knew only about major events – the fall of the Ching dynasty, for instance; also that a state without an emperor had been declared. Other than that I paid little attention, not least because any news I caught about China always involved disturbance, either fighting or an assassination or an uprising, as if China were a country in which only chaos existed.

Siew Lan latched on to this, contrasting the picture of the China we held in our heads with what she had heard about England from her husband. 'England is very peaceful type of country – also powerful. That's why here got English rule. Your boys speak English language, sure to have more opportunities. Remember your husband even he speak English.'

It was true. Peng Choon did speak English. He had worked hard to learn it too, reading every book he could get his hands on. Yet curiously my husband had also wanted to send our boys to a Chinese school. Perhaps he had intended for them to learn English outside; who was to know? Without him around it was impossible for me to teach my sons, and I felt certain that Peng Choon would have wanted them to learn a language – any language – that would give them brighter chances in the future.

I thought about all this but couldn't shake off a nagging feeling. 'What about religion? I want my children pray to Lord Buddha, Kuan Yin.'

'No problem. My Flora now at the English school for girls. She no change religion.'

I sighed, spitting out another mouthful of betel nut juice. Siew Lan always came with an answer to every question. Though my sons' futures could not wait forever, I wasn't yet ready to make such a bold move. 'I have to think,' I told my friend.

With education on our minds, I forgot about my idea for delivering *kueh*. It soon came back, though, and the more I mulled it over, the more excited I became.

By the time I saw my friend a few days later, I could barely contain myself. I stopped her before she could enquire about the school. 'Later,' I said, gesticulating with my hands. 'First I have something to ask you.' My eyes must have shone, because Siew Lan peered at me with a questioning stare.

'I listen,' she said cautiously.

'I want to use a bicycle to carry *kueh*. What you think?'

'A bicycle?' There was silence as Siew Lan digested this. 'Who ride it?'

'Me of course,' I replied without hesitation. 'Who else?'

Further silence, before Siew Lan piped up, 'You?' The incredulity was apparent in her voice.

Upset by her reaction, I retorted, 'What? You think I no can-ah?'

I was used to the sight of those two-wheeled vehicles by then. Although they were not as commonplace as now, I had spied my first bicycle shortly after our arrival in town. But they remained expensive and were beyond the reach of most locals. For years, as I watched riders glide down our hill on the Lahat Road, I had envied them; they fanned me with a breeze as they flew by, and I imagined how much cooler they must have felt as they whizzed along, so much faster than my legs could carry me. When I thought of my daily *kueh* route, the idea of transferring the burden to a machine made my heart beat faster.

'You think I no can learn?' I repeated, a touch wounded.

For once my friend fumbled for words. 'I think . . . hmm . . . maybe-lah,' she conceded uncertainly. 'But who can teach you?'

'Ai-yahh! How can be that difficult? I just get on bicycle and ride,' I said with a confidence I was to regret.

'Hmm . . .' I remember the strange look Siew Lan gave me, a combination of grave encouragement infused with undisguised doubt. 'Maybe . . . not so easy, Chye Hoon.'

To lighten the air, Siew Lan suggested we pay a visit to the English school, which happened to be on our way. 'We can look at bicycles after that,' she added helpfully.

◆ ◆ ◆

I was impressed by the Anglo-Chinese School even on that first visit. This was before the main building was completed; it was under construction then, but the foundation stone had already been laid. In its absence, all I could see was a series of double-storey buildings with elaborately tiled roofs that housed classroom after classroom crammed full of boys. Not all the boys wore shirts and trousers; there were Malay boys in sarongs with *songkoks* on their heads, while some Chinese boys had jackets with Mandarin collars. There must have been hundreds of boys, because the rooms were so full that four attap sheds adjoining the brick buildings were also used for teaching. This worried me, but I was put at ease by the obvious enthusiasm of the teachers, especially the white devil whom we were told was the headmaster.

He was a large man, not fat but lumbering, with arms dangling down his sides like a friendly orangutan's. When he greeted me in Hokkien, I nearly tumbled over. *'Chiak pa boey?'* he said cheerfully. Craning my neck to look into his face, I felt a new respect for this giant of a devil, who had taken the trouble to learn our languages.

The headmaster introduced himself as Mr Ho-Lee and told us he loved our part of the world. He wanted to know how many boys I had, how old they were and whether they already attended school. Mr Ho-Lee's friendliness won me over; it was my first encounter with a white man who didn't look down on us. I knew Siew Lan disagreed, but that was how I felt; the others, including her husband, were politely condescending. The headmaster, on the other hand, conversed easily and freely, frequently flashing his teeth. Whether standing up or sitting down, Mr Ho-Lee conveyed the impression of hearty happiness. He did not laugh; he roared, throwing his head back with gusto. Whenever he did, his bushy moustache – two tufts of hair which hovered above his lips and joined in the middle like a roof – curved upwards like a cat's whiskers. Even his ears looked cheerful, turning pink when he laughed. When I asked about the attap sheds, he assured me they were temporary; the new buildings had already been paid for – by the Chinese community, he stressed – and would be ready soon.

After we left Mr Ho-Lee, Siew Lan and I walked on our own, surveying the other rooms. The headmaster had given us permission to go anywhere we wished and we poked our heads into all sorts of places. We went from a room full of white devils – the teachers apparently – to an enormous hall lined with books from floor to ceiling. There were also rooms in which funny-looking glass tubes hung on metallic clamps. 'This is where they learn science,' Siew Lan whispered reverently. 'Se-Too-Wat tell me this the future.'

As we walked, Siew Lan told me Mr Ho-Lee's story, how he was sent from Singapore to Ipoh to start this school. When he arrived, there had been nothing; Mr Ho-Lee even had to hire coolies to clear trees. Before we left the school grounds, I cast an admiring glance at what this white man had achieved nearly twenty years later. That was when I made up my mind.

It was a decision which would change our lives more than I could have suspected at the time. Early in 1913 I had our four eldest boys transferred to the Anglo-Chinese School, while the younger ones started there when they came of age.

20

Moving the boys to an English school made me wonder what to do about the girls. It was a matter my husband and I had failed to resolve: we had searched for a Chinese school for them at a time when the options were few. Instruction in English, on the other hand, would make finding a school easier, thanks to the missionaries. The same Mr Ho-Lee, when I met him, had asked whether I had daughters. He told me he had taught the first set of girls two weeks after reaching Ipoh – inside his own house. The class of girls grew in number, as did the class of boys, and the girls had finally been moved to separate premises not far away, just off Chamberlain Road.

That was where Siew Lan's daughter, Flora, went for lessons, and my friend did her utmost to persuade me to send my girls too.

'Better for them,' she told me as we rode a rickshaw into town when we had finally set up a time to look at bicycles.

Feeling a thrill as we turned the corner into Brewster Road, I clasped Siew Lan's arm, murmuring, 'We later only talk-lah!' My friend said nothing in reply, but I could hear her thoughts ticking away in the silence. The question was certain to come up again.

Meanwhile the Cycle & Carriage store gleamed in the bright sunlight. Siew Lan's husband called it the only place for bicycles, and there was such an array of vehicles that their glare hurt my eyes. In the initial moments, I had to place my hands over both eyebrows. Squinting in the sun, I saw rows of ugly motor cars, their huge lights and cold bonnets staring straight at me.

A Chinese man came out to greet us. On hearing of my search for a bicycle, he led us inside into the bowels of the shop, where brand-new bicycles were displayed. There were simple black bikes with nothing other than seats and handlebars, bikes with bells, different shapes of seats, fancy handlebars, even tricycles with a smaller front wheel and two large rear wheels. They were all newly imported from Britain – and expensive.

I gasped when I heard the prices. 'What? One hundred dollars?' That was enough to see my four boys through for eight months, even on the increased fees in their new school. 'You no have something cheaper-ah?'

'Sorry-lah, no have,' the man replied. 'Japan-made bicycles more cheap. We here no have them, Japanese shops got-lah.'

I asked to try out a bicycle anyway. Looking clean and lustrous, they were certainly tempting. 'No problem,' the man said. 'Which one?'

I pointed to a medium-sized bicycle with a sturdy seat and a bell on the front. 'Good choice,' the man told me approvingly. 'I am called Lee Tsin-sang. I think you sit on one before, yes?'

When I shook my head, I saw the surprise on Lee Tsin-sang's face. 'Hmm . . . you want to try a tricycle first?'

'No!' I said impatiently. 'I want a bicycle.'

While I stood beside the vehicle, the man lowered the seat. Then he wheeled the bicycle on to the road for me and beckoned me over. All the while Lee Tsin-sang continued to hold the handlebars. I strode towards the machine with my heart pumping, trying to work out how I would get on to the seat in my sarong. Lee Tsin-sang helped me, and

I was soon sitting firmly. With both feet on the pedals, I became terrified of not being able to get down and told him to continue holding on while I made sure my feet could touch the ground.

Once I was certain I could reach the safety of land without having to climb off, I felt ready to go. 'You must pedal, otherwise you fall,' Lee Tsin-sang said.

As soon as he took his hands off the handlebar, the bicycle swerved to the right. The thing had a mind of its own – I was utterly powerless. Everything happened so fast. One second I was in position, both hands firmly on the bar at the front, a foot on each pedal, the next the front bar had turned sideways and my feet were somewhere else – where exactly I couldn't tell – but I was no longer on the seat. I felt myself slipping quickly. I would have fallen hard, right on to the road, had Lee Tsin-sang not grabbed the bicycle from behind with one hand and with his other hand clutched my arm in time to catch me.

Siew Lan came running up. 'Chye Hoon, you good-mah?' she panted.

I nodded, face puffed up with indignation, because I hadn't managed even a single round on the pedals. I wanted to try again.

'Really-ah, Chye Hoon? I scared you hurt yourself,' Siew Lan said in a concerned voice.

With Lee Tsin-sang standing by, I lifted myself slowly on to the hard bicycle seat. I put my right foot on the pedal and turned it round a few times to make sure it worked. Then I took a deep breath. Holding tightly on to the front bar, I gingerly lifted my left foot on to the second pedal. That was when the problems began. The bar swung wildly from side to side, as it had the first time. I wobbled. Trying desperately to put my feet on the road, I came off the seat and knocked hard against the front bar. In that split second a rip could be heard – the sound of my sarong tearing – and I found myself in a heap on the road. The bicycle bell rang from the impact. Fortunately I escaped with minor injuries; when Lee Tsin-sang and Siew Lan helped me up, they found a small tear at the side of my sarong, though only my hands were grazed. However, a bruise appeared the next day, and I could not walk properly.

As I handed the vehicle back to Lee Tsin-sang, I felt deflated. Not only had my pride been dented, but I was deeply irritated with myself. It had looked so easy when I observed others riding, yet balancing on two wheels was clearly no small feat.

'Hard in a sarong,' Lee Tsin-sang said sympathetically, trying to help me save face. 'You want to try a tricycle?'

I shook my head. With their additional wheel, those were even more expensive, and I had no wish to humiliate myself further. As we climbed into a rickshaw, Siew Lan held on to my hands, because I remained shaky on my feet. 'Only your first time ride bicycle. You do very well-ah, Chye Hoon,' she whispered. My dear friend would have thought me crazy if she knew that I hadn't given up on the idea – far from it. But I had learnt one important thing: I would not be the person to ride it.

The next time we saw each other, Siew Lan tackled me again about sending my girls to the English school.

'You already see boys' school – why not go to girls' school too?' She looked hard at me across the table.

Outside, thunder rolled across the Kinta plains. I didn't know what to say. 'You scared what?' my friend persisted. Where to begin? There were so many things. 'Tell me,' Siew Lan said encouragingly.

And so I started, right from where my life had commenced, in Songkhla. As the rains came down that Friday afternoon, Siew Lan sat with me, sipping coffee and chewing betel nut leaves. I caught sight of her gums every now and again, their dark brooding stains peeping out at me. I told her how I had been curious from a young age about the mysterious squiggles Father used to draw with his quill pen and ink, how I even toppled his inkpot and was forbidden thereafter to watch him. I recalled my many battles with Mother, including the time I bit her arm because I wanted to go to school. Siew Lan burst into laughter at this, telling me in the nicest possible way that I must have been a little monster.

I laughed too, but when we began to talk about my daughters, my heart turned heavy. I mentioned the ambitions I had harboured for them, how we had tried, and failed, to find a Chinese school. 'But now have English school!' Siew Lan exclaimed.

'I know,' I said pensively.

'So then, you wait for what? Your sons do well in new school, isn't it?'

That was exactly the problem: the boys had settled in easily – perhaps a little too easily. Within a fortnight my eldest son, Weng Yu, had begun clamouring for Western-style shirts and trousers. 'English shirts better for English school, Mama,' he told me. Following this example, his brothers did the same. When I refused to allow English dress, a war had ensued, during which Weng Yu refused to speak in our house. Silence was his weapon; he ground my spirit with it until I relented, as he knew I would. I forgave my little prince, knowing how the boy's heart ached for his father, as mine did. After all, what did clothes matter? The result was that my sons were now walking down our hill on the Lahat Road in sharp-collared shirts and crisp white trousers.

But I knew our struggle was about more than that. The Anglo-Chinese School had changed the boys, especially my eldest son. 'How?' Siew Lan demanded.

Through the open windows, the rain fell in sheets, beating hard against the gravel road. I struggled for words. The difference was difficult to fathom – a slight sneer perhaps, even an air of superiority.

'Weng Yu?' Siew Lan said, frowning. 'But he such nice boy!' I took a sip of coffee. 'Maybe . . . you just imagine it, Chye Hoon.'

I shook my head. Weng Yu, I pointed out, had also stopped playing with the neighbourhood boys, whom I realised didn't speak English.

'Hmm . . .' was all Siew Lan said by way of reply, but she added, 'You spoil Weng Yu too much.'

Betel nut juice stung the insides of my mouth. I moved the cud, already well chewed, to the front, the part between gums and teeth, where I rolled it from side to side with my tongue. My friend's reprimand brought a sigh. What could I do? Weng Yu reminded me so much of his father that just catching sight of him melted my heart. Besides, he was my eldest son; how could I not spoil him?

'Ai-yahh!' Siew Lan cried out. 'Why we talk about this for so long? Nothing to do with your girls even! Tell me, why not visit girls' school?'

Outside, the rain slowed to a trickle. Clouds had parted, to let a sliver of sunlight through, which brightened the *barlay* floor. I sat uneasily, thinking about Hui Fang, who was then nearly fourteen and unable to walk anywhere without attracting male attention. Her sister Hui Ying, just a year younger, was even better-looking but wholly unembarrassed by catcalls; she would stab any man who dared whistle at her with an icy stare until he lowered his head. I smiled wryly whenever I thought about my second daughter. Her papa's death had blunted none of her battle instincts; instead, she had grown up overnight, one day all arms and legs, the next sitting still, worrying for her younger siblings.

'My daughters soon marry,' I told Siew Lan.

'Yes-lah, Chye Hoon, is like that, but you want them well prepared, isn't it?' Siew Lan retorted. 'In this life anything can happen.'

Though Siew Lan had said this calmly, she had a knowing look which left me in no doubt as to what she meant. I took a deep breath.

'Going to school also may be no use to me, my friend,' I said softly. 'My cooking is more important. Bring us money.'

'Good heart! Why you speak like that? If you know how to read and write, today you also not know what you do!'

'Maybe more hard for me to marry,' I said. I reminded her how marriage had almost eluded me.

'I keep telling you, the world now different. If your girls not know how to read or write, they are at disadvantage!'

I could no longer think. Somewhere at the back of my mind were competing voices, one telling me to send my girls to school as I had once wanted, the other warning me not to. I was aware of an anxiety that would not let go. A picture of the large spider's web I had tangled up and broken earlier that day came to haunt me; I felt sorry for the poor spider as I grabbed the delicate white threads in my hands, twisting them up and throwing the whole lot into a dustbin. The feel of the threads had made my skin crawl, and I had gone immediately to wash my hands.

When Siew Lan touched my arm, I jumped. My friend looked me squarely in the eye. 'Your daughters are already good cooks. Why not let them read and write too?'

A shadow fell across the *barlay*. The sun, which had peeped out previously, now slunk back behind the storm clouds, which continued to adorn the skies. 'I . . . I scared, Siew Lan. I scared . . . lose my boys.'

The unexpected confession brought tears to my eyes, though I had no idea why I was crying. I told Siew Lan how I had failed to consult the temple priest before allowing my sons to change schools. Why, I didn't even ask Kuan Yin for her blessing! What had I been thinking? My feelings, still in a state of ferment, were expelling their poignant odours.

'I . . . I . . . h-have to consult the priest,' I finally stammered to my friend.

21

In the same period I became increasingly worried about my youngest son, Weng Foo. Little Weng Foo had a special place in my heart because he was the only child to have been born after his father's departure for China. Perhaps my troubled mind had affected him, for Weng Foo came out tiny, and his health had always been precarious. Enticing Weng Foo to eat was a running joke in our house. Short of leashing my son to a chair so that Li-Fei could force morsels down his throat, there seemed no other way of improving Weng Foo's figure, which was that of a stick insect on two legs. He caught every cough and cold in town and was often down with fever. Just days after Siew Lan's visit, he complained of a sore throat. Soon, with his head feeling hot, he began coughing like an opium smoker, and it looked as if I would have to take him to see Dr Wong yet again.

Visits to the clinic were a ritual we had started a few years back. In the months after Peng Choon passed away, I had had little time to deal with Weng Foo's health. Whenever he lay awake crying at night, I would rock him in my arms until he went back to sleep. The next day, as soon as I finished my *kueh* rounds, I would take him to see Dr Wong, a physician trained in Chinese medicine who had a clinic on Treacher

Street. We became such regular visitors that the nurses at the Lee Chai Dispensary knew my son by name. Dr Wong's herbal concoctions soothed Weng Foo's ailments but failed to fatten the boy. Or indeed to strengthen him; when the next illness came to town, he would again succumb, and the trip to Treacher Street would have to be repeated.

With the *kueh* business on a sounder footing, I had more time to focus on my children. I wondered what else I could do for my youngest son's health. Feeling Weng Foo's hot head and hearing his splutters, I thought it time I added his ailments to the list of questions I would take to the temple priest. I made an appointment at the Nan Tien Temple. My visit could not come soon enough.

The temple is one of several shrines built within the limestone caves surrounding Ipoh. A newer temple had been opened next to it, but until that day I had never been to either, because the trip to the caves was arduous. From where we lived the journey took a good hour and a half, and longer if the rickshaw puller happened to be tired from his previous efforts, which meant that the pullers often had to be enticed with double the usual fare.

As I sat in our vehicle with Siew Lan, all was quiet along the Gopeng Road. We were each deep in our thoughts, interrupted only by the sound of the puller's soft footfall against ground baked dry by the searing sun. Just outside Ipoh large compounds came into view; these surrounded the mansions of the wealthy, which were concealed behind solid brick walls. Through heavy metallic gates I caught glimpses of what lay beyond – the sprawling pale buildings in the English style of the school my sons attended. Some of the houses were so grand they had long driveways with large porches, obviously designed for several motor cars, as well as fat, incongruous towers. Their fine shuttered windows and red-tiled roofs stretched for miles.

Eventually the houses gave way to a luxuriant emerald on both sides of the road where secondary jungle had been cleared. There were open fields, many overrun with weeds – the *lalang* – that grow everywhere on this land. In between the clumps of *lalang* were small estates dotted with rubber trees, where I could see Klings, the labourers brought in from southern India, at work. Many were cutting slits into the barks of the rubber trees, the streams of white already visible from the gashes they had made. Yet others collected the cloudy liquid from small cups that hung suspended on the trunks. Every now and again, when we spied a clearing a Malay kampong would come into view, and raised wooden houses would peep out from beneath clumps of coconut and betel palm trees.

Always in the distance were the hills. I had loved Ipoh's hills from the moment I set eyes on them. On rain-soaked afternoons when everything outside was cool, the trees became dark, turning the hills black. Light mist occasionally drifted in, its white veil like the brushstrokes on a perfect Chinese painting. On hot mornings I could see the exposed rock more clearly and marvelled at the shapes which had been created: narrow pendants stretching down like long teardrops, and in the opposite direction, thick mounds rising up from beneath, seemingly without effort, sculpted by years of the rain and wind that had lashed down over the Kinta Valley.

The head priest, Tai Fatt Shi Tan, was strolling in the gardens when we arrived. He was a short man, barely taller than my five feet two inches. He was clad in the black slippers and robes of a monk – a simple yellow tunic that fell to his toes, which he wore wrapped around his shoulders. As he greeted us, a line of monkeys with cheeky grey faces scuttled past, swinging their long tails from side to side. A lone fruit seller had set up a stall in the garden, and I bought a handful of oranges from him. In front of us the temple soared. It had been built into the opening of one of the caves, and reaching high up, it beckoned with its air of mystery.

The *fatt shi* walked quickly. We had to run to follow him. Fortunately the main entrance wasn't far. As we hurried along, I saw that the walls of the temple were made of solid brick and had been freshly painted white. Once inside I was surprised by its dark interior. Perhaps that was to be expected, it being a cave, but given the many windows dotted around, I had expected more light. It took several minutes before my eyes adjusted to the gloom within.

When I could see once more, I noticed a round gold-coloured urn filled with ash. Used joss-sticks were planted into the grey mass, some with ends still alight and continuing to flicker red like the dying embers on hot coals. The smell of burning incense wafted through the air. In the distance I heard the hum of sutras echoing through the caves. A shiver ran through me; whether because I was moved by the soft chanting or by a sudden blast of cold air, I couldn't tell.

A long set of steps rose up, so high that my neck hurt just peering at them. I silently hoped the *fatt shi* wasn't about to lead us there. It was then, while craning my neck, that I saw the magnificent shapes hanging down from the roof of the cave. They had been carved into the stone by water, which continued to seep down. Some of the rock glistened like polished marble, and a trickling could be heard every now and again. For a minute I forgot everything. I could only stare at the majestic art before our eyes – the weeping needles and pieces like immortal creatures, part dragon, part lion, all carved into the rock.

'You look. So beautiful-hah?' Siew Lan whispered. 'Yes,' I said. 'See that one there?' I pointed to a low-hanging piece in a corner of the main room we were traversing. From where we were and with the little light we had, the rock face had turned a breathtaking green, the colour of pure jade.

The *fatt shi* led us further inside, deep into the belly of the cave. When I realised we would not have to climb steep steps, I breathed a sigh of relief. The path along which he took us was flat but dark. The lamp the *fatt shi* held in his hand barely illuminated our way. 'Careful here,' he said as we went down a narrow alley where the roof of the cave was so low that we could nearly touch it with the tops of our heads. Walking along that alley, I had to use my hands to guide me, and for the first time I felt Ipoh's hills in the palms of my hands. The rock was solid yet amazingly smooth. It didn't cut into my flesh even when I ran my fingers along its edges.

As we walked, the chanting became louder. The cave eventually opened on to a clearing, where an inner temple stood. There the monks were evidently in prayer. Trees had been planted in the open space, around a small pond in which a handful of turtles were basking. To this day I remember how still it was – not a sound could be heard apart from the chanting of the monks. The air smelt fresh; it was cool, clean mountain air which came straight from the hills. A peace descended on me and I remember thinking instantly that this would be my place of rest, this place where the breath of the gods blew.

The *fatt shi* invited us to sit down under a tree where a heavy stone table and a few chairs had been placed. 'What can I do for you?' he asked. I looked at him, this calm, mild-mannered man who must have been sixty but whose face remained remarkably youthful, with barely a wrinkle in sight. After Siew Lan and I had sat down, he placed a pair of round gold-rimmed glasses on the bridge of his nose and surveyed us before setting his glasses down firmly on the table.

I began my story, explaining the turmoil I had felt for weeks, a turbulence so violent it was affecting my sleep. That was the reason, I said, I had decided to consult more than one priest. I told the *fatt shi* what I had done since my husband passed away, how I'd sent my boys to a Chinese school first and then transferred them to an English school without consulting Kuan Yin. I told him about the change I had noticed in all my boys, especially the eldest, and how worried I was that I had angered the gods through my lack of attention. I wondered aloud whether I should send my girls to school too. I told him about my sickly youngest child, who was in bed with yet another cough. We had been to a doctor repeatedly and I now needed help. What should I do?

The *fatt shi* listened patiently, interrupting only to ask a question here and there. When I had finished, he invited me to join him in prayer. There was a simple altar just inside the shelter of the cave, a table on which a small statue of the Lord Buddha had been placed, illuminated by an array of candles. We laid down my offering of fruit, lit three joss-sticks each and began chanting. The *fatt shi* led the sutra, while Siew Lan and I followed in unison.

How long we stood there I cannot say, but the sun was high in the sky when we left. I loitered in the clearing for as long as I could to savour that glorious mountain air one last time. I was disappointed that the *fatt shi* could not give me an answer then and there. We would need to make the same trip again in a fortnight, when he promised to tell me what I wanted to know.

Meanwhile trouble was brewing. On Siew Lan's next visit, I could tell as soon as she entered our house that something had happened.

'Got problem-ah?' I asked.

'Have war,' she told me.

'Really?' I looked up in surprise. 'Where?'

'Europe,' she replied.

It was the middle of 1914. Siew Lan explained that a war had broken out in which many countries were involved, including Britain. Her husband, she said, had become very sad and told her constantly that he would have gone off to fight if he'd been younger.

'Ai-yahh! Good heart! Good thing then he not young-lah,' I said. I had never understood this obsession men had about fighting. I took in Siew Lan's news about a war and kept it somewhere at the back of my head. Unlike the other problems I was facing, this war that was being fought so many miles away seemed unconnected to me. It was too remote, too much of a white man's war.

Within weeks, however, our *kueh* sales declined. For no apparent reason the townspeople became reluctant to spend money, even on eating. Next the price of tin plummeted and was the talk of the town once more. Mining coolies flooded in, searching for work. Not for the first time, some sought to return permanently to China, while others tried their hand at whatever they could: they swept roads, pulled rickshaws and did odd jobs here and there. My boys mentioned that their school was emptying; classmates whose parents could no longer afford the fees left.

I realised then that the white man's war, despite being fought a distance away, was having an impact on Ipoh. Whether or not I liked it, our destinies were intertwined, and for the first time I understood why many locals supported the British in their war efforts. I paid more attention to Siew Lan's updates as the war, which rumbled on, became almost as real as Weng Foo's numerous illnesses.

In the two weeks between my trips to the Nan Tien Temple, my youngest son continued coughing badly. His chest filled with fluid and he brought up green phlegm. His head, though not burning, remained hot. We had already visited Dr Wong a second time when Siew Lan pressed me to see another doctor, one of the local boys who had come back with a set of Western medical degrees. 'No,' I told her firmly. 'What Chinese doctor do, I understand. The herbs, plants, those I know. But English doctor-ah . . . you don't even know what the medicine made from.' Besides, I pointed out, I was still waiting for word from the *fatt shi*.

Until then, I kept constant watch over my son, barely sleeping for seven days and seven nights.

Two weeks later, at the appointed time I went to the Nan Tien Temple. I was alone, and the *fatt shi* looked grave when he saw me. His answers were brief.

'The gods have said you can leave your boys in the English school, but don't send your girls. As for your youngest son, give him to Kuan Yin to be her godson. That's the only way he can become healthier.'

With that, the priest rushed off. Throughout the ride home I pondered his words. I did not know what adoption by the Goddess of Mercy entailed, but I knew I would obey the gods no matter what it took. At last they had spoken. Sitting back in the rickshaw, I stretched my legs out, suffused with relief, imagining the face of the young man Weng Foo would one day become. In the distance Ipoh's limestone hills shimmered.

22

The following afternoon Siew Lan rushed to our house. She was meant to have accompanied me on that second trip to the Nan Tien Temple, but her son, Don, had fallen ill with fever. Impatient for news, she turned up as soon as Don was better.

'So?' my friend asked breathlessly.

Her look of anticipation melted when she heard what Fatt Shi Tan had said.

'Hmm . . . ,' she muttered. Her normally large eyes narrowed and fixed directly on me. 'So, you think what about his answer?'

'Have what to think?' I said quietly. 'I ask, he give answer, now must listen.'

The delicious smells of sambal frying tickled my nostrils. I had not long been home from traipsing around town with *kueh*; with the back of my head still pounding from the heat, the last thing I wanted was to talk about the girls. I had already decided to leave the boys at their English school, a thought which gnawed at my soul, because with each passing day my sons acted more like our rulers. They refused to wear their sarongs at home. They whispered in

English, even amongst themselves. They consorted with others who did likewise, ceasing to play with the neighbourhood boys who had previously been their friends. There was little doubt my sons were drifting away. Yet the gods had made it clear I should let them be, and I consoled myself with the thought that what I was doing was best for their futures.

The subject of my daughters seemed less straightforward. At the back of my mind lay the certainty that men did not like smart women, and it would be easier for my daughters to marry if they didn't go to school. But the *fatt shi's* instruction not to send them also tore me apart. How could it not when I remembered how I too had once craved to learn?

From the look she gave me, I saw that Siew Lan sensed this ambiguity. Her ringing silence made her own opinion abundantly clear. She arched her right eyebrow sceptically upwards, while I shifted uneasily on the *barlay*.

Seconds passed which felt as heavy as the hours. Abruptly Siew Lan announced that my eldest son, Weng Yu, had turned up at her house while I was away at the caves.

'He want what?' I asked, perplexed.

'He want see Se-Too-Wat. Weng Yu not know how to do his homework, ask questions.'

I sighed. The image of my dimpled son seeking help from a hairy white man with alcohol breath unsettled me, but I didn't have the heart to say so to his wife. Besides, I could not have helped Weng Yu with schoolwork. 'I hope he no disturb your husband,' I said as mildly as I could manage.

'No, Chye Hoon, don't worry,' my friend replied breezily. 'Se-Too-Wat like Weng Yu. He say very good boy. Now already clever speak English!' After a pause Siew Lan added with a knowing look, 'Weng Yu now big boy. Good he speak to a man.'

I coloured, letting Siew Lan's remark drop as the smells from the kitchen told me lunch was ready. The pungent aromas of dried shrimp, chillies and coconut milk wafted into the inner hall. I closed my eyes, inhaling those comforting childhood scents.

◆ ◆ ◆

The Kuan Yin Temple was the first temple I had stepped into after Peng Choon and I arrived in Ipoh, but its location proved inconvenient for regular visits. It stood off Brewster Road at the top of the town, which made it a lot further than the Pa Lo Old Temple, where I had met Siew Lan. After the births of our children, I preferred praying in the quiet of our home, and the early years in Ipoh saw me venturing to the temple less and less. There came a time, after our fifth child, when I began to visit the temple only on festival days. The temples were at their most crowded then: everyone went, including those who only showed up when they needed help and remained godless the rest of the year.

In the weeks leading up to Weng Foo's dedication ceremony, I tested the patience of Tai Fatt Shi Ong at the Kuan Yin Temple, though he never showed it. He was the head priest, a tall man with a kindly face who spoke in a deep, solemn voice that reminded me of Father's. 'Asking Kuan Yin to adopt your son is a big step,' he said. 'You must be ready.' Fatt Shi Ong pointed out that Weng Foo would be entering into a sacred bond from which release would be possible only when the boy sought it himself, which he could do just before marrying. Until then Weng Foo would be expected to revere his godmother, the Goddess. As a sign of his fidelity, Weng Foo would have to renounce the eating of beef, the meat of a sacred animal.

The *fatt shi* presented these details as we meandered through the gardens. Like his counterpart at the Nan Tien Temple in the caves, he too walked at a pace. I puffed and panted trying to keep up, all the while imagining life without the delights of prawns and chicken, pork and fish. I knew that what the *fatt shi* was proposing was far from vegetarianism, yet I wondered where it would all end once my son stopped eating beef.

Beneath the leaves of an acacia tree, its glorious shape spread out above us like a Chinese fan, the *fatt shi* sensed my uncertainty. He reminded me what the act of adoption meant. 'You are giving your son to Kuan Yin,' he said. 'In return, she will take care of him in this and other lives.

'Are you ready?' Fatt Shi Ong asked. When I looked away, the priest proposed giving me more time. 'Come back and talk to me whenever you want.'

My nerves over Weng Foo must have caused me to lose some of the steel for which I had become famous, for it was just then that the incident with Weng Yu occurred.

My eldest son was thirteen and had been at the Anglo-Chinese School for two years. He often visited Siew Lan's house, where he spent time with her husband and son. It was a friendship I grudgingly accepted, since the boy continued to do well in school. The reports Weng Yu brought back at the end of each term, read first by Siew Lan's husband and then relayed to me by my friend, were excellent. Weng Yu had never had trouble at school, which is why when he returned one day to say that his teacher had asked to see me I was surprised.

'You naughty-ah?'

'No,' he replied.

'You say "No, Mama", not just "No".'

Weng Yu looked sullenly at me. He was nearly my height by then, but not so tall that I couldn't stare him down. Our eyes bore into each other's, before my son dropped his gaze, mumbling 'No, Mama' so reluctantly that I could hardly hear him.

'What, Weng Yu? You so soft speak I also no hear.'

'No, Mama,' he repeated, after which he added a phrase under his breath, a hiss he assumed I would never hear – 'Silly old woman.' Through a shaft of light in the inner hall, Weng Yu's words shook motes of dust. He moved off quickly, his willowy figure bat-like across the darkness of the stairwell. None of my children had dared answer back before, and I stood numb. There was my son slipping away, yet neither my jaws nor my limbs could move. I thought of the warrior Hang Tuah and his wonderful sword. Where was my own magic sword when I most needed it?

On the day of Weng Foo's adoption ceremony, I carried a basket in my lap. Its contents had been put together in accordance with the *fatt shi*'s vague instructions. Bring something sweet, a bit of fruit, some vegetables and some clothes, he had said. Four items that sounded so simple, yet they had been anything but. The fruit was easy: oranges, since they were the mainstays in temples. But nothing else had been obvious. *Kueh* for something sweet, but which type? While chanting before our altar, the idea of steamed *kueh* came to me; I associated vapour with cleansing, which seemed fitting for the occasion. There were many I could have chosen, of course, so I opted for one of my favourites. The *seri muka* which lay in my basket were dazzling: to me their diamond shapes resembled little edifices, temples of green coconut custard sitting rather elegantly on top of sturdy bases of glutinous creamy-white rice. The *kueh* had been easy to make, and I hoped Fatt Shi Ong would approve. Even the Nyonya-style vegetables, replete with dried lily buds and thin slices of flower-shaped carrots, I was unsure of. As for 'clothes', I had assumed that anything made of silk would do and had purchased a Chinese silk suit. At the last minute I stuffed as many dollars as we could spare into a red packet, which I tucked deep inside my basket, to be used as amends for any mistake I might have unwittingly made.

Once we arrived at the temple, everything happened quickly. It was so simple that I felt cheated. Fatt Shi Ong, dressed in his usual yellow robe, greeted Weng Foo and me. He led us into a gloomy room with high ceilings, where a table had been set up before the large statue of Kuan Yin. A handful of worshippers were scattered around but I barely noticed them, because my attention was arrested by the statue of the Goddess. Her thin lips, painted a dark red, smiled at me. Her eyebrows, mere slivers, had been painted plucked, while her almond eyes slanted upwards in a knowing look, as if to tell me all would be well. Above the golden orb framing her face, she had thin black hair coiled into a bun, which, except for the absence of five-pronged pins, looked exactly like mine. I bowed in deep reverence.

The *fatt shi* placed our offerings on the table. He spread them out so that the Goddess was surrounded by our gifts. He then handed me three joss-sticks and my son a single one before leading us in prayer, after which he gave Weng Foo another name, Poh Hoi, meaning 'wave of the sea'. At the sound of those words my son beamed; light shone across his thin face; he stretched out malleable lips and flashed beautiful white teeth at me. Weng Foo's smile will forever be in my store of memories, though he never used the name again. Fatt Shi Ong explained to us that by inviting Kuan Yin to be my son's godmother, the boy was forming a lifelong bond he had to keep until he was released. Turning towards me, the *fatt shi* reminded me that release from this bond was possible only on Weng Foo's marriage, at which point he would need to return to this same temple for another ceremony. Until then he was to avoid beef and to offer prayers to the Goddess every year on her birthday.

Turning a final time to my son, Fatt Shi Ong told him in a voice filled with authority, 'Poh Hoi, you have a new godmother, who will look after you. Revere both her and your mama.'

In the next weeks little Weng Foo became stronger. For the first time he kicked a ball with his brothers on the open land behind the Lahat Road. I thanked the Goddess. The peace I had been seeking had finally come.

23

On the week after Weng Foo's ceremonial adoption, I went by rickshaw to the Anglo-Chinese School. The school had been transformed
by then; the new brick building Mr Ho-Lee had spoken about on my
first visit had been completed and opened. It was enormous, set on
two floors and extremely long, with corridors that ran all the way from
one end to the other. The whole school carried an air of grandeur and
wonderful symmetry. With intricately carved balustrades and beautiful
arches, it looked impressive from just about any angle. Yet the school
walls had an unfinished quality, with large segments of exposed red
brick, as if there had been no money left over to plaster them. On
second glance I decided that the patches of bare brick were too evenly
spaced to have been there by accident.

A huge ceremony had been held the previous year to celebrate the
opening of this elegant building. Parents of all the boys were invited,
but with so many illustrious persons attending, I decided not to go. I
had sensed relief on Weng Yu's part, though I told myself I was simply
imagining things.

On walking along one of the famous corridors in the school, I had
to concede that the white devils knew a thing or two about construction.

The place would withstand the test of centuries, unlike our wooden shacks or even the elaborate temples I was used to. I burned with pride at the thought of six sons within such a majestic institution. Gone were the attap sheds I had previously spied; in their place new classrooms stood, each with rows of wooden desks and chairs facing two huge blackboards at the front.

I made my way to Weng Yu's classroom. By the time I arrived, the boys had finished for the day; the room was quiet and only his form teacher remained, together with Mr Ho-Lee.

'Peng Choon Soh, *chiak pa boey*?' Mr Ho-Lee said jovially by way of greeting. The headmaster was as friendly as ever, but he had aged in the intervening period. Noticing deep wrinkles around his eyes for the first time, I wondered how old he was. A new class teacher stood beside Mr Ho-Lee, a fresh-faced devil with fine hair, yellow like shredded ginger and skin as pale as death who looked all of twenty. The contrast between the two was stark. Introducing the new man as Mr Wee-Lem, Mr Ho-Lee explained that Mr Wee-Lem was a recent arrival and could only speak basic Malay. In apologetic tones, the headmaster asked whether we could switch languages – given my Nyonya dress, he assumed I would not mind – to make it easier for the new teacher.

I smiled but immediately found I could barely understand Mr Wee-Lem, whose Malay was heavily accented. 'Your son Weng Yu is very talented, Makche Wong,' he began. 'In music.'

I frowned, unable to make his words out. Mr Ho-Lee stepped in to explain that Weng Yu appeared to have a gift for music. 'His voice, Makche Wong, his voice. Very good-lah!' They might have used another word, but that was what it came down to – Weng Yu's good voice.

'Yes-lah,' I said. 'Weng Yu always sing. His grandfather also a singer that's good.'

'It's not just his voice. He has an ear for music,' Mr Ho-Lee told me.

'That mean what?' I asked. 'Ear for music?'

'We think he should learn to play a musical instrument.'

I raised my eyebrows. The only instruments I knew were Chinese; I couldn't imagine what the gentlemen were suggesting.

'Like what?'

They mentioned a large instrument, one with black and white 'keys' connected to steel strings – something called a piano. 'But they're not the type of keys you know, Makche Wong,' Mr Ho-Lee said hurriedly. He asked me to go with them to the place of worship near his house, where they had brought such a thing. 'We can show it to you there,' Mr Wee-Lem added. 'You can see what it looks like, touch it and hear the sounds it makes.'

I agreed reluctantly. It was a scorching day, and the place of worship was on the other side of the grounds, which meant a ten-minute walk. Even though it was mid-afternoon, it remained searingly hot. Both men put on their hard hats as soon as we were under the sun, while I reached for my paper umbrella. Mr Wee-Lem started speaking again as we stepped forward, whether as an attempt at polite conversation or because he wanted to impress the point upon me I'm not sure. 'Weng Yu really is quite gifted,' he told me once more. 'And he has shown an interest in learning the piano.'

'So, you already talk with my son?' I asked, incredulous. Was this the way of the white devils, that they could have discussed the matter with the boy before consulting his parents?

'We told him we had to ask you, of course,' Mr Ho-Lee replied, peering at me through narrowed eyes as he squinted against the sunlight. The men didn't say anything after that, aware no doubt of my displeasure. If this instrument had already been mentioned to Weng Yu, it would put me in an awkward position. I knew my son would expect to learn it.

By the time we reached the shadow of the church, we were all perspiring. The fabric of my baju clung to my body. I felt hot just looking at Mr Wee-Lem, whose face was bright red. From his temples large droplets emerged that trickled on to his cheeks. Mr Ho-Lee too, despite his short-sleeved shirt, stood wiping his thick brow with those long hanging arms. The church appeared shut, but Mr Ho-Lee had a key for the main door.

As soon as he opened it, a cool descended on our skins. I was amazed by how spartan the church looked – nothing but tall ceilings and white walls and a wooden cross at the front, near a glass window. Opposite a side door stood a tall vertical box, also plain. Compared to the temples I was accustomed to, with fiery dragons carved into the eaves of their roofs and stone lions guarding their entrances, this church seemed very plain. Even the chairs, made of basic hardwood, with rattan stitching on the bottoms and backs, were simple. The only cheer was provided by a small porcelain vase filled with a bunch of sunflowers.

Near the front was an upright object I had never seen before. It was dark brown, box-like and reached almost to my chest, with a long bench seat on one side.

'Sit down, sit down,' Mr Wee-Lem invited me, placing a cushion on the hard wooden seat. As I sat down, I noticed a smell, unfamiliar but not unpleasant, a mix of wood and polish and something else . . . an odour I couldn't place then and have never smelt again. Today I call it the piano smell. 'Touch-lah!' Mr Ho-Lee said encouragingly.

I placed my fingers tentatively on the mysterious piano, feeling its smooth brownness in my hands. It was made entirely of smooth wood, obviously of excellent quality. Just as I began to wonder what lay beneath the breaks in the wood, Mr Wee-Lem lifted a catch, and the instrument opened up – to reveal long finger-like objects, white, in between shorter black ones, all arranged alongside one another in a horizontal row. The teacher started tapping on the white keys, moving his hand gracefully up towards one end of the instrument before shifting it down again near the middle. I could not take my eyes off his fingers. They hovered over the instrument as lightly as if he were playing with air. A melody soared above us, floated back down and entered my ears, before agitating my heart. Its sounds were beautiful, though nothing like the music I was used to.

By the time Mr Wee-Lem stopped playing, my curiosity was aroused. 'That sound come from where?'

The young man smiled before turning back towards the piano. He lifted a cover hinged to the top of the instrument. 'Look,' he said. I stood up. When I looked down, I was staring into a hollow, with nothing inside except for a series of strings and bits and pieces of metal, which obviously held the whole box up. The strings themselves were tightly sprung, arranged vertically in groups of three, in what looked to be the backbone of the instrument.

From behind I heard Mr Ho-Lee's voice. 'Steel strings, Makche Wong. That's what make these sounds.'

I looked up to see Mr Wee-Lem pointing his index finger at the strings. Smiling again, he asked, 'Did you like the music?'

I nodded uncertainly, after which Mr Wee-Lem cleared his throat. 'We would like Weng Yu to start learning this instrument.'

'Learn? He how can learn?'

'A teacher here can give him lessons. Only an extra two dollars each month.'

'Two dollars!' I cried. 'But that's almost as much as his school fees!'

Mr Ho-Lee exchanged words with the class teacher in their own language in what I took to be an admonitory tone. When Mr Ho-Lee turned back to me, his voice had changed. 'Makche Wong, we think your son is exceptionally gifted,' the headmaster said gently. 'I know it's a lot of money. I'm sorry we can't give the lessons for less, but your son will also need to practise. He can play on this piano here as much as he wants.'

'These lessons, they what good for Weng Yu?' I couldn't imagine how knowing the piano would help him in Ipoh.

'Sometimes things work in mysterious ways, Makche Wong,' Mr Ho-Lee replied solemnly. 'God has given your son an outstanding talent. We have to help him develop it.'

I stared in disbelief. Both men knew I had seven sons, yet there they were, telling me to spend double what I was then spending on just one boy, with no clear prospects of any gain in sight. *What if they discover an unusual talent in every one of my sons?* I found myself wondering. *What would happen to us then?*

Shaking my head, I sighed. I felt an ache coming on; it was time to go home. When I arrived, Weng Yu was waiting, with cheeks red and eyes gleaming. 'Mama, have you just come from school?' he asked, panting with impatience.

'Yes-lah,' I replied.

'You saw the piano?'

'Cannot,' I told him firmly.

'But why?' As he cried out, my son's eyelashes turned wet like the morning dew.

'Because expensive. Also no one can explain why useful to you.'

'It's not expensive, Mama!'

As he said this, Weng Yu tilted his head upwards, so that his chin tipped at me. I looked darkly at the boy, using a tone I knew he would recognise. 'Extra two dollars every month, you know or not? So how? You think money grow on trees-ah?'

My eldest son and I stared at one another as the tears poured down his cheeks. He rubbed the back of his right hand across both eyes before spitting out, 'You're just a stupid woman! You don't know anything!'

Before I knew what I was doing, I had raised my right hand. But when I took in the face into which I gazed, with its fair skin and beautifully dimpled cheeks, I dropped my hand. It was my husband staring straight at me.

Weng Yu, still crying, ran off, leaving me as stiff as a statue. As I came to my senses, something niggled in my tummy. I could not wait to pour it out to my best friend.

'I don't believe!' Siew Lan exclaimed when I told her. 'Why he do that?'

We were sitting on the *barlay*, the wooden platform in our outer hall where I received guests. I had no other friend like Siew Lan, who knew me so well that words were unnecessary. I watched her savouring her coffee, holding in both hands the much-loved cup with its green dragons and pink borders as she tilted her head back to pour the last drops of black gold into her mouth. The liquid perked her up and Siew Lan's eyes pierced mine. 'Chye Hoon-ah,' she said, choosing her words carefully, 'you always say Weng Yu so clever sing song. He really want to learn. Why not let him try just one time, two time-lah?'

I lifted an eyebrow. 'What, Weng Yu already talk with you-ah? Your husband also? About this musical instrument?'

Siew Lan nodded, looking not at me but towards the juicy green leaf on to which she had rubbed lime. I waited. She sprinkled pale brown gambier powder over the lime before placing her chopped betel nuts on the powder.

'Ai-yahh . . . Siew Lan,' I said when my friend finally began to chew. 'If he like piano, then how? How to find so much money? One want to learn this, other one want to learn that. I have ten children, good heart.'

Moving the cud to a safe corner in the upper right side of her mouth, between teeth and gums, Siew Lan was about to mumble something when I stopped her. 'Even more bad-ah, Weng Yu never think about money, like so easy to get.'

'Chye Hoon, you cannot let him talk back at you . . . like no manners-ah . . .'

From the open land behind Lahat Road, the call of a turtle dove could be heard. When I thought about the way my son had run to my friend and her white husband, pain scorched me. My worst fears were confirmed, and I had only myself to blame.

Seeing my dejected mood, Siew Lan wisely postponed discussing what she had come to see me about and instead pushed the betel nut tray closer. When I finished wiping my eyes, she handed me a leaf she had prepared. 'Here, take.'

I popped the large leaf-wrapped ball into my mouth, letting its fiery juices burn my gums. The feeling of movement against my teeth soothed me. By the time I spat out a mouthful of liquid, charged like congealing blood, my head was drowsy.

But not so drowsy that my mind had ceased to work. When I heard Siew Lan say 'Weng Yu is good boy. He grow up to be good man, like your husband, also good man. No have cursed blood,' a memory was awakened. Her words trailed in the air. 'You no need to worry, Chye Hoon. Not like your husband waste money, smoke cigarette, or drink or gamble.'

The words came flooding into my ears in a rush, bringing with them a warning I had heard a long time ago.

By then nearly five years had passed, and I could barely recall the details in Peng Choon's letter. When Father had read it aloud, those of us who were listening had been shocked by its revelations.

In it Peng Choon disclosed a family secret. The funds my husband had sent to China had been used not only for the maintenance of his wife and son and his parents and family, as might be expected, but a portion had gone towards paying off a brother's debts, for it turned out that one of his younger brothers was a heavy gambler.

As Peng Choon lay struggling on his deathbed, he was sorry for not telling me about this wayward sibling. The debts were at first small and he didn't think they were of great concern. By the time Peng Choon suspected his brother Peng Shan of having an addiction, he felt foolish at having kept his doubts hidden from me for so long and chose to stay silent.

While he remained in Malaya, Peng Choon had had no way of confirming his suspicions, because his father's requests for funds always came with justifiable reasons. Without hard proof, he gave himself excuses not to worry me. It was only when he arrived back in his village that he realised the trouble Peng Shan was in. The boy spent his waking hours under the trees playing fan-tan or cards and routinely invited men from surrounding villages for games. As Peng Choon observed how his brother's face changed when he heard the soft clatter of fan-tan tiles, how he burst into manic laughter and breathed deeply, he feared the boy was lost.

Every so often a group of village men would head towards the nearest town to enjoy themselves for a few days. It was this which had been Peng Shan's undoing. Playing among friends was one thing, gambling with professionals quite another. Once in town Peng Shan lost heavily. Unable to stop himself, he carried on playing. He told himself he would leave as soon as he had recouped his losses, yet whenever that moment came – as it did occasionally – he would be overcome by weakness; just a little more, he would say to himself. Inevitably his luck would change and he would find himself needing to play even more to recoup what he had lost.

This had been the cycle for many years, until Peng Choon's return. Once home my husband forced his brother to stop all card and fan-tan games. He made him attend the village school and put Peng Shan in charge of the sale of village harvests. Peng Choon paid off his brother's debts, but being a pragmatic man, he was doubtful that his brother would withstand the temptation of the tables. 'Gambling is a powerful addiction,' his letter had read. 'Watch out especially for our boys. They have this vice in their blood.'

I had been unsure what to make of my husband's warning. The turmoil I felt on listening to his letter was compounded by an irritation that he had kept a secret from me. At the same time I wondered at Peng Choon's unusually dramatic words; one of our children a gambler? After Siew Lan went home, I locked my husband's words away for a second time in a drawer at the back of my head, hoping I would never have to open it again.

24

On a subsequent visit Siew Lan was finally able to speak her mind. I knew something was up as soon as she sat down, because my friend couldn't keep secrets. Fidgeting more than usual, she looked around constantly, as if worried we would be overheard. 'You good-ah?' I asked.

'Yes, yes!' she replied rather too insistently. For a while we talked about nothing in particular. I waited, knowing it would come. Soon enough Siew Lan changed the subject. 'Your eldest girl, Hui Fang, she already sixteen years, yes?' she asked, trying to sound casual but with a fluster which made my ears prick up.

I nodded, noting the glimmer in my friend's large round eyes. 'Why you ask?'

Siew Lan cleared her throat. 'I think I have the perfect boy for her.'

I laughed then. From relief that my friend hadn't brought more unwelcome news about my eldest son, and curiosity, because I wondered about the boy she had in mind.

'Tell me,' I said.

'There is a Hakka man,' Siew Lan began. 'He is friend of Se-Too-Wat, many years already-lah.'

That was how Yap Meng Seng was introduced to me – as a businessman of standing and an old acquaintance of her husband's. Siew Lan told me she had personally known Yap Tsin-sang and his family for years. She first met him when her husband had needed help with tricky arrangements in Singapore; he had called on this man Yap, who was described by others as an invaluable link with the Chinese community. According to Siew Lan, Yap Tsin-sang was a comprador – a man who helped British businesses in their dealings with the Chinese. He served as an agent to the bank of which Se-Too-Wat was a client; that was how they had become acquaintances.

After their first meeting Siew Lan told me that she and Se-Too-Wat often bumped into Yap Tsin-sang as they wandered around Ipoh. They began to have coffee together, sometimes with Flora and Don in tow. Siew Lan said Yap Tsin-sang was soft-spoken and well-mannered, a traditional Chinese gentleman. Slowly she learnt more about his family. She was eventually introduced to his wife, Meng Seng Soh, a wonderfully generous Cantonese woman who offered prayers at the Kuan Yin Temple. Unfortunately Meng Seng Soh's health had always been delicate; she died young, succumbing to an illness years ago. Their three children – a boy and two girls – were still small then, but Meng Seng Soh had nonetheless already been contemplating their marriages. A known admirer of Nyonya women, she apparently desired their cooking and refined manners for her son. Before passing into the next life, she asked her husband to find a Nyonya wife for their boy. A few weeks previously Siew Lan had finally set eyes on the young man as he dropped his father in town in the latter's motor car. 'A reliable character,' my friend declared.

With those words, Siew Lan proceeded to sip her coffee. The pause was intended for me to ask any questions I desired. I began peppering my friend with them.

'His father, he ask you to come see me?'

'Yes-lah,' Siew Lan replied. Having heard of both my *kueh* and my reputation for bringing children up strictly, Yap Tsin-sang sought to make enquiries about my eldest girl.

Warmth suffused my heart at the thought that someone wanted my daughter. It confirmed what I had long thought – that girls who could cook and sew and make a home would always be sought after.

'His son is called what?' I asked.

'Yap Wai Man.'

'How old?'

'Twenty-two years.'

'He do what to earn money?'

'Have job in a British bank – that same one-lah where his father is comprador. The boy is a clerk.'

'Salary?'

'Eighty dollars a month.'

'He educated well-ah?'

'Standard Seven at the Anglo-Chinese School, and before, four years at Yuk Choy School. But he clever, sure can study more except . . . school only go up to Standard Seven then. After that no more already-lah.' I nodded, uncertain why Siew Lan was belabouring the point when eleven years of study appeared entirely adequate. I was more concerned about his character. I wanted my daughter to be happy.

'So, what I need to know about him?'

'He is the eldest son; his sisters are younger. He no drink alcohol, smoke also no, also no gamble – all good-lah. Because in his house strict upbringing. I think he in bank got good prospects. Soon go up . . . high position, better pay.'

At that point I had heard enough for a first examination, which the young man passed without trouble. That was to be expected, since Siew Lan would not have suggested him for my family if she hadn't been confident about the match. What was missing was an idea of what he looked like. While I didn't want my daughter to marry a playboy, he couldn't be ugly either. What if he had a pockmarked face or a hunched back or worse, if he was dirty and didn't wash himself? Appearing to follow my thoughts, Siew Lan piped up, 'You need to see what he look like of course. I think I know how to arrange.'

'Really . . . you everything also think of, Siew Lan!' I exclaimed, impressed by my friend's attention to detail.

'So, when you last time go to cinema?'

I frowned. It was so long ago that I had trouble remembering. My first cinema visit had been before Peng Choon's departure, when we had sat with our eldest three inside the Matsuo tent. Hui Ying had stared at the film machine that evening, imagining squashed-up people inside it. Years later I had taken the eldest five to a film at the Harima Hall in New Town, a wooden building with badly arranged rattan seats in which bugs crawled. My main memory of the night was the stench of urine, because the latrines were perfectly positioned for their odours to waft in. Our servant Ah Hong had also hated the crowd of shameless young men, who wolf-whistled and called her names when she wandered around on her own. It was an experience I vowed never to repeat.

'Hmm, I thought so,' Siew Lan said, misinterpreting my silence. 'I invite you and Hui Fang to a film. How about that?'

I looked at her reluctantly. 'You don't like-ah?' Siew Lan asked, puzzled. 'I think you enjoy-lah!'

'I no like Harima Hall,' I replied.

She chuckled. 'Now got new cinemas, Chye Hoon. Much better ones.'

'But Siew Lan, still early, isn't it?'

'Is it? You need to think about what?'

'Well . . . she only sixteen. Still have plenty of time.'

'Ai, you cannot think like that you know. Yap Wai Man not available for long – a boy so good, soon snatched up. We have to make use of this opportunity!' Siew Lan made it sound straightforward, as if we were contemplating no more than a rickshaw ride into town.

Without pausing for breath, she continued: 'Don't worry, Chye Hoon. I take care. I invite Yap Tsin-sang and his son to go to film at the same time. You one thing even no need to do. Okay?'

There was little I could say except murmur 'Yes'.

On the appointed night the Oriental Cinema was brilliantly illuminated. It had moved into new premises on the corner of Brewster Road and Hale Street, two of Ipoh's main thoroughfares. From this position the entertainment centre commanded the attention of the whole town. Every evening its lights could be seen half a mile away. It had never occurred to me that we would go to this palace of modern indulgence, but Siew Lan's plotting would not be denied.

While getting ready, I was dogged by a distinct lack of enthusiasm. Of course I was curious to see this Yap family Siew Lan had talked so much about, but I wished my friend had chosen a different venue. I couldn't understand the attraction of cinemas. They were seedy places where I had to endure things I would never have put up with in real life: the sight of men killing each other, or worse, men and women kissing so shamelessly that when I came out I was flushed to the roots of my hair. I knew this was considered old-fashioned; few in Ipoh felt the same, which is why the so-called entertainment centres went from strength to strength.

My own children would happily have gone to the cinema if they'd been allowed. My second daughter, Hui Ying, kept up to date with films no matter what language they happened to be in. Through forays into town with our younger servant, Li-Fei, my daughter would cast her eye on every advertising poster. She couldn't read the words, but this proved no obstacle to her astonishing memory; on any given day of the week she could have told us every film showing in each cinema if we'd asked. When Hui Ying found out where her eldest sister and I were heading, her face was full of envy.

I passed the girl on my way upstairs. Hui Ying flashed me a forlorn look I knew well, one which burgeoned with hope and last-minute appeal. 'I told you already – your Aunt Siew Lan invite us,' I said in exasperation. 'I how can ask her to let you come too? Because if bring you, then why not Weng Yu? Bring Weng Yu, why not Hui Lin? So you see . . . everyone also must bring then. Become too expensive.'

My daughter observed me furtively, like the monkeys near our house, who sat staring intently until they deemed it safe to move. Hui Ying remained quite still. 'Mama . . . why Aunt Siew Lan suddenly invite Hui Fang somewhere?' As she said this, my daughter scrutinised my face. I made light of her question. 'What a strange thing to ask-keh! You now big already-lah. So she why not invite you to go out?'

Without warning Hui Ying's eyes turned gloomy. 'Mama,' she whispered, 'I no want get married. I no need-lah, isn't it? I want stay here with you.'

The words I myself had uttered years ago echoed back at me. I wondered where the time had gone. It seemed just yesterday that this child of mine was playfully squirming on chairs, unable to sit still. Now here she was, a woman, flanked by curves and child-bearing hips. Yes, I hoped marriage would come soon, but the thought of no longer seeing my daughters hit me with force. I was determined not to let that happen.

'We are Nyonya, my girl. We have *chin-chuoh* marriages. You marry that time, your husband will come with us live here,' I said proudly, forgetting for a moment how quickly the world was being transformed, and with it our Nyonya traditions.

As we approached the cinema, I heard music playing. It sounded like a band. Whenever a public holiday was declared by the white administration and a procession marched through town, the same sort of music played. The tunes were decidedly foreign. They were rousing but noisy, which I assumed was the object, as they were used to alert Ipoh to whatever the occasion happened to be. On that evening the military music advertised what was on offer at the Oriental Cinema. It complemented efforts that had been made during the day, which included a horse-drawn cart that had passed me towards the end of my *kueh* rounds in the morning. The cart had wound its way in the opposite direction, with three boys inside. One pounded a drum using both fists, another beat a large gong in a totally carefree manner, while the third clanged a pair of cymbals together, oblivious to beat or rhythm. On the side of the cart was a poster, which I assumed depicted a scene from the film. It showed white men on horses holding guns in their hands; a few were shooting at another group – men with red skins whose faces were burnt with colour but who wore almost no clothes. As if this weren't enough, two boys ran alongside the cart distributing pieces of paper. The papers held various types of script – the local languages, I assumed – but all contained the same crude pictures. Dread crept under my skin. If it weren't for my daughter, I would never have agreed to such an outing.

When our rickshaw arrived at the Oriental Cinema, Siew Lan was already waiting. Behind her, the bandsmen whom we had heard on our approach were seated on a curved terrace, blowing hard into metallic instruments. They were led by a man who waved a stick about and who pointed it every so often at his musicians. Without exception the band members were dark-skinned, fairer than the Klings who worked on the estates, but still obviously from India. Siew Lan whispered that they were light-skinned Indians from a place called Goa, where sailors from the European country of Portugal had once settled. The men blew into their glossy metal tubes, swaying their instruments up and down and from side to side in time to the beat of drums played by a man at the back.

As soon as we alighted, Siew Lan exclaimed in admiration, 'Wahh! Young lady, you look beautiful!' Before us stood my eldest daughter, Hui Fang, the quietest of my girls, whose face had turned the colour of the scarlet patterns on her sarong.

The compliment brought a warm glow to my face, but I said nothing, in keeping with our tradition of modesty. My daughter looked perfectly rouged and powdered – of that there was little doubt. I had dissolved the pellets myself – rice flour in water – and dabbed the powder on my daughter's face and neck, smearing it carefully until her cheeks were a smooth white. I had applied betel nut juice to her lips, blackened her eyebrows with paste, brushed her hair and coiled it up into a chignon. Siew Lan wasn't the only person to notice her beauty; as we walked, members of the band looked shiftily out of the corners of their eyes. My daughter was decidedly Nyonya that night, beneath the five-pronged hairpins that had once belonged to Mother. I felt confident that any reasonable man would want Hui Fang for his daughter-in-law.

Siew Lan led us inside, up a set of shallow steps, beneath an arch and through the main entrance. The immediate sense was one of grandeur. The building reminded me of my sons' school: the same thick brick walls, the same airiness afforded by high ceilings; plenty of windows and arches and that feeling of solidity like the permanence of mountains. Siew Lan was right – the place was totally different from the Harima Hall. I told her so within minutes. 'Impressive-lah!' I said.

My friend smiled. 'Things changing fast, Chye Hoon, even here in Ipoh.'

25

On that memorable night, as my worldly friend showed us the way up a flight of stairs towards the women's gallery on the first floor, she whispered triumphantly, 'I already got tickets. Only fifty cents each!' They had come from a neighbour of hers who happened to be a friend of the cinema manager's.

'Very good!' I said. I approved of bargains, especially if the item purchased had dubious value.

As we ascended, our glass-beaded leather slippers clattered against the concrete steps. We all looked our best, and no one who saw us would have known how much wealthier Siew Lan was. She wore a deep-brown baju, which showed off the gold-coloured motifs of flowers and leaves on her favourite Pekalongan sarong, while I had on a white long-sleeved tunic that fell sumptuously down to my calves. My baju was matched by a green sarong replete with images of turquoise butterflies. On our heads we wore diamond-encrusted hairpins; in our hands we each carried a basket containing our well-used betel nut boxes and, in my case, also a handful of *kueh*. Once we reached the top of the stairs, the men sitting at a bar stared with undisguised interest. Unlike Penang, Ipoh had never been crowded with Nyonyas, and our number dwindled further from year to year. No man had looked at me since Peng Choon passed away, and I had forgotten what it felt like to be admired in that way. Where once I would have stared back, on that night I became embarrassed. I shuffled behind Siew Lan, looking up only once to steal a glance. The men were a mix of Chinese and Eurasian. All wore Western clothes – shirts, trousers and jackets – most had neckties on, and there was not a single Mandarin collar in sight. Sadly it seemed the days of Chinese dress in Malaya had passed.

It was a relief when we finally entered the viewing hall. We were among the first inside, and the hall remained dim. Only a few of the ceiling lamps had been turned on, but this proved no obstacle to Siew Lan, who led us expertly to a separate gallery on the left. 'This space,' she told us, 'is only for women.' My friend chose three seats in the front row, located at the far edge of the gallery and easily visible from the ground floor. Pausing, Siew Lan suggested the corner seat for Hui Fang before placing me next to my daughter, while she herself sat down beside me.

There was little to observe then, as people did not begin to pour in until much later. My friend used the time to point out the various sections of the cinema: the curtained boxes, which she said were reserved for very important people; the well-appointed first-class stalls – 'So much better view . . . ,' I interrupted just as she began talking about the fourth-class section downstairs.

'You not interested-ah?' Siew Lan asked with a hurt tone in her voice.

I touched her arm in reassurance. 'Of course, but . . . have one thing I must ask you-lah,' I said with urgency. The moment seemed opportune, as Yap Tsin-sang and his son had not yet arrived, and I worried I would forget my question once I had seen them, when other thoughts might cloud my mind.

'You know or not, bicycles now more cheap-ah?' I asked. My friend kept up with the goings-on around town; I expected her to know.

Siew Lan turned towards me. Even in the dim light I saw the surprise in her face. 'You don't tell me! You think about that again-ah?'

'Not me ride it,' I said hurriedly. 'But I think Li-Fei can learn. She
is still young . . . and loyal, and I trust her.'

Siew Lan giggled. 'You not give up, isn't it?'

I let the matter rest while my friend digested what I had said.
With the lights now fully turned on, people were beginning to fill the
seats on the ground floor below us, and I was concerned that Siew
Lan would not have time to share her opinion. 'So, bicycles are more
cheap, or not?' I prodded, in case we became distracted. It was a titbit I
had gleaned from a customer, a comment she had thrown out in passing as we mutually lamented the increase in the prices of everything.
Everything except, evidently, bicycles.

'I have to ask Se-Too-Wat,' Siew Lan finally said.

I felt a tinge of disappointment. 'You won't forget-ah?' I repeated
wistfully. I had wanted a bicycle for so long. The original plan had
never left my mind, but the right moment had taken longer to arrive
than I ever imagined it would. In my life there was only time for essen-
tials; I certainly didn't need a bicycle, since the business was doing well
enough without one. Another person would probably have left things
as they were, but I was nearly forty and beginning to feel the age in my
bones. New aches and pains appeared daily. I was even convinced that
my joints creaked. It seemed time to hire another person to carry my
kueh – on a pole or, even better, a bicycle – provided the machines had
become cheaper in the intervening years.

I had held my breath when my customer mentioned the surprisingly low prices of bicycles. The image of coolie women on two wheels
suddenly made sense. Where once they had walked, the women had
begun to ride on bicycles to and from the riverbeds at which they stood
for hours in cold water, shaking their wooden trays in search of tin.
Seeing the Malays in their tight sarongs and the Chinese with their
looser tunics and glazed black trousers, all balancing happily, I once

again imagined our servant Li-Fei sitting astride a two-wheeled vehicle with a hibiscus tucked into her hair. Curious and willing to try new things, she seemed well-suited to the job, unlike Ah Hong, who like Ipoh's hills was too set in her ways to move.

A nudge on my arm brought me back to reality. Siew Lan was pointing discreetly at the hall downstairs.

'They just come in,' she whispered. 'There . . . the old man with the carved walking stick and the boy behind him.' Following my friend's finger, I saw a man walking slowly towards the centre of the hall below. He cast a brief glance in our direction, and his eyes met Siew Lan's, but the man gave no hint of recognition. He chose a seat on the edge that was just visible from our gallery. His son followed and placed himself next to the old man.

For the next while I had an opportunity to study the boy. He was as Siew Lan had described: not bad-looking but not especially striking either. I judged him to be of medium height, probably around five feet eight inches, not short, but still a few inches shorter than my husband had been. When none of the women who saw him fluttered at his entrance, I decided that the boy must really be as ordinary as my eyes told me and, unlike Peng Choon, lacked charm, which in itself was not necessarily a bad thing. Alas, the boy wore Western clothes, but I could hardly complain about his white shirt and khaki trousers, neat and freshly ironed. The bandsmen had moved indoors by then and the boy sat quietly listening to the music. He occasionally tapped his fingers against his thighs, as if keeping time to the rhythm.

I continued observing the boy long after the lights had been dimmed. I watched for any sign of bad behaviour, anything questionable for a potential husband. He had his father sitting beside him, and I wondered what he would be like on his own or with friends. Would he sit as quietly as he did then, or would he be like the *samsengs* in the back rows, wolf-whistling and catcalling? From the way he nodded towards his father and the quiet manner in which he spoke, it was clear the boy carried the hallmarks of deference and a good upbringing. I estimated that he was likely to be well-behaved generally. Of course I could never know until he started living in my own house, at which point it would be too late. I tried to imagine what it would be like meeting Wai Man at breakfast every morning. The prospect seemed pleasant enough: he didn't smoke, which was good, nor did he shake his legs incessantly the way some men do – also good, since the habit was said to erode family fortune.

But there is only so much you can tell by watching a man seated in the dark.

Having found no detectable flaw in the boy by the time the first offering of the evening came on – a comedy of some sort – I shifted my attention towards his father. I had already noticed the old man's carriage when he was walking to his seat. Despite the stick he used, Yap Meng Seng had a regal bearing like Peng Choon's. I could tell this simply by how upright he sat in his chair, how he held his head high and kept his shoulders back. Every now and then he would turn towards us, scrutinising my daughter discreetly before quickly looking away again, as if he had been taught not to stare. I wondered what he thought. There was an edge in his glance; for a split second I was assailed by doubt. But when he looked at us again, his face had softened, and I knew my daughter had passed a test.

In the course of the evening I drew a similar conclusion about Wai Man and his father. But those were still early days, and there was plenty on my mind. The boy could turn out to be a wife beater or cruel in other ways. I would have to make further enquiries. I would also have to rely on Siew Lan's intuition. This gave me comfort, because my friend was a discriminating judge of character. She had been right about so many people, including her own husband, Se-Too-Wat; their happy marriage, still strong after ten years, was evidence of that.

As I sat in the Oriental Cinema that night, a marriage for Hui Fang remained far from certain, but my heart was already thumping. I wished

Peng Choon were alive . . . he would have been proud, I was sure of that. I spent the evening weaving dreams of the things yet to come: the marriages and grandchildren I wanted. In this way time passed easily, and the shooting and chaos on horses in front of me went over my head, as did the rousing accompaniment of the band.

When Siew Lan came to see me the next week, she strode in with confidence. 'I come to see I can or cannot invite you to eat pig's legs,' she announced. We broke into a giggle: a pair of pig's legs had been one of the traditional rewards for a Nyonya matchmaker, and although no longer expected, the saying had been absorbed into our culture.

'Wahh! Not so fast, my friend,' I cautioned. 'First, their birthdates must not clash. Then the Yap family must accept a *chin-chuoh* wedding Nyonya-style. So, they marry that time, your boy must come here live. Also got other important things, like wedding dowry. The boy I like, but Siew Lan, not as easy as you think-lah!'

Even as I said the words 'wedding dowry', images of house renovations flashed through my mind. In the end I didn't need to worry about those for many months, because that was how long it took us to reach an agreement. Poor Siew Lan had to scuttle to and fro between our house on the Lahat Road and the Yap household in the heart of New Town while she toned down our mutual insults and sweetened our grudging compliments. In the process I was thrust into the position Mother had once been in – because the main stumbling block turned out to be the *chin-chuoh* wedding I insisted on. Like many Chinese men, Yap Meng Seng feared the gossip and ridicule it would provoke. 'I cannot have my son dragged into a woman's home like a stud pig,' he told Siew Lan stoutly.

For her part Siew Lan did her best to keep my confidence up, assuring me things weren't as dire as they sounded. 'Don't worry-lah!' she said calmly. 'He only scared lose face. We sure to find answer.'

There followed weeks of impasse, during which compromise appeared impossible. All was nearly lost by the time I remembered how Peng Choon had finally been persuaded of the merits of a *chin-chuoh* marriage. It occurred to me to tempt Yap Meng Seng with the same arguments. After relaying the story to Siew Lan, we sat hatching a plan.

At her next meeting with the Yap family patriarch, she pointed out the shrewdness of a *chin-chuoh* wedding for a widower like him. Surely his friends would applaud his deft delegation of cumbersome arrangements to the bride's mother! Taking her time, Siew Lan carefully painted a full picture of what he would otherwise have to deal with: matters like decor, the bridal dress, the banquet – things usually left to women and of which he quite rightly knew little. She sensed Yap Meng Seng slowly changing his mind, and I knew that my *chin-chuoh* wedding would come to fruition.

We eventually agreed on a compromise not dissimilar to the one Mother had forged for me: the boy Yap Wai Man would live in our house during the first month, after which Hui Fang would move into the Yap household for the second month. Thereafter I was told my daughter would move with her husband to Taiping, the capital of Perak state, where Wai Man was to be promoted to the position of senior clerk in the bank which employed him. The thought of Hui Fang leaving town saddened me, but there was little I could do: *chin-chuoh* wedding or no, many Nyonya girls were already living away from home, some as far afield as Kuantan on the east coast, travelling to which required the crossing of mountains. I could hardly object to a place reachable by horse-drawn gharry, and thwarting my son-in-law's career was out of the question.

Thus on the tenth day of the tenth moon in the year 1918, I welcomed a new son into my house, and the respected Hakka patriarch Yap Meng Seng became part of our family.

26

In the months preceding the wedding, I was beset by anxiety. My nerves were first stirred by Yong Soon Soh, the flamboyant mistress of ceremonies Siew Lan had introduced to me. She was a figure I had occasionally noticed around town but to whom I had never spoken, a statuesque woman with a waist so corpulent that her clothes always seemed about to burst. Yong Soon Soh was one of the first Nyonyas in Ipoh to parade around in that form-hugging tunic known as the kebaya, now so ubiquitous, and her kebayas were nothing short of eye-catching. With loud embroidery in precisely the wrong places – at her neckline and hem – all eyes were naturally drawn towards those folds of skin. I was no different; when we met, I could barely take my eyes off her bosom and the quivering rolls over her belly. The same garments would have been grotesque on anyone else, but on Yong Soon Soh they somehow seemed appropriate, moulding themselves on her expansive frame with panache.

She waddled into our house, hips swinging and bracelets rattling. Introducing herself as the 'woman who had married off the Nyonya children of Ipoh', Yong Soon Soh burst into a laugh that shook the walls of our house. Like See Nee Ee, the woman who had presided over my wedding in Penang, Yong Soon Soh was well-versed in all the rites and rituals of marriage. 'I do this for twenty years already-loh,' she told me, a wide smile on her round face.

Beneath her buxom exterior and sharp tongue, Yong Soon Soh had a big heart. In our first meeting she asked whether I had prepared my daughter for the night of her marriage. Coming out of the blue, the question made me freeze. I lowered my eyes.

Siew Lan put her hand on my arm. 'You should tell the poor child what to come at least,' she said softly.

'But . . . ,' I stammered, 'time come, her . . . her husband will know how to do-lah.'

Yong Soon Soh remained silent, but when I glanced up, her eyes were lit by gentleness. 'You want me to explain to your daughter-moh?' she asked in a whisper. I nodded, grateful that I would have Yong Soon Soh to help me.

We moved on to other topics after that, subjects far more contentious, in which Yong Soon Soh proved as formidable as she was in everything else. She was a Nyonya of the old school and rather dogmatic, insisting on every ritual with well-rehearsed arguments for why they were needed. Our conversations became so heated that for a time I forgot she had been tasked with explaining the facts of marriage to Hui Fang. Over a discussion one day about the importance of the bride and groom kneeling before both parents, Yong Soon Soh casually mentioned that my daughter was now in possession of what she called the 'truth'. I blushed, finally understanding why my daughter had been avoiding my gaze for days. 'So, she know . . . everything-ah?' I asked.

'Of course-lah!' the mistress of ceremonies replied emphatically without even a hint of bashfulness. 'What the point not tell the girl everything?'

Over the next while the atmosphere in our house remained strained. My eldest daughter seemed to avoid me. I thought back to my own conversation with See Nee Ee, the mistress of ceremonies who had been instructed by Mother to share life's secrets. I had been repulsed; the idea of Father and Mother doing that was too much. Eventually, though, I had accepted this as part of life. My eldest girl, Hui Fang, on the other hand, seemed to take polite embarrassment to new heights.

Detecting little change after a week, I decided to raise the subject. It felt easier, because Yong Soon Soh had done the hard work.

When an opportunity came, I whispered, 'We all must, you know.' Hui Fang nodded without looking up, her cheeks the colour of my *angkoo kueh*. Touching her arm, I said, 'My girl, you have something you want to ask-ah?'

My daughter stayed quiet, neither nodding nor shaking her head, and mute too, as if her tongue had lost all powers of speech. We looked at each other in the yellow glow of the kerosene lamp. 'Don't forget, we are Nyonyas,' I said encouragingly. 'So first month you are at home. Mama stay here together with you.'

In between stormy conversations with Yong Soon Soh, I went shopping. I did more shopping than I had ever done in my life. Siew Lan was tireless in helping me navigate this complicated world, dragging me into outlets I would never have otherwise entered. Without a second's thought we walked alongside white women into classy places with ceiling fans where even the sales assistants wore uniforms.

For once I spared no expense. I purchased fabrics and lace, the best glass beads and embroidery pieces. I chose fluffy pillows, a bolster, or Dutch wife, smooth woollen blankets, even Kashmiri rugs and pink silk for the bedspread. I bought a European four-poster bed and ordered an almerah, or capacious wardrobe, from a well-known carpenter. When this wardrobe arrived – the first piece of furniture we had ever ordered specially – I felt strangely proud, because its workmanship was immediately obvious. Yellowish brown in colour, the almerah was made of beautifully seasoned *chengai*, a tropical hardwood with fine veins. On the inside of one door hung a polished mirror which came from a distant land where the people were swarthy and happy and sang opera all day long. The wardrobe was big enough to fit Hui Fang's trousseau, with extra space for what I estimated would be the bridegroom's requirements.

We also bought jewellery – armloads of it. I showered my daughter in gold: bracelets, chains, pendants, and the occasional jade and diamond stone. Siew Lan told me about a country far away, a place like China, with beautiful lakes and mountains where the perfectly crafted silver watch I acquired for my son-in-law had been made.

In those days I flew around like a madwoman. I rushed from shop to shop, barely catching breath. All the while I remembered how Mother had done the same before my wedding, leaving our house every morning and returning later in the day with mysterious new items in her hands. Arguably I had even more to manage than Mother had, what with a *kueh* business to run and my youngest child then only seven. Yet somehow I survived those frantic weeks and months.

But they did not pass without incident. It was the renovations which ultimately caused my temper to fray. Those were the household improvements I had put off for years – the repairs and painting and upgrading I had always found excuses to delay. When Hui Fang's wedding became imminent, I felt trapped: it was a matter of face, so I had to do something – something grand – not only because we were expecting a hundred guests to inspect the bridal chamber, but also because Yap Meng Seng's dowry was so generous.

I decided rather unwisely to have ten years' worth of repairs and upgrading carried out all at once. 'You want to do so much-ah, Chye Hoon?' Siew Lan asked when she heard my plans. 'A lot, you know.' But I was adamant; if we were going to have work done, then we would have it all done – and properly.

Thus we had water pipes laid and enamel basins installed in the kitchen, the bathrooms upstairs and downstairs, as well as the inner hall, where I liked to wash my hands before sitting on the *barlay*. For weeks there were workmen in our house – a plumber, a painter and a man doing odd jobs – who collectively knocked up dust wherever they walked even though there were only three of them. A thin film settled over our lives, tickling our nostrils and leaving grainy traces everywhere: inside each cupboard, all over our skins and in between the sheets of fresh linen I had brought back from the shops. No amount of wiping or cleaning helped. The dust jarred my nerves, putting me in a bad mood.

With the workmen in our house, wedding activities slowed. A few, such as the setting up of the bridal chamber, stopped altogether. Discussions with Yong Soon Soh also didn't progress as expected: between her combative nature and Yap Meng Seng's obstinacy, arrangements that should have been finalised remained in the air. As we fell behind, I felt increasingly uneasy.

When I walked into the inner hall and caught sight of half-embroidered roses and butterflies, still unfinished despite days of work, panic engulfed me. Poor Hui Fang, who happened to be nearest to me at the time, bore the brunt of my madness.

Grabbing her portable embroidery frame, I pulled it from her hands with such force that a row of pink beads rolled off. 'You give me-lah!' I shouted wildly. 'No use! Slow and no use! We, no matter what we do now, still cannot finish on time! No use!' I screamed so loudly that Ah Hong came running in to see what the matter was. It had been years since I lost my temper like that, and my daughters all cast their eyes downwards, not daring to meet my fiery gaze. Even the usually robust Hui Ying, whose cheeks were ablaze, did not utter a word. Ah Hong, in a state of shock, also said nothing, but the mute yet reproachful look she gave me made me feel instantly guilty.

Still carrying Hui Fang's wooden frame in my hands, I strode into the kitchen, hoping its familiar aroma would calm me. But of course with the workmen there the kitchen was a mess, and the sight of it threw a veil of hopelessness over me. I genuinely feared we would never finish. Sitting down on a chair, I inadvertently used my fingers to scrape away a layer of white – paint dust, I assumed – and I could take it no longer. I burst into tears.

I sat with head buried beneath dust-soiled hands – how long for, I don't know. I was still there when Siew Lan appeared like a miracle. My eldest son, Weng Yu, on hearing my plaintive cries had run to Siew Lan's house. She in turn had rushed over, worried about my state of mind.

'We cannot finish before the wedding date,' I said in a sombre voice.

'Of course can finish-lah!' Siew Lan retorted. 'Chye Hoon-ah, you cannot finish, still not so terrible! Not finish, so what? What can they do?'

I looked up glumly; the mere thought of undoing what we had already agreed gave me a headache. Besides, as this was the first wedding in our family, my pride was at stake.

For the next hour Siew Lan sat listening to the worries plaguing me. She heard about my frustrations with Yong Soon Soh and our endless discussions over ritual. 'She waste so much time!' I declared. She heard how the dust in the house was getting into my hair and my clothes and lately also into my dreams; I told her about the swirling grains I was seeing in the little sleep I managed each night. I lamented my twenty-hour days. We were working flat out, I said emphatically, despite the help she and the hordes of experts and workmen I had hired gave me; how could we work any harder?

Siew Lan listened. Then she made me go through the tasks every single person was responsible for, asking a hundred questions to draw out a handful of details. I had carried out this exercise time and again in my own mind, yet somehow it felt different while I was talking to my friend. What I needed to change became clear. When we finished, I wondered why I hadn't thought of the solutions myself. Siew Lan stretched her arms out, yawning. 'You let me with Yong Soon Soh talk,' she said with a wink. 'The rest you deal with. Tomorrow only-hah; now must sleep.' I nodded gratefully.

The next day my boys were summoned into the kitchen. They learnt to pound and grind, to fan the bellows and use a wok. They learnt the techniques their sisters had already become proficient at, including how to harness the weight of their bodies over the heavy grinding stone, so that they could churn mixtures of galangal, lemongrass and dried shrimp into fine pastes. In this way their sisters were freed to dedicate themselves to needlework and whatever else I needed them for, and we began to make strides.

To my surprise Weng Yu turned out a deft hand in the kitchen. Not only that, but he seemed to enjoy cooking, even volunteering for tasks his brothers hated. Perhaps his strong affection for his sisters overcame all else. In any event he displayed a new talent – a knack for pounding mixtures of onions, chopped chillies and garlic. With eyes watering, Weng Yu would squat over the stone mortar bowl, crushing the ingredients to a pulp by bringing the pestle down repeatedly. It was a skill – yet another unlikely to further his prospects – which came naturally to my eldest son.

As she promised, Siew Lan had a quiet word with the mistress of ceremonies. At our next meeting Yong Soon Soh struck a decidedly more conciliatory tone. We soon came to agreement with the Yap family, and the ceremony itself began to take shape.

For my part I went around visiting *kueh* customers to tell them about my daughter's coming wedding. I knocked on doors, chatting to the women who bought my *kueh*. I told them we would have to make changes and hoped their patience would not be tested. They would be in good hands; my trusted helpers Ah Hong and Li-Fei were excellent *kueh* makers who had worked with me since the business was established. As a bonus I said that Li-Fei would begin delivering the *kueh* on a bicycle so as to improve our service. It would have a loud bell, and they would recognise her by the sound of the bell and by her shouting 'Wong family *kueh*' aloud. Everyone seemed thrilled at the thought of *kueh* on two wheels: 'Wah! A bicycle! What good idea!'

To my surprise sales increased even when I was no longer carrying the *kueh* around or sweating every morning over the steaming pots and flaming woks. In fact, the less I did, the healthier the sales. A few customers later told me about the subtle difference in taste when I was no longer at the helm; not better or worse, they were quick to point out, just different. I suppose that was to be expected. After all, none of my helpers had grown up with Nyonya cooking in their blood. The important thing was that I could begin to really shake my legs, and my business still made money.

27

Ten days before my daughter Hui Fang's wedding, I went to all our friends and relatives to distribute invitations. I must have been unusually flustered. Money would have been on my mind, since a rickshaw had to be hired by the hour, and I had forty houses to visit. I exchanged the minimum of greetings on each visit before taking out the pink handkerchief from my betel box. The single betel leaf that I set down on the hallway table, tied with fine red thread, would invariably elicit squeals of delight. 'Ahh . . . congratulations!' A stream of questions would follow: 'Which daughter? Who's the groom?' Even though I spent no more than a few minutes on chit-chat, these visits took two days in total, and I was drained by the end.

In between the house drop-offs I sat in a rickshaw worrying about the mountain of expenses I had incurred, Yap Meng Seng's dowry notwithstanding. I thought constantly of Mother then. It had taken twenty years for me to appreciate the anxiety she had spared me before my own wedding. Mother had been so successful that I'd had little idea of the comings and goings or how stressful it would turn out to be.

With the frenzy of activity just before the wedding ceremony itself, we shut the *kueh* business for three days. The kitchen on Lahat Road was taken over and became a depository of smells and a domain of increasing chaos. First to arrive were Siew Lan and a group of Nyonya friends, who made the traditional varieties of *achar* or pickled vegetables, which they cooled before ladling into enormous jars. The next morning – the day of the wedding feast – a couple of Hainanese master cooks I hired for the occasion descended on the house. They brought three assistants and two handcarts filled with portable stoves, viscous sauces and cleavers the like of which we had never seen, which they used to decapitate the terrified hens and quacking ducks. Knowing that space would be at a premium, I had arranged for my own servants and helpers to move to Siew Lan's house, where they could prepare *kueh* for Hui Fang's nuptial feast.

While the chefs were working, Yong Soon Soh appeared. Impeccably dressed, with a serene look on her face, she resembled a grand matriarch preparing her troops for a big event. She came towards me first, soothing me with her heaving presence before going round to each of my children. Once she had satisfied herself about our well-being, she led the bride-to-be upstairs by the hand, where they remained sequestered until the guests started arriving.

It was three in the afternoon when people began to trickle in. By five thirty everyone was there, seated at tables across both inner and outer halls of our house. I remember the happiness . . . and smiling faces . . . the warmth that suffused us all. The room was cast in an amber glow – from the elegant English lamps we had rented for the evening. There was laughter and the lazy clanking of glasses. I recall plates and bowls being filled and refilled while I beamed at the compliments given to my daughter, who sat demurely sipping her abalone soup, faultlessly made up and beautifully dressed. Se-Too-Wat, sitting opposite me, enjoyed every dish with gusto despite the heat of the night, which drenched his neat shirt and black bow tie in sweat. I looked at him with fondness, this white man with the ruddy cheeks – still pink after all the years – who patiently read my sons' report cards every term and to whom I now owed a son-in-law.

Throughout the night I was on my feet. I went from table to table, exhorting our guests to eat. As I walked, I soaked up the air of conviviality, thick with the goodwill which settles among friends when they have agreeable food and company.

But it was the conversation with Mr Ho-Lee and his missionary friends that sticks most in my memory. I had told Weng Yu to invite the headmaster; I said he could bring a handful of other teachers if he so wished. Mr Ho-Lee came with three others – two newly arrived missionary women, and a local boy who was also a teacher at the school. They were wildly enthusiastic about the food, especially the Englishwoman known as Miss Win-Te, with her locks of curly dark hair and eyes as grey as the Birch Bridge. When she heard that none of my girls attended school, the shock in those eyes was palpable. After a minute she regained her poise and told me – via Mr Ho-Lee, because she didn't yet speak any local language – 'But why not send them? Our girls' school is not much further than the boys' school.' Repeatedly she and her companion encouraged me to bring the girls in, assuring me that it was never too late, that no girl was ever too old to learn. They told me about girls who had started at a much later age than my daughters who nonetheless successfully mastered reading and writing within a few years.

By the end of the evening Miss Win-Te was begging me. As she left, she gazed directly into my eyes, and I found myself staring into pools exuding such warmth that I knew Miss Win-Te spoke from her heart. 'You must give your daughters the best chance in life, Mrs Wong,' she said.

I remained silent, but I had made a quiet decision.

There was a diffident Chinese man sitting with the group whom I recognised as the class teacher for my youngest boy, Weng Foo. I had met him at the start of the school year when I carried out my annual practice of meeting the men who taught my boys. It helped me to see their faces, to look into their eyes, so that I could judge what sort of men they were. Even if we couldn't communicate freely, I wanted to be able to picture who it was that my sons sat in front of each day. Over the years more local boys had become teachers at the school. The young man who attended Hui Fang's wedding was one such – a local boy made good who spoke in a soft, shy voice. His name was Lim Tsin-sang; I was to discover that he was a poor country boy from the outskirts of Kampar, where his parents survived as vegetable farmers.

But that was to come later. When the Chinese oboe sounded at the midnight hour, Mr Ho-Lee and his group had long departed. Only close friends like Siew Lan remained, honoured guests at a ceremony I would have preferred to omit.

My mind had been in a fog during my own hair-combing ceremony, but I remembered enough to realise that emotion would overwhelm me. I was vulnerable as soon as I heard the strains of the oboe, when, as if in a dream, Yong Soon Soh led my daughter towards the inverted rice measure, placed on a red velvet rug within a large red circle. I watched my daughter walking and in those moments saw her as the placid woman she was, in her simple white tunic, but also as she had once been – the baby with tiny fingers who had been my firstborn, the girl in braids, the demure one who never threw tantrums nor answered back; the girl whose embroidery I had snatched in my hour of despair. The memory brought a sob.

Within minutes Hui Fang was bowing before Peng Choon's tablet. I cried as she bent her head low in deference to her papa. My daughter, who had comforted me in front of the altar table the day I finally shed tears for my husband, had been wise beyond her years even as a child of ten. And when I thought how I had once been disappointed in her being a girl, I was racked with guilt.

By the time Yong Soon Soh's booming voice broke into the silence, tears were flowing freely down my cheeks. When I heard the mistress of ceremonies ask heaven to bless my daughter, I hoped I had not made a mistake with the boy or his family. I prayed that my daughter would be loved and adored, that she and her husband would prosper. I asked the gods to grant my daughter sons so that her husband would be content.

When the music stopped playing, Yong Soon Soh led me to a chair. I was so distraught that I thought I would faint. Then I saw my daughter on the rug in front of me, kneeling, her hands folded in an attitude of worship, and the well of sadness I tried to contain erupted. Instinctively I moved towards my daughter, but Yong Soon Soh stepped in and held me back firmly while telling Hui Fang, 'Now worship your mother, who gave birth to you.' At those words my daughter prostrated herself before me, apparently without prompting. Hui Fang lowered her head until it touched the ground near my feet. All the while Yong Soon Soh continued invoking phrases, to which my daughter responded by bobbing her head up and down. When I was able to take no more, I went forward to raise Hui Fang to her feet.

She faced me with such love in her eyes that I wept. I remembered the times I had attacked her with my temper, yelling for no good reason other than that she was there. Despite such petty cruelties my daughter had forgiven me. I held her tightly, refusing to let go, as if by squeezing her ever tighter in my arms I would make my past wrongs right.

28

The aftermath of Hui Fang's wedding coincided happily with the end of war in Europe. Many celebrations took place in Ipoh, and the festive air provided an excuse for lavish family dinners. I took to inviting Yap Meng Seng to join us, because I knew the old man missed his son, who was living with us at the time. It was the only way I could show gratitude for his magnificent dowry.

The patriarch's visits were always jovial occasions, which began with a sound like the bleating of goats – three hoots from his family car, a rambling open-topped vehicle in dark green which seated four adults comfortably. It had two oval lights suspended over a long, lean bonnet and stubby tyres that could have been legs. The Yap family car reminded me of a bullfrog, but everyone else loved it. People whistled in admiration and stared whenever they saw it on the streets of Ipoh.

His arrival was a signal for the boys to stop whatever they were doing and race to be the first to lay hands on the bullfrog. Little Weng Foo, though not the strongest, was the nimblest. At the first bleat of the horn, he would strike like lightning over the Kinta Valley. The car was unchanged from week to week – a metallic body straddled by squat tyres and the same ugly lights – yet one squeeze of the horn was enough to send Weng Foo scuttling towards the door, as if seeing the car for the first time. Meng Seng – who at the time remained Yap Tsin-sang, or Mr Yap – would appear soon after with my youngest son. They were a sight to behold: the old man with his stoop, flanked by his walking stick in one hand, and my painfully thin son holding the other.

Meals proved a problem. While eating Nyonya fried chicken as a treat, the patriarch began to cough and splutter after just one mouthful. The chicken pieces, which were dipped in a special paste smothered with chillies and black pepper, made his eyes water. Sweat oozed from his temples and rivulets from both nostrils. When the old man finally found his voice, it was thin. 'Water quickly,' he pleaded.

Following such an inauspicious start we decided to lessen the proportion of chillies and spices we used. That in turn was unsatisfactory to everyone else. I ended up spending hours concocting menus with a mix of dishes, some easy on the tongue, others with enough fire to satisfy the chilli lovers. Over time Meng Seng, like Peng Choon, learnt to appreciate Nyonya cuisine. Once he was converted, there was no stopping the patriarch. He acquired a particular love for the hot and sour, and so I recreated Penang specialities I had not made in years. To indulge him, I dredged up recipes from sheer memory. We would make our famous pickles and pungent dishes like stir-fried cucumber in vinegar or tamarind fish curry – food coated in sauces that made the taste buds dance. The thought crossed my mind that I was cooking for a man who was neither husband nor son, which felt strange, though I didn't reflect long on the fact. Tongues inevitably began to wag – or so Siew Lan later told me – not only because Meng Seng spent a lot of time in our house, but also because we developed a respect for one another.

The truth is that the old man was lonely in his retirement. He enjoyed being with my family and took a lively interest in the children, especially their education. When he spoke, he expected to be listened to. In the patriarch's presence, Weng Yu's sway over his siblings was broken and he became just one of the brood, to be interrogated in a way which brooked no argument. Weng Yu barbed his responses with impertinence, while the younger ones were intimidated into silence. Even Wai Man, the patriarch's own son, said less when his father came to dinner. Only my fourth son, Weng Yoon, a boy who could talk his way up Malaya's mountains and down all its rivers, basked in the old man's attention. He filled the empty spaces by proudly recounting all that he had learnt in school.

In turn Yap Meng Seng regaled us with tales of his life. He was a Hakka from Chiao-Ling County – my husband's county – in Kwangtong Province. He hadn't met Peng Choon, though he had heard of him. On one of his earliest visits to our house, Meng Seng told the children about the village where he had been born. He described a haven where the waters were sweet and the fruit was luscious. Hearing those words, I recalled Peng Choon's moments of homesickness, when he too had longed for his fields at the bottom of the hills.

'Meng Seng Pak,' interjected my little prince, Weng Yu, 'if this village is so perfect, why are you here?' I scowled at his tone. Meng Seng himself dealt with the matter calmly. 'Big son, I tell you it's a wonderful place – totally unspoilt. But there were no opportunities. That's why I left, and your father also. We missed our villages, though.'

Ignoring Weng Yu's darkened face, the patriarch began to talk about traditional Chinese medicine and his own mother. He told us he was ten when she had fallen victim to an illness which the village doctors, whose only instruments were what he called 'primitive needles and herbs', could do little about. He watched his mother slowly but surely waste away. He and I became embroiled in an argument about traditional and Western medicine. Meng Seng claimed that if his mother had had access to English doctors, she would have lived, but he offered no evidence to support this viewpoint. I pointed out that all my children had been brought into the world by a Malay *bidan*, that we had always been treated by Chinese doctors, and I was not about to give up a lifetime's relationship for some quack with a piece of high-flown paper but little experience. It was a subject we were to revisit time and again; right from that first occasion we agreed to disagree.

Another time Meng Seng told us what he had seen upon leaving his village. He became subdued, and shadows flickered across his eyes as he brought forth long-forgotten scenes. 'The country was on its knees, half the population dazed on opium,' he said into the still of the night. I listened intently, pricking up my ears.

But nothing else came. On this subject, as on many others, Meng Seng proved different from my husband. For him opium was part of the Chinese landscape.

The first time I heard him talk about his stepmother, I had to raise my eyebrows. This occurred much later, after Hui Fang had already left for Taiping with her husband, when it was just Meng Seng and I chatting alone after dinner. A well of bitterness opened up in the old man. The string of adjectives which flowed out – fierce, tough, outspoken – would have been compliments had they been used on a man, but the tone in Meng Seng's voice left no doubt that he regarded the woman who had ruled his life as a shrew whom his father should never have married. I listened, neither agreeing nor disagreeing.

As we continued sipping tea, Meng Seng shared an idea that had burned in his mind for forty years. He told me that his stepmother had been responsible for his father's demise. 'How?' I asked, intrigued.

'Well . . . ,' the patriarch stuttered, unsure how to express himself. 'She was much younger,' he offered.

'So?' I couldn't see the connection, but when I noticed the pink glow on Meng Seng's cheeks, I guessed his intended words. 'You mean . . . ?' I asked.

'Yes-lah,' he replied hurriedly. I nodded in sympathy, even though I wasn't altogether convinced. Surely his father had willingly participated in his conjugal duties.

Over time Meng Seng and his trove of stories merged in my mind. Sitting with the patriarch sometimes overwhelmed me, because he made me realise how much I still missed my husband. I continually compared the two, asking myself whether Peng Choon would have said this or that. Invariably I ended up being grateful for the husband I'd had; few men would have handed me their income every month or given me free rein to manage our household, as he had.

Not long after Hui Fang's wedding, my two younger daughters and I stood under the main verandah of the Anglo-Chinese Girls' School, where Siew Lan had told us to wait. Hui Fang, already preparing to leave our home and Ipoh, remained in our house.

When we arrived, we found a ready crowd: women alongside girls, whom I assumed were either their daughters or their charges. The girls came in all shapes and sizes. Some were as young as seven, while others were more mature, like my own daughters, who were seventeen and fifteen. The smallest girls let out head-turning shrieks, their volume out of proportion with the tiny bodies from which they had come. The older girls were more sedate; they stood huddled in conspiracy, breaking into hysterical giggles or gesticulating in a code only they could understand. In the drift of chatter I caught snatches of conversation, which told me that the women were at varying levels of intimacy. A few were obviously close friends, while others were acquaintances who had met within the school compound.

In those first few minutes Siew Lan was nowhere to be seen. I looked past the crowd in front of me to the track beyond, the one our rickshaws had pulled into. It was still a dirt track in those days, properly contoured and running straight for several hundred yards before forking into a loop, but a dirt track nonetheless. With the loop, rickshaws and cars could pull up in a continuous stream as they dropped girls off under the shade of the main verandah.

The loop was a simple and ingenious device, one the boys' school lacked. In all other respects, however, the girls' school was inferior, looking the way the boys' school had years before, with low brick buildings and scattered attap sheds. Doubtless, improvements were in the air; already fine lush grass had been dug up, earth uncovered and new bricks laid in the ground, but it would be a while before the girls' school achieved the splendour of the boys'.

Siew Lan eventually appeared on a rickshaw with Flora by her side. Until then I had only seen Flora at home, and I was amazed by the confident young lady who alighted from the rickshaw that day. If this was what school did to a girl, then I wanted it for my own daughters. Of course Flora was more than just self-assured; she was also beautiful. She had grown into a true Eurasian, with porcelain white skin and her Nyonya mother's dark eyes and thick lips. On top of that nature had provided its own quirk – a set of eyelashes so thick and gloriously long that you were instantly distracted. Long eyelashes were rare in Malaya, and I stared in admiration at the curving, willowy reeds which swayed above Flora's eyes. When Flora spoke, perfect Hokkien streamed out of her mouth – a language one did not normally associate with a person who looked the way she did. Even I had to look twice. More than once I reminded myself that this was Flora, Siew Lan's little girl, the one I had known since she was a baby.

Siew Lan herself appeared in a hurry that morning. She beckoned us with a beaming smile and a curt wave to indicate that we should follow her. As she forged ahead, she turned around to apologise, mumbling about having to see Flora's teacher before lessons began. Within minutes Siew Lan had led us to Miss Win-Te's office, where she left us with a smile. 'I come later,' she told me.

I had sent word to Mr Ho-Lee via my sons that I would be bringing my second and third daughters in that morning. Miss Win-Te was expecting us. '*Selamat pagi*, Puan Wong, *selamat pagi*!' she said, welcoming us with a radiant face. '*Masok-lah!*' she added, ushering us in with a wave of the hand. I smiled. Miss Win-Te seemed genuinely pleased to see us; the light was dancing in her grey eyes, and she had also evidently picked up a smattering of Malay. Her facility impressed me, because already I had no difficulty understanding her, something which could not be said for all her compatriots.

As we entered, I noticed a diminutive Chinese woman standing quietly in a corner, her hands held expectantly together just below her stomach. Once the girls and I were seated, the woman came forward to introduce herself. Everything about her seemed taut, from the muscles on her face to the twin pigtails which fell over her shoulders, coiled into knotted plaits like rope. She grappled with her hands as she spoke, clasping and unclasping them nervously.

'I am Liew Siow-chia,' she announced. Her voice was thin and raspy, and I wondered whether this woman ever tried to sing. 'I'll be teaching your daughters,' she continued, smiling. Surprise must have shown on my face. I was expecting a man as a teacher, not this minute woman with a scratchy throat. As if reading my mind, Liew Siow-chia told me forcefully, 'Peng Choon Sau, you don't need to worry. I passed Standard Four two years ago and have been teaching Primary One since. I've taught many girls to read and write.'

She then turned towards my daughters, asking their names and their preferred dialect. I was impressed by the teacher's consideration and how she made no assumptions. An instant camaraderie formed between the teacher and my second daughter, Hui Ying, whose dimples were inscribed into her crimson cheeks as she flashed Liew Siow-chia her most becoming smile. Once Hui Ying got wind that she would be going to school, she had looked forward eagerly to this day and had nearly fallen out of her rickshaw earlier. As for her younger sister Hui Lin, it was difficult to gauge what she really felt. My third daughter rarely offered an opinion. Among the girls it was Hui Lin I knew least. Of her sweet nature there was little doubt; whenever we were unhappy, her turkey-like guffaw would infect the house, chiding us into cheer. But what she really thought about anything was hard to discern.

Soon after, Liew Siow-chia led my daughters to their classroom. I rose, following them out and thanking Miss Win-Te for accepting the girls. The headmistress gave a slight wave of her hand, as if to say that what she was doing was small, that the purpose of the school was exactly to teach girls like my daughters.

Hui Ying and Hui Lin were placed in a special Primary One class for older girls. When we arrived at the allotted classroom, I counted twelve others – all of whom, from the curves on their bodies and their demeanour, I judged to be in their teenage years. Two of the other girls were also Nyonya, one was Indian, and the others Chinese. I watched as the girls introduced themselves, telling the whole class their names and preferred language or dialect.

'Good! We have two new girls today,' Liew Siow-chia croaked, 'so we will go over the characters of the English language.' Turning towards Hui Ying and Hui Lin, she continued in Hakka, our home dialect: 'There are only twenty-six characters. Each one has its own sound, and you put them together to make words.' The teacher impressed me by repeating herself immediately in Hokkien, then in Cantonese, and also in market Malay for the benefit of the Indian girl. Not many locals could speak all three Chinese dialects, and this woman was clearly proficient in all three.

Liew Siow-chia proceeded to draw a series of straight lines on the blackboard. Her white chalk squeaked as she moved it along. 'Ai-yy,' she shouted out, her voice imbued with surprising authority. 'Repeat after me. Ai-yy!' I saw my second daughter, Hui Ying, studying the teacher's mouth as she tried to form the required sound, but her younger sister Hui Lin remained silent, her eyes catching mine, and both cheeks red. Liew Siow-chia, turning from the blackboard, observed us before giving me a sympathetic but firm glance. It was time to go. I smiled and waved goodbye, pleasantly surprised by my first experience of the girls' new school.

As soon as I reached home, I lit three joss-sticks with trembling hands. I had never disobeyed the gods before, and I feared facing the Goddess who had watched over my life since I was a child. For a long while I stood with eyes averted. I thought of Fatt Shi Tan, who told me not to send my girls to school, but also of Flora and what I had witnessed that morning. When I finally raised my eyes to the altar table, Kuan Yin seemed to understand. Through tendrils of misty smoke, she looked at me as if nodding. I inhaled the acrid wafts rising into the air, breathed out the words of my sutras, and felt comforted.

29

My eldest daughter, Hui Fang, did not bloom after her marriage in the way I had expected. She seemed happy enough, and there was certainly harmony between her and her husband, but they never looked at each other the way Peng Choon and I used to. I kept telling myself that every marriage was different, that not all couples would behave as we had or be as blessed in their happiness, no matter how much I desired it for my children. Perhaps the presence of so many siblings inhibited the newlyweds.

Nonetheless I kept watch like a crow, sniffing for the tiniest odour of decay. Even in those early days I sensed an implacable barrier between husband and wife. My heart sank, because if their marriage was a mistake it would be my fault. The thought that I might have condemned my daughter to a lifetime of unhappiness was too much to bear.

Shortly before she was due to move from our house into Yap Meng Seng's, I knocked on Hui Fang's bedroom door.

It was noon and there were just the three of us upstairs: my daughter and I and a sleek Malayan house lizard, which had clambered up one wall. It hung upside down on the ceiling, from where it stared at us through eyes too large for its head. I placed myself beside my daughter on her European four-poster bed with its pink silk spread.

'Daughter,' I said, looking directly at Hui Fang, 'you and Wai Man, everything good-mah?'

Blushing, my daughter nodded. 'Why you ask, Mama?'

'Because . . . ah, I also not know. I . . . I just . . . want to be sure.'

The clacking of the house lizard broke the silence, reverberating like a tongue pulling against the roof of a mouth. Hui Fang said in a weak voice, 'I no complaints so far, Mama.'

It should have been clear to me then. Four weeks into marriage with Peng Choon my reply would have been one of unbridled enthusiasm, any awkwardness due only to a desire to keep some secrets sacred. Nine years after he passed away, memories of our life together still had the power to stir me.

But I had been one of the fortunate ones. For many women marriage meant nights of violence, putting up with stinking drunken breath or turning a blind eye to infidelities – sometimes all three together – plus the burden of tugging children to boot, following one after another like rabbits. As I looked into Hui Fang's face that sunny afternoon, I hoped that she and her husband would grow close, that a fire could be kindled between them. Already I had my doubts, but I kept those to myself. Instead I told my daughter, 'I know you and Wai Man of course happy.' Still smiling, I stroked Hui Fang's smooth hair, reminding her she would always have a home with me. All she had to do was ask.

From the time Weng Yu began attending English school, he spent longer in the bathroom every morning than all his brothers combined. His habits drew comments from the servants, especially Li-Fei, the younger of our two maids, who I think secretly adored him. She described how my son would come down for breakfast in his spotless white shirts, always scrupulously tucked in, with fingernails trimmed and every strand of his hair in place. On my mornings off, even I wondered what Weng Yu could have been doing in the bathroom.

Once, when he left the door slightly ajar, I glimpsed the answer. Weng Yu didn't notice me as he put the finishing touches on his toilette in front of our long mirror. He patted a white cream lovingly on to his head, a cream he had insisted on purchasing and for which he had saved hard-earned pocket money. I watched as my son's deep-set eyes stared dreamily into another world.

Weng Yu's adolescence had arrived, and it assaulted us with indelible marks.

The first signs were heavy stains on his underwear. One morning as the servants and I were in the midst of *kueh* preparation, I spotted the strange look Li-Fei exchanged with Siti, our Malay washerwoman. I tiptoed to the cemented courtyard beside our indoor well, where Siti crouched, scrubbing hard at a pair of male underpants. 'Got problem-kah, Siti?' I asked.

'No, Puan,' she replied. 'But your oldest boy – he now big!' she said, winking at me.

Thereafter Weng Yu became even more self-absorbed. He occupied so much time in the bathroom that even Hui Ying, who never said an angry word against her favourite brother, howled in complaint. She took to banging against the bathroom door, rattling the wooden boards on the floor in the process. 'Come on, Weng Yu!' she would yell. 'We're waiting for you!' Resentment simmered among the brothers as they were forced to troop to the smaller bathroom upstairs. Fights broke out. As soon as the sound of scuffles was heard near the kitchen, I would let loose a shout that left my children in no doubt as to what would follow if they didn't start behaving. My reprimands kept the peace for the day but did nothing to solve the ongoing problem of bathroom occupation.

When Weng Yu's voice finally deepened, the walls of our wooden house sighed in relief. They were no longer shaken by his singing or indeed much by his presence, as Weng Yu spent more time at school, returning home only after his brothers.

Once a week he asked to go to the films – always films in English – to which he would take his sisters, and his brothers when cajoled. I wasn't keen on the cinema, but it was hard to argue when Weng Yu pointed out how the films would help his sisters improve their new English language skills. Besides, the films did not seem to do the children any harm. Every Saturday afternoon my eldest son would appear punctually in the outer hall, clad in a pair of leather shoes, his hair meticulously creamed and smelling of scented water. At first, I asked what the films had been about, but when I heard the stories they told, I stopped. There was little to interest me in the poor thief who ended up a hero in a boxing match, or the rich woman left alone on a ship with her male servant. The children didn't say what happened between this woman and her servant, but I could imagine.

Hui Ying once dropped me a mysterious hint. 'There's a girl Big Brother likes,' she declared with a knowing look in her eye. This was on a Tuesday afternoon, when the boys stayed behind in school for sports.

'What girl?' I asked as my youngest daughter, Hui Lin, giggled in the background.

'An American actress,' Hui Ying replied.

'Really?'

'Yes. But, Mama, you mustn't say I told you – Weng Yu will be very angry.'

'This actress, she look like who?'

Hui Ying thought for a moment. 'She's pretty.'

'Ai-yahh!' I exclaimed. 'You can say that only-ah? At least give description-lah!' I was bursting with curiosity and taken aback at the same time. The idea of it . . . My little prince – my own flesh and blood – being interested in a white woman. *This will pass,* I told myself.

Nonetheless I took the trouble to learn more about the queen of film, a female phenomenon known as Bee-Bee, whom Siew Lan had also heard of. On a quick trip into town, my friend pointed her out on a poster. I had seen the picture many times before but had never realised that this apparition before me, with the petite lips, the thick eyebrows and dark curls sweeping over her head, was the one men talked about. Apparently it was her eyes – haunting, melancholic eyes that stared directly, as if she knew you – which made hearts throb all over Ipoh.

Weng Yu never mentioned Bee-Bee and I never asked, not least because I was soon preoccupied with new challenges. Ah Hong told me about a soiled patch on the *barlay* where the boys slept; she had noticed it when she was cleaning the house. 'Part of growing up-lah,' she assured me, and she would not have mentioned it had she not noticed how Weng Yu was behaving with Li-Fei.

'Ai-yahh! You say what?' I gasped, horrified.

'This evening come, you watch him, Peng Choon Sau,' Ah Hong replied calmly. 'You watch they how with each other.'

Sure enough, when the time came I saw the surreptitious glances my son exchanged with Li-Fei. He was discreet, but he flicked his eyes down her body more than once, the way I had seen men do, face expressionless yet fully alert. From the flush on her cheeks, Li-Fei had noticed too. Recalling her words of adoration from when my son was still a boy, I felt alarm.

I left the dinner table wondering what to do. If Peng Choon were alive, I would have asked him to take Weng Yu aside for a chat man to man. But without my husband there, I kept my worries to myself, too embarrassed to discuss my son's roving eyes with Siew Lan. Soon enough my friend started to worry. 'You more thin. Do what?' Siew Lan asked. I shook my head, mumbling that I was still getting used to my eldest daughter's absence. Siew Lan conveyed her scepticism with just one look, but she kept quiet, knowing better than to put pressure on me.

It wasn't long before my anxiety became too great and I confessed all. Siew Lan's immediate thought was that her husband should speak to Weng Yu, but doubt must have shown on my face, because Siew Lan felt obliged to mention Yap Meng Seng too. 'I think he is good choice,' she said enthusiastically. I was less sure; I explained our differences on many issues. 'Ah, those not important!' Siew Lan exclaimed. 'You see – you can tell him what values you want your son to learn. Think a bit-lah.'

So it was that on my next visit to the Yap household, with Siew Lan beside me, I raised the subject of Weng Yu with Meng Seng. The old man listened keenly, interrupting only to ask for clarification. His eyes were bright, as if he was pleased to step into the role of surrogate father. To stress the importance of what I wanted my son to learn, I relayed a story Peng Choon had once told me, of how his own father had taken him aside while on a walk in Chiao-Ling's hills. High above their fields of rice, he and his father had talked about the responsibilities of manhood. Experimenting with the village girls was strictly frowned on by his father, even though that was all the boys could think about. 'I had finished school by then, and there was nothing to do all day. I couldn't stop looking at the girls,' my husband confessed. He laughed, recalling his bachelor days and what he got up to with delight. But marriage had eventually crept up on him, and with it had come the grim duty from which he had felt a need to escape.

One weekend soon afterwards Meng Seng invited Weng Yu to join him on a stroll before dinner. My eldest son accepted without a second's hesitation, flashing his dimples and even white teeth. I watched as they set off, Weng Yu striding forth proudly, his lanky frame a head taller than Meng Seng's.

By the time they returned, my little prince's body language had changed. Indignation was written all over his dark face and his cheeks were puffed up and flaming. The silence of old had returned; he did not say a word during the entire meal. He kept his eyes on his plate while studiously avoiding mine.

As soon as I had a chance, I quizzed Meng Seng, but the old man simply shrugged his shoulders, telling me that all would be well. For the moment, though, my son was an angry young man.

'He angry about what?' I asked in surprise.

'That I tried to act like his father,' Meng Seng replied drily. 'He's a good boy – just a bit unsure of himself. But then again, aren't we all at that age?'

'But . . . he how with you? The boy say what?'

'He didn't say anything. But I don't think you'll have trouble.'

With little else to add on the matter, we moved on to talking about other things – Meng Seng's life and his opinions, which he always enjoyed expounding. As for Weng Yu, it took weeks before his mood softened. He went often to Siew Lan's house in those days to speak to her, maybe even to the white devil, though she never mentioned it. In due course my son regained his voice, and what mattered to me was that the words I had wanted him to hear had been said.

30

When Meng Seng discovered that I had enrolled my daughters at the Methodist school in town, he was delighted. 'Very good-lah!' he said emphatically. 'Girls should learn to read and write these days so that they can be better companions to their husbands.'

My daughters Hui Ying and Hui Lin made rapid progress. When they came home, they practised what they had learnt during the day, holding up items and repeating a chorus of incomprehensible sounds. They giggled over their mistakes, and their brothers would correct the words they had mispronounced. Weng Yu was diligent in helping his sisters, unlike his brothers, who simply shouted out corrections. Weng Yu would sit with the girls and patiently show them how to twist their lips to form the right sounds. I was pleased to see both girls blooming with their newly acquired skills; it became evident even in their posture, the way they held their head and back. Hui Ying would look around excitedly whenever we went out, trying to spot words she could recognise. When we were on a stroll in Belfield Street one evening, she insisted on reading aloud the sign on every shop. 'Look, Mama! That is the Ipoh Provision Store,' my daughter announced, translating the words into Hakka for my benefit. They had only been in school for a few weeks at the time, and I was amazed at how much they already knew.

One afternoon Liew Siow-chia turned up at our front door. She told me that my daughters were excellent students, the best in their class, and she thought they would make even more progress if they had an extra hour of tuition once a week.

She offered to come to our house to teach them free of charge on any afternoon of our choice.

A warm, heady feeling oozed inside me as I listened to the young teacher; I was so proud of my girls. With such an offer, how could anyone refuse? That was how Liew Siow-chia came to be at our house every Friday afternoon while the boys stayed behind in school for sports practice. She would sit with my daughters at the dining table in the kitchen, repeating words and phrases. She patiently watched them write lines on sheets of paper, correcting the sounds they made and the squiggles they drew.

When they finished, Liew Siow-chia would say goodbye, before dashing off to hail one of the passing rickshaws along the Lahat Road. I sometimes asked her to stay for dinner, conscious of the kindness she was showing my daughters, but Liew Siow-chia always politely declined. One evening a young man appeared a few minutes before she had finished with the girls, a man with round horn-rimmed glasses and the same taut look as Liew Siow-chia had. He introduced himself as her brother. I didn't pay Liew Tsin-sang much attention the first time, merely leading him to the inner hall, where I left him to wait.

When the girls' lesson was over, the young man's deep bass voice reverberated around our house. It had a resonant quality, like Father's. Soon Liew Siow-chia's brother became a regular visitor on Fridays; he would come punctually to pick his sister up, and in the process he struck up an acquaintance with my younger daughters.

Over the months I found out that Liew Tsin-sang had a facility with languages. Having studied at both a Chinese and an English school, he could speak not only English but also Malay and four Chinese dialects. On top of that he was learning Tamil to facilitate his work as an interpreter in the Ipoh courthouse. Thoroughly impressed, I began studying the young man more closely. He seemed rather dark-skinned for one who spent all his days indoors; he could almost have passed for Malay if it weren't for his creaseless eyes, thin as slits.

One night he and his sister agreed to stay for dinner. That was how we discovered the young man's sense of humour: he entertained us with the cases to which he had listened inside the airy colonial building where the courthouse was situated. He had a witty way of bringing stories to life. I laughed as I watched the expressions on his face and listened to the changes in his voice. Liew Tsin-sang's impersonations of the characters walking around Ipoh town rang true, yet when I tried relaying the same stories to Siew Lan, they fell flat; I simply did not have the young man's gifts. When he told us about the man who denied stealing a pair of chickens from his neighbour's garden, the story became action-packed, complete with the voice of the stern policeman and the sounds of terrified hens. The thief was apparently small but the chickens large, and the man had had difficulty holding on to the birds. At that point Liew Tsin-sang rose from his seat to demonstrate in full flow what the passing policeman had described: a tiny man, barely five feet tall, trying desperately to put one leg over a wooden fence while holding in each hand an enormous hen by its neck. As Liew Tsin-sang's glasses fell down his nose, we could see before our very eyes the hens squirming and shitting all over the thief's trousers, pecking incessantly while squawking for their lives. We laughed so much that tears came to our eyes, and it was a while before we could eat again.

The attraction between Hui Ying and Liew Tsin-sang must have started during this period, though I was not aware of it till much later, after our lives had already changed irrevocably.

◆ ◆ ◆

To mark his coming of age, Weng Yu announced a desire to study engineering in London. 'With the ending of war in Europe, there will be much reconstruction,' my eldest son declared. 'I can learn from the best in London, and when I come back I can build roads and bridges, because Ipoh will need them too.'

At the time we had just learnt the good news of my eldest daughter, Hui Fang's, pregnancy. We were seated in celebration around the dinner table, our attention naturally focused on the lucky couple, who were visiting from Taiping. The patriarch, Meng Seng, was notably absent, having gone away for a few days, and I recall scarcely believing my ears when I heard my eldest son.

His pronouncement had come out of the blue. My heart sank. How would we afford such an enterprise? But the idea caught Hui Ying's imagination. 'What a marvellous thought, Weng Yu,' my second daughter said with a distant look in her eyes. Then, peering directly at me, she continued: 'If we can afford it, Mama, this will be a good project. It's prestigious to have a British-trained person in the family. And engineers are well-regarded.'

I cautioned the children not to discuss the matter with anyone outside the family, meanwhile racking my brains to think of who I could talk to, knowing I would have to talk to someone. Since it involved money, discussing the subject even with Siew Lan was out of the question, which left only one alternative: Yap Meng Seng.

As it turned out, the patriarch was pleased to play the role of surrogate father once again. 'I can pay for the costs,' I told him. 'But-leh . . . we how know which course good for him to study?' Meng Seng suggested that I ask Mr Ho-Lee, the headmaster of the Anglo-Chinese School, for help in what he called the Weng Yu Project, a name that stuck.

The following day I set off to find Mr Ho-Lee. From the headmaster's broad smile, I could tell he was delighted by the prospect. 'Ho! Very good!' he kept repeating. 'I will look at his report cards now and give you a few ideas.' I sat in a chair while the man with the gangly arms went through his files. He dug up a thick wad, which he ruffled through at speed. For a few minutes the headmaster remained deep in thought, stroking the thick moustache which curved upwards at the edges. 'I recommend civil engineering, Peng Choon Soh,' he finally concluded. 'Do you know what that is?' I shook my head. 'It's the branch of engineering where the boy will learn how to build large things, like bridges and roads, houses and other buildings. He will learn how to carry out the calculations properly so things don't fall down. That's what you tell me he's interested in – and his grades are fine for that.'

'But London so big,' I said. 'He can study this where?' Mr Ho-Lee replied that there were many colleges which offered civil engineering. He would have to think about the best place for Weng Yu, perhaps somewhere not far from friends of his in London, with whom Weng Yu might be able to lodge. 'How much such a course cost, Mr Ho-Lee?' I asked. 'Also how much to stay? Become very expensive-lah!'

The headmaster gave me a rough estimate – maybe twelve pounds per month to cover all necessary expenses. 'But that's only an estimate. We will need to check what the exact cost is once I've found a college which will take him.' I did a quick calculation in my head: at the pound-to-dollar exchange rate Meng Seng had given me, Weng Yu's expenses would come to nearly fifty times what I was spending in Ipoh – and that was before we considered travel expenses or the cost of warm clothing or unforeseen events. It seemed too risky.

'The important thing,' the principal added, not reading my mind, 'is the set of examinations Weng Yu will have to take next year. He needs to more than pass – he has to do very well.'

Though I nodded, I was unconvinced. I left Mr Ho-Lee's office far from being in favour of the Weng Yu Project and wondered how I would break the news to my son.

31

I first learnt of it after Li-Fei's *kueh* rounds one morning when, with unusual animation, the girl related that she had heard wailing in houses across town. 'Like very many deaths, Peng Choon Sau,' she said in a sombre voice. 'Cry . . . everywhere just cry.' What was I to make of that? I assumed our servant was exaggerating and thought nothing more of it.

By the time I went out, news had already spread. The rickshaw puller who stopped to pick me up looked grave when I told him my intended route: first to Market Street, where he was to wait while I shopped, then across the Hugh Low Bridge and down through town, finally cutting through the Chamberlain Road, where I was intending to surprise my daughters at their school. 'Coffin Street bad,' the man said, shaking his head. He was referring to Hume Street, which locals called Coffin Street because of the funeral homes dotted along it. 'Many dead,' the man added in a grim voice. 'How many?' I asked, remembering Li-Fei's observation of the wailing in houses. 'So many, count even cannot, Ah Soh. Coffin Street no good.'

'Tsin-sang-ah, I want go see,' I said. 'We go so I can see like what-lah.'

With a shrug of his shoulders, we headed off. The streets near our house were quiet; fewer people milled around than was usual for a weekday. As soon as we pulled into the Chinese quarter, we saw coffin makers scurrying around, dragging boxes behind them. I had never seen so many men and coffins at once, and it was with trepidation that I stopped a man. 'Tsin-sang!' I yelled. 'What happen?'

The coffin maker, an older man who wore a cloth cap on his head and a day's worth of stubble on his chin, gave me a glazed look. 'Ah Soh, we finished,' he said sadly. 'This morning in my shop already got ten. Not only me – every shop also got. People just like that go.'

Something had hit Ipoh, and my thoughts turned immediately to the children. I wanted them home, safe. I told the puller to take a different route; it would mean a longer ride, but we would avoid the crux of activity near Hume Street.

Over the next several days we were at a loss as to what precautions to take. Schools remained open, but with many of my customers having to contend with death in their families, business slowed. Rumours began to fly. Within a day or two we heard how quickly the illness struck, even among the healthy; one minute a person would be well, the next a fever would appear and death inevitably followed, often within hours. Some stories were so outlandish that they could not be believed: eyes, we were told, popped out of sockets, something I could not imagine, but there was no denying the rapid spread of the invasion. House after house fell. People in town dropped like dominoes, and all activity ceased.

'Se-Too-Wat say is influenza,' Siew Lan told me. Never having heard the term at the time, I gave my friend a puzzled look. It took Siew Lan a while to describe the unstoppable epidemic which had started in Europe and now appeared to have hit our shores. 'Se-Too-Wat say need to use Western medicine to fight.' I mumbled a reply, not wanting to point out that English medical facilities had not saved the hundreds dying every day in Ipoh. By then the schools and banks were closed and we had ceased making *kueh* – there was simply no demand. Most shops were open only during the day, many not at all. Even those stallholders who could usually be relied on closed their stalls, unwilling to risk contagion by coming into town.

At the height of the plague a familiar figure in gold-rimmed glasses walked down the Lahat Road early one morning. It was Tai Fatt Shi Tan, whom I had consulted at the Nan Tien Temple a few years back. Clad in ceremonial yellow robes, the *fatt shi* wore a black hat on his head, covered with lotus petals. He did not see me. His face was focused in concentration, his lips murmuring a chant as he repeatedly struck a wood block. Beside him a bald attendant chanted in unison, carefully cupping an incense pot into which lit joss-sticks had been placed. The priests came every day for two weeks. They walked all over town, asking the gods to stop the affliction. But their prayers turned out to be insufficient.

On the very morning the priests first appeared, my youngest son, Weng Foo, fell ill. Having insisted that my children remain at home, I thought they would be safe. I couldn't quite believe it when Weng Foo began vomiting. Within the hour his head became hot, so I rushed him to Dr Wong's clinic on Treacher Street. The clinic was full of boys Weng Foo's age. No sooner had we sat down to wait than my son spewed forth the contents of his breakfast on the bench. Out plopped a dirty yellow liquid – the remains of the dumplings I had fed him – alongside tiny chunks of meat, still whole. His fellow patients scattered in different directions and began swearing at him. The commotion brought Dr Wong out of his office. Weng Foo was as pale as a spectre, and one look at my son was enough for Dr Wong to pull us inside. I could tell he was worried. 'How long has he been like this, Peng Choon Soh?' he asked as he felt my poor boy's head with his palm. 'Just since an hour ago,' I replied. Scribbling something on to a sheet of paper, the doctor hurried us towards the dispensary. 'Take the herbs and give them to your son.

Also plenty of water – we have to try to keep liquids down. If he can't hold liquids, let him take the herbs in tablet form.'

By the time we returned home, my daughters had prepared a place on the *barlay* downstairs. While they wrapped their youngest brother in a blanket, I boiled a batch of Dr Wong's herbs. I fed my boy one spoonful at a time. After no more than five spoons, my son stopped swallowing. Within minutes the *barlay* was splattered. My daughters came to the rescue, sponging their brother's head, cleaning the platform and bringing Weng Foo fresh pyjamas. His head felt hot, but because we lacked a thermometer, none of us could tell how strongly the fever raged inside my son.

Weng Foo dozed fitfully all afternoon. I stayed close by; it made me feel better, though my son was too ill to notice me. Remembering Dr Wong's instructions, I gave Weng Foo a sip of water whenever his eyes were ajar. The sight of my son so sick made me weep. With his lips nothing more than thin strips, pale and cracked, the boy was drying up in front of us. Once he whispered how tired he felt, how his whole body ached. After several hours it became clear that Weng Foo would be unable to drink his herbal medicine, and I resorted to the tablets Dr Wong had dispensed. That was when I glimpsed the strange mucus all over my son's tongue. I gently scooped a layer off with a spoon. It felt slimy in my hand, this thick white film which coated Weng Foo's once-pink tongue. No matter how often my daughters and I scooped the coat off, more came.

Meanwhile Weng Foo's head and neck boiled like a stove. Sometime during the afternoon Weng Yu went to the Chinese pharmacy on his own initiative to buy a thermometer so that we could ascertain his brother's exact body temperature. With the thin glass stick in his hand, Weng Yu was about to approach his brother when I yelled, 'Don't go near him!' From what I had seen in Dr Wong's clinic, I had a hunch that the illness was more dangerous to boys than to girls, and I didn't want anyone else in my family becoming infected.

For once my little prince obeyed without argument. He looked terrified. When he spoke – to tell me where I should place the thermometer on his brother's body – the tremor in his smooth bass voice was unmistakable. After ten minutes I removed the glass stick from beneath Weng Foo's armpit and handed it silently to my eldest son, whose face turned grave. With sorrowful eyes he said, 'Mama, it's not good. His temperature is one hundred and two. Normal should be ninety-eight.' Although Weng Yu spoke gently, he was so affected that he had to turn his face. He walked with head bowed, his footsteps echoing along the wooden floors.

Every few hours Weng Yu returned to the outer hall and asked me to take a temperature reading. I followed his instructions mechanically. I had been unable to eat all day and was exhausted, but that did not stop my heart from racing. We noted the steady rise in Weng Foo's body temperature. Just two hours later, when his breath became laboured, the thermometer showed 103. Still the fever raged. By nine o'clock that night, when the reading had turned to 104, my son was struggling for breath.

We took turns watching over Weng Foo in the outer hall. We wrapped him in a blanket so that he didn't catch a chill, gave him sips of water whenever we were able, sponged his head and rubbed his chest with a spicy oil to dispel wind. In short, we did all we could to let my son know that we were with him. The only other place I frequented during those interminable hours was the family altar, where the tablets of my ancestors and husband and the statue of Kuan Yin stood. I stared at the white porcelain image of the Goddess, unable to reconcile the smiling woman before me who sat placidly in a cross-legged lotus position with the vision of my suffering son nearby. 'Goddess, you are his godmother,' I pleaded. 'I beg you, listen to my cry!'

At midnight Hui Fang arrived from Taiping with her husband, Wai Man. Knowing the patriarch had a telephone in his house, I had sent our servant Li-Fei to the Yap household earlier in the evening while it was still light, to ask that Meng Seng apprise my daughter and son-in-law of their little brother's sudden illness. Li-Fei had travelled so speedily on her bicycle that I half expected the patriarch to follow her back, but he did not come, not realising the gravity of what had befallen us. On their arrival, Wai Man told me that his father would call on us first thing in the morning.

My daughter and son-in-law insisted on climbing on to the *barlay* to see little Weng Foo. When they came out, Wai Man's face was pale. Quivering, he said, 'Mama, I think I should fetch Dr Khong. He is a family friend. No harm seeing two doctors, is there?'

I swallowed. Little Weng Foo's shoulders were heaving, his mouth agape as he struggled for breath. I nodded my assent.

In no time at all Wai Man returned with a tall Chinese man, who walked in briskly carrying a black bag. After introducing himself, Dr Khong asked a barrage of questions, all the while stroking a noodle strip of a moustache with the thumb and index finger of his left hand from the centre outwards. He wanted to know when the illness had started, what Weng Foo had been given by way of medication, and anything unusual we had noticed. He asked whether we had seen mucus on the boy's tongue. As he listened to our answers, Dr Khong stood impassive, but the flicker in his eyes gave away his fear.

By the time Dr Khong examined Weng Foo, my son's fever was nearly 105. After laying a palm on his forehead, the doctor placed a glass tube – similar to the one my eldest son, Weng Yu, had bought – into the crook of Weng Foo's armpit. The doctor then took out a long rubber tube with a two-pronged fork on one end and a round metal plate on the other. 'To listen to the heart,' Wai Man whispered. My poor son was barely conscious by then. When he opened his mouth as instructed, we could see a heavily coated tongue. New symptoms appeared: uncontrollable sneezing accompanied by fits of shivering, as if my son was epileptic.

Before leaving, Dr Khong handed me two bottles: one containing a liquid, the other full of tablets. He asked us to feed the boy every hour with both. The liquid was described as a syrup to soothe my son's throat, while the tablets were for fever. We did as we were told and looked continuously for signs of improvement, but none came.

When Weng Foo began to complain of severe pain in his head and joints, the thermometer showed that his body temperature had risen past 105. My son opened his eyes and attempted a weak smile. Holding back tears, I stroked his forehead, which felt like a furnace, all the while whispering to him to sleep.

I was standing before the image of Kuan Yin when the end came.

I heard a cough and splutter so violent that I ran into the outer hall. Droplets of sweat had formed on Weng Foo's forehead. When I put my hand on his skin, it felt clammy. His face turned blue even as I was rubbing oil on his chest. I hoped the pungency would relieve him, but all my son did was tremble with a convulsive jerk. When he fell limp in my arms, I knew he had left us.

I put my face down on his chest and sobbed.

32

The first light of dawn streaked the skies around six thirty. I sent Li-Fei on her faithful two-wheeler to Siew Lan's house to apprise her of our misfortune. While my maid was gone, a handful of neighbours – the ones who had been alerted by my plaintive calls through the night – arrived in our house, as did Yap Meng Seng. I will never forget the look on the old man's face as he hobbled in: the shock in those wide-open eyes at the sight of what greeted him, shadowed by the remorse of a farewell unsaid to the little boy who had always been the first to greet him.

I was in no mood to console the patriarch. I had lost my voice and was walking in a daze, as much from lack of sleep as from the suddenness of my son's passing away. The emerging day and everything in it felt unreal. Shafts of sunlight poured in through an open window, washing the body of my son as he lay covered in a sheet on the *barlay*. I felt as if I were standing outside my own body, unable to think or plan or make a single decision, as numb as when I had received news of my husband's demise ten years before.

Seeing the state I was in, Meng Seng decided to act. He announced that he would go to Hume Street by car to search for a coffin and undertaker. Weng Yu insisted on accompanying him. They knew my preference for cremation, but when they arrived at the town's main thoroughfare for funeral shops, they found the undertakers so overworked that they were left with little choice. Bodies were being crammed into whatever containers could be made in time, because the dead had to be buried or burnt quickly to reduce the chance of infection. The only thing the living could choose was the type of service – Hindu, Moslem or Buddhist/Taoist; everything else depended on where and when workers were available and what was humanly possible. We were so pressured that my little Weng Foo was buried at one thirty that same day inside a hastily made cardboard coffin like a pauper's. 'The best we could find,' Weng Yu told me with tears streaming down his dimpled cheeks. 'I'm sorry, Mama.'

When it came time, I nearly fainted. Siew Lan had to hold me throughout, and it was my little prince, Weng Yu, who held the hands of his brothers and sisters as we headed out. I barely remember my son being lowered into that child-sized plot in the Chinese cemetery off the Tambun Road.

I was too distraught to even say goodbye properly; it was my daughters who sponged the boy, sprinkled him with scented Florida Water and dressed him in a suit. This remains one of my great regrets.

For many weeks afterwards the atmosphere in our house remained muted. A silence descended, fed by grief.

I wandered aimlessly between kitchen and outer hall, unable to rest yet incapable of much else. There were days when I could barely get out of bed. My second daughter, Hui Ying, took over the household. She managed it with Ah Hong's help, and with Siew Lan's too; whenever my friend visited, they would sit huddled in the kitchen, whispering to one another.

Beliefs I had long held lay crumbling in the wake of Weng Foo's demise. If Kuan Yin, his godmother, could not protect the boy, who could? Doubts about the medical treatment I had sought assailed me. These were spurred by Yap Meng Seng, who let slip that he thought his friend Dr Khong could have saved Weng Foo if he had been consulted earlier. 'He was trained in Britain, and brilliant! Next time, why not see both a Chinese and Western doctor at the same time?' the old man suggested. 'Surely there is no harm in that.' I could have pointed out that children were dying in Ipoh's British-run hospitals every day, but I didn't think of this till much later.

My solemn mood affected everyone, including the children, who stopped fighting over petty things. Even my third daughter, Hui Lin, the best-natured of the brood, showed signs of strain; she continued practising English words with Hui Ying, but with noticeably less enthusiasm. All the boys, including Weng Yu, behaved with more consideration towards one another; no longer were there struggles for bathroom occupation in the morning. The two youngest, twelve and thirteen at the time, regretted the unkind words they had once used against their brother. With recompense no longer possible, they hesitated before opening their mouths, worried about what might come out.

The deep lethargy into which I fell was broken only by necessity. The deaths in town ceased one day – as mysteriously as they had commenced – at which point we were forced to carry on with our lives. School resumed. Mr Ho-Lee at once asked to see Weng Yu in his office. While the fever raged, I had postponed telling my son what I really thought about sending him abroad. When Weng Yu returned home one afternoon with both eyes shining, I knew I was in for a delicate moment.

It seemed his headmaster had received a response from friends in London, who had independently recommended the same educational institution. My son said the name of the place – a name longer and even more complicated than Se-Too-Wat's. It specialised in science and engineering, exactly what Weng Yu was looking for. And the school was prepared to accept my son, provided he passed his upcoming examinations in mathematics and English.

Weng Yu told me all this without catching breath, much as the night years ago when he had recited the story of the Princess Hang Li Po. When the boy eventually paused, I saw the animation in his face; he seemed truly happy for the first time in weeks. In spite of my own poor spirits, I felt a surge of anticipation and set aside the thoughts about money which were already filling me with dread.

Weng Yu told me that the course would last five years. Yet when I asked about costs, he became vague, as if these were a mere afterthought. I recalled my previous misgivings about Weng Yu's attitude towards money, so desultory, as if he had a right to the sums involved and did not need to bother. But I didn't confide my fears to anyone, because I could only have told Siew Lan, and I did not want her to know about our financial worries.

Casting doubt aside, I visited Mr Ho-Lee at the earliest opportunity. I was shocked by the headmaster's appearance; he had aged so much in the intervening weeks of crisis that I could scarcely believe this haggard man with the hollow cheeks was the same one I had spoken to only months previously. His hairline had receded, and even his ears drooped. 'We lost many boys,' he told me in a sad voice. 'Such a waste of life . . . Anyway, Peng Choon Soh, good news about Weng Yu, isn't it?' At the mention of my son, Mr Ho-Lee cheered up. He rose from his chair, carrying his lumbering frame towards a filing cabinet, from where he retrieved a wad of papers. When he sat down again, I saw that the kindly smile which had once lit up his face was still intact.

'I must know how much, Mr Ho-Lee,' I said.

'Of course, of course!' the headmaster replied, adding with a puzzled look, 'Weng Yu didn't tell you? I gave the boy all the information.'

'No,' I said cautiously. 'He not sure . . . about anything like that.'

'Ai-yahh, these young people!' The headmaster saw my concern but laughed it off, proceeding instead to silently add up a series of figures on his papers.

'The total cost per month, Peng Choon Soh, is around fourteen pounds. For everything – tuition, books, lodging, transport – but there would be nothing left over. So if your son wanted to go to the cinema, for example, it wouldn't be possible.'

My heart sank at the new number: it came to two pounds more than I had been expecting, which would mean having to find another eighteen, maybe even twenty, dollars a month. I could not see how we would raise the funds when we hadn't even counted the cost of passage or warm clothing for my boy. The uncertainty must have been obvious in my face, because Mr Ho-Lee immediately asked, 'You want time to think-moh, Peng Choon Soh?'

I nodded. 'Lot of money-ah. Must carefully think,' I said before adding, 'You very good,' to which Mr Ho-Lee merely gave a wave of his large hand. When we parted, the smile he flashed, so broad and wide, brought wrinkles to the sides of his eyes.

'When you're ready, let me know. We shouldn't delay for too long.'

Over the next days the spring in Weng Yu's step told me that my son had already begun imagining himself in London. When Siew Lan burst into our house, grinning, it was to chide me on my devilish secrecy: 'Ay! How come you no tell me you send your son to England?' It seemed my little prince had gone to see the white devil, to whom he had poured out his heart; over many hours they had spoken of London and little else. There could be no turning back. I hurried to meet with Yap Meng Seng, showing up one morning after my helpers had finished *kueh* preparations. The patriarch listened patiently, coffee cup in hand, while the numbers tumbled out of my mouth.

'One hundred and twenty, one hundred and thirty dollars even. So much money-ah! Month-month also need. What to do? I calculate already; I think I can support my son. Just enough-lah. We got rubber estates, also got rental . . . but must economise. Oh, you maybe not know . . . my late husband leave us rubber smallholdings, also give three shophouses in Old Town. We have good tenants. But much risk-lah!'

My words trickled into the air alongside beads of anxiety. I paused before continuing. 'Price of rubber fall that time, like few years ago, what I do? Then tenant no pay, also what I do? Also,' I added, my mind racing, 'ticket still not counted, warm clothes also not counted. Then he fall sick, what I do? England is very expensive.'

Everything poured out in a deluge, but I couldn't stop myself. Meng Seng sat with a bemused expression on his face. When I stopped talking, he told me decisively, as if he had long expected my visit, 'Chye Hoon, have no worries. I will pay his two-way passage and get him warm clothing. I think you should ask Wai Man and Hui Fang if they can spare something each month – my son has just been given a raise, and they may be able to contribute to contingencies. The Weng Yu Project is worthwhile, and I want to help.' Raising his voice, the patriarch said, 'You have my promise that any time there is a shortfall – and I mean any time – either because the price of rubber falls, or if one of your tenants doesn't pay rent, whatever the reason I will make up the shortfall.'

His last pronouncement brought a lump to my throat. But I held the tears back, because any show of emotion would have embarrassed the patriarch. Looking directly into his eyes for a long minute, I said softly, 'Meng Seng-ah, so kind of you. Emergency only we use your money.'

The old man cleared his throat. 'We are family now,' he replied gruffly. 'I have more than enough. I want to give the boy the chance he deserves.'

Thereafter Mr Ho-Lee proceeded with a formal application to the science college and also booked a bed in a youth hostel – a safe place, he assured me. 'This is very exciting, Peng Choon Soh!' the headmaster said, his moustache curving into a smile. 'Good for Ipoh-lah.'

Despite my qualms I could not help but be a little infected by everyone's enthusiasm. My son, a British-trained engineer! His father would have been so proud.

33

The birth of my first grandchild marked a turning point in our lives. I wish I could say that I was present at his birth, but alas Hui Fang chose to have her baby in Taiping, inside a hospital.

When I heard about my daughter's decision, I was livid. I was sure it had been the patriarch's idea. Though my faith in traditional medicine had been bruised when Weng Foo passed away, the Western-trained doctor had not saved him either. In any case, babies were different: I could see no reason for not having them in the comfort of one's own home. I had once had the misfortune of stepping into a hospital when I visited a sick Nyonya who was one of my customers, and I couldn't imagine the indignity of lying in such a large room among strangers, being barked at by a doctor, a man, who told you to push . . . pu-u-sh . . . without ever conceivably knowing what your pain must feel like.

It was during one of their monthly visits to Ipoh that my daughter told me she was not coming home for the birth. I was surprised but not unduly concerned. 'Taiping sure to have good *bidan*,' I said. 'You want me go to Kampong Laxamana to ask?'

Looking away, Hui Fang replied in a timid voice, 'Mama, we . . . we go enter into a hospital.'

I was at a loss for words. 'You really want like that-ah?' I finally asked.

'Yes, Mama,' my daughter replied, relieved that an outburst had been avoided.

'So, Wai Man also want like that?' Hui Fang nodded, taking care to repeat that she too preferred to be in a hospital. Continuing to prod the girl, I eventually prised the admission out of her that the initiative had been her husband's, and that her father-in-law had played a role.

The patriarch would have to be tackled. To make sure he was in a good mood, I fed Meng Seng first. Only when we were sipping tea did I ask outright, 'Hui Fang go enter into hospital to deliver her baby your idea-ah?'

A shadow of surprise flickered across the old man's face. He seemed torn between stamping his foot and justifying his interference. But Meng Seng never lied. He nodded. 'Yes,' he said a little hesitantly before launching into a robust answer. 'Look, Chye Hoon, I know you want the best for your daughter. Me too. Taiping General Hospital is one of the best in this country. It has modern equipment. That's why I told her to go there.'

From my stiff face, the patriarch knew what was to come.

'Meng Seng, you know I have ten children,' I began, 'all born at home . . . with a *bidan*, each one also healthy. At home for baby good, for mother also good. Hospital like . . . like . . .' At that point I left the sentence unfinished, struggling to describe the repugnance I felt for hospital rooms.

The patriarch took the opportunity to barge in. 'If I may say so, Chye Hoon, you were just lucky. Many women die, you know.' The man sat there looking so smug that all I wanted to do was shake him. Because I couldn't, I did the next best thing – which was to scream.

'You not know . . . give birth . . . like what!' I yelled so loudly that Ah Hong peeped through the doorway. 'My own mother also never want baby come out in hospital. They . . . they . . . evil,' I finally said, unable to find a better word. It's unfortunate that what emerged from my mouth in those few minutes came from the heart, not my head, because it gave the patriarch an excuse to disregard my words as hysterical ranting. I knew what I wanted to say, but the feelings were impossible to describe using any language I'd been taught. As a result Meng Seng simply looked at me with kindly eyes, as if I were a child, until I became so frustrated that I told him I needed to go to bed.

Realising the futility of trying to change the patriarch's mind, I found out as much as I could about hospital births. Siew Lan, despite her other attempts at modernity, had also had both her children at home and shared my scepticism about babies born in hospitals. We heard how, once the infant came out and the doctor had cut the cord, a nurse would remove the baby from its mother and put it into another room! This sounded so cruel that I couldn't believe it really happened, until one of our friends swore it was true.

When I listened to such stories, I was filled with despair. I offered to be with my daughter in Taiping during her eighth month, but the couple insisted that would not be necessary. The result was that I didn't witness the coming into this world of my first grandchild, a lovely boy called Choong Meng. I wasn't there to cradle him, shower his face with kisses or hear his earliest cries, a disappointment I shall always carry in this life. I did not see my grandson until he was ten days old; he came swaddled in cloth, a sleeping infant with a snub nose and tiny black hairs on an otherwise bald crown. Even at that tender age Choong Meng gave the impression of severity, thanks to lips which pouted naturally downwards and a prominent bottom lip hanging loose.

Looking at the little mite, I felt a pang at the way our world was changing. We elders were becoming less involved in the lives of our children, less valued, our wisdom and experience considered irrelevant. I wondered what Choong Meng would wish to learn from me in the future. Possibly nothing; my grandson would grow up to regard me as a fool – ignorant, slow and incapable of teaching him. I didn't like what was happening, but there was little I could do to turn the clock back.

Yet the very fact of his presence brought new vigour to my weary bones. It was an awakening, like a miracle.

I thought often of my grandson and was desperate for his parents' visits to Ipoh. I would have travelled the eighty miles to Taiping had it not been for Weng Yu's imminent examinations and departure for England. Already dreading my eldest son's five-year absence, I was torn between spending every remaining minute with Weng Yu and seeing more of my grandson, a physical impossibility unless I could be in two places at once.

Fortunately my daughter realised how important my grandchild's one-month celebration would be to me. She and her husband made a special trip, giving me the chance to fetch the tortoise-shaped *angkoo* moulds from the back of our tiny pantry, to clean them inside out and to place all ten wood blocks on the kitchen table in readiness for a heroic culinary session. We had our hands full that day: with my younger girls, two of their brothers and the servants in tow, we made the traditional dishes, which turned our table into a riot of colour. There was saffron-seasoned turmeric rice and red Nyonya chicken curry, also bowls of hard-boiled eggs, their shells dyed pink for cheer, and for sweetness orange-red *angkoo*, the most famous of our *kueh*.

After the *kueh* were steamed, we arranged them inside the beautifully lacquered *sia nah* that Wai Man placed on the passenger seat of his car. He spent no more than an hour driving the *kueh* round to the houses of friends and family. I marvelled at the speed of change: not twenty years before, Peng Choon had tied the lacquered containers with strong rope to the ends of a wooden pole and hauled them all over town. The task had taken him more than one evening, yet here was my son-in-law delivering the same to even more houses, without so much as a drop of sweat on his brow.

A string of well-wishers came to our house, including Siew Lan, who spent hours cooing over the little Choong Meng. My friend was delighted by my grandson. Her large eyes, around which fine lines had formed, sparkled as she played with his tiny toes. 'Ai-yahh . . . so cute . . . so cute,' she kept repeating. When we finally sat down on the *barlay*, Siew Lan had a store of compliments for me too. 'Even more weight, Chye Hoon!' she exclaimed, indicating my girth with her hands. Seeing the horror on my face, my friend broke into a smile. 'Only little bit-lah! Good for you, you know!'

I sighed. 'What to do?' I said in a half whisper. I had noticed the weight gain myself. Though my figure had always been of the stout variety, the five miles I'd had to walk six days a week every week during the lean years had kept expansion in check. Once the bicycle became part of our business, though, there was no concealing my increasingly comfortable life. The change took place gradually: the thickening of both arms; the way tiny rolls of skin began to hang off; the tightening of the sarongs around my waist. Ultimately it was the mirror from which I could not hide, for the face reflected back at me was no longer oval but a tenuous circle, with a generous chin to boot.

I was getting old. I said this aloud to my friend, but Siew Lan shook her head vigorously. 'No-lah! You have many years left.'

'No, my friend,' I told her. 'My children already leave home. First Hui Fang, now Weng Yu.'

We talked then about my eldest son, who was largely absent during those months, his head buried in mounds of books. Every afternoon he stayed behind at school so that he could revise in the library, which he said was quieter than our house. My son's ambition surprised and pleased me; I had never seen him so focused and was secretly delighted by this dedication and diligence. In the last two months before his examinations, even his Saturday outings to the cinema were suspended. This brought howls of protest from Hui Ying, who told her brother that he needed to take a break every now and then – 'The brain must rest,' she would say – to no avail.

'I have to study,' Weng Yu insisted. 'It's my only chance.' Eventually my second son, Weng Koon, then nearly sixteen and already the cheekiest of the boys, offered to take his brother's place until the examinations were over.

These took place over a two-week period in December 1920. Weng Yu walked around like a madman in that fortnight, with eyes blazing in concentration and jaws so taut that I worried he would crack his teeth. There were moments when the tension inside our house became unbearable. Arranging our meals around Weng Yu's revision schedule, I strictly forbade the others from making any noise. Every one of us felt as if we too would enter that sombre examination hall with Weng Yu to sweat over long lists of befuddling questions.

I prepared Weng Yu's favourite dishes to celebrate the end of his last examination, but when my son returned home he was so fatigued he went straight to bed. For the next month we breathed again. After that, anxiety crept in, because we knew it would not be long until the results were announced, in March.

That year – 1921 – Weng Yu was named one of the top scholars in the state of Perak. He passed his examinations with such flying colours that he was mentioned in the local newspapers. He gained distinctions in five subjects, some of which I hadn't even heard of until he began his revision. I knew about English language and mathematics and English history but was amazed when Weng Yu told me he was studying art and drawing. 'You can study art?' I asked, incredulous.

'Oh yes, Mama!' Weng Yu replied enthusiastically. From the way he shook his head up and down, I suspected that my son was probably good at drawing – another dubious talent, for what worse way could there be to earn money? As for geography, which I had never heard of either, I made my son explain what the word actually meant. 'Oh, we learn about crops and weather and terrain,' he began.

' "Terrain" is what?'

'You know . . . whether a place is flat or mountainous . . . What crops can grow depends on that sort of thing,' he replied in his usual airy manner.

'So, is agriculture-ah?'

'No! It's a study of countries really.' That description – 'a study of countries' – awakened my curiosity, yet as soon as I probed further I was disappointed.

'You learn about which countries?'

'Well . . . England mainly, but other countries too,' my son said. 'In Europe, for example. It's world geography.' Taking a deep breath, I left it there. I had made a decision to give my boys an English education, and it was too late for regrets. What would come would come.

When the examination results were announced and I heard that my son's name was mentioned in the newspapers, the doubts I carried inside my head evaporated. I walked around with a stupid grin on my face, even stopping complete strangers along Lahat Road to tell them about my son's triumph. We celebrated with absurdly large meals, which Siew Lan and her husband and Meng Seng joined. At the first of these, to Weng Yu's delight the patriarch presented him with a beautifully wrapped case. Inside was a heavy silver chain looped around a pocket watch, also silver, with a sparkling white face and unusual black lines around its rim. I was told the black lines represented numbers but were written the old-fashioned way, hence they looked different to the squiggles more commonly seen on watches of the time. The watch was so expensive it even had a name, two syllables that sounded like Los-Kof. It was the best pocket watch then available in Ipoh, made in that country Siew Lan had once told me about, the one that was like China, with its mountains and lakes.

Amidst the celebrations I never lost sight of the fact that I would soon have to say goodbye to my little prince. Time marched forward relentlessly, hastening the day when my eldest son would leave for unknown shores.

Our farewell was simple. Holding Weng Yu close for as many minutes as I could, I whispered a goodbye into his ear before wiping away my tears. I was surprised by how sad my son looked. I had only expected excitement on his face, not the dark bags under his deep-set eyes or the harrowed air which fell across his cheeks, dampening the dimples that were his and his father's hallmarks. Meng Seng and Wai Man had kindly agreed to drive ten people to Penang, but with my business to run and the other children to care for, I could not spare the days away. That at least was what I told everyone. I had other reasons too, feelings I could not speak about. As soon as the departing parties left in their two cars, I went into the inner hall to stand before the tablets, where I released my sadness in front of our ancestors, my husband and Kuan Yin.

For hours no matter how many tears I shed, more followed. The silence in the house oppressed me. Whenever I recalled images of my son, I started to cry, no matter what the actual memory was. I forgave his waywardness, his fascination with a white actress, even his insolence. I would have gladly taken him back with open arms if that had been possible.

When I had exhausted my tears, I sat alone near an open window. I did the same the next day, watching the storm that unfurled in the afternoon. The skies darkened ominously. Everything – from the trees shivering in the wind to the smell in the air, with its tinge of dampness, and the rustle all around, like the noise of air being sucked in – told us to expect rain, lots of it. Soon flashes of light were seen, followed by the roar of clapping thunder. Eventually the heavens opened and the rain started to beat down, drops as large as pellets lashing hard on the streets outside.

It poured as it had not poured for many months, flooding the sun-seared valleys of the Kinta District. The land itself, acres of open plain surrounded by green furry hills, seemed to invite the rain and the wind. These rolled in relentlessly, gathering in fury as they churned into the fierce thunderstorms for which Ipoh was famous.

When I rushed to close a window, I saw a streak of lightning tear across the sky, the type of rushing flash whose ferocity you feel in your bones. I saw it high in the skies above the plain. The light moved at a giddy pace, crackling in the air, and the accompanying drum roll echoed back and forth from the limestone hills.

When it was over, the sun shone once again. A rainbow rose up, a perfect band with strips of red, yellow and purple, arching magnificently over the hills of Ipoh.

PART IV:
UNCHARTED
TERRITORY
SEPTEMBER 1921–1930

34

It was Siew Lan who told me the story of the mine, a small pit in a godforsaken corner outside Ipoh town. She had heard the tale from Se-Too-Wat, who in turn learnt it from friends at the Ipoh Club.

The concession had once belonged to a white devil, a man with flowing red hair and beard who, on discovering he was short of the funds he needed, offered his prize to another white man. Those were pessimistic days, because the ending of war in Europe, which we initially heralded, had brought little joy to our territory. Our jubilation plummeted, along with demand for rubber and tin. Coolies once again poured into Ipoh town, so that when the concession in this distant spot came up, no one had the nerve to make the necessary investment. A Chinese group eventually took it over. Instead of prospecting for tin themselves, however, they left the hard business of working the land to an old woman, a widow to whom no one gave a second's thought.

She was reputedly already fifty, this Chinese woman whose skin was a shell baked brown by the Malayan sun. Her back was curved from years of stooping over a *changkol*, but everyone who knew her spoke of her incredible strength and how she could be prevailed on to work like an ox. Just five years previously the woman had wailed over the mutilated body of her husband, a mining coolie who had the misfortune of falling from one of the rickety ladders Peng Choon once told me about. After her husband passed away, the widow, who already knew much about tin, joined the throngs being hired as small-time panhandlers. Naturally when the opportunity came up at this neglected mine, she seized it. The widow could not read and write, but she was wise. Wary of being cheated, she hired a Chinese lawyer, who advised her to seal the contract with her thumbprint.

When it came to finding those precious black lumps, the widow turned out more adept, and perhaps more persistent, than the men before her. Working the mine with a small group of coolies, many of whom were women, she managed to eke out a living.

Digging late one afternoon, the woman hit a vein of black stone. The stone she found had all the qualities she was seeking: hard, lumpy and streaked with white crystals. Only there were more white crystals than she had ever imagined. Using bare hands at first and then a *chang-kol*, she began digging furiously; the harder she dug, the more of the black stone she found. Fate rewarded her determination. By the end of the day the woman and her helpers had filled more tubs than they were able to carry home.

Her discovery came at a critical time, for her lease was due to expire within the week. The next day the widow presented herself at the offices of the Chinese syndicate to ask for an extension of her lease. Alas, news of her find had spread overnight; despite heartfelt pleas, the syndicate refused the widow's request.

But the woman did not give up. She organised shifts to work the land day and night for the entire week until her lease expired, so that none of what she'd found would be stolen from under her nose. Together the woman and her helpers dug up tin said to be worth eighty thousand dollars. Being a generous soul, the widow shared the loot with her helpers. Despite that, she was able to retire comfortably.

Rumour had it that she had moved to Penang, where she was waited on hand and foot inside a grand house.

No sooner had the woman been banished from the land whose wealth she had uncovered than the land itself dried up. No matter what they did, the men who followed were unable to find any more of the black stuff. Within months the mine closed down, but the tale of the poor widow continued to spread, giving hope to the multitudes then seeking shelter beneath the Hugh Low Bridge. From their rubbish-infested hovels beside the Kinta River, they could not imagine ever scraping together enough for a passage back to China or India.

I was in a more fortunate position, but the tale of the poor widow had allure even for me. I thought often of the woman, of her kindness and most especially her tenacity. I was to recall the widow's story many times in the next few years, when my spirit was ravaged. I had to remind myself that any trial, no matter how difficult, could be overcome.

Within days it was my eldest daughter, Hui Fang, who occupied my waking moments. When she, her husband and the children returned from Penang, where they had seen Weng Yu off, our house came alive again. Everyone talked excitedly all at once. My second daughter, Hui Ying, who babbled on about what she had seen, made me smile. She marvelled at the size of Weng Yu's ship: 'As high as a two-storey shop-house, Mama, and as long as forty shophouses joined together!' She talked about a huge temple they had visited, a white edifice with a golden roof set high on a hill, from where they had glimpsed the distant sea. It was the same temple Mother had once described in a tone of reverence. 'You must go and see it, Mama!' Hui Ying told me, so enthusiastically that my eyes flicked across the room, where they were unwittingly drawn towards her elder sister beside her.

For the first time I noticed how gaunt my eldest daughter looked. Hui Fang's eyes were those of a cadaver and her cheeks appeared sunken, the skin textured like a Chinese plum in the early stages of drying. When I went to bed, I was convinced the shadows across my daughter's face had nothing to do with the twilight streaking our inner hall.

As soon as an opportunity came, I knocked on Hui Fang's door. It was a lovely Malayan morning, all blue skies and sunshine, with not a cloud to be seen. Light streamed in through the open windows, bathing Hui Fang's room in warmth. She sat perched on the pedestal that had once been the bridal bed, nursing her son.

I smiled, waiting for the awkward silence to pass. On the wall outside I heard the frantic pecks and twittering of long-tailed swifts assembling a nest. Soon enough my eldest daughter began to speak – about my parents. 'Kong-Kong and Po-Po very frail, Mama, so thin, I also shocked. I scared . . . I not know . . . They maybe sick, Mama.'

Her words reminded me how I too had wanted to travel to Penang. I longed to see Mother, but it had seemed prudent to remain at home, because my head was in such a mess, my heart even more so. The sight of my little prince stepping on to his ship would have been more than I could bear. I had contented myself with sending Mother our packages of food, replete with chilli and coconut and the smells of love.

I nodded sadly, knowing I would have to brace myself for the day which would eventually come. Meanwhile here was my daughter, with a boil inside her heart. Trying to coax it out, I said, 'You last night very quiet, Hui Fang.'

At this my daughter turned away, keeping her eyes near the hollow of her nose as she watched baby Choong Meng nibble at a nipple. A single touch was all it took; as soon as she felt my hand, Hui Fang began to cry.

'I think . . .'

Seeing that my daughter could barely get the words out, I folded her into my arms. Hui Fang's breath on the sleeves of my baju brought back memories. This was the way we had once been, my eldest daughter and I, a long time ago.

When Hui Fang lifted her head, I patted her eyes dry with the handkerchief I always carried inside the folds of my baju.

'I think . . . I no good wife, Mama,' my daughter blurted out, making my head pound. A flame flared up inside me.

'Ai-yahh! Why you like that say? Wai Man tell you-ah?'

Hui Fang shook her head. 'Then . . . you where get that idea?' Searching my daughter's eyes, I saw that they were empty, drained of spirit.

'I think . . . he have . . . he have . . . mistress.' The words seemed to choke her. Outside, the long-tailed swifts on the wall squealed, breaking into the peace of morning.

'Why you think that?' I whispered, my mouth dry.

Hui Fang told me about Wai Man's outstation trips. He went often, sometimes coming home with a cloying smell on his clothes, an odour Hui Fang immediately associated with another woman. The trips had begun while she was halfway through her pregnancy and increased thereafter. Worryingly they had no savings. It was her husband who controlled their money. He gave her enough for food and other expenses, but there was never anything left over. When she challenged him on where his salary went, he brushed her off with vague explanations, telling her about this, that and the other, disjointed bits which failed to answer her question. There were moments she feared she was imagining things, when she thought she was simply going mad, but then the fragrance would invade her house again, this smell of cloves and lemon she knew wasn't hers.

When she finished, I felt a burning in the pit of my stomach. My son-in-law seemed such an unlikely candidate for infidelity. I could barely imagine him charming a woman, let alone cheating, and yet my daughter's story had the ring of truth. I could see that Hui Fang knew it too from the wretchedness written all over her face.

'Daughter,' I said as I held her hand, 'I need to think what to do. Remember you here always have home . . . always.'

Throughout the day I had to fight an intense urge to run to Siew Lan's house. I was bursting with feeling and unable to make sense of the random thoughts flying into my head. Kuan Yin seemed of no help. In front of her porcelain image it was my daughter's hollow eyes I saw, and when I shook joss-sticks in the air, all I did was to chase shadows. By mid-afternoon I could no longer contain myself. I set off for the English quarter in a rickshaw.

When I arrived at Siew Lan's, the sight that greeted me so took my breath away that I forgot the very thing which had seemed pressing just moments before. For there was my friend, standing not in her usual baju but in a frilly Western dress similar to the one worn by Weng Yu's favourite actress. The dress was loose and sleeveless, pulled in at the waist and with a skirt which reached near the knee. A gasp escaped my lips.

'You do what, Siew Lan?' I asked in alarm. 'You also go modern-ah?'

My friend exploded in mirth. 'You should see your face, Chye Hoon!'

Siew Lan spoke haltingly, as if reluctant to reveal why she was in Western clothes. 'No-o, I . . . I . . . no go modern,' she said.

I pointed to the thin crêpe-like material the colour of bean curd which fell from her body in soft folds. 'Then all this what for?'

It took a change of attire and many sighs before my friend disclosed her news. 'You cannot tell anyone,' she said in a complicit whisper. 'Se-Too-Wat and I go overseas, maybe next year. Go to London and Paree. We want Flora go to see her father's country.'

My eyes widened. 'Ooh!' I exclaimed, blowing air out loudly. I tried to picture Siew Lan in Europe but failed, not having any idea of what

Europe could look like. The furthest I managed was seeing big streets and mountains and lakes and people dressed in large coats. 'So . . . in London you no can wear baju-meh?'

Siew Lan chortled. 'Of course can, only I think wear their dress easier-lah. Must walk a lot, you know. Not like here. Here we ride rickshaw go everywhere. There I have to walk.'

'We of course want to see Weng Yu,' Siew Lan continued. I nodded gravely, my thoughts elsewhere. 'You hear from him already-ah?' she asked. When I shook my head, my friend gave me a searching look. 'Chye Hoon, have problem-ah?'

I hesitated, wondering how I would bring up the subject. Siew Lan and Se-Too-Wat were friends of the Yap family's after all, and Wai Man was a boy she had personally recommended. Even as I reasoned with myself I knew there was no other way. I had to tackle the issue head-on.

'Hui Fang think Wai Man have mistress.'

Siew Lan blinked hard. Her drooping eyelids shut tight for a noticeable second before she raised her eyes to meet mine. The air between us changed, becoming at once sombre and anguished, but Siew Lan's face gave nothing away. Afraid she would not believe my daughter's story, I prepared to defend Hui Fang. Fortunately that proved unnecessary.

'She sure-ah?' was all that Siew Lan asked. I repeated the story exactly as I had heard it from my daughter's lips that morning. When I finished, my friend looked glum. 'Ai-yahh, I sorry, Chye Hoon,' she said, her eyes gloomy.

'Not your fault!' I exclaimed. While sipping tea, I added, 'More important is think what to do.'

With nothing concrete to hold on to, we found ourselves going around in circles. My friend pointed out that we had no proof a woman was actually involved; the boy could have taken up an unsavoury activity – gambling for instance. 'I not say that is good,' she added hastily. 'Just that . . . we anything, also not know. You no got evidence, how to confront a man, isn't it?'

I laughed. 'But Siew Lan, wives always no have evidence-mah. How to find proof? Only have what their hearts tell.'

'This different,' my friend insisted. 'We know more that time, we can meet Meng Seng.'

At the thought of the old man, I breathed deeply. Confronting the patriarch would be delicate, since Weng Yu's future depended on him, and therefore so did mine. Siew Lan of course had no idea about these arrangements, and I certainly was not about to tell her.

Meanwhile, when my friend suggested she speak to Se-Too-Wat, I swallowed. It must have been clear I didn't like my family affairs being discussed with a white devil, even if that white devil happened to be her husband.

'Chye Hoon,' Siew Lan said in a gently admonitory tone, 'you no let me talk to Se-Too-Wat, then must find someone in Taiping-ah!'

I sighed.

'Besides,' Siew Lan continued forcefully, 'you before want Chinese husband for your daughter, isn't it?' I nodded. 'Hah! Then like this-lah! Chinese men always have mistresses and concubines.'

I breathed even more heavily, not liking the implication of Siew Lan's words. It wasn't true, I thought, recalling my own loyal husband. But with so many bad examples among the towkays and prominent Chinese men, how could I argue? I left Siew Lan's house thoroughly dissatisfied, while her words rang triumphantly in my ears.

'White men better to women, Chye Hoon.'

35

While Siew Lan and I scrambled to uncover the truth about my son-in-law's activities, Weng Yu's first letter arrived.

The whole family jostled into the inner hall after dinner, eager for the grand unveiling of a missive that had travelled across oceans. My breath quickened in anticipation. I expected descriptions of London, its people, the stars in its night sky. Instead my son wrote about architecture. I could scarcely believe it. When Hui Ying's sonorous voice finally stopped, we had heard only about windows on the roofs of buildings, carvings on pillars and ubiquitous metal railings outside of houses, painted black and supposedly impressive. What was the boy thinking?

The same scene repeated itself through the years. Weng Yu's letters were always opened with fanfare and read aloud in the pale glow of twilight, yet they left me disappointed. From the height of a dark mahogany chair Peng Choon had imported from China, I wondered what life in London was really like for a Baba boy.

My little prince never told us. On the rare occasions when he did write about his feelings, he said that he missed the Malayan sun. London, with its air of grey dullness, could be drab even in the summer; there, colours didn't dazzle the eye the way they did in Malaya.

His words left the impression of a subdued country in which beauty was kept in check, like the contrast between the English and Chinese quarters in Ipoh town. Weng Yu reinforced my view that the white devils, even if faithful to their wives, were different – so different that we could never truly understand one another.

When Siew Lan mentioned that my son had written to her husband, I was astonished. We were on the *barlay*, where my friend was spreading white lime across a betel leaf held flat on her left palm. She then chopped betel nuts with my guillotine knife and at the same time told me how impressed Weng Yu was by the motor vehicles around London.

'There got bus two storeys-kah!'

'What? Like house-ah?' I asked.

'Yes-lah!'

Sipping my Chinese tea, I peered at the brown dregs that had sunk to the bottom of my cup. Holding the cup in both hands, I felt the grainy etchings along its smooth surface, carvings of dragons and borders that were painted in Nyonya green and pink.

'Weng Yu talk about other students-ah?'

In answer Siew Lan spouted a series of facts: that my son was among fifty students; that two others were from Malaya; that they had lectures six hours every weekday and three hours on Saturday morning—

'My son say or not the white students-ah . . . they with him how?' I interrupted.

Siew Lan trained her large brown eyes at me in a frown.

'Ai-yahh! Chye Hoon,' she said, inadvertently exposing gums blackened by betel nut juice. 'They all students-lah! They all same. Se-Too-Wat say your son do well. He very like London!'

A rivulet of dark red appeared on one corner of Siew Lan's mouth. I took a deep breath. It was clear I would have to read between the lines of Weng Yu's letters.

At the end of his first year, my little prince announced that he would seek new lodgings with a kitchen, because he could no longer put up with meals of boiled liver and sausages. That was how I realised he had used up the bottles of condiments I had carefully packed. A room with a kitchen in London sounded expensive, and it made me wary. I wrote straight away to remind my son to take care of his funds. When Weng Yu assured me he could stick to his budget, I became less anxious, but then I worried about his having to move further from his college. That was what those years were like – filled with anxiety because my son was so far away.

I was not the only one to notice the vagueness in Weng Yu's letters. Liew Tsin-sang, the brother of the girls' teacher, chuckled so much one evening after our family meal that his horn-rimmed glasses quivered. When I shot him an enquiring look, the young man said apologetically, 'Sorry, Peng Choon Sau, sorry-lah! I just don't understand! Weng Yu stands on the road to watch the wedding of two rich strangers and then . . . you don't even hear who he spends every day with! Strange boy-lah!'

I smiled awkwardly. By then I was certain that the young man had designs on my second daughter, Hui Ying. Having caught sight of him once when Hui Ying walked into the outer hall, I had seen how even his ears coloured, and how he had eyes only for her during meals, when he would offer her choice pieces of meat and fish.

I did not know what to think of the courtship being played out openly before me. With Weng Foo's demise and my eldest daughter's troubles, beliefs I had long held were shaken. While I wasn't in favour of young people choosing their own husbands and wives, I did not have the heart to put a stop to the obvious affection this earnest young man felt for my daughter. For one thing I was indebted to his sister, whose free tuition over two and a half years had helped my daughters attain Standard Three in half the time it took others. The young man himself was much like the son-in-law I had chosen for my eldest daughter, but now I asked myself whether I had not made a serious mistake. Did Liew Tsin-sang's politeness and prospects matter more than my own daughter's wishes? I brooded over this long and hard. If it indeed turned out that my daughter liked the young man, which was far from clear at the time, I could not refuse her. But equally, if her feelings were elsewhere, I would not try to persuade her. I would have to speak to Hui Ying in due course.

◆ ◆ ◆

In the midst of these storms a competitor arrived in Ipoh.

In truth, there had been a handful of women through the years who, envious of my success, had tried hawking *kueh* around town. Though most of these came from a Nyonya background, there were the inevitable Chinese copycats who thought they could simply add dashes of coconut milk here and spoonfuls of colouring there to turn their own delicacies into Nyonya *kueh*. They soon learnt. Each had come and gone; none had lasted more than a few years, some not even months. To make *kueh* every day as we did required passion, supreme dedication and much persistence, because they had us to contend with – the Wong family of established *kueh* makers.

When Li-Fei informed me about a certain Heng Lai Soh, whose Nyonya *kueh* were gathering a following among the townspeople, I didn't think much of it. I only took heed when the pouch of coins the girl handed me became lighter and remained so for many days.

'How come?' I asked, trying to sound casual.

'Because of this Nyonya lady-lah. I tell you already. Her *kueh* good to eat, you know! Everyone also like.'

Heng Lai Soh apparently came from Malacca, which meant she served some of the *kueh* differently. She employed an Indian man, Muthu, to carry her wares around town, and Li-Fei had peeked into his baskets out of curiosity. 'Hmm,' I mumbled. 'They look like what?'

Li-Fei said her *kueh* were pretty enough. 'Colour not so good to look. But I see one or two types only-lah, Peng Choon Sau. *Pulut tai-tai* and *ondeh-ondeh*. Her *pulut tai-tai* not so blue, *ondeh-ondeh* not so green. But still nice. And she sell more cheap than us.'

This last point worried me. I supposed it was inevitable that someone would come along sooner or later. We'd had no real competition for ten years, and I always wondered what I would do when it happened.

It was time to investigate. I discussed the matter with Siew Lan as soon as I could, and she, being a dear, loyal friend, assured me that our *kueh* tasted better. 'Ai-yahh, Chye Hoon! You no need to worry-lah!' she said. 'I see her *kueh* in town. Not as nice as yours! Really! You no believe, go and ask Hong Seng Soh-lah!'

This in turn led me to the Nyonya woman, whose house stood further along Lahat Road, down the short bit of track known as Thirteenth Street. Herself a widow, Hong Seng Soh had been our loyal customer from the start. On my very first day she had come out to offer condolences and to buy three pieces of our white and green *seri muka*. Eleven years later she was definitively older, and toothless to boot. 'Peng Choon Sau,' she replied cautiously, exposing two rows of gums blackened by betel nut juice. 'Your *kueh* good, her *kueh* also good. I buy from both. What you want me to say?'

I explained that I wished to know the differences between us. Were there types of *kueh* the other woman was better at? 'Yes,' Hong Seng Soh said to my horror. '*Rempah udang*. More spicy than your one! But your nine-layered *kueh* and *pulut tai-tai* and *angkoo* more nice to eat than her ones!' Hong Seng Soh thought for a minute before adding, 'And she sell cheaper. So have to buy from both. Otherwise I no money left-lah!'

As Hong Seng Soh roared with laughter on her doorstep, I wondered whether we should reduce our prices. Was that a wise thing to do? I remembered Peng Choon's story about Ipoh's first mechanic, the man who had lost loyal customers when, despite fierce competition, he insisted on retaining his prices. Was I behaving like that mechanic, stubbornly burying my head in the sand when the world was changing?

I decided I had to see this new woman for myself. On learning that she prayed at the Pa Lo Old Temple, I visited it in the hope of bumping into Heng Lai Soh.

A meeting did not take long. As I walked in one day with Siew Lan, my friend nudged my elbow. With a flick of eye and head, she indicated where I should look. In a corner, bowed before the image of Buddha, stood a slim woman who couldn't have been more than thirty, dressed in an ultra-modern white kebaya with intricate lace on its hem and sleeves. The sarong she wore caught my eye too, with its diagonal slivers of green and yellow adorned with motifs. In the dim light I made out pink roses and leaves of various sorts, as well as butterflies etched in brown ink.

When the woman raised her head and saw us watching her, she smiled. Without a moment's hesitation Heng Lai Soh walked over to introduce herself. From that simple act, I knew that she, unlike the others, would be here to stay. This impression was confirmed by the way she sized me up through narrowed eyes which curved slightly upwards. She seemed to know exactly who I was. 'I've heard so much about you, Peng Choon Sau. A real pleasure to meet.' The smile she flashed, full of teeth and vermillion lips, was polite enough, if somewhat forced. We bade each other goodbye knowing we would meet again.

Yet when I left the temple I was in no doubt as to what I needed to do. Having seen Heng Lai Soh herself, I concluded that our *kueh* would always be different. Heng Lai Soh was a modern Nyonya, one of those who would take shortcuts because she lacked the patience for true Nyonya cooking. She would always have to sell her *kueh* more cheaply. I kept our prices the same, telling customers that if they wanted to eat the best Nyonya *kueh* in Ipoh, they had to pay. But I also knew that we would need to work harder to keep our customers loyal, and occasionally perhaps even tempt them.

That was when the idea of loyalty chips came to me, chips like those we children had once used for games in Songkhla. Anyone who purchased more than one dollar's worth of *kueh* would get five cents of *kueh* free. To keep count, customers would receive chips: square pieces of rough brown cardboard with the Wong name stamped on them; for every five cents' worth of *kueh*, a customer received one of these cards. Anyone who had collected twenty cards could return the whole set to Li-Fei in exchange for five cents' worth of *kueh* absolutely free.

With this in mind we set to work gathering cartons and boxes from the owners of provision shops in town. At home we cut the surfaces up into squares and stamped them with the Wong family seal, an old Chinese seal Peng Choon had once used; it lay dusty with age, but its character remained intact.

Se-Too-Wat loved the idea of my cards, as did I. Yet all Li-Fei heard at first were grumbles. 'Must buy one dollar, then only get five cents-ah! So little . . .' Yes, those were the rules, Li-Fei told them. They didn't have to play the game of course; no one was forced to collect chips. But not a single person said no – they all took their cards, which was what I had expected. In this way customers who set out to buy only three cents' worth of *kueh* sometimes bought more to add to their collection of cards. The cards gained in popularity after my daughters Hui Ying and Hui Lin painted them with pictures of our *kueh* in lively colours, when even the children of Ipoh began to clamour for them.

36

It took many months for Siew Lan to help me ascertain the truth about my son-in-law. A showdown with the patriarch Yap Meng Seng became unavoidable, but that was a decision I made only after much hand-wringing and soul-searching, when I found myself defending Hui Fang before even Siew Lan, who began doubting my daughter's state of mind.

'You say what?' I shrieked. 'You think she mad-ah?'

'No, no, of course not,' Siew Lan replied hurriedly. 'But a woman after have child is different. You know what like-lah, Chye Hoon . . .' My friend's voice trailed off into the distance.

To placate me, she told me that after Flora's birth she had imagined Se-Too-Wat guilty of all kinds of misdemeanours. 'Hui Fang maybe . . . not normal yet,' my friend added a touch defensively.

Seeing that I was unmoved, Siew Lan again offered to speak to her husband, as she had at the outset, but she added a condition: I had to give my consent. Warily I agreed. Once apprised of the situation, Se-Too-Wat surprised me. He made discreet enquiries so quickly that within days we had an answer. When it was clear that Wai Man's job hardly required him to travel, Siew Lan proposed a move I never would have thought of: 'We hire someone to follow the boy.'

'You mean . . . a spy?' I said, taken aback.

'Yes!' my friend replied coolly, as if this were the most normal thing in the world. She reminded me how we had had her servant Rokiah follow the coolie Ah Boey when we first became suspicious of his meagre *kueh* earnings.

'But that is different!' I exclaimed. Wai Man was a member of my family. How could I ask anyone to spy on him?

I eventually relented, because I could think of no other way to learn what we needed to know. Finding a spy proved worryingly easy. With so many coolies out of work, there were men on every five-foot way looking to earn a few dollars. The challenge was identifying someone we could trust. In the end Siew Lan chose a man with whom she had had some dealings. She warned me that she couldn't vouch for him, but he looked the best out of a sorry lot. He called himself Ah Long and was as scrawny as his fellow street dwellers, yet Ah Long had retained some of that dignity which distinguishes us from animals. He tried to keep himself clean – to the extent that was possible for someone living on a concrete walkway. In the absence of a toothbrush, he picked his teeth ardently, and he patched the holes on his one singlet and trousers. Despite having come upon hard times, Ah Long wasn't afraid to look us in the eye. I liked what I saw there: eyes small but alert, dimmed neither by opium nor the hundred guilty acts we were yet to uncover.

Nonetheless we took precautions. We gave Ah Long a new suit and bought him a single ticket on the omnibus which ferried passengers from Ipoh to Taiping twice a day. Siew Lan was able to remember enough from her Taiping days to provide exact directions to my daughter's house and my son-in-law's workplace. She arranged a room for Ah Long by telephone so that all we gave him as a cash advance was two dollars, enough for a week's meals and small contingencies. He had strict instructions to find out where my son-in-law went every day. Only when he had answers was he to make a reverse-charge call to Siew Lan by telephone, at which point she, who knew Taiping well, would descend to verify his discovery. If he completed his task, he would be paid ten dollars, but if he lied, Ah Long would get nothing more and would have to find his own way back to Ipoh.

Though the plan sounded easy, a problem soon arose. After three days Wai Man disappeared from Taiping, and the coolie had no means of following him. Until then my son-in-law had evidently led a chaste life, going to the bank every morning and returning each evening as one would expect. On the morning when he drove out of Taiping, Ah Long noticed his direction of travel and told Siew Lan that the boy had headed towards Ipoh. I was incredulous. 'Really-ah?' I asked Siew Lan.

'Just mean he went south, Chye Hoon,' my friend replied. 'We not know he drove where exactly.'

Ah Long's version of events confirmed my daughter's story, but it also put our plan in disarray. I berated myself for not having foreseen this. Hui Fang had told us her husband often went out of Taiping, yet we had failed to account for something so simple. Into this tangled web Siew Lan's white husband gallantly stepped, inadvertently becoming the central player in our plot. Perhaps more than anything else it was this which elevated him in my mind. I was forced to look at him afresh and saw for the first time not only spidery hairs and cheeks still pink from wear, but also the kindness in his sharp green eyes. Where before Se-Too-Wat remained a white devil I had to put up with because he happened to be Siew Lan's husband, after our Taiping escapade he became a true family friend.

It fell on Se-Too-Wat to drive the thirty miles in a hired car, so as not to be recognised. Once there he paid Ah Long before patiently tailing my son-in-law around the small town. It must have been tedious as well as uncomfortable, for the weather was hotter than usual, and Se-Too-Wat had never fully adjusted despite years in the tropics.

Occasionally even indoors the forest of hairs on his arms made him pour with sweat. On his return, a noticeably browner Se-Too-Wat reported that Wai Man had travelled to a bungalow in Kuala Kangsar, a village halfway between Ipoh and Taiping, where the bank had a small representative office. As soon as my son-in-law's transactions were complete, he shot off to a single-storey wooden house of the type built for government workers, set within a large compound, where my son-in-law apparently spent the night. Se-Too-Wat could see that this was no guest house. He surmised that Wai Man was visiting a lady, but it was not until two days later, after my son-in-law had departed, that he finally had a good look at the female in question. Sophisticated-looking, he told us, clearly Chinese, wearing Western dress and with a good figure.

When I heard this, I felt sick in my stomach. I wanted to walk home, but Siew Lan insisted that her husband drive me. 'You very pale, Chye Hoon,' she said. Though none of us mentioned it, our minds were on Yap Meng Seng, for we knew then that a meeting was inevitable.

I set off to see the old man several days later. I shall never forget his reaction . . . the confidence oozing out and his smugness. 'My boy wouldn't do that,' he proclaimed, haughty eyebrow unmoved. I screamed, gesticulating wildly in the hope of shaking the man, until we ended up almost tearing at each other's throats like angry chickens. I was so furious that I boiled over, tempted even to snatch the oval reading glasses from the bridge of Meng Seng's bony nose. It took all my restraint to contain myself. I could not see how I would make this arrogant man acknowledge that I was neither mad nor stupid.

'You no believe me, you ask Se-Too-Wat-lah,' I finally cried out in exasperation.

The patriarch turned pale. 'What does he have to do with this?' he asked as he removed his glasses.

'You call him-lah . . . Go on. Then you see-lah your precious son is how good.'

As I turned to leave, I made sure my words rang down his driveway. 'Call Se-Too-Wat, then come see me. You like or you no like, also we have to talk.'

The next week brought an unexpected visitor to our house: Liew Tsin-sang, who arrived alone bearing a basket of fruit. When I saw how nervous the young man was, I guessed the reason for his mission.

He sat down awkwardly, cleared his throat and spluttered. Finally, after rubbing his hands together, he told me in a shaky voice that he wanted permission to take Hui Ying out to a film that Saturday afternoon. Swallowing hard, he continued, 'Peng Choon Sau, I hope very much that you will agree.'

I smiled at the earnest young man before me. 'Hmm,' I began, at which point Liew Tsin-sang's dark face turned pale. He looked at the floor as if the earth had just trembled. 'Tell me, you and my daughter, your intentions are what?'

The boy cleared his throat once more. 'Hmm, I . . . I . . . like your second daughter a lot,' he stammered. 'I think I would like to marry her.'

'You only think?' I asked in as gentle a voice as I could.

'No, no . . . I . . . I didn't mean it like that,' he mumbled. 'I would like to marry her,' he said in a louder voice.

'Hui Ying, her feelings, you know or not know?'

Liew Tsin-sang shifted uncomfortably in his chair. 'I believe I have reason to hope. But I don't know for sure, Peng Choon Sau.' I watched the lump in the young man's throat bob in and out as he swallowed. He fidgeted with his hands. 'I wanted to ask her out before, but I was afraid . . . in case she said no. You see' – and here Liew Tsin-sang spoke in a softly confiding tone – 'I . . . I . . . like her . . . very much, you see.'

I tried to imagine this flustered young man as he went about his daily business in the courthouse. Could I see him with my daughter? Yes, but such a grave decision could no longer solely be mine. In our new world my second daughter, Hui Ying, would have to make up her own mind.

◆ ◆ ◆

When Yap Meng Seng finally came to see me, the contrite look on his face told me he had found out about his son's mistress. Taking laboured breaths, the old man sipped the tea Ah Hong handed him.

'Not much I can do, Chye Hoon,' he muttered.

'He is your son.'

'But he's grown up already. He earns his own living now. He won't listen to me-lah.'

'So what, you not even try-ah?'

Meng Seng looked away in embarrassment. Huffing, he puffed air loudly out of his nostrils so that a noise escaped from the top of his throat, a low wheeze which broke our tense silence. The next minute the patriarch's right leg began to shake violently up and down, jerking continuously with such force that his whole body rocked. I watched in amazement. From my silence it was clear I expected an answer.

'I can tell the boy what I think,' Meng Seng finally said. 'But I can't promise anything will change.' He opened his mouth to say something else but just as quickly closed it again, as though he feared he might provoke me.

Several days later he came to tell me that Wai Man flatly refused to give up his mistress. According to the old man, my son-in-law became angry when confronted. He told his father to mind his own business. It was the first time his son had raised his voice, and Meng Seng shook at the recollection – 'I've never known Wai Man in this mood, like a man possessed.'

I covered my mouth with one hand. Without thinking, I turned towards the patriarch and told him simply of my wish to see my daughter. The old man understood, even suggesting that he bring her to Ipoh himself, together with my grandson.

It was while Hui Fang and Choong Meng were staying with us that my second daughter, Hui Ying, asked for my permission to become engaged to Liew Chin Tong.

The request was not unexpected. I had watched Hui Ying blossom in the previous months. 'My girl,' I said, brushing her left cheek with my right hand, 'I hope you with him happy.'

I apologised that I would not be able to give her a grand wedding, but Hui Ying brushed this off without a second's thought – 'It doesn't matter, Mama.' Then, in a tone far more mature than her twenty years would have indicated, she added, 'What's important is that we love each other.'

The sight of Hui Ying in the Malayan sunlight that day remains one of my clearest memories: her almost translucent skin shimmering, beautiful doubly creased eyes sparkling with joy. I marvelled at how different it was for these young people. Why, they even talked of love! When Peng Choon and I were getting married, love could not have been further from our minds. And yet he and I had built a solid relationship, which turned into . . . what? Gratitude? Loyalty? Love perhaps? I wasn't sure. I knew only that eleven years later I continued to be distraught at his having passed away early.

In those days I stood constantly before our altar table, watching the coils of smoke as they rose towards the ceiling, where they were absorbed into the darkening cracks. In anguish I presented myself before Kuan Yin and our ancestors. A mere three years had passed since Hui Fang's wedding, yet time had wrought such irrevocable changes in our lives that even the Goddess of Mercy had trouble responding. With my youngest son dead, my eldest son thousands of miles away and my oldest Nyonya friend starting to wear Western dress, we were in the grip of a relentless march. The tide was taking us I knew not where, but it was so powerful that I felt moved by its force, for there was no question of my not allowing Hui Ying to choose her own husband.

This decision was reinforced by a conversation I overheard one afternoon just outside Hui Fang's bedroom, where I caught muffled sobbing and the sound of my eldest daughter's voice. 'You marry for love,' she cried out to another person, who I guessed was her second sister, Hui Ying. 'I marry for Mama. Now look at us . . .'

'Big Sister, don't cry,' came Hui Ying's reply. 'Mama would welcome you home, you know that.'

There followed minutes of silence before I heard my eldest girl again. 'I how can leave my husband, Hui Ying? I have to think of my son. Besides, where to find man now? Man also no want me.'

About that Hui Fang was right. Sadly some things remained the same. The patriarch had asked for my eldest daughter to return to her marital house and her unfaithful husband; 'Otherwise people will talk,' he said, adding that he would personally see to it that my daughter and grandson were well provided for. When my son-in-law eventually turned up at our house, he was wholly unrepentant. He strode in, announcing that he was taking his wife and son home. 'A wife belongs with her husband,' he said in a loud voice.

His cavalier attitude bothered me. I asked as casually as I could, 'Husband cheating on her okay-ah?'

'Mama,' Wai Man replied stonily, glaring at me, 'that is a matter between husband and wife.'

I saw my son-in-law in a different light that day and wondered why I had never before noticed the swagger, the way he threw his voice when he spoke. He was no longer the boy my daughter had married but a big fish in a small pond. Unfortunately my Hui Fang proved no match. When ordered to pack her bags, she went willingly. I reminded my daughter that she could remain in Ipoh; there was space for her in the *kueh* business. But I left the final decision to her. Within minutes both my daughter and grandson had been bundled out of our house.

37

Hui Ying's wedding to Liew Chin Tong took place on the second day of the second moon in 1923, the year of the Water Pig. It was a simple affair, presided over by Yong Soon Soh and attended by family and close friends, a mere dozen or so guests.

Yong Soon Soh was delighted to be called on. 'Few people want Nyonya weddings now,' the mistress of ceremonies confided sadly. She had added years to her age and as many inches to her waist but was no less lively. She continued to make a noise wherever she went, wobbling with terrifying energy as she rattled the bracelets on her wrists and ankles. My eyes were drawn to the bursting folds beneath her kebayas. I marvelled at the woman's tenacity, convinced that the brooches which held her blouse together would one day fail. I wondered what Yong Soon Soh would do then. In my fantasies she simply waddled into the distance while daring others to stare.

Once we began discussing the ceremony itself, it was clear the mistress of ceremonies had changed. Where before she would have argued over the slightest detail, now she kept nodding in agreement, signing off on ritual simplification with a minimum of fuss. Over tea one afternoon I probed her. She sipped delicately from her cup – the only thing I ever saw Yong Soon Soh doing delicately – before replying with a hint of dolefulness in her voice.

'Times already different, Peng Choon Sau. We too have to change or else . . . one day maybe . . .'

Looking across at one another, our eyes met.

'. . . no more Nyonya,' the mistress of ceremonies whispered. Hope and fear shivered across the space between us. Anxiety hung in the air for a fleeting moment, and then life carried on as before.

Except that in my case it didn't, because in those few short weeks I made a discovery which shook me.

This came about innocently when I began making enquiries about the Liew family. To my utter surprise I unearthed information not only about Liew Chin Tong and his sister, but also about another family whose secret had lain buried for years – in Gopeng of all places, a one-street settlement about twelve miles south of Ipoh. The Liew family didn't even live in Gopeng; their wooden house, which Liew Chin Tong described as a hut, was situated on the jungle outskirts.

Liew Chin Tong and his sister grew up with nothing except a table and two chairs between them. Their hut was surrounded by *belukar* and banana trees. Besides a handful of chickens, they had only the children of the neighbouring shacks for company. Their parents were labourers: their mother was a washerwoman and offered her services in the houses of the rich every morning, while their father, who served in a coffee shop, worked their small plot in his spare time to make ends meet. Although Chin Tong and his sister never went hungry, there were times when they ate only rice and boiled yam or sweet potatoes. Meat was a treat enjoyed a few times each year when their chickens were fat enough for slaughter.

From early on both children had to work. They tended the vegetables, fetched water, fed the fowl, hoed the soil, removed weeds with a spade and hauled a *changkol*. When not helping with chores, they would huddle beneath a palm tree with the other little ones from neighbouring houses, who gathered to play games and more often than not to listen to Liew Chin Tong's stories. He had that gift even at a young age. Stories would come into his mind and, watching the faces around him, he would raise and lower his voice to hold the children's attention, oblivious to the flies buzzing in the sunlight or the mosquitoes swarming at dusk. Inside their cool, dark hut, Liew Chin Tong clung to his sister in their one bed until the day she bled, at which point he was relegated to the damp floor, with just a thin plank separating him from the stony ground beneath.

Then, in a bizarre twist of fate, their lives changed. One morning their mother had only just returned from her washing rounds when a white man called with an unusual question. Speaking in Cantonese, the man told their mother that a new school had started in Ipoh. It had a hostel, he said, to accommodate children from outstation. Although the school was run by missionaries, there was no need for the children to change their religion. They would be taught in English – for free. Would their mother consent to sending them away to school?

Never having expected to face such a dilemma, the poor woman did not know how to react. She directed the man towards the restaurant where their father worked, saying that he too would have to give his permission. Both parents wanted to send only Chin Tong, but the boy, having lived through the trauma of losing his siblings at birth, refused to leave home without his elder sister. Brother and sister arrived together in Ipoh, never to look back.

Once Chin Tong and his sister gained employment, they started providing for their parents. Chin Tong told me they gave the old folks twenty dollars a month each from their salaries, more during the New Year festivities, so that their parents could live comfortably without having to work. But as with many of my generation, the ethic of work was too ingrained. Chin Tong's parents were unable to just sit and shake their legs. They continued to tend their plot even when they were already hobbling on sticks.

When I told Chin Tong that I looked forward to meeting his parents, the young man gave me a sheepish look. The elderly couple were not planning to attend his wedding apparently. 'Good heart-lah!' I exclaimed. 'They of course must come! You marry, they no come, how can?'

'They're stubborn, Peng Choon Sau,' Chin Tong replied. 'My parents have their own ideas . . . hard to change them.'

When it was clear that an independent emissary would be needed, Siew Lan rose to the occasion, volunteering to make the trip to Gopeng with her husband. She said he went from time to time to visit a plantation in which he had a small interest. While Se-Too-Wat set about his business, it would be no problem for her to drop in at the Liew household.

A week later Siew Lan appeared at our house in a curious mood. She seemed wary, her mournful eyes flustered, as if she was impatient to spill a weighty load, yet at the same time she appeared indecisive. She spread chalky white lime across a choice betel leaf in long, deliberate strokes. Then without warning she began.

'They ask many questions, especially the mother.'

The mother had wanted to know about Nyonya traditions, with which she wasn't familiar, and Hui Ying's brothers and sisters. On hearing that the eldest girl was married to a Yap boy, the eldest son of Yap Meng Seng, the old lady had smiled in such recognition that Siew Lan wondered whether she had ever met the patriarch. 'Oh no,' Liew Chin Tong's mother replied, shaking her head. 'Him, no. But I before for his concubine work. In Gopeng here-lah.'

At that point it was Siew Lan's turn to have her interest piqued. She quizzed the couple. The wife talked while her husband made tiny gestures to discourage his wife from saying too much. He kept emphasising that it had all happened a long time ago and in any case wasn't their business. The concubine herself wasn't from Gopeng: she was a sing-song girl Meng Seng had met in Ipoh. He had simply installed her in Gopeng out of convenience, the old woman said, away from prying eyes. Siew Lan assured me she hadn't known this aspect of the Yap family story, although she added, 'My husband knew.' Siew Lan said this in an even tone, but I caught the flash in her brown eyes. 'We had argument all the way home . . . big fight,' she enunciated. 'I very angry, but Se-Too-Wat, he say Hui Fang not with father marry, with son marry.'

When Siew Lan finished, I blew air out from between my lips. My friend had to curb the desire I had of rushing over to Yap Meng Seng's. I wanted the satisfaction of shouting at him, until she pointed out that shouting would be of little use. Once Siew Lan succeeded in curing my instinct, an ache erupted inside my head and I had to lie down.

The news convulsed more than just my wedding preparations, for I started wondering whether every one of the men we knew kept mistresses and concubines.

Perhaps even my husband had had a mistress tucked away in some remote village somewhere and I had never known. I discarded this idea as unlikely, because if it had been true, someone would surely have come forward after his passing away to claim an inheritance.

As for the others, the men like Se-Too-Wat who purportedly did not keep mistresses, I began to doubt them too, especially their loyalties. They seemed to show greater fidelity to their male friends than to their wives. I considered myself wise, yet it had never once occurred to me that a man as stalwart as Yap Meng Seng could have cheated on his wife. If he could, then any man could. For the first time I was thankful that my second and third daughters had attended school and would have the means of earning for themselves should the need ever arise. It was too late for poor Hui Fang, but I insisted that her second sister, Hui Ying, continue with school even after marriage. By the time she left, she had had the equivalent of seven years of education and could have become a teacher.

◆ ◆ ◆

Shortly after Hui Ying's wedding, Ah Hong ran into our house shriek-ing at the top of her lungs. 'We-ng Foo . . . We-ng Foo . . . outside . . .' With eyes wide open in terror, my faithful servant dragged me by the arm. 'Is him, Peng Choon Sau . . . I know is him,' she kept murmuring.

The commotion attracted the attention of my living children, who trooped out with me towards the five-foot way at the front. The noise we made must have scared off my late son's spirit, because by the time we arrived he had disappeared, and there was nothing in his place except thin air.

It took a while for us to calm Ah Hong down. When I saw how she continued to shake, I made her sit at the kitchen table, but even tea did not soothe her nerves. Every few seconds her eyes would dart around the room, on guard against apparitions and heaven only knows what else. The fading light of dusk did us no favours, because shadows began creeping into the normally bright air well. With a faraway look, Ah Hong told us what she had seen. 'He was there, standing, the wall there. He wear black, all also black.'

I did not know what to make of this sighting. Weng Foo's spirit had evidently succeeded in returning to us, but I could not see what he was hoping to achieve, standing alone on the five-foot way with his back against the wall. 'You hear he say anything-moh?' I asked Ah Hong. My voice must have contained a hint of doubt, because for once the faithful servant looked at me with petulance.

'He call-ah. Hong Ee, like he always call-lah,' she said adamantly. 'Is his voice I sure.' It became clear Ah Hong would tolerate no doubts over what she had seen. She even had a ready explanation when I pointed out that my son had lain in his coffin in a white shirt and white trousers. 'He of course change clothes already-lah.'

Afterwards both she and Li-Fei refused to sweep the five-foot way unaccompanied. They would tiptoe out together just after lunch when it was still light, one carrying a broom and dustpan, the other holding a wind chime in her hand, as if by augmenting the clanging of the chime already suspended above our front doorway they would be more certain of chasing away any evil spirit. 'Ai-yahh! He not evil spirit – is Weng Foo-ah!' I cried out.

To no avail. The girls insisted on an extra wind chime for protection. 'We scared ghosts, Peng Choon Sau,' they explained. 'Not the boy himself.'

When after several weeks nothing more was seen, the incident subsided from everyone's minds and household activities returned to normal.

At the time life was going well. My heart was gladdened by many things – the *kueh* business for one. With the aid of our brown loyalty cards, our sales held up well against Heng Lai Soh, formidable competitor though she was. Between us, she and I split the market for Nyonya *kueh* in Ipoh, always surviving the worst that life could throw at us.

We were helped by the audacity of the towkays, whose construction projects continued irrespective of external conditions. Further down the Lahat Road a large number of shophouses suddenly appeared, providing a new community of hungry customers within Li-Fei's easy reach. Not only that but New Town, once regarded as a foolhardy plan that would fail, never ceased expanding. The boundary of Ipoh was by then so far beyond its original limits near the Kinta River that the town was beginning to impinge on Wong family land – the six plots my husband had had the foresight to acquire before leaving for China. This meant that our land had appreciated significantly in value. I did not know how much we had made, but I felt a warm tingle whenever I thought about our land, knowing that I could always sell a plot at a tidy profit if we ever needed the cash.

I was also pleased that my eldest son had settled well in London. For the first time Weng Yu wrote about his classmates. We heard about the tall boy in well-cut suits who had become Weng Yu's friend after my son's fine performance in the examinations; also about the plump curly-haired boy so brutally teased by his own kind that he preferred to sit with the Malayans. Then there were the eccentric boys who practically lived at college, building the latest toys to grip Britain, and many others, all with unpronounceable names, whose brown hair and large noses blended in my mind. Weng Yu told us how the boys' attitudes changed after he outshone them in examinations. Where once they had wondered if people in Malaya lived in trees like savages, now they came up to my son for help with assignments. They even asked about his home town, their questions showing genuine curiosity instead of derision. Finally I could feel Weng Yu open up, and his affection for us came through in his letters.

These communications entertained me in unexpected ways. I laughed when my son told us about a large park in London where he often went walking. He had not been fond of exercise, and I was unable to imagine Weng Yu striding amongst the trees. Hui Ying pointed out that the weather in England was different. Perhaps the cooler climate suited Weng Yu better, as he had never liked the sun. I remained sceptical, convinced there was more to the park than met the eye. I asked many questions, yet all I was told was that it was a magnificent place, with areas that included a lake, a trail for horses, even a corner where anyone could get up on a crate to start talking about absolutely anything they wished. 'Why do like that?' I enquired. To make their opinions known, I was told. When I wondered whether any of the speakers ever talked about the opium problem in Malaya, Liew Chin Tong laughed. 'I don't think they would have heard of Malaya, Mama,' he said.

It was Hui Ying who first read Weng Yu's letters aloud. Later on, one of the boys took her place. Regardless of who the reader was, I was left with the odd feeling of something being concealed from me. I heard all about Weng Yu's visits to museums, sometimes even about his concert outings, but never that he had a companion – a woman with a mop of curls on her head and eyes as blue as the sea.

38

After ten months of marriage Hui Ying finally fell pregnant. I was delighted; her good news put the incident of Weng Foo's apparition firmly into the recesses of my mind. I became engrossed in the process of welcoming another grandchild.

With Hui Ying and her husband living with us, *chin-chuoh* style, I thought it wise to ascertain whether they were intending to have the baby in our house. Liew Chin Tong was reluctant, but Hui Ying, who shared my opinion on this matter, prevailed.

Thus it was that I set off to Kampong Laxamana to locate my old *bidan* Soraiya's daughter. I had no trouble finding the house or recognising the girl, who welcomed me with a warm smile. 'Of course I remember you, Makche Wong,' Siti Aishah said in Malay. 'I will come for your daughter.'

Having settled the difficult matter of the *bidan*, all that was left was for me to pamper my daughter endlessly. I made the right dishes for her and sat back in satisfaction as her girth expanded. And how Hui Ying grew! By the time Siew Lan left for Europe with Se-Too-Wat and Flora on their long-awaited trip, my daughter's belly was so large that she found it hard to walk. 'Wahh!' Siew Lan exclaimed. 'Big! Must be boy.' I beamed, even though I would have been happy with either a boy or a girl.

As the months progressed, Liew Chin Tong became increasingly anxious. Just after Siew Lan and Se-Too-Wat's departure, when Hui Ying was nearly in her sixth month, he began dashing home during his lunch hour to check on his wife. We would hear the front door open, followed by the distinctive sound of Chin Tong's footsteps – like a herd of elephants, according to Li-Fei – as he trundled into the inner hall, where my daughter usually rested. In the evenings, when he returned the first thing he did was to rush towards my daughter, laying both his hands on her round hardness to reassure himself that his child was safe and well, even though he had no idea what he should be feeling for. One evening I saw, etched all over Liew Chin Tong's face, the terror of past traumas and how the memory of his lost siblings continued to haunt him. My heart went out to the young man. When he glanced up and saw me looking at him, his narrow eyes acknowledged my sympathy. We sealed our unbreakable bond with a smile.

For my part I remained perfectly relaxed. Having seen ten children safely into this world, I was imperturbable when it came to all things related to women and childbirth. I felt some concern only during Hui Ying's seventh month, when I noticed a grimace on her face, as if she was in pain. 'It's uncomfortable moving, Mama,' she told me, indicating the difficulty she was having simply shifting in her chair. Registering her complaint, I spent more time in front of the altar over the next several days chanting to Kuan Yin. Still, as all appeared well, I wasn't unduly worried.

Shortly thereafter Siti Aishah, Soraiya's daughter – the woman I had wanted to be Hui Ying's *bidan* – knocked on our front door. 'I must ask forgiveness, Makche Wong,' she said in embarrassment. 'I've been called to my grandmother's kampong, so I can't attend to your daughter. Ask forgiveness-lah.' She gave me a minute to absorb this devastating news. 'But I brought Noridah with me,' she continued, pointing to a woman behind her. 'She has been a *bidan* for twenty years. All the children in Kampong Laxamana she and I together have delivered.'

I looked first at Siti Aishah, then at Noridah, then back again at my old *bidan*'s daughter. My heart shuddered in bewilderment. The thought *This no good* crossed my mind, but I cast it aside. Although Noridah's face was seasoned with maturity, I didn't like the idea of a stranger delivering my grandchild. And yet my first *bidan* herself had once been unknown. Until Hui Fang's birth I could not have picked her out from any other *bidan* in Ipoh. I took another look at Noridah and made my decision while standing on our doorstep. In truth I had little choice, for even if I were to wander into another kampong, I would still have known no one, which meant that a stranger would deliver my grandchild. Noridah at least came with a recommendation from someone I trusted.

After the women had had coffee and *ondeh-ondeh*, Noridah examined Hui Ying. She patted my daughter expertly enough, placing her hands on strategic spots, not just on her belly, but also on her pelvic region and hips. I watched as she asked my daughter to breathe in and out. Before they left, Noridah took me to one side. 'Makche,' she whispered, 'I not know yet, but . . . feels like this birth will be difficult.'

'Why?'

'The baby is not in good position.'

The foreboding I had felt at the start of the women's visit gripped me once more, and when she saw my fear, a shadow passed across Noridah's aged yet still beautiful eyes. As the *bidan* regained her composure, she sought to reassure me. 'We will know nearer the time only, Makche.' Then, putting her hand on mine in a gesture of farewell, she told me she would do her best. She promised to arrive at our house a full week before the baby was due so that we could prepare for any complications.

Despite Noridah's reassurances, I became a slave once more to a dream I had not had since Peng Choon passed away. It would begin gently enough, in a pitch-black tunnel through which I glided. I would become aware of a menacing presence, a thing with no face which made me want to escape. I would try to get away, but it was too dark to see and the presence invariably engulfed me as I fell further and further . . . Even deep in sleep I wondered what the gods were doing. Before the answer could come I would wake, drenched in sweat.

Until that morning I don't believe I ever screamed out. I still don't know whether I did scream or the sounds from my daughter's room awakened me. Not that it mattered, because once my eyes were open and I heard loud moans, I imagined the worst. I leapt out of bed and banged on my daughter's bedroom door. Ah Hong came running up the stairs. 'Good-mah?' we both demanded as soon as Chin Tong stuck his head out. 'Good, good, Mama,' my son-in-law said in a shaky voice. From the glow of the kerosene lamp which Ah Hong carried in one hand, I could see the muscles on Chin Tong's face stretched taut with anxiety. 'Ahem . . . ,' he said, swallowing hard. 'Hui Ying is having trouble . . . ahem . . . finding a comfortable position.'

Through the open door I could see my daughter on her back. Her face appeared puffed with perspiration. It was undoubtedly hot beneath the white mosquito netting, and with her extra weight – for Hui Ying was like a bouncy tyre by then – I wasn't surprised she found it uncomfortable. When I went in briefly, I found my daughter labouring for breath but otherwise content.

The sight of my bedraggled son-in-law haunted me, and I wondered whether to give in to Chin Tong's preference for a hospital. But then I comforted myself with the knowledge that we women had brought countless generations into this world. The methods we used had been tried and tested over hundreds – no, thousands – of years. I would have to trust in them and in the gods, in Kuan Yin.

◆ ◆ ◆

I knew it was Weng Foo as soon as I saw him. He stood inside our kitchen near the terracotta pot we used for storing water from the well. It was still light. I saw him clearly, leaning against a wall in a corner of the open air well. He was dressed in black from head to toe, just as Ah Hong had described.

As we locked eyes, I was sure that the spirit shook his head and scowled. I blinked hard to convince myself that I wasn't imagining things. When I opened my eyes again, he was gone . . . and all that was left was coldness on my skin. I blinked a second time, willing the apparition to come back, but nothing changed; the air well remained bare except for our yellowish-brown pot with its glazed green pattern of a tree. Goose pimples broke out on my arms. I longed to speak to someone and wished with all my heart that Siew Lan were around.

Shaken yet unable to open my heart to anyone else, I went in search of oranges for our altar table. On returning, I stood before the altar as I had so many times in the past, holding lit joss-sticks in my hands and watching the tendrils of dense smoke curl upwards. From fiery ends the choking clouds emerged, before dissipating into the atmosphere to placate the Goddess and our ancestors.

Meanwhile Hui Ying entered the last stages of her pregnancy. By then she had become enormous. She was so large she even had trouble standing up and could barely move about. Her husband would not let her lift a finger; whenever he was at home, he insisted on helping her up and down the stairs. While he was at work, one of the servants was always on hand to see to my daughter. I of course did whatever I could. We helped with everything, including accompanying Hui Ying to the latrine, a room at the back of our house where the convenience stood. This was truly a throne, with a circular hole which dropped straight down into a large bucket that was emptied daily by a Chinese man. To reach the hole you had to go up three steps to a place one of my boys had jokingly called the high heavens. In those last days the high heavens proved too steep for my daughter; she had to be lifted for her daily toils.

On the day that Noridah first returned, the skies were overcast.

The *bidan* spent fifteen minutes in our inner hall examining Hui Ying with her hands. I watched as Noridah's fingers touched every inch of my daughter's rounded belly, pausing long and often at various spots, especially in the crevice where my daughter's pelvic region began. Laying her hands still, Noridah concentrated on feeling the life inside my daughter, and the muscles on her face tightened. I studied the *bidan* anxiously, but Noridah gave nothing away. After she completed her explorations, Noridah took a bottle out of her bag and announced that she was taking my daughter upstairs for a massage. When the pair emerged, Hui Ying looked like a new person, with cheeks glowing and her breathing considerably lighter. She smelt of kaffir lime and lemongrass, a result of the herbal oil Noridah used that had evidently given my daughter such relief.

When I accompanied Noridah to the door, I asked whether anything had changed. The *bidan* pursed her lips, put both her hands in mine and whispered that the baby was still turning. She would only be able to tell later on in the week.

As promised, Noridah came every day after that. She repeated the same procedure at each visit: a thorough examination followed by an hour's massage. It was only after her fourth visit that the *bidan* took me aside. 'The baby still not in right position . . . head and legs are a problem,' Noridah said in a low voice. When she heard my intake of breath, the *bidan* touched my hand. 'Don't worry, Makche. Your daughter is strong. And I also will do my best to help her.'

The *bidan*'s attempts at optimism did little to calm me. My daughter's discomfort grew, but I did not know what else to do. On the sixth day Hui Ying's pain was so intense that Noridah stayed by her side the whole day. Around five in the afternoon the contractions began, and it was clear that a long night lay ahead. Noridah would have to stay. I sent Li-Fei on her bicycle to Kampong Laxamana to fetch the *bidan* a change of clothing.

The next hours proved as excruciating as Noridah had anticipated. Unable to leave my daughter, I remained beside Chin Tong and the *bidan* the entire time. Hui Ying's groans became louder through the night. By five in the morning, when Chin Tong was asked to leave the room, my heart was in my mouth. Because of her heaviness, Hui Ying lay on her back, and I could see Noridah having trouble coaxing the baby out. It seemed to me that there was something in the way blocking the little one's passage into this world. I wondered whether it would help to have my daughter standing, but the *bidan* shook her head, continuing instead to exert pressure on Hui Ying's belly. When the pain became too much, Hui Ying started to scream. Her shrieks were unbearable. I had to cover my ears many times.

Noridah used her hands to urge the baby out, all the while encouraging my daughter to push. Finally, after screams which raised the hairs on my arms, Hui Ying managed to expel the baby's legs. At the very same moment blood began oozing out of my daughter's wound, and my heart jerked. I put both hands over my mouth as the colour drained from Hui Ying's face. She turned pale. Droplets of sweat were visible on her forehead. Noridah whispered words of sweetness into her ears, telling her how well she was doing and that it would soon be over. Soaking a piece of cotton wool with the herbal oil she had brought, the *bidan* tried to staunch Hui Ying's bleeding.

But the baby's head appeared stuck, which meant a last effort would be needed. Noridah worked quietly to spur Hui Ying on. '*Sayang,*' she said in a gentle voice, 'one last push.' When my daughter replied that she had no strength left, Noridah calmly dabbed her wet forehead with a cloth. 'Your baby's legs are out . . . just one more push . . . then you can rest.'

With heroic force, Hui Ying pushed, at the same time letting out a scream that reverberated across the neighbourhood. It made her husband rush in, just in time to see a stream of blood gush out of his wife. I did not look at my son-in-law till minutes later, after I had taken my dead grandchild – a poor baby girl – from the *bidan*. Noridah meanwhile was frantically trying to soak another piece of cotton wool in herbal oil, because the swab she held in her hand was already drenched in my daughter's blood. When I saw how quickly the blood flowed, red and thick, with no sign that anything we did had an effect, I realised we had to act quickly.

I turned towards my son-in-law. 'Please,' I begged, my voice nearly breaking. 'Please fetch a doctor.' Chin Tong's face was drained of colour, but he understood at once. Releasing his wife's hand, he ran out of the room. Later Chin Tong told me he continued running all the way into Old Town, where he was able to hail one of the rickshaw pullers who had started work early. It took them half an hour to reach Dr Khong's house and another fifteen minutes for the two to return in the doctor's car. By then Hui Ying was barely conscious. We had used up all the cotton wool in our house and were doing our best with any piece of clean cloth we could find. I'm far from faint-hearted, but I had seen so much blood pour out of my daughter's body that I was close to collapsing when the two men arrived. Somehow I held on, because I knew Hui Ying's life could depend on it.

When I looked up at Dr Khong, the horror on his face told me my daughter was in grave danger. He took out a syringe from his black bag and injected her with a clear fluid – 'To stop the bleeding,' he explained. Then, twiddling his moustache with his right hand, he muttered a few words to Chin Tong in English before rushing off – to where I have no idea, but my son-in-law explained that we were going to get Hui Ying to a hospital. Not long afterwards an ambulance arrived with sirens shrieking, and two men descended with a canvas bed. Hui Ying was still bleeding, though not as badly. I was beside myself by then, my throat parched and my hands trembling. The men placed my daughter inside the ambulance. Chin Tong and I were allowed to travel with her as we sped to the hospital, which was then located in Old Town, not far from our house. It could not have taken us long, yet those few minutes crouched in the ambulance are the longest in my memory.

When we arrived, it seemed that we were expected. A white man received us, flanked by two nurses, and the trio bundled my daughter off. I followed my son-in-law blindly as he led me down long bare corridors that had a smell which made my stomach churn. We finally reached the room into which they had taken Hui Ying to see if they could repair the tear the baby had made inside her body. My son-in-law told me all this in an even voice without any hint of blame, but I paced up and down the waiting room berating myself. Why had I not listened when the portents of ill luck had lined up one by one before my very eyes? I prayed silently to Kuan Yin, hoping it would not be too late to save my daughter.

Eventually the white man came out, his face the colour of ash. His message made the tears flow down my son-in-law's cheeks, and I understood that my wish would not be granted. Without a word Chin Tong took my hand and pulled me into the emergency room, where we saw Hui Ying on a bed covered in white sheets. My daughter's eyes were fluttering weakly, but from her smile I knew she had seen us. Hui Ying took her final breath as I stroked the hair on her forehead. When she was gone, I walked out into the endless corridor, not knowing where I was going.

39

For weeks afterwards I wandered with my soul detached from my body. A dark hollow formed inside, as if my innards had been scraped clean. I knew I could have prevented my daughter's death; I could have acted the night I heard her screams; even further along the way, I could have fought fate. In the glaring light of hindsight my remorse was terrible.

Overnight I aged. Before losing my daughter, a handful of grey hairs graced my head; afterwards they sprouted from hour to hour, multiplying so quickly that within weeks whole patches of white could be seen. Sitting before the mirror one morning, I was aghast. There on my head sat a white crown, its threads wiry like cotton wool, beneath which a shrivelled bag of bones protruded – the woman I had become, my skin as furrowed as baked earth.

This pathetic sight woke me from my stupor. Shaking my coconut-white mane, I lifted its end deftly with my left hand, coiled it into a bun behind my neck and then fastened it with small black pins, as I had seen Siew Lan do several years back. I stared. The mirror, ever faithful, told me that my new bun was no less pretty than the chignon I had worn every day since the age of twelve, even though the bun wasn't held up by five-pronged pins or garlanded with blossoms. And it had taken only five minutes. I understood then why many Nyonyas had adopted this new form and wondered at my previous obstinacy. When Siew Lan had begun wearing her hair in a simple bun, I had scoffed. 'No work, just easy life. Everything also everyone want make easy. How can be like that?'

The bun on my head brought with it a burning compulsion to change, perhaps to become 'modern', though I had little idea what this meant.

I descended into the kitchen, where the air was thick with the sweet smell of steaming coconut milk. There I found Ah Hong busy supervising Li-Fei and the two hired hands in the making of *kueh*. All were surprised to see me, as I had barely stepped outside my bedroom in weeks. When Ah Hong complimented me on my new hairstyle, I smiled before surveying the room.

In a far corner Li-Fei was pouring finely diced winter melon into a large wok. A mesmerising white cloud rose up, which disintegrated into puffs as it spread its wonderful fragrance of pounded chilli and dried shrimp across the room. Sprawled on the kitchen surfaces were rectangles of cut banana leaves and large pots of glutinous rice, sticky with coconut milk. These and other comforting Nyonya scents dragged me out of my malaise. In that early dawn, when I bit into winter melon, a vegetable fit for emperors, my spirit revived. Once again it was my roots which saved me.

Days later, when the letter arrived from the Kinta Electricity Department, I surprised my children by agreeing to have electrical points fixed up in every room in the house, even the latrine. By the time our house could be lit by the quick flick of a switch, Liew Chin Tong had moved out. I had used every argument I could to persuade him to stay but without success; our house just carried too many memories. Fortunately Chin Tong visited often, knowing there would always be a place in my heart for him.

I felt immensely sorry for my son-in-law. At Hui Ying's funeral he had looked like an expiring animal, with eyes that stared vacantly into the world. For days he could barely get out of bed. I was too distraught to tend to him then; that task fell to my youngest daughter, Hui Lin, and the servants. They did what they could, making sure he had one square meal each day and feeding him plenty of tea.

The jolt of seeing me in a new hairdo must have roused Chin Tong, because he began thereafter to recover noticeably. He hauled himself out of bed the next morning, shaved off the stubble on his chin and announced that he was taking a stroll in the People's Park. When he had regained his colour, he resumed the routine he had once followed. He would wake to watch the sunrise, dash off after a breakfast of steamed dumplings, spend all day inside his airy courthouse and then return in the late afternoon, bursting with stories.

In those weeks the hours of twilight proved our toughest challenge. We would sit comforting one another in the tranquillity of the inner hall, Chin Tong with cup of tea in hand, I with Nyonya *kueh* in mine. As we each tried to conjure up the magic that dusk had previously wrought, we would chatter endlessly, desperate to prevent the silences which sometimes descended. My habit of devouring the Wong family *kueh* started then. Until Hui Ying passed away I had kept my sweet tooth in check, preferring to sell *kueh* for profit; in the months afterwards I succumbed to temptation and indulged heavily. At first I ate only what could not be sold, dousing leftover *apom* in palm sugar sauce or gobbling up the badly cut pieces of tapioca *kueh* I inevitably found on various tables. But I enjoyed them so much that I took to sniffing in our kitchen like a hungry vagrant. I ate *kueh* for breakfast, taking just one or two, then three or four, then more. Slowly but surely I gained weight. My sarongs grew tight, and folds of skin showed beneath my bajus. Though my girth never matched that of the mistress of ceremonies, I was still unhappy with myself. By the end of the year I was thirty pounds heavier, but I found the habit of eating many *kueh* a day impossible to stop.

For as long as he lived in our house, Liew Chin Tong never once missed taking an after-dinner tea with me. One balmy night – a night so hot that even the creatures outside could not settle – Chin Tong cleared his throat just after the croaking of frogs had reached us from the open land behind the Lahat Road.

'Mama,' my son-in-law said, at once looking away. 'Weng Yu . . .'

Nearby a mosquito hovered, oblivious to the concentric dark green coil we burnt to keep them at bay.

'Yes?' I whispered, wondering what would come next.

'Weng Yu . . . ahem . . .' Another clearing of the throat. 'And this . . . this white woman . . . Helen . . .'

At the sound of her name, I recalled the uncanny feelings I'd had whenever Weng Yu's letters were read to me. 'Tell me,' I said, ignoring the itch on my wrist. My son-in-law sat immobile, as if considering a weighty legal judgment.

'I think you must be prepared, Mama,' he finally declared.

Outside the frogs continued to screech; inside the air remained still except for the belches of acrid smoke released by the burning mosquito coil. The look I gave my son-in-law made his horn-rimmed glasses fall halfway down his nose, until he admitted that Weng Yu had made references to Helen in his letters. Chin Tong said it had been Hui Ying's idea to conceal the truth, because my daughter worried that her brother's infatuation would upset me. An angry welt rose on my right wrist. I scratched it vigorously and made a disgruntled noise in my throat, even though I knew my daughter had been right. She and my son-in-law had hoped Weng Yu's enthusiasm for the girl would diminish with time, but that had not happened; if anything, Chin Tong feared that my son's ardour had grown. The inevitable would soon come, and he felt it prudent to tell me. 'You must be prepared, Mama,' he said again.

I went to bed crestfallen, still scratching my wrist. As soon as I awoke the next day, I stood before Kuan Yin and our ancestors. The redness on my wrist had subsided, but I had hardly slept. I placed a handful of oranges into a white porcelain bowl etched with blue butterflies and flowers. On a matching plate I lay three pieces of *kueh kochee*, beautifully wrapped in oiled banana leaves, and set both plate and bowl down on our faithful altar table. Then, lighting three joss-sticks as I had always done, I began to chant.

While I mouthed the sutras, my mind wandered. I thought about the things I had seen in Ipoh during my twenty-five years in the town, how it had mushroomed from a small settlement on one side of the Kinta River to a modern town straddling both banks. There were now many more people, the horse-drawn gharries had been replaced by rickshaws and bicycles, and there were even motor cars.

But not all the changes had been good. Our lives were now permanently invaded. Signs of the white devils were everywhere: in the clothes we wore, the language we spoke, the films we saw, the deference we showed, kowtowing without question. Some Nyonya and Baba families had even forsaken their own ancestors and gods and embraced the god of the white devils, the one they worshipped on Sundays. That was something I could never do. Change I was willing to entertain, wholesale abandonment of everything dear never. It would be like giving up Nyonya *kueh*, the food which had sustained my family through the years. How could I have done that? I couldn't.

With these thoughts swirling in my mind, I remembered the resolution I made on the day I had coiled my hair into a simple bun: to become modern. But what did that really mean?

White streams rose from the joss-sticks in my hands. Higher in the air, where the streams broke into ringlets, I saw the handsome face of my eldest son, with his deep-set eyes and dimpled cheeks. Why had I ever allowed Weng Yu to go to England? It was beginning to seem like a big mistake.

40

As soon as Siew Lan returned to Ipoh from her grand European tour, she sent her servant Rokiah over with a basket of juicy mangoes and a message that she would visit as soon as she had unpacked. I was delighted to have my friend back in town, but so much had happened that I also felt a tinge of trepidation. How could I tell her everything just as she was settling in?

True to her word, Siew Lan swept in soon after, resplendent in an eye-catching red kebaya and a beautiful brown sarong she had bought in Penang. A boisterous welcome greeted her. 'Lan Ee!' the two youngest boys, Weng Onn and Weng Choon, shouted. I was so overcome that I hugged my friend for many minutes and stood breathing in her scent, ignoring Rokiah and the rickshaw driver, who trailed behind with a large number of boxes. With my arms around her body, I could tell that Siew Lan had gained weight too. Her belly pushed against mine and her shoulders felt well padded. She was still beautiful, even with the extra inches and the lines on her forehead, which had spread to both eyes and cheeks. Having been away from the tropical sun, Siew Lan had grown fairer, but her skin was also less taut, as if the years had suddenly caught up with her.

'This is what, my friend?' I asked, pointing to the absurd load her servant had scattered about. There were boxes everywhere: on the table in our inner hall, on chairs and on the floor. When I stepped inside the kitchen, I found boxes there too.

'Oh . . . just small things,' Siew Lan replied with a dismissive wave of her hand. 'Hope you all like.'

She was about to encourage Hui Lin to tear open the ribbons on an exquisite box when my friend gave me a peculiar stare. 'Your hair, Chye Hoon!' she exclaimed. 'Wahh . . . you do modern-ah?' she asked in a teasing tone. Then, looking around, Siew Lan noticed the lights on the ceilings. 'Wahh! Electric lights! I not here that time, so many new things!'

As her eyes continued to scan, I could feel her question coming. Within minutes Siew Lan blurted out 'Ai! Hui Ying-leh? She where?' so cheerfully that it was enough to bring a lump to my throat.

No one said a word. My gaze remained on Siew Lan, who looked carefully back at me. I saw the old sadnesses in her almond-shaped eyes as they measured my fuller hips and waist before studying my face. While waiting for me to speak, Siew Lan did not once take her eyes off me. 'She . . . she pass away, my friend,' I replied, my voice weak as the emotion I thought I had conquered came gushing back.

Siew Lan's look turned to one of mute horror. She understood at once, and a sob escaped into the air. Wailing openly, my friend rocked back and forth in grief. She stayed doubled over for many minutes, her face covered with both hands, as if she was unable to quite believe what she had heard.

When Siew Lan finally raised her head, we wrapped our arms around one another. We were each quiet in our memories, I bitter in my regrets and guilt, Siew Lan sorry she had not been there to bid Hui Ying farewell.

Yet the evening brought cheer too, because of my friend's safe return and the presents she had carried thousands of miles. Siew Lan had forgotten no one. There were neckties and sweaters for the boys, brooches and perfumes for the girls, suede shoes for my sons-in-law, sarongs and a pearl necklace for me, and even condiments for the household. She was exuberant about what she and her daughter had seen in Europe, especially its huge shops – 'Got one shop two storeys just for toys!' Siew Lan exclaimed. 'Got so many things to play, cannot also imagine!'

They had met Weng Yu, of course, who had reportedly lost weight. 'We take him out to eat . . . You must eat, I tell him!' The boy and Se-Too-Wat had apparently spent hours together.

'Do what?' I wondered.

At that point Siew Lan gathered all the fingers of her right hand together into the shape of a beak opening and closing. 'Talk, talk, talk all the time, just talk.' She said the two would sit up late into the night and on weekend afternoons would stroll through parks.

My ears pricked up at this revelation. 'He say anything about his studies-ah?'

No, Siew Lan replied, except that the work was becoming harder. To relax, Weng Yu listened to European music. He had asked to go to two concerts and an opera, a request which delighted Se-Too-Wat. Flora too had enjoyed the performance, which took place inside a very elegant music hall. 'Room so big-ah, Chye Hoon, you need spectacles to see sing-song people.' Gasps echoed around the room. But then Siew Lan confessed that she had found the evening trying – 'So different-lah, not like our opera! And tickets so expensive,' she grumbled.

When my fourth son, Weng Yoon, asked about their sea voyage, Siew Lan would not be drawn. Seasickness, she claimed, had blotted her memories. Cautiously I asked whether she or Se-Too-Wat had met with my son's landlord, and Siew Lan narrowed her eyes into a scrutinising stare. 'No-o-o,' she said, her tone even but with a slight inflection, as if half asking a question. I could tell from her eyes that she had no idea what I meant, so I let the subject drop as elegantly as I could.

Out of the corner of one eye I caught Chin Tong squirming in his chair. 'Oh, silly idea . . . not important-lah,' I said calmly. 'Weng Yu to us a lot tell about his landlord, like good friend, so I think you maybe meet him.'

From the odd look Siew Lan gave me, she understood this was a subject we would revisit in due course.

In those days Yap Meng Seng sometimes turned up at our house. He continued to drive the same ugly green motor car, the one with the lights at the front which stared at us like a frog. Only, with more cars in Ipoh by then, it was of less interest to the boys, and they no longer ran out to greet him.

If he arrived early enough, the patriarch would join us for dinner. More often than not he would come after seven, when we had already finished. He and I would then while the evening away sipping tea in the inner hall, as we once used to. There were subjects we avoided, like Hui Fang and his son. I had also never found an opportunity to let the old man know that his secret had been revealed. Uncertain whether to drop a hint, I asked myself what purpose it would serve and could come up with no good answer. Meng Seng only resumed his visits after Chin Tong had stopped living with us, and I guessed that the old man remained keen to keep aspects of his life quiet.

Nonetheless one night, when he casually mentioned that my daughter and his son appeared to be getting along better, I gently let Meng Seng know that I had learnt the truth. 'Yap Tsin-sang-ah,' I said, deliberately using the polite form of address, 'I want to tell you . . . I all also know. We no need talk-lah – so long ago, now not important. But I know . . . you see . . .'

The old man coloured before swallowing. He struggled for words but just as quickly regained his composure, the way men tend to so that no one else will see their shame. His voice was gruff when he spoke. 'We all do silly things when young, don't we?'

After a suitable pause Meng Seng introduced a subject he knew would catch my imagination – the fact that my son Weng Yu had written to him. I demanded to know what Weng Yu had said. 'Calm down, Chye Hoon,' the patriarch told me when he saw the fluster I was in. 'It was a very ordinary letter – this and that, nothing much. You know Weng Yu. He talked a lot about a famous park he goes to.'

Meng Seng explained that when the boy had enthused at such length about things in London, he had started to worry that Weng Yu was in danger of forgetting his roots. But then the patriarch reminded himself that this wasn't just anyone's son – he was my son, a boy brought up in the strict Nyonya-Baba tradition. He would need to give Weng Yu time. Yet when successive letters had reinforced Meng Seng's concerns, he decided to write. He warned Weng Yu about the foolishness of forgetting his own culture and people. It wasn't a long letter; he sent it two months ago and had not heard back.

For once the patriarch and I were in agreement, and I thanked him. Meng Seng's company was especially welcome at night. After Liew Chin Tong left us, the house had become quieter, because my second and third sons left home just then. My third son, Weng Fatt, went to teach at a school in Tapah, thirty miles south of Ipoh, while my second boy, Weng Koon, travelled even further, to the town of Seremban in the south, which in those years took most of a day to reach.

But a new visitor also appeared in our midst, a young man whose presence I had first noticed at Hui Ying's funeral, when he spent so much time with our family that strangers would have thought him already a member. Not only did the boy attend Hui Ying's wake, but he also walked with us all the way to the caves just outside town for her cremation. Although his face looked familiar, I could not remember where I had seen him previously. He was soft-spoken and unobtrusive, someone you wouldn't pay attention to. It was only when he introduced himself again that I recalled a face from Hui Fang's wedding years before, when he had sat with Mr Ho-Lee and his friends.

Lim Tsin-sang surprised me by turning up again just weeks after Hui Ying's funeral. I wasn't even aware that he knew my youngest daughter, Hui Lin, so when he asked for my permission to take her out on that Saturday, I sat up to scrutinise him. He had evidently come in his best clothes: white short-sleeved shirt, blue tie and khaki trousers, all neatly pressed. He shook his legs nervously until he caught me staring at him, at which point the jerking movement ceased, but the young man's face became as red as *angkoo kueh*.

I left it to Hui Lin to decide whether she wished to accompany Lim Tsin-sang to the cinema, but it was hard to restrain my natural curiosity. I could not help noticing the shade of his skin, dark like Chin Tong's and our Malay brothers', and the pimples scarring his face. Yet it did not surprise me when Hui Lin agreed to go out with him, for Lim Tsin-sang had dark, captivating eyes that were almost half-closed and tingling with liquid softness, like a woman's.

It was raining the day the letter arrived, and it rained every day thereafter for five months.

Liew Chin Tong was at our house that evening, which could have been either coincidence or more likely was a plan devised by my daughter Hui Lin, who on opening the missive had sent word that she needed help. My son-in-law came rushing to the rescue, armed with his horn-rimmed glasses and the voice that could tell a thousand stories. Weng Yu's letter began innocently enough, with greetings and generalities and the like, until a page at which my son-in-law paused. In his low, lulling voice, Chin Tong told me that my eldest son, who at the time was commencing his final year at college, was seeking my permission to become engaged to Helen.

When Chin Tong began extolling the white girl's virtues, I stopped him. 'Enough!' I said roundly.

'But, Mama,' Hui Lin interjected, 'Big Brother is serious about this young lady. Don't you think you should know why?' For once the girl's light-hearted air had deserted her. She stared glumly at the floor, as if at a funeral.

Reluctantly I let Chin Tong continue. I heard how Helen had attended college, how well read she was, that she loved art and music as much as Weng Yu, and that they often went on walks together. At last things fell into place, and I guessed that my eldest son had had a female companion all along to the musical concerts and the walks he took in his wretched park.

To rub salt into my wound, Weng Yu announced that Helen's father had given the couple his blessing. His blessing! I was astonished. What did the man know about us or our country, and what exactly did he think he was blessing? The union between his daughter and a man from one of the inferior races his people had conquered?

I stopped listening. Recalling the story of the warrior Hang Tuah and how he had earned his magical sword, I felt a bitter taste in my mouth. Here was my own son, a boy over whom I had slaved, whom I had even sent abroad, pushing my own retirement into the future, and for what? So that my little prince could marry a white woman when he graduated and live away from his family, roots and country? The muscles of my neck contracted involuntarily. Of all the women in this world, the boy had chosen one to whom I could not say even one word. No, this marriage could never be; eternal bonds would be impossible. Like Hang Tuah, I too would have to sharpen my sword.

When Chin Tong finished and a hush descended, I catapulted into action. Instructing my daughter Hui Lin to pick up paper and pen, I began to dictate. My daughter tried to stop me. 'Don't you want to think about it, Mama?' she asked.

I shook my head. 'I not stupid,' I said, looking Hui Lin in the eye so that she could see how determined I was.

As the younger ones sat quietly, I spoke in a firm voice. I told my eldest son that I had reflected much on the matter and could never accept his marrying a white woman. Marriage meant eternal bonds. Hard as I tried, I failed to see how those could be formed between us and members of a race who considered themselves superior. I wouldn't even be able to talk to Helen, nor she to me. I reminded my son that I had worked day and night to pay for his education in London, expensive by Malayan standards. The whole of our family had made sacrifices for him. We had skimped, buying less when we could. We ate cheaper meals and we had given up visiting the cinema, all so that we could keep him abroad. The last thing I wanted was his unhappiness, but he had presented me with something to which I simply could not agree. However, I was willing to make a promise: if he returned home, I would give him free rein to choose his own wife. There were many talented, kind and beautiful local women in Malaya.

I felt considerably lighter by the time I finished, but I foolishly did not stop to think how my son would react. It never occurred to me that Weng Yu would use Siew Lan's marriage to Se-Too-Wat as the basis of his reasoning, so I didn't bother telling my son about Siew Lan's own reservations or the fears she harboured for her children.

Not that any of this would have made a difference, for Weng Yu was then in the grip of madness. If the money I sent hadn't reached his pockets, I would at least have heard a few words. As it was, Weng Yu never wrote home again. It was enough to break my heart.

41

For the next twelve months we heard nothing from London. We knew my son was working towards his final-year examinations, but we had no idea how his preparations were going.

In the same period my fourth son, Weng Yoon, passed the highest examinations in Perak with surprisingly good results. Like his eldest brother before him, Weng Yoon became one of the top scholars in the state, and an article about his achievements appeared in the local paper. To celebrate, we held a dinner in his honour. A dozen people attended: Siew Lan and Se-Too-Wat of course, as well as the former headmaster Mr Ho-Lee, who had left Ipoh by then but happened to be in town on a short visit. A few teachers were also invited – Lim Tsin-sang for one, although he was hardly a special guest, having been such a frequent visitor to our house. Meng Seng came, as did my daughter Hui Fang, from Taiping, and her errant husband, and of course Chin Tong, together with his sister.

Not having seen Mr Ho-Lee for many years, I found the change in the headmaster's appearance striking. I can only assume that he thought the same about me. His hair and moustache were now as white as the clouds, and there was considerably less of both. The thinning strands allowed pink scalp to peep through when he was seated, and his forehead looked broader because of this raised hairline. The headmaster had lost none of his cheer, though – his booming laughter reverberated around the room as he took turns with Chin Tong to regale us with stories. A tricky moment came when Mr Ho-Lee asked after Weng Yu, as he was of course prone to do. The hush that fell must have told him all was not well, but Mr Ho-Lee had been in our part of the world long enough to understand not to probe further. With a bland smile I told the headmaster that my eldest son was about to take his final examinations. He was extremely busy and wrote less often. Mr Ho-Lee merely nodded and gave us a reassuring glance, as if to say it would all work out in the end, before graciously retreating.

Concerning the saga of my son, I told Siew Lan everything. With her being married to a white man, this was a delicate matter, and I raised it only after my friend was groggy from the effects of betel nut juice. The cud inside her mouth stopped moving at once, causing her left cheek to bulge.

'Your son, he also cannot see!' she mumbled in agitation.

I asked whether Weng Yu had spoken to Se-Too-Wat during their visit to London, to which Siew Lan shook her head vigorously, her eyes round with astonishment. Holding the brass spittoon just below her chin, she expelled a blood red stream in the manner of an expert betel nut chewer. The liquid spurted out with the force of a waterfall to land squarely in the cradle of the spittoon, where it settled. 'Ai-yahh, Chye Hoon! You think I not tell you-ah?'

With anguish on her face, my friend recounted her experiences on the boat. I listened, eyes agog and ears alert. 'First class for whites,' Siew Lan informed me. 'My husband is white person, so I can stay. Women no got white husband cannot stay. People not nice.'

'Your husband, he not do something-ah?'

'How can do something? Not his boat-lah.' With this pronouncement had come another bloody cascade straight into our spittoon. Siew

Lan lifted out the well-chewed nest from inside her mouth delicately, as if it were gold leaf. She was in a talkative mood. 'Stay in second class, no problem. But go to first-class room, walk also cannot walk. Many people stare and stare.'

'What? At you?'

'Yes-lah.' My friend nodded vigorously. 'Flo-lah also. My daughter not look like Chinese, but also not look like white person. So all people look at us . . . I also not know how to say. Not rude. But not nice.'

Things were better in London, she said, though there had been an incident. One evening she and her daughter were stopped by a man in a dark uniform and hard hat and spoken to very rudely. My friend only picked up a word here and there, but she recognised insolence when she heard it. The policeman's manner altered when her husband, who had been loitering at a shop window a few paces behind, went forward and confronted him. The experience made Siew Lan long for home.

We sat quietly then, each uncertain how to continue. I stared at Siew Lan's lips, stained black red by betel nut juice. For the first time in years we were on the verge of speaking frankly about the white devils, and both of us were reluctant to head into this dangerous territory. It was my friend who broke the silence.

'Chye Hoon, you know I happy in my marriage.' I nodded. In spite of the sadness which threatened to overwhelm me, I smiled at the memories of her husband in his white suit.

Siew Lan took a sip of coffee. 'Here more easy. We so *champor-champor*, even *ang moh* nicer. In London very hard-lah.' Looking at her dark face, I pointed out that what she said was different from the idyllic picture my son painted of London. 'I know . . . I know,' Siew Lan murmured, shaking her head while absent-mindedly moving an index finger around the rim of her cup, with its pink borders and green dragons. 'Your son refuse to see-lah! I think he in London one Eurasian also not know.' I was inclined to agree.

We only learnt how Weng Yu had fared in his examinations because his college sent details of his results, which turned out to be shockingly bad considering how much we had lavished on him. Although my son gained an overall pass, he failed two of his papers, barely scraped through in another ten and scored good marks in only two subjects. This was a far cry from his previous performance, and I decided that the affair of the white girl must have affected his head. Whenever disappointment welled up inside me, I had to remind myself of the final outcome – that Weng Yu, my son from Ipoh, was now one of the best-trained civil engineers in the entire world. We had succeeded in the Weng Yu Project.

Once my son graduated, I stopped sending money. Perhaps this was a mistake, but I had agreed to fund him only until he completed his studies. We had never discussed what would happen after that, though it was clear I could not provide for him indefinitely. He would either have to come home or fend for himself.

Unbeknownst to me, Meng Seng took it upon himself to write to Weng Yu when he found out about the intended engagement. By his own account the patriarch's letter was gentle. Meng Seng made clear that in affairs of love no one was to blame; indeed he complimented my son, telling him that a boy of his calibre and looks was bound to attract girls. Unfortunately we lived in a world in which the white race regarded itself as superior. If my son doubted that, Meng Seng reminded him of the Ipoh Club, which had operated a white-only policy for as long as Meng Seng could remember. Malay rulers were occasionally allowed into the place, as were a handful of Chinese towkays, but to all intents and purposes the club remained a preserve of our white rulers.

Meng Seng underlined his point: Helen, he told my son, was not just a member of any race but of the ruling race, and this had implications for marriage. If my son were to marry her, her own people would be the first to treat her with contempt – for lowering the tone of their race, because her husband would be viewed as a Chinaman and her children as half-castes, neither white enough for them, nor brown enough for others. Weng Yu himself would suffer, not least among his own people, who would wonder why a local girl wasn't good enough for him. Thus marriage between a local and a white person was destined to end in failure.

Meng Seng encouraged my son to reconsider. No two people, he said, could live apart from society; they had to interact with the world around them.

Weng Yu's reply, when it came, was defiant. Meng Seng told me that its tone had surprised him. The Weng Yu he remembered was a boy of few words, not the firebrand whose short page shimmered with fury. My son told Meng Seng bluntly that he disagreed with his views. People of mixed descent looked happy on London's streets. As for Malaya itself, the marriage between Siew Lan and Se-Too-Wat stood out. Could he, Meng Seng Pak, honestly put hand to heart and declare their marriage a failure?

These robust words echoed in my head. I had been given the gift of Mother's culture and instead of guarding it with my sword I had put my weapon aside and sent Weng Yu to London. Now my worst nightmare was unfolding. I was going to lose my little prince.

By the time the rains began late in 1926 we had still received no news.

Even early on during that monsoon season the rains seemed heavier than in previous years. It was not long before the banks of the Kinta River overflowed. I imagined Weng Yu's letters lost, carried away by the torrents of water that swept everything before them.

With an eye on the *kueh* business, I surveyed the heavens. We had been fortunate the year before, not losing custom even though it had rained every day. Much of Old Town had as usual been flooded. Despite that, the ever-industrious Li-Fei had found a way across the Kinta River to New Town – how, I will never know, as the girl was sparing with the details. There, hungry customers were so grateful to see a bicycle carrying goodies that they bought more than their normal share. In the end the only thing that affected us was the closure of the Old Town market, because there came a point when we simply could not buy the fresh coconuts or pandanus leaves we needed and were forced to stop making *kueh*.

Remembering our difficulties then, I made my way to the People's Park for a peek at the Kinta River. By the time I arrived, the park was covered in a sheet of water, and I could get no further than the entrance. A crowd stood by, an assortment of characters with nothing better to do than stare at the rising tide.

Hours later the waters had reached that part of the Lahat Road lying in the valley below. As I looked down the hill on which our house was situated, I saw the unstoppable expanse rushing in. When I had selected our house years previously, I had chosen the spot precisely to avoid the floods, which recurred every monsoon season. I had little idea then that this judicious piece of foresight would one day save my family.

Once the water arrived at the bottom of our hill, it accumulated quickly. With nowhere else to go, the water inevitably rose. Soon people were wading along what used to be the bottom of the Lahat Road, their calves covered. From the safety of our five-foot way, I saw motor cars being abandoned as their occupants made their way slowly towards us, cursing loudly.

Within hours the valley below resembled nothing like anything I had ever seen before. Debris floated everywhere: bits of wood, rubber tyres, pieces of newspaper, even rubbish from the drains. Few people were out by then. Only one or two brave souls tried to walk between houses. It was obvious from their slow progress that the obstacles in their way were insidious. The water itself – rain mingled with what had oozed out of the latrine pots that lay uncollected in the unfortunate houses below – was a deeper brown than the tanned-leather shade of the Kinta River.

That night, as the servants were cooking the evening meal in our kitchen we were surprised by shouting at the front of our house. The familiar voice belonged to none other than Yap Meng Seng, who had evidently hired a sampan to traverse the lowlands, before walking up that part of our hill which remained dry.

From his demeanour I sensed bad news. 'Phone call from Penang,' he told me. I digested this with a sinking heart. 'Your mother passed away last night. I'm so sorry, Chye Hoon.' All I could do was stare helplessly into empty space. My immediate thought was that I would not be able to leave for Penang. As if reading my mind, Meng Seng said, 'Station Road all flooded. Nothing running . . . no trains, nothing. Hard to travel now, though maybe the rain will stop soon.' Looking up at the dark skies, we had our doubts, but we kept these to ourselves. I thanked him before saying goodbye. In return Meng Seng agreed to keep check on the trains and motor buses running out of Ipoh town.

The next day it suddenly stopped raining. For several hours not a drop fell. The waters at the bottom of the hill began to recede, leaving behind a trail of horror and a stench so foul it even invaded the air in our corner up on the hill. Smelling like a thousand night-soil collection vans, it reminded me of the first morning I had set foot in Ipoh with Peng Choon, when I had wondered why he had brought me here. From what I could see, the waters continued to reach the ankles of those below; in any case, until I heard from Meng Seng I was loath to make my way into town, in case I was disappointed.

Then without warning the rains came again. This time it was clear there would be no stopping the outpouring of the gods. The waters came down with a vengeance, flooding the town as had never happened before. I used our supplies sparingly, but with seven of us in the house there came a point when we started to run low. For the first time since the rains began, I felt fear. Eventually we finished our yams and sweet potatoes, and my fourth and fifth sons bravely ventured into the fetid mess to see if they could reach the provision shops in New Town. They came back surprisingly dry – thanks to the enterprising coolies who plied the sampan trade throughout the floods. My sons brought on their backs heavy sacks to ensure our survival. When they described what Old Town looked like, I found it hard to take in. Not only were the main streets covered with a blanket of water, but the currents had been strong enough to break panes of glass. Even the glass front of the largest shop in town, a favourite with the white devils, had been swept away.

It was only a fortnight later that I was able to make my way to Penang. By then it was too late to say goodbye to Mother, but I reached the island in time to catch a last glimpse of Father. Soon after Mother's demise, he too passed away, from loneliness and a broken heart. Numb from shock, I bowed frigidly before Kuan Yin. All I could do at the temple was to clutch a handful of ashes while praying for my parents' souls as they floated somewhere on this earth.

42

One afternoon Li-Fei came running into the kitchen with flushed cheeks. Her right index finger, pointing outside, shivered in the hot air. 'Weng Yu! Weng Yu come home-lah!'

I ran into the outer hall to find a stiff young man beside two large suitcases. The boy greeted me formally without even a smile – in English. He used the only English word I could recognise, 'Hullo', followed closely by 'Mama'. Had I awakened in a nightmare? The boy looked like my son – indeed he had Weng Yu's voice – but surely this could not be him.

By then everyone in the house had encircled Weng Yu. All were there: my daughter Hui Lin, my three youngest surviving sons, both our servants, Ah Hong and Li-Fei, and Liew Chin Tong, who was dining with us that evening. The stranger in the midst of this commotion showed little pleasure at seeing us. After saying hello politely, he stood imperiously with his arms and back straight like the white devils in the English quarter.

There was little doubt my son was playing the part of an English gentleman. For one thing he was dressed like one, in a long-sleeved white shirt and khaki trousers so well pressed that they were barely creased despite his journey. On his head he wore a topee, the hard hat with the tiny brim and round top favoured by our rulers. The biggest shock came when he opened his mouth, for the boy claimed to have forgotten his native dialects.

I was incredulous. Though my eyes tunneled into him, Weng Yu did not look at me, which left me uncertain whether to give him a piece of my mind. Once again I imagined Hang Tuah as he fought a foreign warrior with his beautifully carved *keris*, but instead of wielding my own sword I took the easy way out. My eldest son was home after all. I had neither the heart nor the energy to shout at him. I waited, hoping that in time my little prince would come to his senses.

Over dinner Weng Yu refused to eat with his hands; such behaviour, he told us, was uncivilised. To avoid a scene, I asked Ah Hong to hand my son a fork and spoon. Conversation could only proceed at the pace of sand drying, since everything had to be translated for my benefit. From the glances they gave one another, it was clear his siblings were as bewildered as I was. What in heaven had happened to this son of mine?

In no time Weng Yu began to act as if he were the newly returned head of our family. He interrogated his younger brothers with his head tilted to one side so that the end of his nose gazed petulantly down. His brothers soon turned a deaf ear. Only his sister Hui Lin was able to communicate with Weng Yu. With charm and humour, my daughter somehow burrowed a way through Weng Yu's iron armour. He invited her in whenever she knocked on his bedroom door, and the two would chat for hours. He knew that Hui Lin shared much of her life with me, but he nonetheless told her many things, presumably because he wanted me to learn about the sores festering inside his heart.

In the days following Weng Yu's return, I spent troubled hours before our altar table. I made special offerings of vermicelli topped with sugar crystals. With head bowed and my hands tight around burning joss-sticks, I remembered our ancestors, who had come to build new lives in boats with eyes painted on their prows. I would think of Father and Mother and also my husband, Peng Choon. Staring at the tablets with their dark wood and mysterious writing, I wondered what they would have done with my recalcitrant son. Mother, I felt certain, would have put her foot down sooner and never have allowed a son to forget his own language and culture.

At least my son had returned. I consoled myself that he had not married the white woman.

Weng Yu forged an independent life at home, never once asking me for money. I gave him shelter and food, as any mother would, but nothing else. Nor did he seek it. 'Mama's done enough for me,' he said to Hui Lin, an acknowledgement that pleased me, coming as it did out of nowhere. It was given freely, without any hint of a grudge. These oblique words of thanks led me to hope that the boy remembered the many sacrifices we had made for his sake.

In other ways, though, my son's bitterness could not be shaken. 'I not even know I glad or not he come back!' I confessed one day to Siew Lan.

'Good heart, don't talk like that-lah,' she scolded me on the *barlay*. 'I think Weng Yu will change. He talk a lot yesterday,' she added, referring to the visit my son had paid her and Se-Too-Wat. Physically Siew Lan observed that he seemed much as he had seemed in London, only much thinner. 'Se-Too-Wat think he anxious, a lot of things happen-lah, but he not want to say.' What exactly it was that had taken place in London none of us knew, though we guessed it could only have been related to the English girl.

During his twelve months at home, Weng Yu came and went as he pleased. When one of the servants asked where he was going and when he would be back, he snapped. When I asked, he answered, albeit gruffly. It was clear he didn't want anyone meddling in his affairs, and apart from Hui Lin, no one bothered Weng Yu. From time to time, when I wondered about his future, my son would declare confidently that with his qualifications he should have no trouble finding a job; it was simply a matter of time before he landed a position appropriate to his stature. As I watched him swagger out of our house one morning, I could hardly believe that this boy, who behaved as if he owned the world, was the same boy I had brought up.

To my embarrassment my son refused to visit Yap Meng Seng, the man without whom he would never have been able to travel to London. Instead Weng Yu maintained a mysterious schedule. He would leave the house early in the mornings and sometimes return for lunch, other times not, though he always came home for dinner. Occasionally he disappeared again as soon as he'd eaten, staying out as late as ten o'clock at night. We could not think what he was up to. When I asked him, I received a cryptic reply. 'You'll see, Mama' was all he said. Siew Lan didn't know either. It wasn't until Weng Yu invited Hui Lin for a walk that his secret was revealed: my eldest son had been surveying the whole of Ipoh town – every road, every bridge, even the newly constructed embankments for combating Ipoh's annual floods. By then the town had grown, and it was no longer possible to go round on foot. For help, Weng Yu had approached an old school friend, a boy who had his own car. He drove my son towards the furthest reaches, which allowed Weng Yu to take measurements and make notes as required.

One night my little prince gathered us all around the dining table. On its surface he unfurled sheets of smooth paper, each covered with fine drawings – networks of parallel lines marked with thin black script. Gasps escaped from my children. 'Wahh! Big Brother . . .' I wondered aloud what the papers in front of us contained and was at a loss for words when my son explained that the sheets when put together formed a large hand-drawn map of Ipoh town. 'But you have to imagine you're looking from above,' he said as if this were the most natural thing in the world.

His passion was infectious. I followed Weng Yu's fingers as they traced out known landmarks. He pointed out the Lahat Road on one of his diagrams; then, moving across to an adjacent piece, he proceeded to show us all the main roads and bridges, even the embankments. As he moved his finger from spot to spot on this wondrous map, Weng Yu talked animatedly. Eventually he moved to that part of the map where the Wong family lands were situated. I had heard that the area was being developed, a fact my son confirmed. His index finger wagged towards the spot. 'Here, Mama!' he said. 'It's now called Green Town.'

Green Town. The image of a house rose up before me . . . a house built in wood and painted a lime green. I put the picture away and returned to the conversation taking place between my children. By then Weng Yu was describing the problems facing Ipoh's roads and bridges. He went into vivid detail, as if speaking about a beautiful woman. He told us what he thought would be needed to transform Ipoh town and proceeded to lay fresh sheets on top of the table. Each sheet contained a finely etched network of roads, bridges and embankments, but there were many new markings and plenty of script everywhere, sometimes in thick black ink.

'This,' my eldest son announced, 'is my vision for the Ipoh of the future.' I stared with open mouth, impressed in spite of myself. Weng Yu's enthusiasm reminded me of the night he had told us the story of the Chinese princess, when my son had gone from start to finish without once pausing for breath. The memory struck me forcefully. Weng Yu stood with a lively face, his long, elegant fingers pointing at the roads he would widen and the bridges he would strengthen. 'So they can take more cars,' he told his dazed audience. He added that the embankments which had been built weren't adequate; therefore, he had marked out reinforcements.

In short, I finally understood that my son was single-handedly proposing to redevelop Ipoh town.

Not imagining that the white devils would welcome such radical ideas from a local, I warned Weng Yu, but he derided my objection. 'It's different for me, Mama,' he said loftily without even a hint of hesitation. 'I'm a British graduate.' His younger siblings looked at one another, amazed their brother could have such peculiar ideas, embarrassed too by his poor display of manners. Keeping my thoughts to myself, I merely looked at my son. I hoped he was right.

To prove me wrong, Weng Yu came back several evenings later with a deep flush on his face. He told us that his friend, the one with the car, who was now the chief clerk in the Kinta Public Works Department, had taken him to see his boss, the chief engineer. The chief engineer was a white devil, of course, but he had listened intently to Weng Yu's plan. 'You see, Mama!' my son said victoriously. 'He's even arranged for me to see two senior people in Batu Gajah. We're going next week.'

On the appointed day I watched as Weng Yu left the house for the administrative capital of the state. Immaculately dressed as always, Weng Yu went armed with a black briefcase that held his precious plans – reams of the special paper on which he had patiently sketched everything of note in Ipoh town. When my son returned, the air of defeat in his sagging shoulders was enough to tell me what had happened. The visit had not been the success Weng Yu had hoped for. Though his plans had not been rejected out of hand, the reception had been decidedly lukewarm. I felt for the boy, but part of me was secretly pleased, because I hoped it would wrench Weng Yu out of his dreamworld.

After several months it became clear that the white administration was not going to take Weng Yu's plans up. They didn't even offer him a job. At the time Ipoh sorely needed civil engineers, but Weng Yu had not inherited his father's tact; he had a habit of letting the whites know exactly what he thought, as if he were equal in station. Qualified he may have been, but white he certainly was not, despite the airs he put on. No local, no matter how talented, would have been allowed to run a department – that was the remit of the white man. Weng Yu remained adrift for a year, growing more disillusioned with each passing day. His face hardened in disappointment, while his eyes seemed to lose soul. In that period he stopped visiting Se-Too-Wat and Siew Lan. I tried to talk to my son, but it was like trying to cut through water with a sword.

◆ ◆ ◆

For all his weaknesses, Yap Meng Seng redeemed himself. When Weng Yu did not visit to pay his respects, the old man turned up at our house instead.

I was mortified at the sight of the patriarch, but I needn't have worried. Entering unhurriedly, the old man gave me a warm smile, saying in a loud voice that he happened to be passing. Age had caught up with him, and Meng Seng's hair was now completely white. Why the man suddenly grew a moustache I shall never know. It was the type favoured by older Chinese men, the sort whose sides hung down past his lips like a pair of white fangs. It made him look much older than his years as he hobbled in on his stick.

When Meng Seng saw Weng Yu, the patriarch extended his free hand. I held my breath as Weng Yu hesitated, but in the end the boy did not dare refuse the proffered hand. Though his manner was stilted, my son addressed the patriarch appropriately and replied when he was spoken to.

Meng Seng even took pains to enquire after my son's welfare. I was awestruck. Our years together in the bosom of the family had given me little understanding of this man of extremes: filled with the arrogance of males of his generation yet able also to be utterly humble. He asked many questions of my son, more than were needed for polite conversation. When he offered to help Weng Yu find a job, I had to hide my tears.

I held both the patriarch's hands in mine before he left, the first time I had ever done so. This display of feeling caused his cheeks to burn. He turned away quickly. 'Don't mention it,' he said with a dismissive wave of his free hand.

Most men of his age would not have come by. I said as much rather loudly, inducing a heavy silence in our inner hall. Weng Yu did not reply. He walked into his room and slammed the door.

43

After two years of visiting our house, the young man Lim Tsin-sang sought my permission to become engaged to Hui Lin. I thought it was about time he proposed and told him so. With a look of embarrassment the teacher apologised. 'My personal circumstances, Peng Choon Sau. Please understand,' he said. 'I didn't have money before to marry your daughter.' As the only surviving child of aged parents, both vegetable farmers, who had to be supported, Lim Kwee Seng had had to save hard for my daughter's hand. Smiling, I told him that Hui Lin herself would have to agree. There was little doubt in my mind that Hui Lin would accept this serious young man, with his dark skin and eyes like a woman's, but I had to give my daughter the final word. When I asked whether Kwee Seng would consent to a *chin-chuoh* marriage, his answer delighted me. 'Of course, Peng Choon Sau,' the young man said enthusiastically. I beamed. This was just the sort of son-in-law every Nyonya mother dreamt of having.

Given the changing times, it was no surprise that my third daughter's marriage to Lim Kwee Seng was a far simpler affair even than her second sister's wedding. There was much ceremonial simplification, forced on me by my own children, who insisted that I had already done more than enough. Their words made me wonder whether my physical deterioration was becoming noticeable. I had become much heavier after Hui Ying passed away. Even walking up the stairs made me weary.

Yong Soon Soh, gloriously fat as ever, presided once more. I insisted on a dinner and the hair-combing ceremony, but even there we broke with tradition. The bridegroom's parents were invited to the dinner on the eve of the wedding, a novelty that pleased everyone, especially Yap Meng Seng, who at the time of his son's wedding to Hui Fang had strenuously argued against his exclusion.

Then after the feast we downed our tea with large helpings of Nyonya *kueh*. This was my idea, and our guests loved it. As soon as the *kueh* were carried in, our tables became a riot of colour. There were the pinks and whites of my famous nine-layered *kueh*, with their peeling alternate slices; the blues of *pulut tai-tai*, spread thickly with our signature coconut egg jam, a burnt orange in colour; also the greens and whites of *seri muka*; and of course the princely yellows of banana fritters served cut into bite-size pieces and deep-fried. By the end even my little prince sat licking his fingers.

The wedding was memorable in another way. I had placed Weng Yu beside Se-Too-Wat in the hope of softening my son's heart. They had Europe and other things in common after all. I wasn't far wrong. Once they began chatting, Se-Too-Wat casually mentioned a friend of his in Singapore, another white devil, who apparently worked for an important-sounding body that was looking for engineers. Siew Lan's husband passed on his friend's address and suggested that my son write to enquire about a job.

A week later, when the boy sent off his application letter, I interceded with Kuan Yin. An official-looking envelope came back, and we waited with bated breath. When Weng Yu was summoned to an interview, the whole family breathed a sigh of relief. My son made his own travel arrangements to Singapore, not bothering me for his train fare or expenses.

The interview must have proceeded well, because he was offered a job. When he eventually wrote, I found out that my eldest son had become an assistant building inspector. This sounded extremely grand. I was suffused with pride that I had a son who was a somebody. Weng Yu was put on a year's contract at a starting salary of $150 a month. While this wasn't going to make him a millionaire any time soon, I thought it generous, especially when his housing and travel allowances were taken into account. I gave thanks to Kuan Yin that my auspicious seating plan had played a role, however small, in helping Weng Yu land his first job, and prayed that this turn of events would give my eldest son the boost he so sorely needed.

It was only after Weng Yu had left for Singapore that Hui Lin and Kwee Seng told me what had happened with the white girl. The details made me blush: things Weng Yu would never have told me, such as the scent of roses Helen sprinkled from a bottle on her skin each morning. My son had clearly been besotted.

When Weng Yu read my response to his engagement request, his reaction had been one of fury. The more the boy mulled it over, the more incensed he became. By the time Meng Seng's letter followed, his wrath was fully stoked. Exploding in passion, he shook both my letter and Meng Seng's in front of his landlord. 'Look how narrow-minded the people in my home town are!' he said contemptuously. This turned out to be a mistake, but Weng Yu was not to realise it until much later.

His landlord, an army retiree, read both letters over many times. The man said little but within a fortnight had announced a long-delayed holiday to Ontario in Canada, where his brother lived. Helen would accompany her father, as it had been a while since her uncle had seen his favourite niece. Although Weng Yu didn't cherish the idea of Helen being so far, he was hardly in a position to object. The girl herself stormed out of the room with blue eyes blazing – to no avail. When the time came, the army man insisted that my son not accompany them to the port. It was too far, he said, so the couple bade each other farewell at home. Weng Yu spoke of his anguish and also apparently of hers. Helen pressed a photograph into my son's hands, a picture Weng Yu showed his sister.

For weeks Weng Yu heard nothing. When he eventually received a letter from her father, the message came as a shock. The army man told my son that, after much thought, he had decided it would be better for everyone if Weng Yu tried to forget his daughter, and she him. When my son realised he had no means of contacting the girl, he despaired. The separation began just months before his final examinations and affected his studies badly. He couldn't sleep, couldn't eat and was unable to work. Had it not been for a few kindly lecturers, he would surely have failed. As it was, he barely scraped through.

Weng Yu was unable to believe he would not see Helen again. He felt sure she would defy her father, if she only had the means. After graduation Weng Yu found work as an apprentice and chose to remain in London, where he knew Helen would return by the end of the year.

When he next set eyes on her, Weng Yu barely recognised the young woman who walked stiffly towards him. Helen looked as wonderful as in his memories, smelling of roses and with blue eyes glinting, but her lips were tight and her back upright like a pole. On one of her fingers Weng Yu glimpsed a large diamond-studded ring.

'I met a man,' she said. 'We're engaged to be married.'

The next day my son purchased a ticket for home. Without the girl to whom he had given his heart, a future in London seemed bleak. I knew then that many moons would have to pass before the boy's wounds could heal.

At the end of his first month of work in Singapore, Weng Yu wrote home. The letter came with a cheque: twenty dollars for me. It wasn't a big amount, but the fact that he had even thought to send a gift thrilled me. All was not lost with my eldest son.

Weng Yu was then sharing a flat with an old classmate from Ipoh, a friend who was happy to put him up until the outcome of his interview was known. Thereafter the boys came to an arrangement to share the modest premises above a shophouse. I worried when I heard where my little prince was living, but he assured me that the neighbourhood was quiet at night.

Weng Yu continued sending a cheque at the end of each month. For a while we heard little else; we had only a vague idea of what he did from day to day. Out of nowhere a letter arrived with nothing but complaints. My son was evidently fed up with colleagues and bosses alike and ready to resign. The boy's impetuous nature alarmed me. Resigning from a job, no matter how much he hated it, seemed unwise when he had only begun work a few months previously. I discussed his situation with men who had the relevant knowledge – Meng Seng and Chin Tong, and even Se-Too-Wat, through his wife – and was gratified when they all agreed with me. On the basis of their advice, which I thought would carry greater weight with my son, I counselled Weng Yu against any hasty decision. There were many types of people in this world, I said; unfortunately we sometimes had to work with those we found troublesome, occasionally even with people we detested and had no respect for.

My words must have given the boy pause for thought, because he calmed down. Weng Yu was part of a team responsible for widening Singapore's roads and strengthening its bridges – the very thing he had envisaged for our town. At the end of twelve months Weng Yu was given a permanent contract. His salary was raised, as were his allowances. When the next cheque came, my son had written it out for thirty-five dollars. He apologised that he could not send more, because he intended to start a business and was saving hard. That, he told us, was the only reason for staying on in Singapore, because not a day went by when he didn't feel like resigning.

I had mixed feelings when I heard about Weng Yu's business ambitions. Of all my sons, he was the least astute. He was undoubtedly good-looking, and talented when it came to singing and drawing and pounding chilli-shrimp paste, but he had none of the boldness and practicality every businessman requires for the hard times that inevitably come, nor did he possess the charms needed to woo customers.

Nonetheless, the fact that my son revealed his plans gave me hope. I longed for the day when we could be as we had once been, mother and son, our hearts at peace. I hoped it would come before I left this earth.

By the middle of 1929, dark clouds were sweeping the world. Ipoh continued to flourish, but I heard rumblings from Siew Lan, whose husband started fretting. Independently Yap Meng Seng, whom I had always known as a staunch optimist, took to predicting doom. He claimed the world was about to change. When I asked in what way, the patriarch replied that he sensed a deep slump coming. The business transacted by his bank was on the decline, and this had accelerated in recent months. It was unusual, he said, to see the same thing happening in Malaya, Hong Kong and Singapore all at once. Even in London and New York, business was falling. Although his words were uncharacteristically dire, I took them with a pinch of salt. After all, there had been many falls in demand for tin and rubber before. What could be so different this time?

I was to see in due course. None of us could have envisaged the severity of the downturn, and it's fortunate that my fourth son, Weng Yoon, had left for England by the time the full force of what hit us became apparent, because I would never have let him go otherwise.

When Weng Yoon spoke to me about his desire to study law in London, the tremors were barely being felt. The word 'London' caused me shivers of a different kind, yet as I listened my pride also swelled: this fourth son of mine was nothing if not audacious, for he had quietly saved every cent he earned from four years of teaching at the Anglo-Chinese School to realise his ambition. I had always suspected Weng Yoon of having inherited my spirit, but the style in which he confirmed this stunned me.

Entirely without any prompting, Weng Yoon took the initiative to consult the patriarch, a course of action which pleased Meng Seng. Promptly repeating his predictions of an imminent worldwide slump, the old man said it was a good thing Weng Yoon was not planning to rely on funds that had yet to be raised, but he nonetheless worried whether the pool of money the boy had accumulated would be sufficient. A three-year stay in London, he warned, was expensive. Meng Seng offered to pay for Weng Yoon's sea passage to and from home just in case. If world conditions became catastrophic, the patriarch further assured my son that he would step in. Being inexperienced in business, Weng Yoon would have never considered these factors. He and I were grateful for the old man's thoughtfulness. After the disappointing example set by Weng Yu, I could scarcely believe that the patriarch would agree to stand surety for another of my sons. Meng Seng must have been able to see that this fourth boy was a grounded young man, not given to fanciful dreams and therefore likely to succeed, if for no other reason than because he refused to give up.

To seal his blessing, the patriarch held a farewell dinner in Weng Yoon's honour at the Kum Loong Restaurant, one of the best in Ipoh for Chinese food. The meal must have cost a fortune, for the kitchen at Kum Loong was presided over by a newly installed Hong Kong chef and there were twenty of us in a private room, enjoying delicious shark fin soup and juicy roast suckling pigs with crispy skins.

Weng Yoon, not having acquired his father's chiselled features, was not as handsome as his eldest brother, but he more than made up for this deficiency with his sharpness of brain and tongue. Weng Yoon's arguments with his sister Hui Ying were legendary, as were the debates he had won at school. The legal profession seemed apt for so loquacious a person. As I watched my son that night, I was certain that this pugnacious young man of twenty-three would return to become somebody in Ipoh.

With little warning Weng Yu reappeared in town one day. His grumblings about the men he worked with had increased over time, but I was still surprised by so abrupt a resignation. When pressed, Weng Yu revealed that a recent arrival from England had been promoted over him. 'I decided that resigning was best, Mama,' he said. I stared at my son, who at that moment looked dreamily out of the window with his nose pointing down at the world. 'I want to start my own business.'

I had grave concerns over such a plan. Repeating Se-Too-Wat's and Meng Seng's warnings, I wondered aloud whether it was a good time to launch a new venture. I was met with an icy glare.

'What do you know about business, Mama?' Weng Yu asked.

I retorted, 'Now twenty years already I have run one.'

The impact was immediate, for my son's voice softened. 'Ah, but, Mama, mine is a different type of business,' he said proudly, as if it would not be subject to the rules of supply and demand.

I already knew that I didn't like what I was seeing every day in Ipoh town. I was beginning to agree with Se-Too-Wat and Meng Seng: hard times were about to descend, and only those of us who kept our wits would survive.

PART V:
THE TWILIGHT YEARS
1931–8 DECEMBER
1941

44

For the first time in my life I lost interest in the coins Li-Fei brought back from her *kueh* rounds. I would separate the copper and silver pieces into blocks of ten the way my husband had taught me, but my mind would wander as soon as I began to count. Halfway across the piles of coins, images from the past would assail me, and I would stop, lose count and have to begin again.

I had never been so distracted. For respite I went in search of the delicacies which had saved our lives. The texture of coconut layers flopping on my palm, the feel of grainy rice balls inside my mouth, with their fulsome aroma of roasted peanuts, pandanus leaf and palm sugar, comforted me, but even they could not restore my concentration. For many mornings in a row my routine of money counting took twice as long as it had previously.

Once, Hui Lin found me at my dressing table, muttering as I absent-mindedly caressed a silver five-cent coin with its raised head of a white man. 'Daughter, I not know how to explain,' I said in response to Hui Lin's raised eyebrows. If our neighbours had known what was bothering me, they would certainly have called me ungrateful, because up and down the Lahat Road everyone congratulated me on my good fortune: the women envious of my daughters' marriages, the men of my sons' prospects, what with one a British-trained civil engineer, another a law student in London, the rest teachers in well-regarded schools.

Yet unlike Mother, I had failed to pass our culture on to my children. Weng Yu had even been in danger of not returning to his homeland. That had fortunately been thwarted and he was now at home, but Weng Yu bore none of the hallmarks of a Baba. As for the others, they too wore Western clothes and spoke mainly English. It was only with my daughters that I dared hope. Perhaps with the girls, who wore the sarong kebaya and spoke Hakka and Hokkien by choice, I would succeed in passing on our values.

I consoled myself that language and costume were merely outward signs. More important was what we held within our hearts and virtues like respect for our elders, our ancestors and our gods. On those perhaps I had succeeded. Only time would tell, but already I felt distinctly uneasy. I had once vowed to safeguard the magic sword I had been given with every breath I took. Now its powers were fading before my very eyes.

As suddenly as he forgot his local dialects, Weng Yu one day began speaking directly to me again. The words simply burst forth in perfect Hakka, a dialect many describe as coarse, but since it was the language taught to me by my beloved husband, it sounded magical to my ears, especially when spoken by my son.

'Mama, *ngi cho ma kai-ah?*'

Weng Yu's enquiry, uttered in that wonderfully deep bass that reminded me of Father's, was accompanied by a bewitching smile.

'Big Son, your Chinese sound very good-ah,' I told him happily. Weng Yu's cheeks reddened. It was clear the anger in the boy's heart had dissolved, because he invited me for an evening stroll. My prodigal son had finally returned.

As the stars in the Malayan sky peeped down on us, Weng Yu spoke of his plans and where he would locate his business. 'Mama, I will be using that shophouse we have, the one at the top of Hale Street,' he said in a matter-of-fact tone, as if relaying information, without so much as an attempt at asking permission.

Because we had been estranged for so long, I was reluctant to say anything that might put our relationship at risk. I looked up at the black rug of sky above, at the swathe of dots forming the River of Heaven. I held my tongue even though the ideas that poured forth from my son's contoured lips filled me with dread. He dreamt of becoming Ipoh's foremost civil engineer, but in his mind wealth came easily. Such naivety made me nervous, yet our first walk in years was hardly the best time to point this out. On that perfect Malayan evening it was enough that Weng Yu spoke in Hakka. Any unwelcome words would have to wait.

As it turned out, Weng Yu was very much in a hurry. Just days later we visited the shophouse Weng Yu had picked out for himself. I could see why my son had chosen it. Being at the far end of town near the border with the English quarter, it was well located; in fact, it was in such an ideal corner that I had always wondered how Peng Choon had managed to acquire the shop – it must have cost a fortune even in those distant years.

Once I knew that Weng Yu was going to give notice to the tenant who rented our shophouse, I realised I would have to accompany my son on his visit. Our tenant on Hale Street was a tailor by the name of Yap Min Kang, a quiet man who had been renting the premises for ten years and who happened to be our best tenant. Unlike others, Yap Min Kang paid his rent on time and always with a cup of tea. As we approached his premises, I thought back to the occasions when I had watched the tailor snip bales of cloth. I would stand transfixed, my eyes on the spinning wheel of the black sewing machine, which he turned by hand. Rolls of beautiful fabric adorned the front. Everywhere was the comforting smell of fabric and toil. I regretted what we were about to do, because I was sorry to see Yap Min Kang go.

Weng Yu, on the other hand, was wholly businesslike. 'We need the shop back. You must leave within three months,' he told the man curtly. Even though my son had never been one for small talk, his brusqueness alarmed me. What would it be like being one of his clients? When Yap Min Kang pleaded for another two months' grace, in addition to the three months' notice we served him, the request seemed reasonable for a tenant of such long standing, and I blushed at Weng Yu's refusal.

Naturally Yap Min Kang turned towards me. I had to look away; I could not meet the man's gaze. Noticing our exchange of glances, Weng Yu rounded on the tailor. In a raised voice he told Yap Min Kang that in accordance with Chinese custom, he, the eldest son, was head of our family, and his decision was final.

I stood at a loss for words. How was it that my little prince, a boy I had raised with my own hands, understood so little about Nyonya culture? Weng Yu had seen how I had been the head of our family while his father was alive, as was typical for us. Even Peng Choon, a man born in China, had understood and respected this and given me free rein to run our household, going so far as to hand me his income at the end of each month.

Weng Yu reminded the tailor one final time of the date by which he was to vacate our shophouse before striding out in his imported white shirt, khaki trousers and beige topee. As he walked, his arms swung back and forth in some imaginary British march. I shuffled behind in my sarong with head lowered, eyes fixed in shame on my pink-beaded slippers.

Yap Min Kang came to see me before his notice period was up, begging for an extension of two months. 'Please, Peng Choon Sau,' he said, 'I need more time.' When I looked at the man, my heart was touched.

'Yap Tsin-sang-ah, we see-lah,' I told him. Then I did something I rarely do: I told a lie. 'My son very anxious, work urgent-lah. Otherwise of course can stay longer. We see-lah. I ask for you. Hah?' Yap Min Kang nodded sadly and went away.

That weekend, after a delicious lunch of Siamese laksa, I broached my subject. 'Weng Yu-ah, you give Yap Tsin-sang another two months, you make me very happy. He long time now our best tenant.'

My son looked at me with disdain. He told me gruffly that he needed the space immediately, so his having to wait three months was quite long enough. He added, almost growling, 'Now that I'm home, it's not for you to decide such things, Mama.' His tone told me an argument would ensue if I were to take a harder line.

As bad as I felt for Yap Tsin-sang, I had to choose my son. If we quarrelled openly, gossip would spread around Ipoh. For the sake of family I let Weng Yu have his way.

Conditions had become extremely difficult by the time the tailor vacated our shophouse. The trickle of mining coolies who found themselves unemployed soon turned into a torrent, and the human tide flooded Ipoh. I had seen this many times before, only it was much worse now, for the coolies were joined by a host of others – tradesmen, clerks, even funeral parlour workers. It wasn't that fewer were dying, but with so many unable to pay, the undertakers were forced to charge less and therefore resorted to firing workers.

In those days I avoided walking into town. I could not bear the sight of so many lying about with nowhere else to go. The scale of human misery became impossible to ignore. Even on the short journey from our house on the Lahat Road to the People's Park, where I went on daily walks, I would trip on homeless stragglers. Until then I had always thought the unemployed lazy. I assumed they spent their days squatting on their haunches, smoking the voluminous water pipes that were passed endlessly from person to person. But with half the Chinese population out of work, it occurred to me for the first time that they couldn't all have been useless layabouts.

The ones unable to move – the old and the infirm – were the worst off. The younger men could at least find some way of scraping enough for two meals a day, but their older, sicker compatriots could only scavenge around dustbins early in the morning and late at night, when the coffee shops had closed. The rest of the time they lay heaped on top of one another along the covered walkways, dreaming of better days to come.

I had to wander into town occasionally, and it was inevitable that I should catch whiffs of the desperation in the air. On one walk I was shocked by what greeted me below the august Hugh Low Bridge. This bridge had always served as shelter for the homeless, but I could scarcely have imagined how permanent a home it had become to a growing crowd. In addition to the cardboard boxes and the thin sheets the men slept on, I saw rags serving as partitions between little rooms, and even photographs placed daintily along the banks of the Kinta River. On one corner where the river curved, a makeshift altar stood: an image of one of our gods, tattered and peeling, with candles in front. When I described the scene to my son-in-law Kwee Seng, he confirmed that the men who had previously been herded into prison by the white authorities now remained perpetually beneath Ipoh's main bridges.

Soon the newly unemployed made their presence felt in other ways.

Li-Fei began bringing home ever more unsold *kueh*. This did not worry me at first. In some ways I was even pleased, because we gave what was left to the unfortunates below the Hugh Low Bridge. Sales of our *kueh* had always ebbed and flowed, and I was confident they would pick up again – people had to eat after all. In 1931, however, the trend of poor receipts continued for weeks, which then dragged into months.

When Li-Fei no longer had to replenish her tiffin carriers for a second morning round, I began to fret. The stacks of coins I had to count kept dwindling, until the day came when we barely made ten cents. That was when our astute servant made a remark which forced me to sit up. 'Peng Choon Sau,' she said, 'you should go to town. Very many hawkers now-ah! Big problem-lah!'

At the earliest opportunity I asked Yap Meng Seng to take me around town in his car. Sure enough the streets crawled with new food stalls, many clearly opened by the recently unemployed. I could hardly blame them, but I knew I would have to respond to this threat. Along the Anderson Road there were a handful of fruit vendors, three or four satay stalls and several Chinese noodle stalls, all on a stretch no longer than a quarter of a mile. Then, back on Theatre Street, we found a new phenomenon: stalls offering *lok-lok* – wooden skewers of fish, cockles, liver and other types of offal, all of which could be purchased by the stick and dipped into a tub of boiling water. A large number of people stood around the *lok-lok* vendor, happily dipping their sticks into a steaming vat before dousing the skewers greedily into a large communal bowl containing what looked like a hot sauce. I didn't taste anything. I merely walked up and down, taking in the faces of those against whom our *kueh* business would have to compete.

For several days I sat deep in thought. Not wishing to act hastily, I consulted Meng Seng before discussing my ideas with Siew Lan over tea and betel leaves. With times being what they were, people in town were looking to do no more than fill their stomachs. It was not a climate in which Nyonya *kueh*, regarded as mere delicacies, would thrive. On the other hand, having nurtured a loyal following over twenty years we couldn't simply abandon our dedicated customers; we would have to tread carefully. I decided to offer *kueh* on three days of the week; the rest of the time we would make another dish, something that would give our customers a complete meal. The only question was what.

Recounting the scenes that had greeted us along the Anderson Road and parts of New Town, I remembered the brisk trade done by the hawkers – Chinese and Tamil coolies who had learnt how to handle a wok. They would never be able to compete with me for Nyonya food, so whatever we offered had to be true to our traditions. When I mentioned the hordes sitting around the noodle stalls, it was Siew Lan to whom a flash of inspiration came. 'Of course!' she said, smiling as she spat out a mouthful of charged betel nut juice. 'Noodles, cheap and filling! Why not make your Siamese laksa, Chye Hoon? Can sell I'm sure.'

I could see her point: with noodles changing hands for only two to three cents per bowl, there were plenty of takers slurping with gusto. Over the next week I began experimenting with the laksa recipe Mother had passed down. I varied the proportion of noodles one day, prawns the next and did repeated calculations to see whether a decent profit could result at three cents per bowl.

It took a week for us to conclude that Siamese laksa required too much work for day-to-day catering. If noodles were what customers wanted, there was a simpler dish we could make which would be equally delicious: Penang Nyonya laksa. This even had Nyonya in its name, and everyone knew I came from Penang. After additional days of testing, we were ready. I couldn't use as much fish in the gravy as I wanted, but the aroma rising from our pots was so wonderful that I judged we would surely attract customers.

In my desire to save on costs, I had envisaged Li-Fei transporting our laksa – noodles, gravy and all – on the back of her bicycle set on two poles as if it were a shoulder, with a pot dangling from each side. The contraption we built proved precarious, and it became clear that I would have to invest not only in a new tricycle, but also in fitting it out with a wooden cart, the type the other vendors used, so that Li-Fei could transport our warm offering door to door.

I took another week to reflect, nervous at the thought of so much expense while the town was engulfed in a depth of poverty we had never before seen. Where previously I would have rushed in head first, then I deliberated long and hard. In the midst of this deep reflection, I asked to tour the town a second time with Meng Seng. 'Go on-lah, Chye Hoon.' The old man was in the process of growing a beard, and I watched as he patted the tuft of hair below his chin. 'I have a feeling you'll do well.'

Thus it was that the Wong family started offering Penang Nyonya laksa alongside our already well-known Nyonya *kueh*. The laksa was an instant success. For months in a row we sold all the noodles we made. Unfortunately the appearance of our laksa had the effect of driving some of our *kueh* customers straight into the hands of our competitor, Heng Lai Soh. Because there were days on which we made only laksa, customers unable to buy their favourite *kueh* on the day of their choice gravitated to the other established Nyonya *kueh* maker. I was horrified. Overnight years of goodwill evaporated just like that, and no amount of cajoling or sweet talking could bring our customers back. The servants at the mansion down the road stopped taking our *kueh*. Even Hong Seng Soh, the Nyonya in one of the thirteen houses, who had been our customer from the outset, no longer came out at the sound of Li-Fei's bell.

In those difficult days we were forced to redouble our efforts. I decided we had to wake up earlier so that we could make both laksa and *kueh* every morning. I hired extra hands. All the women in our house – the servants, my third daughter, Hui Lin, and I – were exhausted by the time evening fell, but we had to act before we lost even more *kueh* customers. We tailored our *kueh* offering too, making sure we had a substantial taro or radish cake every day so that the impoverished could eat their fill without feeling they were frittering their money away.

Amidst these challenging conditions, Weng Yu launched his business. He started in haste, opening his premises as soon as the tailor had departed, with a minimum of renovation to our old shophouse on Hale Street.

Despite having decided to leave my son alone, I was unable to stifle my curiosity. Late one morning after counting the coins Li-Fei had brought back, I headed out by rickshaw to the top of Old Town for a little peek.

Our shophouse stood much as it had for twenty years. Its solid grey concrete had suited the tailor perfectly, but I could not imagine visiting a newly qualified engineer in such premises. For one thing its walls needed painting, and the floor was unchanged from the time the place had been built. Looking down at the barren concrete, spotty with craters and trapped bubbles, I felt distinctly uncomfortable for my son.

I tried to convey these doubts in a way that would not provoke my little prince. How could I tell him that as our premises stood, they would fail to inspire confidence? In the shadows of its murky walls, mosquitoes buzzed lazily, drowsy from the blood on which they had feasted. One of these irritants hovered before my nose. I swiped it whilst telling my son he needed to turn the shop into a proper office, perhaps even to spend some money. This elicited a sharp intake of breath. Weng Yu became flushed, not least because we were within earshot of the assistant and draughtsman he had hired.

'I don't need to do anything here, Mama,' he replied forcefully. 'People will come because of my British diploma.'

My son's thick lips curved downwards in the look Mother used to have whenever she sulked. Unable to find the words, I left, but my frustrations came tumbling out later to Meng Seng, who summed things up memorably. While sipping tea in the inner hall, the patriarch muttered under his breath, 'To attract prosperity, one must already appear prosperous.'

No one else could have phrased it so well. What the old man said was surely true, as I myself knew from dealings with professionals, limited though these were. When I went to see doctors, I was influenced by what their clinics looked like. I noticed if they were clean and bright or messy and gloomy. I saw what sort of furniture they held and of course whether they were empty or full of patients. It couldn't be so different for an engineer, even if he did have a British diploma. I feared that my son was in for an unpleasant surprise.

45

Just before dawn one morning, as I neared the bottom of the stairs the world started to spin. By then I was used to visiting the latrine many times each night, accustomed also to the ants that crawled along to sniff at my secretions. I knew they shouldn't have been there, but this was a fact I didn't wish to think about. Like others my age, I was adept at putting unpalatable worries about health to the back of my mind, preferring instead to focus on the *kueh* I consumed every morning. With the passing of the years, I seemed able to eat to my heart's content. Gone were the juicy folds around my belly; instead I had bones sticking out everywhere – from the hollows of both cheeks, from around my ribs, along arms and legs and even on my wrists. I ate as much as before, but instead of gaining weight I had the wonderful fortune of losing it. It occurred to me that my change of luck must have had some connection with the appearance of the tiny red ants in our latrine, but with so much going on I chose to tell no one. Why bother them when the weakness in my bones must surely be due to old age?

That morning my knees buckled. One minute I was upright, the next I slid. My collapsing frame made such a noise that everyone came running. I couldn't have fainted completely, because I remember what happened quite clearly. On its way down my head brushed against the wooden banister – not so much a knock as a scrape, accompanied by a thud, though that could have been just the sound of my palpitating heart. Then I was on the floor, staring into the darkness.

Our old servant Ah Hong was the first to arrive. When I looked up, I was greeted by a blurred vision; it was her voice I recognised first. 'Peng Choon Sau! You good-mah?' Too drained to speak, I nodded.

I tried to lift myself, but my daughter Hui Lin stopped me. 'Slowly, Mama,' she said softly. She and my son-in-law Kwee Seng helped me sit up. I heard someone light a fire in the kitchen. It must have been Li-Fei, because Hui Lin had asked for tea to revive me.

While I sat quietly with a cup of green tea, my son-in-law declared that a trip to the hospital was advisable. I had fallen, he said. It would be best to be examined by a doctor. I was about to tell him that I felt fine, if a little shaken, but something in the young faces stopped me. An indecipherable exchange passed between my daughter and her husband, a flicker of fear I had not seen before. With everyone looking so glum, it seemed churlish to refuse. After all, what harm could there be in consulting a Western doctor?

Once my son-in-law had left, Hui Lin, Weng Yu and my other sons helped me slowly up the stairs one step at a time so that I could lie in bed while waiting for the ambulance. It was just as well I moved, because the ambulance took over an hour to arrive.

That was how I found myself once again inside a noisy car as it sped along, siren blaring. Except this time I was the centre of attention. A young man fussed over me, while Hui Lin held my hand. Forced to lie on my back, I was unable to see a thing. I became dizzy from the spins and turns the vehicle took on its tortuous route towards the General Hospital. By the time we arrived I felt more ill than I had at the start of our journey.

This time there was no waiting team; the ambulance men simply wheeled me inside, while Kwee Seng and Hui Lin followed on foot.

My daughter held my right hand as we passed through endless open-air corridors. I was aware of an army in white uniforms: men and women, locals as well as *ang moh* bustling to and fro, speaking in a tongue I could not understand. The smell I had previously noticed when we had brought my second daughter hung even more pungently in the air. Out of curiosity I raised my head once, just before we turned a corner, to be rewarded by the sight of a worker scurrying past. In his hand he carried a bag bursting with a dark red fluid the colour of liver. When I realised what the bag contained, I felt as if a boulder had knocked me over. All the colour must have drained from my face, because the doctor who examined me was concerned about my pallor.

He came bounding towards us, a picture of health and cheer even at five in the morning. He bent to touch my cheeks, and my overwhelming memory is of his ears, lobes of skin slightly pink and so long that they wobbled like Nyonya jelly. After the doctor exchanged a few words with my son-in-law, I was told his name was Dr Pillay and that he was the Assistant Medical Officer. When I indicated that I was well enough to sit up, the entire team swung into action. In no time at all I faced the world from a chair. The doctor and I sized each other up. I saw that he was a fair-skinned Indian with a narrow nose. Hoping to put me at ease, Dr Pillay flashed a set of perfectly white teeth. Around his neck hung the black tube I recognised as the heartbeat instrument I had seen hanging around the necks of various doctors. Placing his right hand around my left eye, Dr Pillay pulled my eyelid up. That was when we really did stare eyeball to eyeball, and I noticed the droopy moroseness of the doctor's own eyelids.

Dr Pillay prodded me for a good ten minutes. Every so often he barked orders at a nurse, also Indian. At one point, with the handles of his heartbeat tube inside his large ears, he placed the metallic surface at the other end firmly on my baju while telling me to breathe in and out deeply. To my surprise I was able only to take shallow breaths; anything else exhausted me. 'Do you feel tired?' Dr Pillay asked. Via my son-in-law I told him I had been weak for a while, but since I was getting old this was hardly surprising. Dr Pillay's response was to shoot me a quizzical look. He fired off questions which made me blush. He wanted to know, for example, how often I went to the latrine. Then he asked if I had noticed anything unusual when I passed water. Had I seen ants, for instance? I glanced first at my daughter Hui Lin and then at my son-in-law, who both had expectant looks on their faces.

When she saw me hesitate, Hui Lin spoke up. 'Mama, do you know?' she asked, and I had to nod despite my reluctance to confess.

The surprise in my daughter's eyes made me slightly ashamed. 'I not want anyone to worry . . . ,' I offered lamely.

As soon as he heard about the ants, Dr Pillay announced that he suspected diabetes, or 'passing sweet urine', as the Chinese call the illness. Unfortunately the doctor told me he would need samples, one of my urine and another of my blood. My blood! I brought my hands to my face and gasped. The doctor, who seemed oblivious to my fears and my gathering tears, turned towards his nurse and began shouting orders. Hui Lin came to stand beside me, whispering, 'Don't worry, Mama, everything will be fine,' but as soon as I caught sight of the needle I felt faint. It loomed large in my mind, unlike the narrow acupuncture needles I was used to seeing in Dr Wong's clinic. 'No!' I screamed. Kwee Seng assured me there would only be a small prick and I wouldn't feel anything. My son-in-law tried to show me how tiny the point of the needle was, but instead of calming me their intervention increased my anxiety.

After another exchange between the doctor and my children, it was decided that I should lie down. The doctor and nurse helped me on to a bed in one corner of the room. I was crying openly by then, which no doubt distressed Hui Lin, who soon joined me. Together we sounded like a funeral cortège. When I finally felt the prick in my arm, the pain wasn't as bad as I had imagined, and I surprised myself by remaining conscious throughout. Still, my head was spinning afterwards from the thought of so much blood draining away.

We were told the test results would take two weeks. When three weeks later I returned to the hospital, Dr Pillay's grim diagnosis was confirmed. Medication wasn't available in Malaya, he said, and even if it had been, it would have been prohibitively expensive. 'So, you anything also cannot do-ah?' I asked in a mixture of astonishment and relief – astonishment that we would be given nothing, not even a small tablet, but also relief, since it meant I would not be subjected to humiliating rituals.

Dr Pillay nodded, large ears wobbling. His lack of medical weaponry didn't prevent him from barking out a command: 'Aunty, you must stop eating Nyonya *kueh*!'

Finally the good fortune I had enjoyed in recent times appeared to come to an end. Now more than ever my life would rest in the hands of Kuan Yin.

In the days following my diagnosis, the most that my children allowed me to do was to sit on our *barlay* chewing betel nut leaves with Siew Lan and the other well-wishers who called. The enforced idleness was challenging. Instead of resting, I kept up a constant shuffle from our inner hall into the kitchen. I shouted out commands, lifted the lids off pots and pans and generally made my presence felt. The household sighed in relief when an unexpected visitor arrived, bringing with him a proposition which finally kept me occupied.

The man was none other than Yap Min Kang, the tailor whom Weng Yu had evicted from our shophouse. He came to see how I was and to ask for assistance. The favour he sought – help with a deposit he needed for premises he wished to acquire – would take my life down a path I never could have imagined. Given the circumstances of his eviction, I could hardly refuse the request. I listened. The shop he was eyeing up was in a good location. I visited it the next day and was once again mesmerised by the smell of the rolls of cloth he kept everywhere and the sight of his scissors snipping. I judged his business to be sound.

In case he was unable to repay the money I lent, I asked Yap Min Kang for thirty rolls of fabric as security. In addition, he agreed to pay me interest of 2 per cent every month on the loan. Such income was what made the whole enterprise appealing. The rate I offered was less than half that charged by the Indian men in town – the Chetties, immigrants from India who controlled the moneylending business in Ipoh – but at the time I simply thought I was doing a favour to someone I had known for ten years.

It did not occur to me to ask for paperwork. On the day we sealed our deal, Yap Min Kang simply turned up at our house several times carrying rolls of fabric under his arm until he had brought thirty rolls. When that was completed, I invited him to the *barlay* for a cup of tea. We shook hands, I handed him his money and that was that.

I never expected word to spread about this small act of mine. Within days strangers came knocking on our door, all asking for loans. Like the tailor, none of them had a guaranteed income. Most were like me – women who couldn't read or write and who felt uncomfortable signing the pieces of paper demanded by the Chetties. Surprised by the deluge, I spent a week pondering what to do. Lending to Yap Min Kang was one thing, but what of the others?

In the end I lent selectively, my choices guided by intuition. I scrutinised the faces of those who came to see me; anyone with shifty eyes I refused to do business with, which meant turning most away. The rest I made enquiries about, finding out who their parents and family members were and visiting their premises. I always turned up unannounced so that I could examine the businesses for myself. All that I had was the word of my borrowers; we never signed any papers. 'Chye Hoon, you crazy-lah!' Siew Lan declared through a mouth stuffed full of betel leaf cud, influenced no doubt by her husband, who would never have entered any agreement without papers. Yet none of my borrowers ever missed a payment; they were simply grateful someone had been prepared to lend them money. My fiery reputation no doubt helped. Besides, I always asked for some form of security, a portion of which I kept throughout: rolls of fabric from the tailor, three bicycles from another man, catties of tin from a panhandler and so on.

In this way I generated additional income for my family. At the end of each month I would send my youngest son, Weng Choon, around town to collect the debts people owed. He went on our bicycle with the bell, ringing in receipts during those lean years.

46

Meanwhile my eldest son struggled. Clients did not come to see Weng Yu just because of his grand qualification. For fifteen months my son could barely earn enough to keep his two members of staff. He kept no income for himself and stopped giving me a monthly allowance.

Weng Yu limped on, unable to bring himself to ask for help. It was only after twelve months that he finally swallowed his pride and came to borrow a small sum from me. He was bright-eyed, telling me excitedly about the renovations he wished to implement on the shophouse, as if they were his idea. Of course I lent him the money free of interest – I wanted to see the boy succeed after all.

Towards the end of 1932, chinks of light came from among the dark clouds. The first piece of good news arrived from London – from my fourth son, Weng Yoon, who by then had commenced the final year of his law degree and was doing exceedingly well. The next glimmer of hope was brought by Weng Yu, who marched in one day with a wad of banknotes in his hand. 'Mama!' he said, thrusting the notes towards me. 'For you!'

I looked enquiringly at my little prince. 'What for?' I asked. My son's smile brought out his dimples, and for a moment he looked just like his father.

'Business has picked up,' he announced happily. 'I should be able to give you an allowance from now on.'

When I counted out the money, it came to twenty-five dollars, a pleasing amount. For weeks afterwards Weng Yu's cheeks continued to be flushed. Imagining that business must be good indeed, I wondered whether I had been mistaken. Could it be possible that this dreamy artistic boy of mine might actually have a talent for making money?

I soon learnt from Hui Lin the real reason for her eldest brother's good mood: he had met a girl. My daughter said little about the object of Weng Yu's interest other than that she was the daughter of one of his clients, a prosperous merchant who had recently built a mansion along the Gopeng Road.

The sound of such wealth alarmed me. I knew I would have to keep my promise to let my son choose his own wife in Malaya, but that did not stop me from burning with curiosity. By asking a question here and there, I had within a week found out everything important about the girl without having to leave our house.

Her name was Mei Foong. She was the second daughter of a Chinese immigrant, a man called Kwok Man Leung, whose wife, a devout Buddhist, had steeped their home in traditional Chinese values. The first thing people spoke of was the girl's beauty: shining hair tied up in two braids which fell lustrously down her shoulders and fair skin, without a blemish anywhere. Beauty concerned me less; I wanted to know what sort of first daughter-in-law she would make. It took persistence before I heard about Mei Foong's impeccable manners. From an early age, I was told, she and her siblings were taught to have respect for their elders and the right attitudes of worship. They apparently stood daily before their ancestors and their gods, which set my mind at rest a little. Of course Mei Foong enjoyed trappings I could never have afforded. These included a personal maid, who was on hand to dress her, fan her when she perspired and generally look after her every need.

Despite Weng Yu's burst of good fortune, I could not see how my son would maintain a girl of Mei Foong's background in the lifestyle to which she was clearly accustomed.

Mei Foong was reputedly clever, having received seven years of education at the Anglo-Chinese Girls' School – enough to be able to earn a living as a teacher. Though the girl conversed in Cantonese at home, she also spoke Hokkien and of course English, which she would have learnt at school. All of which, Siew Lan told me, made her highly desirable as a wife, and if Weng Yu didn't snatch her quickly, someone else would.

I sighed at this unexpected conclusion. I had worried that some unworthy girl would snare my handsome British-educated eldest son, but Siew Lan pointed out that the advantages in this case were very much the other way round. If the Kwok and Wong families were to be united, it would be the hand of fate; there was little I could do to either hasten or prevent it. Moreover, I could not find anyone with a bad word to say about the girl or her family. Rich they were, spoilt she apparently was not. Even Meng Seng, always sparing with compliments, spoke highly of Mei Foong's father. In his limited dealings with Kwok Man Leung, he had known him to be a man of his word.

Whatever happened, I could not intervene. I forced myself to sit back, awaiting signs from Kuan Yin.

The pounding on our front door was frantic, as if a disaster had befallen Ipoh. I unlatched the bolt to find Rokiah on our five-foot way, her face crushed in misery. 'Come quickly-lah, Makche Wong!' she cried out in Malay. 'Tuan has fallen. Please hurry!'

At the time I was dressed in the checked green-and-white baju and sarong I wore only at home, their fabric faded from years of scrubbing. It says a lot about my state of mind that I did not even think to change. Despite looking like a beggar, I dashed out with Rokiah towards her waiting rickshaw. The man ran as quickly as his legs could manage, while Rokiah told me how Se-Too-Wat, who had complained of feeling unwell for a number of days, had collapsed in the living room. Fortunately their boy, Don, now a grown man of twenty-five, was on hand to fetch a doctor. Still, Rokiah whispered that she wasn't sure the Tuan would survive. 'Very pale . . . as if life had left him,' she confided.

When we arrived, an ambulance was parked outside along the driveway, and two men in white paced up and down. I could hear Siew Lan crying inconsolably, and I knew then that we had come too late. I entered the house to find my friend arguing with a third man in a white uniform. Every now and then her son weighed in. They spoke in English, so that neither Rokiah nor I had any idea what was going on.

As soon as she saw me, Siew Lan rushed up and threw herself into my arms, burying her face into my right shoulder. 'Chye Hoon . . . Oh, Chye Hoon.' In between my own tears I looked up to see the boy whom I called Tong deeply affected by our distress.

'Don't worry, Mother,' he told Siew Lan in Hokkien. 'I won't let them take him away.'

When the men in white eventually left, Siew Lan regained enough composure to let me know what had happened. Evidently the ambulance men had wanted to remove Se-Too-Wat's body so that they could cut him up. 'What for?' I asked. Tong replied it was because no one knew the reason for Se-Too-Wat's death. He told me it was probably a heart attack, because his father had had heart problems for a while, but the medical authorities didn't know for sure. Without cutting him up, they would never really find out.

This unfortunate thought drove my friend wild again. 'You think!' Siew Lan exclaimed. 'He dead already, still want to cut him up. What for? He not going to come back-lah . . . Imagine go disturb old man like that!'

Soon Meng Seng hobbled in to offer his condolences. Between us we helped Siew Lan and her children in whatever way we could: I with supervising the preparations of food and drink, the patriarch with the renting of tables and chairs and a canopy outside in case it rained. Hundreds of people were expected, because Se-Too-Wat had been a prominent member of the white community, and my dear friend Siew Lan was of course well respected everywhere.

Until the day of the funeral I stayed at their house to keep my friend company. Not surprisingly Siew Lan walked around unsure of the ground beneath her feet. She burst into tears at the slightest provocation, and I was glad I was there to hold her hand. During the day my friend would wander between guests. In the evenings she sat next to me in the garden, chewing betel leaves and sipping coffee with that distracted look which told us she was lost among memories.

My eldest son, on learning that Se-Too-Wat had passed away, wept. After he dried his eyes, Weng Yu came to help Siew Lan and her children. His tall figure strode the garden, leading guests towards chairs and carrying cups of coffee and tea.

I was so busy that I had little time to grieve. It was only after the funeral service, held in a church and in English – which meant I could not understand anything – that images of Se-Too-Wat rushed at me in furious assault. That was when I cried for this white devil who had become a dear friend through the years. I recalled the day Se-Too-Wat married Siew Lan and how smart he had looked in his pristine white suit with the red carnation attached to his lapel. I sobbed at what I owed the man: a husband for my eldest girl and a job for my eldest boy, without which Weng Yu might never have begun a business. I remembered how Se-Too-Wat, arms dripping with sweat, had willingly borne the prickly heat of Taiping to tail my errant son-in-law.

Whenever I thought of our Taiping adventures, I became ashamed. Until then this white man had been an irritant, his spidery hairs more important to me than the kindness in his heart. Now that he was gone, I realised how good Se-Too-Wat had been to our family. I wished I had thanked him when I still had the chance.

47

After her husband passed away, Siew Lan felt bereft. 'Like my right arm chop off already,' she explained in unusually macabre fashion. My friend lost her pleasure in life, eschewing even the betel leaves she once adored. 'Teeth also no have. How to chew?' she grumbled.

As the weeks passed, the skin around Siew Lan's fingers grew into crinkly cages; lines became permanent features on her face. Her hair turned white, and though I knew this to be the consequence of no longer using dye, it still came as a shock. Even those of us who saw her regularly stared, unable to take our eyes off the veins of white. I would arrive at her house to find Siew Lan crying, her heart stirred by some object or other that reminded her of Se-Too-Wat. A memory loomed in every corner, and my poor friend found no peace. She even considered selling the house they had lived in, complaining that it was too big for just her and the servants.

I sympathised. After Peng Choon's demise, I too had wanted to flee Lahat Road. If it hadn't been for the children and my worries over whether Peng Choon's spirit would find us, I might well have moved us to a new home.

The same concerns plagued Siew Lan. She wished to make any new house easy for Se-Too-Wat's spirit to locate, which meant it could not be far from the English quarter, nor could the house be too large. Moreover it had to have all the conveniences to which Siew Lan had become accustomed, such as the English toilet most of us could only dream about. The first time she had shown me the contraption, we had stared at the white porcelain while giggling over the sitting position it required. With its long metal chain and its flush of water, the toilet struck me as peculiarly English – clean, self-contained and not for us.

But Siew Lan now announced that she could not live without her white bowl, which made finding another house a tall order. I looked in every neighbourhood where there was a house for sale. 'Toilet can build,' I told my friend. 'Place must find first.' My search took me even into Green Town, the leafy area where the plots of Wong family land stood.

Despite my best efforts Siew Lan was never ready to make a decision. Whenever the time came, she would deflect me with reminiscences. One day it was the pair of magnificent mahogany chairs in their small sitting area; another day it was the rolls of fabric she and Se-Too-Wat had brought me shortly after Peng Choon passed away. There was always something to recall.

At first I thought that what Siew Lan needed was time. I expected her to make a decision eventually, as she had always done throughout our friendship. Yet when the weeks passed and our options dwindled, my concerns grew. My friend continued to vacillate, apparently unable to make up her mind. On the one hand, she sobbed that she simply had to leave because it was too painful to stay; on the other hand, whenever an opportunity arose she grew flustered, too afraid to leave the neighbourhood with which she had grown so familiar. 'What to do?' she asked rhetorically. 'So hard-lah!'

Reaching across the *barlay* one day, I said to her, 'No, Siew Lan, not hard. You make up your mind only-lah. Move also can, no move also can. If you move, must pray a lot-lah. Just like that. Not hard.'

This brought a flood of tears. 'Sometimes . . . ,' she told me breathlessly, 'he in the room.' Siew Lan's fingers shook so much at this confession that she had to put down her well-loved Nyonya cup, the one whose pink borders and green dragons had faded with time. Siew Lan said she could feel Se-Too-Wat at night and wondered whether her time too had come.

'Chay! Why you say such things-ah?' I retorted, horrified.

I sighed, knowing then that Siew Lan would never move from the house she had shared with Se-Too-Wat.

The business of moving house was a matter to which I had given much thought, because when I saw our land in Green Town, I once again imagined a wooden house painted completely in lime green. I knew I too would have to make a choice: remain cocooned in Lahat Road, where I knew Peng Choon's spirit was safe, or head for the promise of Green Town, to the land he had given us.

Green Town was by then a sprawling neighbourhood dotted with fine houses, many of them built for government servants. Rubber smallholdings abounded, but with a hospital and an English-speaking school nearby, Green Town had potential. Our land had continued increasing in value, a thought which pleased me. I loved the neighbourhood, not least because Peng Choon had picked it. Siew Lan's indecision made me realise that if my dream of a Green House were to become a reality, I needed to act.

As for Siew Lan, she never moved. She stayed in her house with its English toilet, ensconced by the trimmed hedges and memories which washed over her in waves.

Weng Yu was equally downcast after Se-Too-Wat passed away. For many weeks his face remained as mournful as the ponies that had once dragged gharries across Ipoh town. Two months elapsed before he came towards me as I sat with my betel box on the *barlay*. He stood at the edge of the wooden platform, uncertain whether to join me or to stay where he was. From the look on his face, I could tell that the gloom had lifted. I invited him to sit.

Stepping up wearily, he crossed his legs one way and then another before clearing his throat. 'Mama,' he began hesitantly, 'it's time I got married.'

'You meet already a girl?' I asked. After nodding, Weng Yu remained strangely silent. When I prodded my son to reveal more, he mumbled that Hui Lin must surely have told me. 'What? But is you want to get married. You should with me speak,' I said, thinking what odd behaviour this son of mine had. Fancy wanting to marry and not saying more than three words!

There followed the much-curtailed story which his gregarious sister Hui Lin had already related. Days later, when Weng Yu brought Mei Foong to our house for her first family dinner, I had the satisfying opportunity of scrutinising my intended daughter-in-law at close quarters. The meal itself was a test I had devised to see how the girl would deal with spicy cuisine in a dining room devoid of the comforts she was used to. The young lady seemed unperturbed. She came gliding across the threshold in a Chinese tunic and trousers made of fine silk, her back straight and head held high – a regal bearing which reminded me of Peng Choon's. Though her clothes were loose-fitting, I could see that the girl had a slender figure and long creamy fingers unsoiled by work.

She was a striking beauty, of that there was little doubt. As well as the hair I had heard so much about, she had a fine complexion, discreetly enhanced by a coating of powder, though she would have been equally striking with no make-up. Her lips were coloured, not the bright red I was used to but a modern pink – the result, I guessed, of the new wave of imported goods that had reached our shops.

Throughout the meal Mei Foong's famous manners were on display. She didn't eat with her hands. She and Weng Yu were given their rice in bowls with a pair of chopsticks each, for which she seemed grateful. The girl tried and praised every dish. Having evidently been warned about the spiciness of our cuisine, she had come with a strategy in mind, and I watched as she mixed her dishes up to tame the effect of the chillies, which must surely have set her tongue on fire. Mei Foong delicately broke up the morsels of fish in her parcels of *otak-otak* before taking a sip of water, and then she would lift strands of *kangkong* fried with our infamous chilli paste and follow that with a spoonful of clear vegetable soup. It helped that she was accompanied by her personal maid, a tiny girl who seemed determined to keep her cool. The maid, attentive to every bead of sweat on her mistress's forehead, shook a triangular paper fan throughout dinner.

Despite her wealth, Mei Foong's kindness was obvious, for she treated her maid respectfully. After we finished, she insisted her maid not follow us into the inner hall. 'You must eat now, Chang Ying,' she said simply, thereby forcing Chang Ying to have her own meal with our servants. I was impressed and more than surprised that there was nothing I could find fault with. Indeed, my younger sons were in such awe of Mei Foong that they were clumsier than usual throughout the night, incapable apparently of filling their lettuce leaves or eating their braised pork without spilling gravy everywhere. What I remember best was Mei Foong's aura of tranquillity and the fragrance which lingered in the air after she left. When I recognised it as the smell of roses, presumably from the foreign scented water she dabbed on her skin, I coloured, remembering the story of Helen.

Weng Yu was adamant that his would be a Western wedding, and I had to conceal my disappointment. 'Mei Foong and her family, they don't mind-ah?' I asked quietly.

My son would have none of it. He assured me that his fiancée's family were happy to break with tradition. 'We have to be modern after all,' he told me drily. Conscious of my promise not to interfere, there was nothing I could say, especially since going 'modern' was all the rage in those days.

Even Siew Lan chided me for being supposedly conservative. 'You must not be so square, Chye Hoon,' she said playfully. 'Look at our buildings. These days they also round!'

My friend was referring to a new three-storey block on the Laxamana Road with, of all things, a curved corner. It was part of another spate of construction which had accompanied the recovery in Ipoh, except that this time the boom was no longer just about having more buildings, but also about making them taller, bolder. This famous curved building was an example. I thought it highly impractical, but everyone else loved it and the place, called the Lam Look Ing Bazaar after the towkay who had built it, became a focal point in town. I was one of the few who had never stepped foot inside, despite Siew Lan's attempts to change my mind. Having heard about the hotel and the dance hall on the top floor filled with pouting girls, I simply had no desire.

In the midst of such rapidly changing times, Weng Yu married Mei Foong in 1933. The only concession my son made to Chinese custom was to let me consult the priest over a choice of dates. Apart from that everything else was supposedly modern, though the food at the banquet remained Chinese. The official marriage was even conducted inside a registry office, an act considered seriously fashionable by some.

Afterwards a grand reception was held, to which hundreds of guests were invited. Knowing my limited financial means, Mei Foong's father had kindly agreed to foot all expenses. When I saw the decorations laid out on each of the round tables, all beautifully covered in white linen, and the ten-course Chinese banquet that was served, I was thankful for Kwok Man Leung's generosity. Not that I would have begrudged my son the wedding of his life, but we would never have been able to afford such a sumptuous feast for so many guests.

It was exhilarating to see my little prince marry in such fashion. My jubilation was the greater because my surviving children were all present – even Weng Yoon, my fourth son, had by then returned from London, a qualified lawyer with the right to set up his own practice. Yet I was conscious also of a weight gnawing at my heart, for it was clear that Weng Yu would never pass the values so dear to me on to his children. I was square, as Siew Lan had put it, and I realised I could never be otherwise.

My most enduring memory of Weng Yu's big day was the three-tiered cake which greeted the bride and groom at the front of the reception hall. From a distance the cake resembled three thick slabs one on top of another, each covered in white icing and dotted with artificial roses in red and yellow. It was only when my son and daughter-in-law had cut through the lowest and biggest tier that the secret within was revealed. To our utter astonishment a handful of pigeons flew into the air, soaring above us in the hall. Everyone clapped, never imagining we would live to witness such a spectacle.

The next day, my pride overflowed when I was shown a picture of the moment as captured by a local newspaperman. The photograph itself was in black and white, but the scene in my mind is forever in colour. There, sprawled across two pages, were the pigeons fluttering over my son and daughter-in-law, he resplendent in black bow tie and white suit, she wonderfully glamorous in a lace-bedecked gown, the skirt sweeping down to her ankles and hovering over a pair of stunning red shoes. It seemed a wholly auspicious start to my little prince's married life.

◆ ◆ ◆

The birds that flew out of Weng Yu's wedding cake had a strange effect on the Wong family: within just twelve months two of my other sons had also entered into marriage.

The first of these entanglements was somewhat unfortunate. Weeks after Weng Yu's wedding a letter came from Seremban, from my second son, Weng Koon, who at the time was still a teacher in that town. My daughter Hui Lin read it aloud to me, and when her breathing grew short and sharp I knew that a girl was involved.

'Tell me,' I commanded.

It transpired that her brother Weng Koon had married a Cantonese girl without informing me. I was so stunned that I had to ask Hui Lin to repeat herself.

After she confirmed the bare facts, I began yelling into the steamy afternoon air, 'He why do like that? His wife got problem-ah? She deformed-ah?'

I continued hurling abuse in this vein at both my son and his wife, whom I hadn't even met. I wondered what I had done wrong in this life. Why were my children turning their backs on me? This second boy of mine had truly taken disobedience to new heights. Why, even his eldest brother had not dared to go behind my back. All felt lost, for without filial piety, our family, indeed our whole community, would be adrift.

When Hui Lin added that Weng Koon had asked to bring his new wife for a visit, I shrieked in disbelief. My screams disturbed the neighbourhood cockerels and dogs, which crowed and howled in unison, causing a symphony to rise over the hill on Lahat Road. Hui Lin, fearing that the slightest provocation would stoke my anger to new heights, wisely let my rage cool itself. By the time I cried out for the fourth time – 'The boy of course say something else in his letter!' – she knew that the moment had come.

Touching me gently on the shoulder, Hui Lin whispered, 'It's done, Mama. You cannot change it. Please go and rest. All this shouting is bad for your health.'

When I told the patriarch what had happened, he threw me subtle but unmistakable looks. In a gentle voice Meng Seng reminded me that Weng Koon was still my son. 'Chye Hoon, don't be so hard.'

Only it wasn't hardness I felt but pain and frustration. I could no longer control what my children chose. I simply had to accept their choices or risk losing them. I was a mother who preferred square corners, while my children delighted in the latest shapes, such as that of the exotic building on the corner of Laxamana Road. I lay awake at night confused and regretful, yet also ruling out any welcome for my son or his new wife.

48

After their marriage, Weng Yu and Mei Foong moved into a shophouse on Chung Thye Phin Road, beyond the girls' school in New Town. The location, though close to her parental home, was almost an hour away by rickshaw. As a result I saw little of my son and daughter-in-law in the early years of their marriage, except when they came for dinner.

It must have been on one of those occasions when I gleaned that all was not well. At least not with my daughter-in-law. Picking over the half dozen or so dishes we always set out in our most beautiful china, Weng Yu seemed happy enough, but there were moments when I was sure I caught flickers of sadness in Mei Foong's eyes. My son, detached as usual, didn't seem to notice.

Not that Mei Foong would ever have complained, least of all to me, certainly not about my own son. She was faultless as a daughter-in-law: refined, courteous and ever respectful. Yet even she in less guarded moments let slip hints.

The first came when she told us how much she had loved school. Mei Foong's normally calm eyes lit up when she talked about her favourite subject, which turned out to be, of all things, mathematics. Instead of the lulling tone I had come to expect, her voice became animated and her cheeks turned the colour of the pink eggs we gave away on a baby's full moon. In vivid detail Mei Foong described the branch of mathematics at which she had excelled – the study of shapes and measurements and drawings.

She revealed then that she had once dreamt of becoming a teacher. This made everyone's ears prick up. 'What do you think of that, Elder Brother?' Kwee Seng teased my son. 'Your wife might go out to work!'

Weng Yu gave his brother-in-law a scathing glance. 'No wife of mine will ever have to work,' he declared in his booming baritone, inadvertently lifting his head so that his nose peered down at the rest of us. It was a posture to which we had grown accustomed, but his wife exchanged a look with him.

What passed between them I could not tell, except that when she next spoke her voice was steely. 'No need to shout. I'm sure it was a joke, wasn't it, Kwee Seng?' I watched dumbstruck as my son's manners improved, to the extent that even his nose stopped staring down at us during the rest of the meal. For the first time I felt a grudging respect for the petite woman before me who seemed able to influence my son. I might have lost my way with him, but I began to perceive an ally in his wife.

That night I thought about Mei Foong's revelations. I recalled how, when Father first taught me to count, I had been spellbound by the abacus and had spent hours moving the beads up and down, until I conquered them with a palpable feeling of triumph in my chest.

My daughter-in-law said that she had dreamt of becoming a teacher. Not that she had wanted to become one; rather, that she had dreamt of it. I remembered that I too had dreamt of school and of learning. Then, when I realised this would never come to pass, I kept the only thing I could: my spirit.

I wondered how much Mei Foong had really wanted to marry. Mei Foong, unlike me, had attended school and would have had other options. Though a teacher's salary could never have bought the comforts she was used to, it would have given her independence. As it was, the girl had neither: not the chance of fulfilling her dream, nor the comforts of the truly wealthy – for it would have been impossible for my son to keep her in the style in which she had lived previously. The Chinese tunics and trousers she wore took on a shabbier appearance; her face too began to look subtly different. Gone were the creamy skin and the distinctive pink on her lips, to be replaced by what were seen on ordinary women – the white of common powder and the red of local lip rouge. Her scent of roses had also turned into a fragrance decidedly less powerful. When I asked whether she minded giving up the imported toiletries she had once used, Mei Foong smiled, replying matter-of-factly that one had to cut one's cloth according to the size of one's wallet.

She continued to visit us throughout her first two pregnancies, a phenomenon which bothered me. Not only that, she even went regularly to see her uncle who lived on Belfield Street in Old Town, not far from us. This traipsing around Ipoh with a belly hanging over the side of a rickshaw was not something I thought wise, but Mei Foong simply laughed. 'I'm fine, Mama,' she said in that deep voice of hers in such a way that I could feel her strength.

Towards the end of 1934 Mei Foong gave birth to a boy they named Wai Sung. Though desperate to see my latest grandchild, I worried about stepping into the hospital, fearing I would be dragged against my will into a room where some waiting doctor would stand. Only after my fourth son promised that nothing of the sort would happen did I visit. By then the baby was already two days old.

We went in three rickshaws. When we arrived, Weng Yu was standing stiffly near the window as if unsure what to do. From a distance he watched his wife cradle their son. As soon as Weng Yu saw us, though, he beamed, slipping into the role of proud father. 'Meet my baby boy,' he announced.

During the hour we were allowed to stay, I observed Weng Yu's peculiar aloofness for a man whose son had just been born. When I asked what he was thinking of, my son smiled – that wonderful smile in which he showed off his perfect teeth and handsome dimples. 'Many things to think about, Mama,' he said. 'Fathers have more work, you know!'

Wai Sung was a lovely pink child with a snub nose, which stood out in the room. We couldn't understand where that nose had come from, seeing that our noses were long and thin. 'His grandmother's nose,' Mei Foong informed us. He also had amazing hair, so abundant that it covered the top and sides of his head thickly in mats and even reached down below his ears, a sight that elicited exclamations throughout the room. 'Wahh! Lot of hair! Good-lah, he'll never be bald!'

◆　◆　◆

Over time the ants swarming into our latrine grew in number. Despite my valiant attempts at hosing the floor, the creatures returned, darting about wildly and sniffing at empty space. They were perpetually in our kitchen, caught by the water basins protecting our food cupboard. Whenever the basins – in which the legs of the cupboard stood – were emptied, their waters were inky black with creatures.

Other than the ants, I did not feel so different. I breathed more heavily during walks, but then again who wouldn't at my age? It was only when I collapsed in the People's Park one afternoon that I felt fear. I fell suddenly, exactly as I had when I went tumbling down the stairs. One minute I was standing on two feet, the next my knees folded into themselves and my head hit the ground. When I opened my eyes, I could barely see. Everything around me had turned white, full of blurred dots. It crossed my mind that I had perhaps reached the other side. Blinking furiously, I opened and closed my eyes many times until the dots disappeared. Standing over me was a stranger, who asked if I was the Nyonya matriarch of Wong family *kueh* fame. In a weak voice I said yes. The woman helped me to my feet, walked me to the edge of the park and once there promptly hailed a rickshaw, which carried me all the way home to Lahat Road.

The following evening my fourth son, Weng Yoon, sank his stocky frame into the chair beside mine. It was a hot, sticky night, and the sharp hissing of cicadas floated in through the open air well. Without warning my son told me that it was time I retired.

This was not what I was expecting to hear. Weng Yoon was then extremely busy with his legal practice; it being barely a year old, he worked all hours from dawn to dusk, and when he did come home he brought work with him. After dinner, while I strolled along our street or sat sipping tea, Weng Yoon would be at the kitchen table with his bundles of papers laid out in piles or rolled into clutches, each neatly tied with a pink ribbon. The last thing he should have been doing was worrying after his old mother. I told him so, but the boy would not give in.

'Ai-yahh! If no work, I how to spend my time, Son?' I argued. 'Nothing to do, how can-ah?'

'Mama, how many women your age run three businesses?'

When I pointed out that I could hardly be said to run anything, we faced each other like warring buffalo. Weng Yoon raised one of his bushy eyebrows in a thunderous look he no doubt employed to great effect inside the courthouse where he spent his waking hours, but the boy forgot that I was his mother. I was not going to be put off by a child who had once nestled inside my belly. I reminded my son that our servants took care of the *kueh* business. As for moneylending, I indulged only sparingly, and the two rented shophouses didn't even need me – it was his youngest brother, Weng Choon, who took care of rent collection once a month.

'But there are repairs, Mama! You should be resting.'

We continued in this vein, until I promised to think about retirement. 'This is big decision,' I said. In the distance the cicadas screeched in sympathy.

I decided to seek the opinion of the patriarch, who himself had retired many years before. I was surprised when he told me to take Weng Yoon's advice. 'His heart is in the right place,' the old man said with a faraway look in his eyes. Meng Seng's beard was then already the white of coconut milk on its first squeeze. When talking, he liked to caress its arid strands. The more ponderous he became, the faster his fingers would work, as if each stroke gave him a new idea. He described the visit my fourth son had paid him on his return from London. Unlike Weng Yu before him, Weng Yoon had shot off to see the patriarch and almost went down on his knees. 'I had to stop him,' the old man said with a quaking voice.

Meng Seng subsequently gave Weng Yoon a financial guarantee so that he could start his business. I never heard the exact details, but I knew Weng Yoon could not have established his legal practice if it had not been for Meng Seng's unflinching support. Which was enough to tell me, yet again, how much my family owed this exasperating man.

The patriarch seemed happy to while away his time, but I wondered what I would do if we didn't make *kueh* and laksa. The day would surely come, but I would delay it for as long as I could.

When Mei Foong was pregnant with their second child, she came to visit us more often. Seeing how her first pregnancy had passed, I became more relaxed at the idea of an unborn grandchild being rocked on a rickshaw, though I can't pretend I liked it. I guessed that my daughter-in-law was bored at home, as my son had hired two servants by then: the first to cook and clean; the second to look after Wai Sung, which meant that Mei Foong wasn't much needed.

It was then that she and I started talking. Or rather, I started talking: my daughter-in-law merely listened. With each visit I poured out more and more of my heart, until the day came when I had told Mei

Foong all my troubles. She knew about Helen and how hurt my son had been, also what he'd been like on his return, when he had refused to speak our dialects. Though she said nothing, Mei Foong's eyes widened. Finally, as if she had made some sort kind of decision, she turned to touch my hand.

'Mama, you and Weng Yu will be united someday.' The words, when Mei Foong spoke them in that quietly stirring fashion of hers, had a palliative effect. I believed her and felt immeasurable relief.

It was Mei Foong who encouraged me to build the Green House. While describing the Wong family lands, I told her about my vision of a wooden house painted completely in lime green; also how I had resisted the move for years out of fear that Peng Choon's spirit would never find us.

'But it's been twenty-five years, Mama! You have to live your life.'

'You say these words, very correct. I also like that think.'

'Why not build your house now on one of the plots of land?'

'But my sons also will need the land.'

'One of them can live with you,' the girl answered without any hesitation.

The more I thought about Mei Foong's idea, the more I liked it. It would be easier than buying another plot, as I had been vaguely considering. Siew Lan thought Mei Foong's plan a good one too, though my friend, who continued to be dogged by unshakeable fatigue, was distinctly less effusive. 'Only if you anything also no need to do,' she told me. 'We now no strength already-lah, cannot here go there go, like before.'

One night after dinner, with a wink towards my daughter-in-law, I raised the subject with Weng Yu. It was another wonderful Malayan evening when the River of Heaven blinked down on us. With my fourth son, Weng Yoon, also present, I told the boys that as one of them was a civil engineer and the other a lawyer and both were British-trained, it would be best for them to divide the land their father had acquired.

We would need six equal plots – one for each surviving son – each with the necessary papers, which everyone in modern Malaya demanded. I would build a house on one of the plots, I said, a brand-new wooden house painted green, as befitted a dwelling in that part of town.

My sons looked at me in astonishment. Weng Yoon immediately reminded me of my diabetes, but I parried him by pointing out that what I requested would have to be carried out in any case. 'You scared for my health, then you do quickly-lah. I want to live in my house while I still strong.'

My fourth son breathed deeply. 'Mama, please . . .' When I retorted that I wished to die in my own house, not in a home rented from someone else, Weng Yoon could think of no response. I had won, but I decided there and then that building the Green House would be the last thing I would do. It seemed fitting; finally I would do something entirely for myself, with my children's help, on the land my late husband had left us. I felt like the warrior Hang Tuah once more, wisely wielding the sword I had been given. The Green House was my dream. It would also be my legacy.

49

When I knew that my dream of a house in green would come true, an astonishing contentment settled on me, a feeling broken only by Siew Lan's persistent complaints of fatigue.

'I always so tired-lah,' my friend said when I went to visit. 'Sleep and sleep also still tired.'

'You see doctor already-ah?'

'Of course, Chye Hoon! I take all those herbs also, still no good. We now old already-lah. What to do?'

Though I said nothing, I was worried about my friend. Black sacs hung below her large eyes, and the folds of her kebaya gathered ever more loosely around a shadow of skin and bone. I made up my mind to speak to the patriarch when I next saw him, to ask whether he knew another doctor whom Siew Lan could consult.

The following day Weng Yu's and Mei Foong's second child, a baby girl called Lai Hin, entered this world. My granddaughter's birth proved rather dramatic; indeed, if fate hadn't intervened, her arrival could easily have been a catastrophe, for Mei Foong went into labour at her uncle's house on Belfield Street.

When the contractions began, my daughter-in-law was unruffled, thinking they would settle and she would have time to get home and thence to hospital. But instead of there being periods of lull, the tugs grew increasingly violent. Mei Foong sensed she was dealing with a headstrong child, one in a hurry to enter the world and who would not be stopped. Within a half hour her waters had broken, and my daughter-in-law knew that her body would expel the baby before help could arrive. Her uncle, a widower, stood helplessly watching the pools of liquid inundating the floor, barely able to listen to his niece's tormented screams. Fortunately an aunt happened to be there who had borne six children. With plenty of experience on birth matters, albeit not in the capacity of a midwife, this aunt had the presence of mind to scrub her hands and then to shout for rags and pieces of cloth, anything they could find, while she massaged Mei Foong's belly, giving whatever relief was possible with nutmeg oil and her gentle palms.

By the time the ambulance came, my granddaughter was already out in the world.

I received the news half an hour later, just as I was preparing to leave for Siew Lan's house. For a fleeting instant I felt torn, but then the excitement of another grandchild took over. How could it not? I told myself that I would see my friend in the afternoon, when it would be more comfortable once the sun was lower in the sky.

My granddaughter, a little girl bristling with energy and covered in thick mats of hair just like her elder brother's, was a joy to behold. Her hair was darker than anything I'd seen on one so young – black like starless nights – and shiny too, as if it would start to glow. It was only after reaching the hospital that I heard the circumstances of her birth. Panic engulfed me. Losing my head, I screamed at Mei Foong, stunning everyone in the process, most of all her husband. I couldn't understand why my daughter-in-law would put her baby at such risk. Perhaps because of the harrowing story of her birth I had a soft spot for Lai Hin from the outset. The impatience she displayed during her journey into this world I took as a sign that she might have inherited a little of the Wong fire.

On returning to Lahat Road from the hospital, we found a distraught Rokiah wailing in the kitchen. My heart sank when I realised that both our servants were crying too. 'Ahh . . . ahh . . . Makche Wong . . .' Rokiah herself seemed beyond comfort. Tugging at my arm, she gestured towards the front door. I followed meekly, numb from shock.

Rokiah was too disconsolate to speak during our rickshaw journey. My main concern was whether Siew Lan had suffered pain. On this point Rokiah shook her head but I didn't believe her – I had to see for myself. The image of my friend sitting upright on a chair with both eyes still open was to remain with me for the rest of my life. Her body lay limp on one of the very chairs she had reminisced about – a well-polished mahogany chair Se-Too-Wat had acquired in Singapore. Her son, Don, had reached the house by then, and he helped Rokiah and I carry Siew Lan to bed, where we lay her down before gently closing her eyelids.

Knowing what would come next, Don went quietly downstairs, leaving us alone with his mother's body. While Rokiah was in the kitchen preparing the warm water we needed, I began speaking to my friend. I whispered to Siew Lan that I couldn't believe she had left so suddenly without any warning at all, so that I hadn't even had time to say a proper goodbye. I told her how sorry I was that I hadn't seen her that morning. The words choked in my throat, but no tears would come. Instead, gripped by an inexplicable urge, I released Siew Lan's hair from its coiled bun. I stroked the long strands, first with my fingers, then with a brush I found on my friend's dressing table. Her hair was completely white, but it still felt healthy, the strands thick and smooth; they glided like silk on my fingers.

When Rokiah returned with a basin of warm soapy water and a sponge, we undressed Siew Lan and started to wash her. We spoke to her throughout, Rokiah in Malay, me in Hokkien. We said many beautiful things, and I hoped Siew Lan could hear us. I reminded her of how we had met at the Pa Lo Old Temple those years ago by chance, two young women in need of companionship. I remembered the creases etched into her face even then, the sadness of past disappointments she carried in her eyes. I told her that I had been wrong about Se-Too-Wat – he had indeed been a good man. I knew this, I said, not only because of the way she began to glow after their marriage, but also from the kindnesses he had freely bestowed on my family. As Rokiah chose a fresh kebaya and sarong for her mistress, I prayed that Siew Lan's and Se-Too-Wat's souls would be reunited.

The next few days passed as if in a dream. I remember little about what went on. I just know there were people constantly coming and going – family, friends, well-wishers who had only known Siew Lan to say hello to on the street. Food and drink appeared miraculously, organised by Siew Lan's children, Flora and Don, with help from the patriarch, who despite his own frailty retained his wits about him. My eldest son seemed much affected by Siew Lan's passing away. Though he visited with his wife, they did not stay long. There was incessant noise throughout. Priests in yellow robes chanted all day and late into each night, accompanied now and again by the beat of an enormous gong they had carried in.

When it came time for the cremation, a long cortège filed out towards the Gopeng Road, led by a multitude of priests, who carried four gongs between them. These they beat intermittently with great vigour. There were so many mourners that traffic in New Town came to a standstill for hours until we had all passed through.

It was a scorching morning. I could walk no further than the few hundred yards to the corner of Hugh Low Street before exhaustion overcame me, and I climbed into the motor car my fourth son, Weng Yoon, had hired. Everyone, including those of us riding in the relative shade of the cars, was sweaty and bedraggled by the time we reached the Sam Poh Temple outside town. Yet the sight of that august structure soaring into the air lifted my weak spirits. As Weng Yu and Mei Foong held my hands, I whispered that I too wanted this to be my final place of rest. 'Chay, Mama! Don't say such things please,' Weng Yu begged.

Once inside Ipoh's limestone caves, I was revived. Cool air blew in, breath of the gods which fed the wondrous hills I had loved from the first moment. I imagined my best friend's soul being freed from her body, rising into new worlds beyond. In this magical place of rock and ancient trees, my turn would one day come.

The day after my friend's funeral, Flora and Don appeared on the five-foot way outside our house. Don, with his dark complexion and round, flat face, was a replica of his Malayan mother, while his sister beside him, with her rosy cheeks and brooding double-creased eyes crowned by exceptional lashes, could have passed for European. In her hand she carried a plain receptacle, the sight of which made me shiver. We three stood smiling dumbly at one another, until I finally found my voice and invited them to enter.

Flora glided in. With her head held gracefully high, she moved like a swan on water, her white dress billowing in the breeze. I marvelled at her poise in the face of such a tragic loss. Flora explained in an apologetic tone that she and Don couldn't stay long – she had to return to her job in Kuala Lumpur. Too miserable to attempt small talk, I nodded, unable to focus on anything except the object on her lap, a plain vessel with three distinctive lines etched around its body. What Flora said I have no idea. Her voice washed over me until the moment she faltered and I caught the words 'Mama . . . alone by herself . . .'

I looked up to see Flora's beautifully dark eyes misting beneath their willowy lashes.

At the sight of her tears, I berated myself once again for not having called on Siew Lan when I still had had the opportunity. If I had not procrastinated, I could have bid farewell to my friend of thirty-six years. As it was, all I had left were memories and the urn on Flora's lap. I could barely bring myself to hold the urn. Someone else had to take it from Flora.

After Flora and Don left, I found the urn sitting forlornly on our altar table beside the jar that held my husband's ashes. I picked the vessel up with both hands. As I ran unsteady fingers along the three lines on its body, I was shaken again by grief and regret. It was only much later, after the pins and needles had started attacking my feet, that I realised I had forgotten to thank Flora and Don for this gift of their mother's ashes.

◆ ◆ ◆

Siew Lan's demise changed our lives. My little prince, it seemed, was especially affected. Within a fortnight of her funeral, Weng Yu went to pay his respects to the patriarch and even took Mei Foong along.

'He say what-ah?' I asked the old man.

'Oh, it was just a social call,' Meng Seng replied with a wave of his hand. 'They dropped in to see how I was-lah. Very nice of them.' Then, narrowing his eyes and stroking his moustache, he added mysteriously, 'I think the boy has repented.'

The comment raised my interest, as Meng Seng well knew it would. 'Why you like that talk-kah?' I demanded. 'My son say sorry-ah?'

The patriarch shook his head, but when he next spoke his voice conveyed a distinctive air of satisfaction. 'I think, Chye Hoon, you can finally stop worrying about your son. The boy has seen sense . . . much more humble now, not like before.'

When my eldest son and his wife next came to dinner, I was stupefied. Not only had the boy's swagger mellowed, but he even took care not to point his nose down on us. Remembering Meng Seng's words, I wondered how it could be that it had taken Siew Lan's leaving us to make my son sorry.

'My husband was impressed by the number of people at her funeral, Mama,' my daughter-in-law explained one afternoon.

'What you mean?' I asked.

Mei Foong's response was a deep sigh. 'You know what Weng Yu is like,' she said softly.

I shook my head in incomprehension.

'He has his own ideas. He sees this woman, uneducated, doesn't work . . . and yet half of Ipoh turns up to pay their last respects. So he had to ask himself why . . . What did Siew Lan Ee have? He searched his heart.'

'I told my husband it was time, Mama,' Mei Foong added, her voice turning steely. 'Time to make up with the family who has given him so much. Going to see Meng Seng Pak was my idea.'

At last I dared to hope.

In the ensuing months, when Weng Yu's conciliatory manner persisted, I finally believed that my eldest son had come home to his roots. If he could serve as a role model for his younger siblings, I would not have lived in vain. There was still a chance that Siew Lan's dire prediction 'Maybe one day . . . no more Nyonya' would not come to pass.

50

In those days I often found myself taking out Siew Lan's favourite Pekalongan sarong, the only possession of hers I had kept. The shapes and colours of Java on the cloth – previously vivid in blacks, reds and greens – were by then barely visible, and no one else could understand what I saw beneath its faded lustre, or the volley of memories the sarong evoked. I would retrieve it from inside my almerah just so that I could hold it in my hands. I would place it on my dressing table and stroke its well-worn material, smooth from the years of washing.

On some days, feeling the cloth on my skin was not enough. Like a jilted lover I longed to hear my friend's voice, to smell her scent on our *barlay*. In desperation I would pick up the pale purple sarong and place it tight against my nostrils, pathetically attempting to evoke her fragrance. It was only after my third daughter, Hui Lin, saw me sniffing at the sarong that I became self-conscious. Though she said nothing, her astonishment was obvious. I became more furtive thereafter, breathing in my best friend's aroma only behind locked doors, where my secret would stay safe.

◆ ◆ ◆

By the time Mei Foong came to see me, the Wong family land had already been broken up into the six parcels I had asked for. Weng Yu and his fourth brother, Weng Yoon, showed me their drawings, outlined on rolls of special paper in fine black ink, just like the plans my eldest son had once made of Ipoh town. The shape and size of each plot were visible, as were the tree-like figures denoting the small rubber estates, which made the neighbourhood so leafy. Having encouraged me towards my dream, Mei Foong took a continued interest in the Green House, and I thought she had come to discuss the next phase of work.

The servants were preparing lunch when she shuffled in, wearing a faded Chinese tunic and the type of black trousers favoured by the amahs. Mei Foong was weighed down by the third child she was then carrying, and the sight of trousers on her legs caused my tongue to desert me.

'Comfortable-ah?' I finally asked, not knowing what else to say. Smiling, my daughter-in-law nodded.

When a long and ponderous silence ensued, I sensed that Mei Foong had come to ask my advice. From our kitchen floated the tantalising aroma of chillies and dried shrimp frying. Though my eyes were failing, my nose and taste buds were as sharp as ever; one whiff was all it took for my mouth to water. I savoured the thought of lunch while waiting for Mei Foong to come to the point. It took ten minutes before she confessed.

'I'm worried about Weng Yu.'

'Why?' I asked, nostrils dancing to the wonderful smell of sambal.

'He's changed in recent months.'

'That mean what?'

'He . . . comes home later than usual.'

I was unsure what my daughter-in-law was saying. It didn't help that from where I sat she appeared as dim as a ghost.

'I need your help,' the figure whispered.

'You want me to do what, Daughter?'

'Talk to my husband,' Mei Foong replied, more forcefully this time and in a tone full of expectation, as if I could perform miracles.

There was a sizzling sound . . . something being poured into a hot wok, followed at once by a smell which I recognised as *petai* – the crunchy, fiery Malayan bean – being cooked. Shaped like a beetle, the bean is an astonishing laxative, which provokes unique explosions all over Malaya. *Petai* was also my favourite dish, and its odours trailed through our house for days.

'Maybe my son just got more work,' I said when I had regained my concentration. Mei Foong shook her head.

When our servants banged the gong to announce lunch, Mei Foong rose, said she had to hurry home for her afternoon nap and then disappeared as quickly as she had arrived, leaving me with nothing but an enigmatic message.

'Mama, if you can't help him, no one else can.'

Late next morning, after counting the coins Li-Fei had brought back, I set off towards the shophouse on Hale Street that Weng Yu had refurbished. Hard as I tried, I failed to think what Mei Foong could have meant. When I climbed out of my rickshaw, I was saddled with a niggling feeling that the girl knew more than she had said.

As soon as I stepped inside Weng Yu's office, I could tell that neither of the moving apparitions was my son. One of the hazy persons I recognised as my son's assistant, a boy who seemed oddly nervous. He wished me good morning and then stood with his hands together, as if he didn't know what to do. Breathing heavily, the assistant told me that Mr Wong had gone to see a client.

'Weng Yu when come back?'

Neither the assistant nor the draughtsman seemed to know, a fact I found amazing. My son was running his business very badly. I imagined a new client walking in as I had done and wondered what his reaction would be on finding the boss away, whereabouts unknown. The client would take his project elsewhere of course. There were enough engineers in town to provide Weng Yu competition – of that I was certain. Men who could build houses and bridges just as well, even if they didn't have British qualifications. It was inconceivable that my son could continue in this undisciplined fashion. I shuddered at what I would have to say to the wayward boy.

Meanwhile the assistant offered me Weng Yu's chair, a high stool my son had imported from Europe. Made of unforgiving wood, it stood on three legs instead of four and was so hard on my posterior that I had to move on to a local cane chair. Not knowing where my son was or how long he would be away, I soon decided to head home.

I would normally have hailed a rickshaw there and then, but in those years I was assailed by nostalgia. Following an urge to retrace the walk I had taken with Peng Choon during our first tour of Ipoh, I strolled towards Leech Street. It was only a few minutes away on foot.

Along the next block from my son's office, my ears caught a distinctive sound – of tiles clanging and men laughing. The shophouse looked just like ours, except that its front door was closed and the bright blue shutters of its windows flung wide open. From inside came raucous voices and the noise of mah-jong tiles crashing against one another. A sudden clattering erupted, with voices shouting in both jubilation and commiseration all at once and in Cantonese. 'Pong! Eat!' someone yelled. 'Wahh! Eat like that-ah!' a low voice cried out. 'Ai-yahh! Such pity-lah! I why throw that tile?'

Something prompted me to knock. What it was I shall never know, except that the thought came with a lucidity which stopped my heart. I climbed the shallow steps leading from the street up on to the five-foot way. Once on the five-foot way I stood for a few minutes, staring hard at the wooden and very blue front door before banging with my clenched fist. The portly middle-aged man who opened it looked surprised to see me. 'Wong Weng Yu here-mah?' I asked. 'I am his mother,' I added in a firm voice. The man nodded curtly before turning around. 'Weng Yu!' he said, shouting towards the back of the shop. 'Your mother!'

At those words play ceased. No one stirred while the man at the front door helped me over the raised ledge at the doorway entrance that kept evil spirits at bay. From afar a figure made its way towards us. Through the acrid pall of cigarette smoke it was hard to tell whether the moving man was my son, though he bore Weng Yu's gait. I could barely breathe. Electric fans hung from the ceiling, but their blades turned lazily, hardly stirring the stale streams rising into the air.

Fear gripped me. I was reminded of the opium den into which I had once ventured with Father. I recalled the two men who had come tumbling out as they pummelled one another. Nearly thirty years had passed, but my heart still beat fast at the memory of what they had said, at the way they had cursed their mothers. The blood roared through my veins.

Amidst revulsion I was aware of a strong smell of roses, the same fragrance Mei Foong had worn early in her marriage. When my eyes adjusted to the darker interior, I realised that there were women at the mah-jong tables, holding cups and cigarettes in their hands.

Everyone was scrutinising me then, men and women alike. Those who sat close by stared openly. The others further away probably did too, but I could only sense their eyes from where I stood. For the first time I regretted the bright red baju I had put on.

When the figure walking towards us finally stopped, it turned out indeed to be my son. His face was as red as my tunic, which at least told me that Weng Yu knew shame, yet when the boy opened his mouth he shocked me.

'What are you doing here, Mama? Who told you to come?' he screamed, making me jump.

Though Weng Yu had always been a gentle boy, as I stood near him my heart thumped. My lips became strangely immobile. I was aware only of breathing and smoke, the perfume of roses and the smell of coffee.

Eventually the sight of my son in so incongruous a setting propelled me to speak. I gave Weng Yu a choice: either he came to our house that night, or I would come to his and we could talk in front of his wife and children. It was up to him.

By the time I finished, my throat felt parched, even though I had said just a few words. Weng Yu's face darkened. Without answering, he began shouting once more.

'This is no place for you! I want you to leave now, Mama!'

'You come tonight or not?'

'Mama, I'm thirty-five years old,' my son said irritably. 'Not a child any more!'

'You tell me-lah, you come or not?'

That was when I felt Weng Yu's hands on my right elbow, nudging me away. His elegant fingers dug into the sleeves of my baju and I looked at my son in wonder. How could someone so unathletic be so strong? I had a sensation of standing on a cliff edge and being dragged by stronger forces. A scuffle broke out between Weng Yu and the middle-aged man who had let me in. As they pushed at each other, I heard the older man telling my son to let me go.

It felt like a long way to the front door. The room stretched from the front of Hale Street to the tiny lane at the back. Nothing untoward happened. No one shoved or threatened me, but I was shaking when I left. Holding back tears, I shivered all the way home. When we reached our front door, the coins fell from my hands as I paid the rickshaw puller. I rushed to the washbasin in our inner hall, where I crouched to hurl fear out in great oozy clumps. When I looked down, I saw the remains of my breakfast.

As soon as I could, I went to Kuan Yin's altar. My heart was filled with shame and my head with regret for the foul deeds I must have committed in a previous life. How else to explain my fate?

Then, while standing in candlelight enveloped by white wisps twirling into the air and flanked by the shadows of my ancestors and late husband, I remembered.

Shoving my joss-sticks into the dark earth of the urn, I headed straight to my bedroom and the dressing table. I opened the bottom drawer, where I kept every letter I had ever received in my life. Rifling through the sheets, I found at the very bottom the crumpled papers my late husband had sent from his deathbed, yellowed with age. I peered at their faded Chinese writing and wished for the first time that I could read. I went to ask my daughter Hui Lin for help, only to find that she had no idea what the characters meant, as she had never attended a Chinese school. Later, when the boys returned, I found to my dismay that they had largely forgotten their Chinese. It was with difficulty that they deciphered enough characters between them to convey the gist of their father's message. As my children read out parts aloud, I could hear my dead husband speak from beyond.

'Beware,' he had warned. 'They have this Chinese vice in their blood.' I wept, never imagining that Peng Choon's words would one day come true.

◆　◆　◆

That night it rained heavily, a veritable Ipoh downpour, in which the waters gushed down in sheets. The atmosphere in our inner hall was fraught. None of my other children took Weng Yu's gambling seriously.

'Mama, this may just be a pastime,' Hui Lin said while throwing a nervous laugh into the air. Weng Yoon's thick eyebrows knitted into a frown while he reminded me that the world was changing. 'Nothing wrong with a game of mah-jong now and then, is there?' My son-in-law Kwee Seng wisely stayed out of the fray, mumbling that he didn't have any experience of these things. Neither did I, but when a boy who should have been at work was found in a gambling den, I knew we had a problem. I said as much aloud.

Our conversation was broken by the sound of rain beating hard against our wooden shutters. Through the open air well, the water pouring in was caught by the drains, which carried it back into the earth.

At eight o'clock Weng Yu strode in striking a nonchalant air. He was wet but impeccably dressed, with not a single crease visible on trousers or shirt and with every hair in place. His head shone from a new cream he was using. Under the glow of the electric lights, only his inflamed cheeks and the muscles on his face, so taut that both his dimples had disappeared, revealed any anxiety. At the sight of Weng Yu, his siblings stood up and began to troop out, but I stopped them, knowing instinctively that I wanted Hui Lin and Weng Yoon with me. This infuriated my eldest son. 'I'm head of this family, and you want to talk about me with these two?' he protested.

'This is family matter,' I said firmly. 'Is important Hui Lin and Weng Yoon listen what we say. Here live with me, they are the oldest.'

When Weng Yu continued glaring, I thought he would get up and walk off, but just as quickly he sat down again, albeit in a huff. Keeping his eyes steadily on his knees, my son bristled like a cat.

I thought of the warrior Hang Tuah and his magical sword. Somehow I would have to find my sword tonight.

How I managed to speak, I have no idea. Nothing had prepared me; I was led only by intuition and an aching heart. I poured out my deepest feelings, reminding my son of what he knew and telling him things he didn't. I started with how I had taken him from his hanging crib the night he couldn't settle. I recounted the tour we had taken, he and I, around our house, until I had sat with him inside our inner hall. I described cradling him close against my breast, so close that I could feel his breath against my neck.

My son's eyes moistened at these revelations. I told him that life after their father's death had not been easy, and there were times when I didn't think we would survive. Yet survive we did, thanks to my hard work and the grace of Kuan Yin and our gods.

I may have made mistakes, I said, but I hoped my children would forgive me, because I had always tried to do the best for them. When I told Weng Yu that Siew Lan had even accused me of spoiling him, he reddened. I was a mother, I said. How could I not love him and hope he would change?

Then when he had asked to study in London, everyone in our family had made sacrifices. As I said this, Weng Yu took a deep breath. We had been happy to do this, I added, because we were proud of our joint enterprise. He was our eldest boy after all, and we wanted him to be an engineer, a somebody. How thrilled we would be by his successful return. But then had come news of his escapade with a white girl, during which I lost hope of ever seeing him again. At the mention of Helen, a shadow flickered across Weng Yu's eyes.

Outside the renewal of the earth continued. Rains lashed Ipoh town, turning its baked fields into swamps and giving succour to the trees. I reminded Weng Yu that he was so changed on his return from London we could hardly recognise him. The aching in my heart must have been evident, because Weng Yu swallowed and hung his head. A boy from Ipoh who did not speak Hakka or Hokkien or Cantonese – what sort of son had I brought up? In the end the gods had smiled on us once more, and all had turned out well. Weng Yu had found himself an amazing wife – a beautiful woman from a wealthy family who was refined, well brought up, educated – a good wife and companion. Now that he had two lovely children, a boy and a girl, with another on the way, it was imperative he took care of what was precious in this world, especially the little ones, who relied on him.

'My son, think of your wife, your children. You how can gamble instead of work? Think of what Mama do for you . . . Also your brothers and sisters.'

Weng Yu's cheeks puffed in indignation. 'I am not a villager, Mama.'

He jerked out of his chair and marched towards the door. My daughter Hui Lin ran to stop him, but Weng Yu pushed her away. I followed, shuffling one foot in front of the other as quickly as I could while I tried to grab Weng Yu's arm.

'Son, you no leave like this!'

Turning an anguished face towards me, Weng Yu cried out, 'Mama, why are you always meddling where you shouldn't? And when you should do something, you don't.'

'What is meaning, Weng Yu? You say what?'

'You let Big Sister go back to that useless husband of hers, didn't you? Why? Because you chose him for her.'

We stared at one another then, my little prince and I, not as mother and son should, not as we had once done before the cockerels crowed, but in blank incomprehension. I peered into Weng Yu's soul, and the uncontrolled fury I saw there threw me back. I could not think what to say.

'And when Second Sister gave birth, you could have done something, but you didn't. Why don't you leave me alone too?'

The torrents had stopped by then. A light drizzle was falling; into this, Weng Yu stumbled like a man intoxicated. I watched him disappear into the night. As I held out my hand, the fine Ipoh rain caressed the sleeve of my baju. *Help us, Kuan Yin,* I said silently. I closed the door wearily, my heart bleeding, yet thankful that I had finally spoken.

51

In the months following my confrontation with Weng Yu, I lost sensation in my toes. The numbness came on gradually. I noticed nothing until I saw black bruises on the sides of my feet, pustules like those which graced the heels of the mistress of ceremonies Yong Soon Soh. With the pustules came a loss of control that terrified me: I could not feel my toes, which did not tingle even when I crashed my feet against the heavy almerah in my bedroom. I stumbled around like a drunk, my gait unsteady as if I had been drinking.

Once he saw the state of my feet, Weng Yoon insisted on dragging me back to the hospital. The trip served little purpose. We were seen by a Chinese man, who very kindly not only confirmed my diabetes but also pointed out that I was growing clouds in both eyes. It was only a matter of time before I became blind.

With such joy to look forward to, I waited impatiently for my Green House to be completed. It was my one glimmer of cheer, like a star in the night sky. I monitored progress by badgering Weng Yoon every night for an update on what the builders had added that day. Construction seemed absurdly slow. I couldn't believe how long it took to put up what was merely a single-storey house with four bedrooms. No wonder the mansions of the towkays took years to complete. Weng Yoon had taken me to the building site early in the project but declined to do so again, because, he told me, my presence had been bad for morale. I had shouted at the contractor, whom I thought was cheating us on materials, and also at the labourers for working at too leisurely a pace. After years of mellowing, my previous fire returned with a vengeance, because I no longer saw the point of curbing my tongue. Why bother if I could pass into the next world at any moment?

The Green House might have been completed sooner if our workers hadn't been put on two projects at the same time, a fact Weng Yoon omitted to tell me. When he took me to the building site, he had merely pointed out the plot of land next to mine. The plot – which happened to be his – was then no more than a piece of undeveloped land overgrown with *belukar*, uninviting in the way all virgin land is. Unbeknownst to me, Weng Yoon was doing so well for himself that he had decided to build a house – for himself and the girl to whom he had lost his heart.

I had an inkling he was keeping something from me, because Weng Yoon disappeared every Sunday morning. It wasn't difficult to guess where he went. Even I knew that the white devils prayed on Sundays. Where I failed was in connecting this unexpected religious interest with a girl. I didn't find out about her until the night Weng Yoon announced that my Green House was ready. In the same breath he told me he had been courting a girl in Penang whose name was Dora (or as I would say it, Do-lah) and who apparently came from a respected Nyonya family. The boy looked so happy, grinning from ear to ear, that I couldn't have objected even if I'd wanted to.

Weng Yoon was careful to leave the contentious issue of his intended's religion to the end, when he explained that his would be a church wedding in Penang, because Dora was a Christian and he too had become one. Weng Yoon watched me closely as he said this, in preparation for an eruption. It never came. My fourth son's announcement was further confirmation, as if I needed one, that I had failed to safeguard the sword Mother had passed on to me. I looked sadly at Weng Yoon and at my other children too. One by one they were turning to the ways of the whites, and there was little I could do to stem this tide.

With the completion of the Green House, my promise to retire loomed large. Weng Yoon asked when my last day would be and calmly waited for an answer. Having kept his end of the bargain, my fourth son clearly expected me to keep mine.

It was 1938 by then, and we had been making our family *kueh* for twenty-eight years. In our early years Siew Lan boasted that I had single-handedly introduced Nyonya *kueh* to the town, a claim which made me blush. It was true that we had given the townspeople a taste for these delicacies, but with Heng Lai Soh, the other long-standing *kueh* maker, providing stiff competition, I could scarcely take all credit.

Nonetheless we had been responsible for a few stirs: the delivery of *kueh* on a bicycle; the introduction of a vending cart-and-tricycle for selling Nyonya laksa and *kueh* together; and of course the brown loyalty cards with the famous Wong family seal. After so many years, catering was as much a part of my life as it was the servants', and I worried about what would happen when these activities came to a sudden stop.

I mulled over the idea of sharing our catering profits with our servants and leaving the business in their charge, but neither Ah Hong nor Li-Fei seemed enthusiastic. When I raised the question, each assumed that my health had taken a turn for the worse and took fright. My daughter Hui Lin didn't relish the idea of managing a business either, and her sister Hui Fang lived too far away. With a pang I thought of my second daughter, Hui Ying, whom I felt sure would have carried on our family tradition had she lived.

Without a successor, I had no choice but to shut everything down – *kueh*, catering and all else. For many nights I could not sleep; I tossed, turned and succumbed to nightmares. I ceased moneylending activities too, although this proved easier. Our family continued earning an income from the two shophouses that were still rented out, but it was my fourth son, Weng Yoon, who took charge of rent collection.

It was *kueh*, though, that had been closest to my heart. For six mornings in a row I hired a rickshaw to take me around town, where I knocked on the door of every house that had provided loyal custom through the years. On each doorstep I said thank you in person. It felt like a series of mourning calls. Every visit unearthed new memories and brought a few more tears. By the end of that week I was wrung dry of emotion.

On the last morning I woke earlier than usual. I watched both servants put our thoroughly blackened kettle on to the stove for boiling water. As they lined the steaming baskets with muslin cloth and set the baskets on the heat, I stood in the open air well, savouring the aroma of pandanus leaves rising into the atmosphere. The sight of Li-Fei squeezing coconut milk by hand took me back thirty years – to the time when she was still an apprentice and unable to twist the muslin cloth properly. Now that Li-Fei had become a mature lady, her thick arms left not even a single drop of milk wasted. She could also beat, ladle and wrap. In short, she had turned into an expert Nyonya *kueh* maker.

When the girls finished all six batches of *kueh*, Li-Fei loaded the tiffin carriers on to her tricycle while I made my way to the waiting rickshaw at the front of our house. All morning as I sat partly exposed to the Malayan sun, I felt my life grinding to an end.

There's no denying that retirement came as a shock. I continued to wake at four every morning, unable to stay in bed despite not having to supervise any cooking.

With hours of idleness I could not think what to do with myself. I took to morning strolls in the People's Park and to chatting with our neighbours along the Lahat Road. Though I had never been keen on gossip, with so much time on my hands even I indulged in nosing into matters in which I had no business.

The late mornings were the hardest. At eleven o'clock, which had been the hour of my money-counting session, I would start seeing coins in my head. I eventually took to emptying the contents of my safe. I would pour the coins on the kitchen table and gather them into piles in sets of ten, as I'd always done, even though I no longer had to count anything. I did this every morning, playing with the reddish-copper one-cent coins and fingering the silver pieces – the five cents and ten cents and twenty cents – until my hands were greased by the smell of dirty money. Not that I cared. The piles of metal and paper, the banknotes I kept tied into fat wads with thin rubber bands, reminded me of what I had done well in this life.

On hauling myself out of bed one fateful morning, I found I could not stand. My knees crumpled just like that. The noise when my head hit the floor woke my daughter Hui Lin, who ran in from the next room before I could even shout for help.

This happened a fortnight before Weng Yoon's marriage to Dora, and I missed their wedding as a result. Weng Yu's third child, a baby boy, was born shortly afterwards, and I could not even make it to the hospital to see my grandson Wai Kit. It didn't help that relations with Weng Yu remained strained. Beneath his cool exterior my son tried to do the right thing, coming in person to inform me about my grandson's birth and visiting with the baby as soon as he and his wife were able. I could not tell from Mei Foong's demeanour whether anything had changed, but with a move into the Green House due within days the question of Weng Yu's gambling had to wait.

To ease my disability, my fourth son, Weng Yoon, bought a sedan chair, a cumbersome contraption with a seat on top that was carried by hired coolies. The men were instructed to handle our things first and then to move me. I, meanwhile, had to wait in the inner hall of our Lahat Road house while our lives were wrapped and transported. Unable to restrain myself, I shouted, often and thunderously, whenever a precious object was at risk of being damaged. When the time came for me to be hoisted on to the sedan chair, the men were so shaky that I thought I would surely fall. I screamed like a baby even after the men's arms had steadied. I calmed down only when the Green House rose before my eyes – a vision from my dreams, a wonderful wooden house painted completely in lime green.

The house was everything I had imagined it would be; the only thing I had not bargained for was my own loneliness. Weng Yoon and Dora were then away on something called a honeymoon – yet another Western convention the young ones had adopted. My daughter Hui Lin and her husband, Kwee Seng, could stay with me for only ten days. While they remained, they were wonderfully attentive; my daughter even took pains to search the neighbourhood for a gardener and an odd-job man. She did not give up until she found two Malay men whom she felt able to trust, who as well as tending the land had the indelicate task of hoisting me and carrying me on the sedan chair.

With the help of Samad and Kamil, I could survey our new neighbourhood from the comfort of my throne. The two would haul the chair on to their shoulders, criss-cross the newly planted garden to show off Samad's handiwork and then take me from one end of our street to another. Our street connected two larger roads – Ashby Road on one side and Abdul Jalil Road on the other – but it was just a small lane at the time, so tiny it didn't even have a name.

Much of the neighbourhood remained undeveloped. Opposite was vacant land covered in *belukar* and lalang, alongside remnants of a rubber estate thick with mosquitoes. My own Green House was flanked on both sides, but this was a rarity. On one side stood the mansion my fourth son, Weng Yoon, had built, still unfinished, and on the other was a sturdy wooden house designed in the Malay style and inhabited by a Malay family, the Ja'afars.

Though I loved the peace of the neighbourhood, the Green House felt much too large for just me and my faithful servants. Our most regular visitor in those days was the patriarch Yap Meng Seng, who, on enquiring after my retirement, proceeded in the next breath to tell me in great detail about his. I heard about the grand dinner his bank had thrown and the speeches people had made, including the white bosses, and how they had showered Meng Seng with expensive farewell gifts – imported watches, pens and bottles of brandy sold in the exclusive shops. For weeks afterwards his former clients stopped him on the streets of Ipoh to congratulate him on a job well done.

I could not help reflecting on the contrast between Meng Seng's retirement and my own. Though I had served Nyonya *kueh* to Ipoh for twenty-eight years, no one had honoured me with a grand dinner. I supposed that was inevitable; I wasn't even sure I would have wanted anything big, but a small gesture would have been warming. Instead it was I who had thanked my faithful clients, not the other way round. I wondered whether this was simply the difference between working for a large organisation and working for oneself. Who was to know? The *kueh* business had been like a child to me, perhaps even more important in my life than the bank had been in Meng Seng's. For once I felt sorry for myself.

After a sleepless night I was determined I would shake off this unbecoming self-pity. I asked Samad and Kamil to take me on a tour of our garden, a grassy plot that would bring me pleasure in my twilight years. Pointing with my index finger, I instructed the pair to grow trees, living shoots that would bear the fruits I had come to love in Malaya – mango, papaya, banana, guava, rambutan. These trees would be mine, I told the men, and they must zealously guard the fruit they bore.

52

The New Year began with an unexpected loss. My daughter Hui Lin ran in one morning holding an envelope in her left hand and with a panicked look on her face. Even in my half-blind state I could tell that her fingers were shaking.

'What, daughter?' I asked.

'From Second Brother in Seremban,' she replied, panting.

In a sombre voice Hui Lin said that her sister-in-law, the Cantonese girl I had refused to welcome, had succumbed to cancer of the womb. There had been little warning; the girl simply faded within weeks, leaving my distraught son with three young children to tend to.

I let out a cry. No matter what had happened, Weng Koon was still my son, my own flesh and blood, and his children were my grandchildren. I asked Hui Lin to write at once, saying how sorry I was that in my new state of immobility I could not attend my daughter-in-law's funeral, but I told my son how I longed to see him and his children.

Before the dust had even settled, Hui Lin visited again, this time to tell me about her sister-in-law Mei Foong's strange wanderings through Ipoh town. 'I saw her on Osborne Street, Mama,' my daughter confided. 'Something is wrong.'

'What you mean?'

'She looked sad, very sad. I asked whether she was well and she didn't answer, just looked through me and carried on walking.'

This image of Mei Foong meandering around town with a lost look haunted me, but I could not think what to do. I spent days shouting at the servants. When I tired of that, I would pray before our gods and ancestors. When that too brought no relief, I asked to be moved into the dining room, where I could at least inhale the good, clean mountain air which blew in through the courtyard. It was there while surveying the pink sky over Ipoh's hills one evening that the idea came to me. Why not invite Weng Yu and his family to live with me in my splendid new house?

The more I thought about it, the more right the plan seemed. My grandchildren would give me the company I desperately craved, and at the same time I could watch over Weng Yu.

It proved easy to persuade my eldest son to move into the Green House, so easy that I feared he might already be in debt. Such thoughts were dispelled when Weng Yu bought himself an automobile – in two-toned cream and black, brand new and imported all the way from Britain. I resisted asking my son how much the car cost, but it must have been an enormous sum.

After Weng Yu's family moved in, my house was filled with laughter, with tears, screams and hushed whispers and the patter of children's feet – all that I had missed during my months of solitary living. I moved from the grand room in front to a smaller room at the rear – the only room in the house which opened directly on to the open-air courtyard adjoining the dining room. Fresh air blew in from my beloved hills, and each morning and evening I sat with my bedroom door ajar while taking in continuous breaths, as if the breezes from Ipoh's limestone hills were a luxury I could not get enough of. As well as facing the hills, my new bedroom was close to the modern kitchen I had planned in consummate detail. Every day without fail the wonderfully aromatic smells of Nyonya cooking drifted in to remind me of all I had been given by the gods.

My son and daughter-in-law took over the master bedroom, the largest room in the house, slightly set back from the outer hall and the only one fitted with its own washbasin. I did not miss it; I preferred my cosy burrow with its hill breezes. My grandchildren had their own rooms too, the two boys and their amah occupying one, while my granddaughter Lai Hin was given her own room. Thus in a single stroke my Green House began to beat with life.

Each of us soon settled into a routine. Mine began long before the first crow of the cockerels, when I found myself awake in bed with eyes wide open, impatient for the coming day. Shortly after four, two dim figures entered my room. What came next – the moments which should have been private and were not – filled me with shame, until I fell during a valiant attempt in the latrine. I had no choice then but to accept my growing fragility, and thereafter I allowed the servants to help me instead of imagining them my enemies.

After rising, I sat at a corner of the dining table and waited. Ah Hong and Li-Fei always put the kettle on the wood-fed stove to make my breakfast. They filled the air with the smells of my childhood: ginger being sliced and garlic chilli paste fried; pandanus leaf being steamed and coconut milk freshly squeezed. When I had eaten my fill, the atmosphere in the kitchen changed, for it was then that the servants my son Weng Yu had brought with him entered to prepare the Western nonsense he had learnt to consume in London. They invariably fried meat that stank, purchased from an unhealthily cold shop where the produce was kept in packs of ice.

When my grandchildren woke, they burst out of their bedrooms with the energy that I too must once have had. The eldest two, Wai Sung and Lai Hin, rushed towards me to show off their gleaming teeth. To them each new day was an adventure, and their boundless enthusiasm invigorated even my old bones. Next the youngest, Wai Kit, appeared, swaddled in rolls of cloth and held in the arms of his amah.

My son and daughter-in-law were always the last to wake. Watching them, I found it impossible to tell whether anything was amiss. Only when I spoke privately to Mei Foong did I learn that my son had continued gambling. 'But Weng Yu plays much less now, Mama. Only one or two hours during the day. He knows he must come home every evening.'

It was true that the boy dutifully appeared each evening without fail. I foolishly regarded this as progress, consoling myself with the thought that bad habits could not be broken overnight. Besides, Weng Yu gave me an allowance of twenty-five dollars each month and contributed to household expenses, and I had nothing to complain about.

In those days it was my grandchildren who occupied my attention, especially my granddaughter Lai Hin, whom neither parent graced with much care. Her eldest brother, Wai Sung, was Weng Yu's favourite, given free rein to do as he liked, while the recently born Wai Kit was doted on by Mei Foong for reasons only a mother could know. That left my poor granddaughter without a champion; if it had not been for me and Ah Hong, who loved the girl as if she were her own child, my granddaughter would have felt quite alone in this world. I sensed even then that Lai Hin was close to me in spirit: strong-willed at the age of three. Within hours of their arrival I had to reprimand her for trampling all over a patch in the garden. In sweeter moments Lai Hin amused me with questions. She was as insistent as I had once been, a child who would not give up until she received an answer.

When Lai Hin asked where I came from, I began recounting the stories Mother had passed on. I told her about my days in Songkhla, about the men and women who had arrived from the sea and the goddess Nu Kua, who had made the sky blue for the little children. Lai Hin would appear in my bedroom every afternoon, sneaking in like a cat and waiting until I had opened my eyes from my usual nap, at which point she would jump up and down for her stories.

The afternoons with my granddaughter were energising. My youth seemed to return alongside the memories I unearthed. Lai Hin brought me untold joy. She was a gift from the gods, a sign that perhaps not all my deeds in previous lives had been so terrible.

53

When a large shimmering car appeared on the driveway next door, I knew that my fourth son, Weng Yoon, had returned from the world tour on which he had taken his bride. He knocked soon afterwards to introduce me to his wife, Dora, a young Nyonya woman who wore her hair in the traditional chignon held by five pins. Within minutes of stepping into the Green House, she had brought tears to my eyes. She came towards me, bowed deeply in her beautiful blue kebaya, and in a voice ringing with sincerity told everyone how honoured she felt to be meeting the woman who had brought her husband into the world.

Over the months Dora and I shared our recipes. Her cooking was exquisite even by my fastidious standards. I watched as she supervised the servants in our household, marvelling at her eagle eye for the smallest detail. Dora's recipes, like mine, had been handed down over generations – how many generations, Dora herself did not know; she thought at least three, from the time of her great-grandmother, who was also a Nyonya from Penang. I thought Dora's Siamese laksa tastier than mine, a confession I made only to Dora and only much later.

Dora was fluent in Hokkien, Cantonese and English, which meant she knew everything and talked to everyone. When war broke out in

Europe, I heard it first from Dora, who appeared at my house in a state of agitation. I could not understand the fuss, seeing that we'd had wars before; after all, China had by then been at war with Japan for two years. 'Yes, Mama, but this may be different,' my daughter-in-law said. Despite her gloomy statement, nothing much happened. Life went on as before in Ipoh, except that my sons kept talking about the fighting between different European countries with more excitement than seemed warranted. One minute such-and-such an army would be in this country, the next it was another army somewhere else, always in places I had never heard of, knew nothing about and with no conceivable connections to Ipoh.

The only other topic which elicited as much reaction from anyone was Weng Yoon's monstrous new car. The beast stretched the length of my bedroom and was so wide that when it crossed the smaller bridges in town, any car unfortunate enough to be travelling in the opposite direction had to give way. I can't say I thought it beautiful; the car had the same ugly lights which festooned Meng Seng's, a pair of orbs sticking out incongruously at the front like the eyes of a toad. The monster attracted attention, not to mention envy, which embarrassed me the first time I sat inside. All eyes focused on me, the Nyonya *kueh* maker who was now driven around for leisure.

Once I became accustomed to being stared at, I must confess that Weng Yoon's car made me purr like a well-fed cat. I much preferred it to Weng Yu's smaller car, though I worked hard to conceal this.

In family life too Weng Yoon was the more successful. He was deeply taken with his wife, even naming his house after her. He gave it an English name which sounded like 'Toh-kot'; I was told the first part came from Dora's own name, while the second part was the English word for court, appropriate given where my son spent his days.

◆ ◆ ◆

On my sixty-first birthday Weng Yoon insisted on a celebration. 'Ai-yahh, no need-lah! I don't want to feel old,' I pleaded.

To no avail. Having avoided a large celebration the previous year on account of the work then being carried out on the Green House, I was unable to circumvent my son a second time. Weng Yoon took me to one of the fancy establishments that had opened in town, where the fifteen adults and nine children of our branch of the Wong clan gathered. Our meal was replete with every conceivable delicacy, including dishes that were the preserve of the wealthy. We sipped a rich broth in which delicate slivers had been scattered – the abalone so beloved of many in town. We feasted on giant succulent prawns and whole roasted piglets, their skins gently crisp. Though delicious, the dinner was inordinately expensive. We could have spent a fraction of what my son paid and had as much pleasure at home.

The highlight came when I set eyes on the two boys and the girl – the children of my second son, Weng Koon – whose arrival in this world I had missed. The eldest was then five, the youngest only two. We had not met until then. When I felt their little hands grasping at my sarong and looked down to see impish faces peering up, full of mischief and trust, I regretted having missed their early years. It was too late to turn the clock back, but I resolved to be less pig-headed from then on.

Over dinner, war dominated the conversation. I had little desire to find out any more about the fighting or hear which country's armies were advancing where. It bored the little ones too – they squirmed like worms. As soon as we finished eating, I announced story time. A magical effect came over the room: everyone woke up at once. The adults stretched, yawned and swayed arms in the air, while the children, eyes brightening, became my captives. My granddaughter Lai Hin led the charge with shouts for her favourite tales. This grandchild of mine didn't tire of listening to the same story repeatedly; whatever she liked she asked for every day. At the time she was obsessed with the story of Nu Kua and would keep gazing out at the skies the way I had once done, searching for that elusive hole she could never find. I wasn't surprised when she asked to hear the story again, even though the girl could have recited every sentence backwards to me. Feigning excitement, I described for the hundredth time how the world had been created and the skies made blue for the little children.

After I finished, nine little faces looked up at me, stunned into silence. From across the room I heard Weng Yoon announcing his plan to stand for elections to the Perak State Council. I wondered what this meant and resolved to ask Dora. At the next table I could just about make out Weng Yu's face, like a mask the Chinese opera singers wore, beautifully painted but inscrutable. I guessed that he couldn't be happy at the way his younger brother was beginning to overshadow him, yet there was also no avoiding this inconvenient truth.

On a sultry afternoon Mei Foong came scuttling towards my room, a fan in one hand and a silk handkerchief in the other. From the colour of her eyes, she had obviously been crying. Lai Hin, who was sitting near my bed, looked up in surprise at her overwrought mother. The child climbed out of her chair to touch her mother's hand, all the while silently searching both our faces in the hope we would reveal what was wrong. Curiosity tinged her eyes, but there was also a fear holding her back from blurting out words that must have been on the tip of her tongue. Lai Hin left the room without protest, in contrast to her usual practice of pestering to be allowed a longer stay.

As soon as the bedroom door closed, my daughter-in-law burst into tears. In between sobs Mei Foong murmured that her husband was in trouble.

A deep wariness rose within me. 'Is about gambling-ah?'

Mei Foong nodded, explaining that my son had creditors at the mah-jong club to whom he owed a lot of money. She didn't know how much, but it was a big amount – enough to make it difficult for Weng Yu to part with a single cent for the next few months. I sat in silence, understanding that my son would no longer provide a monthly allowance or contribute to household expenses.

Outside, the stray dogs which roamed Green Town's leafy surrounds in packs serenaded us with a strange howling. Their baying unnerved me. I remembered a cry from long ago, the call of the man in Songkhla village who had sat crumpled with head buried in both hands. He had gambled everything he owned and lost.

'Are you all right, Mama?' Mei Foong's voice broke into my reverie.

The girl was busy fanning herself. It was one of those hot, sticky Ipoh days, the sort on which dogs stuck out their long pink tongues when they panted. I could smell sweat in the room. As I watched Mei Foong's trembling fingers, I realised it was not her heat I smelt but her fear.

When I spoke, my own mouth felt parched. I could hardly recognise the raspy voice that was supposedly mine. 'I also not know what to do,' I croaked. A pause before I asked, 'You want me do what?'

'Have pity on us, Mama, if not for my husband's sake, then for your grandchildren. Let us live here for free, at least in the next few months.'

'Good heart, daughter, of course!'

Through the half-open window, a wolf-like call reminded me that a bigger problem loomed, a challenge more intractable than food and lodging.

'You think already what we do-ah?' I asked. 'We how to make your husband stop gamble?'

Shaking her head, Mei Foong ceased fanning herself, as if deep in thought. The heat built up in my little room, trapped as it was within four walls, a closed door and a half-shut window. Suddenly I felt tired . . . so tired. At my age I didn't need this drama. But then I thought of my grandchildren, and especially little Lai Hin, who needed me.

'I not yet know what we do, but I need your help,' I said.

'Of course, Mama, but what can a mother-of-three do when she doesn't work?'

I stared at my daughter-in-law, astonished by this display of helplessness. Where had her steel gone? If I could only tap into the reserve of strength I had once glimpsed, we would make a formidable team. I told her about the home arrangements Peng Choon and I had put in place, how at the end of each month my dear husband had handed me his entire earnings so that I could run our household. The girl's eyes widened, as if to convey the impossibility of Weng Yu ever agreeing to a similar arrangement. I assured my daughter-in-law there was no alternative. How else could she control his spending?

She looked away.

'We must together work, Mei Foong. Otherwise cannot,' I said in such a sharp tone that she looked up. My daughter-in-law did not reply, but there was a new acquiescence in her eyes.

When Weng Yu returned that evening, his swagger was the only hint of his errant ways. The boy walked in exaggerated fashion, as if to assure everyone of his respectable day on Hale Street, a day spent with clamouring clients. He mentioned the names of men supposedly in the process of acquiring plots of land, men from whom there would be much demand for houses. Weng Yu's lyrical voice and beautiful use of the Hakka dialect lulled us all. Only when I paid close attention to what my son said, noting the inflection in tone, the evasiveness which gave the boy away, did I see how shamelessly Weng Yu slid from lie to lie. I felt ill. Trying to catch him in his deceptions would be like using a sword to cut through water.

54

For seven successive nights after Mei Foong's visit, my sleep was interrupted by dreams.

I dreamt that Mother was in my room with Nu Kua, the woman who had made the skies blue. Or perhaps it was Mother turning into Nu Kua – I couldn't tell. It was dark when Mother came into view beside me. I knew it was Mother from the shape of her lips, which curved downward as they used to when she was displeased. She was dressed in a familiar baju panjang, the one in green and white squares she had worn at home with a brown sarong. She even gave off the smells she used to have when I was young, a pungency mixed with comforting sweetness, as if she had continued frying garlic and steaming pandanus leaf in the next world.

I didn't know who the other presence in the room was, but I sensed the spirit to be benign. When Mother called her name, Nu Kua, children came from out of nowhere, cloaked in tunics whose ample sleeves spread outwards. My grandchildren Wai Sung and Lai Hin were among them but neither paid me any attention; they merely glided towards Nu Kua. Or was it Mother they sought? In the thick blackness Mother and Nu Kua blurred as they merged into one, beckoning the children away.

I woke up with an ache in my head and with Mother on my mind. I felt shame, because I knew Mother would never have allowed things to progress to this state. She would have curtailed Weng Yu's activities long before they fell into such disarray.

For several nights Mother and Nu Kua visited me in my dreams, bringing the children with them. Eventually the children and Nu Kua stopped coming; it was only Mother who turned up.

When she and I were alone, Mother took me on a long journey. We traversed a vast expanse of blackness until I could go no further. At that point I asked Mother the question that had been plaguing me. 'What should I do, Mother?' My voice sounded hollow, as if I were travelling through a cave. Mother turned towards me. Though she didn't say a word, a smile radiated from her face. *You know what you need to do,* she seemed to say. Then she was gone.

On the designated day I watched my son as he walked towards his car. I stared at his feet, at the handmade shoes carved out of crocodile skin, shoes that must have been exquisitely expensive. It was no wonder the boy was in debt, I thought, as my son reversed his car out of the garage. After my son had sped away down our street, I asked to be carried into the second hall beside the master bedroom, where my prayer altar was set up. I spent the day face to face with Kuan Yin, my ancestors and my husband. Offerings of *kueh* and oranges had been laid and candles lit in the knowledge that the ensuing battle would be the biggest I would ever have waged.

At the usual time Weng Yu returned from the office. We had popiah that evening, a Nyonya dish in which diners wrap a choice of meat and vegetable filling into paper-thin spring roll skins made of rice flour. The filling ingredients are chosen for texture as well as taste and liberally doused with chilli before being folded into their white cages. Because each person wraps her or his own roll, it allows for camaraderie among diners and is ideal for breaking the ice between strangers. I was conscious of a different kind of coldness that evening, but one no less frigid and difficult to conquer.

In the vein of our previous confrontations, I made sure Weng Yu had first enjoyed his fill before luring him into my territory: I asked him to help me to my bedroom. I assumed he would sit with me, if only for a few minutes, but my son had other ideas; he was already heading towards the door when I called him back. 'Stay awhile,' I said. 'I like talking to you.' My imploring tone must have surprised the boy, for he complied without objection. He placed himself in the only chair in my bedroom, a broad rattan seat I had acquired as a retirement present to myself. Like a coiled python I attacked without preamble.

'Big Son, I know you still play mah-jong. I also know you lose money-lah.'

Observing Weng Yu carefully as I said this, I heard his perceptible intake of breath.

'No need to get angry,' I said evenly. 'Mei Foong just worried. She think of the three little ones. I know you too think of them.'

'Of course-lah, Mama, of course,' my son replied indignantly. 'It's just that I've had such a spell of bad luck. Luck comes and goes, you know.'

The conviction with which my son said this left me in little doubt that he believed the nonsense he was spouting. He carried on assuring me that everything would 'be fine in the end'. When he saw my scepticism, his thick lips curled into a sneer, as if to indicate that an old woman like me couldn't possibly comprehend the complexities of the gaming tables. 'I just need a change of luck. When my luck is good, it's very good, you know. Nothing touches me then,' Weng Yu declared with the certainty of one possessed.

I looked sadly at my son. Inside my soul there echoed the cry of a hundred elephants dying.

'Weng Yu, you know how many people gamble and make money-ah?' My son became sullen. When he gave no reply, I asked a practical question. 'You owe how much?'

The boy refused to say. He kept his lips pursed tightly until I screamed so loudly that the entire household heard; only when cornered in shame did my son confess. 'All right, Mama, keep your voice down.' He then whispered a number which horrified me: 'Three thousand dollars.'

I could hardly believe my ears. I had made three thousand dollars only in the good years, when business had been booming. To lose so much money so quickly . . . There could only be one possible explanation.

'You play big-ah?' I asked. 'How can lose so much? Each game, how much?'

'Sometimes ten dollars, sometimes fifteen,' my son replied nonchalantly.

I looked at Weng Yu with even greater sorrow. There it was again, that casual attitude to money I had seen years before but had done nothing to curb. The boy behaved as if money grew on trees. I understood then that dealing with Weng Yu's debt would be the biggest challenge of my life.

I sought inspiration from the only place I knew: in front of Kuan Yin, Goddess of Mercy. Leaning on my faithful servants for support, I would shuffle towards the chair near our altar table, from where I would gaze at our well-worn figure in porcelain. Though yellowed with age, Kuan Yin calmed my nerves. I marvelled at her posture, left leg bent at the knee and tucked beneath her right leg in that look of timeless composure. The Goddess responded to my devotion with an idea so bold that it made my hands tremble. Had the sign come from the Goddess herself, though, or had I merely imagined it? This time I had to be sure; mine was too important a mission.

With Dora's permission I asked the driver her husband had hired to take me to the Kuan Yin Temple off the Brewster Road, where I could consult the chief priest. Our gardeners, Samad and Kamil, carried me out of the house and into the car, then from the car into the temple on my wooden sedan. While I was inside, they sat outside near the bank of the Kinta River under a tree, whiling away time with the coolies who liked to take shade there. Dora stayed with me, watching what the chief priest and I were doing from a discreet distance. As I set eyes on the woman with the high cheekbones who had taken care of me through the years, it became clear what I had to do.

The next day we resumed catering. Upon retirement I had been inundated with requests for Nyonya delicacies – at the weddings, funerals and festivals which seemed to take place in Ipoh every month. I had always declined, even when the requests had come from the most loyal of customers, for fear of setting an unwelcome precedent. I knew that as soon as I said yes to someone, another request would follow, and enmity could arise if I were perceived to show favouritism. With Weng Yu's misfortune, a perfect opportunity presented itself. We could cater to Ipoh's apparently insatiable appetite for Nyonya cuisine – not on a daily basis as we had previously done, but on demand by former clients whenever they wished to celebrate special occasions. I would keep occupied, do the town a favour and make money at the same time.

Or so I thought. Unfortunately the enterprise turned out to be far tougher than I could ever have foreseen, because I'd forgotten how short people's memories are. By the time we resumed catering, Wong family *kueh* had not been seen on the streets of Ipoh for two years, and almost everyone had forgotten us. During our first two months not a single order came in. We would surely have sunk had it not been for my tenacity, for I was not prepared to leave this world until I had fully discharged every ounce of my son's shame. Nothing was going to stand in my way.

I knew it could take months, possibly even years. I let my son and his family live with me for free and used my lifetime's savings of one and a half thousand dollars to repay half Weng Yu's debts, but I still needed to find the other half. I tried to estimate how long it would take us to earn this. In this my wayward son was of little help; pride clogged his tongue. He would only say that in his best month he brought home more than two hundred dollars.

'If your month not good, how bad?' I asked, but my question brought nothing more than a sheepish look and a series of mumbles.

For the next two years the goal of seeing Weng Yu's debt repaid consumed my every waking moment. It drove the way we lived and the way our house was organised.

First, I demanded that my son hand over a hundred dollars each month. Next, I added to my daughter-in-law's stable of household tasks, putting her in charge of what had once been my responsibilities: supervision of the servants' routines and the gardeners' work. Mei Foong thus began to manage every aspect of the daily affairs in our household. No longer having to watch over the servants, I was free to dream up menus and to spread the word that we were catering again. I did all this from a throne in our outer hall. To alert the townspeople, Li-Fei was given time off in the mornings to ride around Ipoh on our bicycle. She rang her bell everywhere, making sure the town knew that the Wong family kitchen was open for special treats.

When despite our best efforts no orders came, we were forced to eke out a living from my savings and the income from the two shophouses we continued to rent out. I even went as far as looking into what prices our rubber smallholdings would fetch. It turned out they wouldn't bring more than several hundred dollars. I decided to keep them in case our circumstances became truly desperate. Whatever Weng Yu handed me went towards paying off his creditors, though he sometimes fell so far short of my hundred-dollar target that I fretted. It occurred to me more than once that my son was continuing to frequent the mah-jong tables. Whenever I imagined him among the smokers and carousers, scrambling tiles in his hands, I spat into the brass jar that had served me loyally for many years. Long were the hours I spent wondering whether I should look for Weng Yu's creditors.

After an especially agonising month, I sent Weng Yoon to the club in Hale Street. By then I viewed my project as a business, a miserable one admittedly, but a business nonetheless and subject to similar rules. Once I associated it with business, Peng Choon's words came screaming into mind: every business incurs costs, my dear husband had once said, and costs are the only things you can control; therefore, keep them low. If Weng Yu was indeed ringing up new debts without my knowing, I had to find out.

It proved no small matter persuading my fourth son to participate in the plot. Despite their eldest brother's known weakness, his siblings continued to look up to Weng Yu, and it was with deep reluctance that his brother headed towards Hale Street. I had to shout at the boy before he agreed to go. When he returned an hour later, Weng Yoon was accompanied by a balding specimen whose pale face rarely saw the sun. The man's shoulders stooped in the way of the old, even though age barely lined his skin. He wheezed too, as if the very act of speaking cost him his breath. In between bouts of coughing the man, Foo Chong Wee, explained that he had been nominated to act on behalf of all of Weng Yu's creditors – twenty in total, of whom one was a woman.

I invited Foo Chong Wee to sit. We took tea in our faithful Nyonya cups with their green dragons and pink borders. Admiring our tableware, Foo Chong Wee said he had seen me at the club. When I told him I intended to ensure that my son's debts were fully repaid, his eyes narrowed. Not liking the hard gleam of cunning shining at me, I let the man know exactly who he was dealing with. 'You help me, I help you. If not, everyone lose,' I said in no uncertain terms. My tone seemed to gain the man's respect. His eyes softened, and I established that Weng Yu still owed three thousand dollars. While not pleasing, this at least confirmed a number we could work with, provided my son didn't continue adding to it. I told Foo Chong Wee that if the group wanted to be fully paid back, he would have to give me a report at the end of each month so that I knew as soon as my son increased his debts. When the consumptive man agreed to my demand, I felt huge relief, as if I had already won the battle.

55

Mei Foong proved an excellent worker. It was her first taste of real work, and the results delighted us both. While Mei Foong did not have to grind or pound or chop, she did have to run our kitchen, take charge of the house rotas, replenish supplies, and manage every aspect of the garden. The garden, though not huge, needed constant tending, because of the many fruit trees and rose bushes I had asked to be planted. The days when Mei Foong had swept into our house with a maid trailing by her side seemed a distant dream, but my daughter-in-law did not lose an ounce of grace. Even in shabbier dresses, Mei Foong retained an aura of the refinement which some in town described as 'class'.

When catering orders failed to come in after two months, I began to worry. I sent a message to our former tenant the tailor telling him to spread word that I was prepared to resume moneylending to the right clients. As often happens in life, things picked up all at the same time: our first catering order came in just as a woman from Kampong Jawa arrived to see me about a loan to expand her business selling the Malay dish of *nasi lemak*. I wept in relief before Kuan Yin. My sword, which had brought us safely through this life, was poised to save us again.

In Ipoh news spreads through word of mouth, and a single catering order was enough to change our fortune. Requests began to trickle
in. As more people heard about us, the orders turned into a stream. At
the same time my moneylending activities increased. Finally we made
progress in reducing Weng Yu's debt, a state of affairs confirmed by
Foo Chong Wee during his monthly visits. Our chats over cups of tea
became rituals I looked forward to. For a while all seemed well.

Yet for the first time in my life I also felt invisible. I had an inkling
of being cheated: by my sons, my daughter Hui Lin and even the servants, as well as everyone who visited the house, with the exception of
my grandchildren and those to whom I lent money. People would speak
over my head as if I weren't in the room.

It had begun when I decided to stop holding my tongue and simply said whatever came to mind. I told my daughter-in-law Mei Foong
about how I'd had Ah Boey the ting-ting man followed, and suggested
we do the same with her husband. Mei Foong looked at me as if I were
mad, although she nodded her head.

Soon everyone treated me in the same way, wagging their heads
up and down when they meant no and trying to conceal all manner of
uncomfortable truths no matter how small. It was therefore not surprising that I began to doubt Foo Chong Wee's assurances. The man
insisted that Weng Yu's debt pile was declining at a speed I could not
have anticipated. I didn't believe him, yet there was little I could do or
say. Every time our eyes met, I sensed Foo Chong Wee holding back,
but in the end I had to let it go. I contented myself with keeping track
of what my son handed me each month, what we ourselves made from
catering and moneylending, and what Foo Chong Wee told me he and
the other creditors were still owed.

Even the patriarch Meng Seng didn't behave as he had always done.
For one thing he stopped pontificating. I had a niggling feeling that this
sudden loss of words had everything to do with me, for he would listen
while giving me scrutinising looks, though that could just have been

my eyes playing games. For reasons known only to himself, Meng Seng chose to keep a white beard and a moustache; the former hung like a flag beneath his chin, while the latter, meticulously trimmed, arched over his mouth. He knew about Weng Yu's debts of course, because I couldn't stop talking about the boy's vice, and there were times Meng Seng would gaze at me with such deep sympathy that I almost wept. The patriarch told me not to worry.

'You can depend upon it, Chye Hoon. Weng Yu's debts will be repaid before you leave this world.'

Just before my sixty-third birthday, when I thrust $150 into Foo Chong Wee's hands, he counted out a few bills and then handed back a thick wad of notes.

'Weng Yu only owes twenty-five dollars more-lah. That's it, all finished.'

'Cannot be!' I shouted. 'What about the interest?'

'You've paid it all, Peng Choon Sau,' he responded calmly.

'But we still owed three hundred dollars,' I said, confident about my ability to count. I remembered the figure we had discussed on his last visit. It could not have shrunk so suddenly.

'Peng Choon Sau, you're mistaken. It was only twenty-five dollars you owed.'

The hands I held around my Nyonya cup shook. With my right index finger, I traced the simple line of gold around its pink rim. Was I going mad? I could think no more. I sobbed, weighed down by exhaustion and confusion and the enormity of what I had done. Relief churned my stomach. Grabbing the brass spittoon, I almost missed the jar when a dull yellow liquid came gurgling unexpectedly out of my mouth. Foo Chong Wee had to avert his eyes. In the open courtyard we heard the call of a turtle dove.

When my fourth son, Weng Yoon, was told the news, he and his wife Dora insisted on a celebration of my 'monumental achievement', a term which made me blush. We would celebrate my birthday at the same time, they said. I agreed, but only on condition that the gathering was held in my Green House, that it include only family and that Nyonya food be served.

If truth be told, I had little desire to celebrate. I remember almost nothing about the event, not even the food my daughter-in-law Dora prepared. An entire table was laid out with Nyonya *kueh*, but I couldn't say what they were. I remember a rainbow of colours: the greens and whites and blues and reds that were undoubtedly beautiful to look at, though I, with my pulse so weak I could hardly breathe, touched little. Life was slipping away. Only my spirit kept me going, but even that was faltering. I wondered how long it would hold up. As soon as my spirit waned, I knew that the time would have come.

In the world outside everyone was still at war, and even the Americans had joined in the madness. Like most people in town I wasn't unduly alarmed; with our white rulers, I couldn't imagine anyone attacking us, except perhaps another white power, but they were too busy killing each other to bother with Malaya. I was sure, when it came to war, that the whites would defend the country they had lived in for so long, out of loyalty if nothing else.

Our family celebration was memorable for the photographer whom Weng Yoon invited to the Green House, a Japanese man who worked for the Mikasa Photo Studio on Belfield Street. The man spoke some Cantonese, but he rolled his words in such a peculiar manner that I couldn't make head or tail of what he was trying to say, which did nothing to make me feel at ease. It was the first time I had ever been photographed, and I turned cold as I faced the square box on its three-legged stand. My granddaughter Lai Hin reached for my hand to reassure me in the instinctive way children have, but it was clear my nerves persisted, for I barely managed a grimace in the photograph.

A pall of moroseness hung in the air. The Wong brood feigned contentment before the camera. The men were exceptionally loud, Meng Seng perhaps loudest of all, even to my failing ears, as people become when they attempt a cheer they do not feel. My mind wandered towards times past and the loved ones I had lost. I thought especially of Siew Lan, my friend with the worry lines who had seen the births and deaths of every one of my children. I mourned them all, especially my little prince, as I sat wishing I could turn the clock back.

Over the following months the contrition which appeared on Weng Yu's face gave me hope that the boy might have repented of his vice. I never felt able to ask and never knew what he really thought until the day he walked into my room.

It was a bright morning. I was in bed struggling for air when I heard a knock on the door. My son had not come a moment too soon, for I could feel my spirit fading fast. Through the haze that my vision had become, I made out Weng Yu's familiar shape as he strolled in. He pulled the rattan chair forward so that I could see his face. He looked pale, his cheekbones as taut as the skin of a drum.

'Ha-llo,' I said, managing a weak smile.

My son responded by folding my left hand into both of his. Thereafter he sat without saying a word, simply watching the rise and fall of my chest. As the minutes passed, I could hear his breathing, which at first matched mine but soon became heavier. At some point I realised that Weng Yu was sobbing. His shoulders heaved and he began to wail like a sick animal, filling my room with a noise so terrible that I hoped his children were far from us.

Before I knew it, my son was kneeling by my bed with his head digging into the folds of my baju; deeper and deeper his nose sank, until the wetness of his tears seeped into my left ribs and I began to shiver.

'Mama, I'-m, I'-m sor-ry,' he said when he finally lifted his head. Seeing how the boy wept, I reached for his quivering lips with my fingers. There was no need for words. He had come. With a beating heart he had come. I could feel the sorrow in his bones, and that was enough.

We sat in silence, my son and I, me taking air in slow, laboured gulps, while he looked on, his hands around mine. I savoured the warmth of those hands, hands which had formed inside my own belly. Thanking Kuan Yin for answering my prayer, I wept.

After I regained a little strength, I asked Weng Yu what was happening in the world. I heard that the war had taken another turn: the Japanese had just attacked an American port; now no one knew what would come next. There was despair in Weng Yu's voice. He told me things could get worse; everyone was worried the Japanese would attack Malaya.

I paused to take in the vision on a chair, of a man with the hint of dimples on his cheeks. I thought of Peng Choon, the husband who had helped make my life in Malaya what it was.

'Japan boys come here is fate. Use your brain, Big Son, work hard. Your life you can change. Some things you cannot change. They are fate.'

With those words I turned away from the sad eyes of my little prince and looked out of the window. In the distance were my beloved hills, blue from the shimmering heat.

EPILOGUE

Hours after my mother-in-law passed away, Malaya entered a state of war. Overnight Japanese forces landed on a beach in the north-east of the country. No one knew what would happen next, and we scrambled to make arrangements as best we could. Despite the turmoil, crowds gathered for the three-day wake, which was presided over by wailing priests, who beat a gong every hour. In keeping with the air of mourning, my sister-in-law Dora made wokfuls of Nyonya *kueh* in all colours except red.

At the funeral, traffic in Ipoh stopped, just as it had when my mother-in-law's good friend Siew Lan McPherson was sent off years previously. Beneath the shadow of weeping needles, part dragon, part lion, carved into the rock she had so loved, hundreds paid their respects to the matriarch who had brought Nyonya *kueh* to town. Even her rival, the woman known as Heng Lai Soh, came, full of tears and sorrow.

My husband sobbed inconsolably. He had been with his mother when she took her last breath, had held those hands, calloused by toil. 'Mama would have given her life for me,' he said with voice breaking, 'yet for too long . . . I was ashamed of her.' The recollection burnt his cheeks. He was full of her stories – we all were, because in death she loomed even larger than in life. For once my husband regretted the mah-jong and cards that had tempted him, instead honouring the Chinese ancestors who had arrived in boats with eyes painted on their prows.

When my turn came, I recalled a story my mother-in-law had told our daughter Lai Hin. It featured Hang Tuah, the warrior with the magic sword whose courage had always inspired Mama.

Hang Tuah served many Sultans of Malacca over the course of his life. The final ruler had sent him to Mount Ledang, home to a beautiful princess the Sultan wanted to marry. Mount Ledang was a haven in the clouds which the princess had no wish to leave. Not wanting to embarrass the ruler, the princess gave Hang Tuah a list of the gifts the Sultan would have to bestow. She asked for a golden bridge to link Malacca with her home in the clouds, a bowl of blood drawn from the Sultan's firstborn son and seven jars of virgins' tears.

Hang Tuah knew that these wishes could never be fulfilled. The taste of failure was bitter; the warrior fell on his knees and wept, howling so loudly that everyone around him ran away. Unable to face his Sultan, Hang Tuah never returned to Malacca. With a tremendous roar, he flung his magical *keris* into a nearby river before disappearing into thin air, never to be seen again.

My mother-in-law told this story repeatedly in her later years, perhaps imagining her soul rising like Hang Tuah's. She believed we each had power, if only we could harness it. 'We also have magic sword,' she insisted. 'Just must find first.'

Unlike Hang Tuah, my mother-in-law succeeded in her final mission on earth. I shall never know whether she realised that others had helped to repay my husband's debts, most of all the old man known as the patriarch. The effort had been collective, but Mama remained its driving force to the end.

Throughout the cremation, a cooling breeze blew, as if even Ipoh's hills were bidding the grand old lady farewell. She would have loved this touch of mountain air – 'breath of the gods', she had always called it.

Our lives changed after she passed away. Barely a week later, before we even had time to sort through her belongings, Japanese bombs fell over Ipoh. They looked innocent in their downward drift, like a series of eggs floating from the blue skies. But once they touched the ground, they shook the earth with a force we had never known. Those droplets ushered in a less gentle age, which I'm so glad my mother-in-law was spared.

ACKNOWLEDGMENTS

The main character in this novel was inspired by my feisty Nyonya great-grandmother, whom sadly I never met. She was much discussed in our family and I am indebted to my mother, Chin Fee Lan, for the stories she told me when I was growing up. What my mother said made me yearn to find out more. This novel is one of the results.

This story took a year to write and another year to edit. I carried out extensive research in Malaysia, where I was hosted by family members who agreed to be interviewed. Aunts, uncles and cousins spent many hours with me. In the process they revealed family secrets which fed my imagination, thus allowing me to create a richer tapestry of characters. Though I cannot mention everyone by name, I must especially thank Aunt Chin Mei Leng and Uncle Foo Khong Yee for putting up with me for months, when I ate too much and was unsociable. Not only was my aunt a reader of early drafts, but she was also my chief investigating officer, connecting me to anyone whom she thought could help. Then there was Aunt Lorna Chin, who invited me to her restaurant, Sri Nyonya, in Petaling Jaya, where she showed me how to make some of the *kueh* described in this book using old family recipes.

My late grand-uncle Chin Kee Onn was the first writer in our family. The same matriarch inspired his novel *Twilight of the Nyonyas*, on which I have drawn for colourful details about Nyonya weddings. I am also grateful to Dr Ho Tak Ming for his authoritative tome *When Tin Was King*, which tells the history of Ipoh, my home town. Dr Ho's book, as well as his time and patience with my questions, made my research much easier.

As with any debut novelist, I relied on plenty of beta readers. Thank you to Oksana Kunichek, Kirstin Zhang, Alex Catherwood, Nadine Leavitt and SJ Butler for reading parts or all of this manuscript and for the feedback you gave. If I have forgotten anyone, I apologise; the omission is unintentional.

My developmental editor, Nathalie Teitler, helped me grow from being a first-time writer who had never written fiction to the author of an epic family saga. She was instrumental in helping me shape this story; my novel would certainly have been poorer without her.

My agent, Thomas Colchie, and his wife, Elaine, were the first people in the publishing world who were excited by my manuscript. Thank you for remaining undaunted and for not giving up the search for a publisher.

When I disclosed at writing workshops how long my debut novel was going to be, there were gasps of disbelief. I would like to thank Amazon Crossing, and especially my editor, Elizabeth DeNoma, and her team for choosing this story, for their belief and their support.

Last but not least, a very big thank you to Svetlana Omelchenko: first reader, trusted critic and muse to whom I owe too many creative ideas to count.

GLOSSARY

- **Air well**   Open-air courtyard found inside many traditional shophouses and houses.
- **Amah**   Servant whose primary responsibility is to look after one or more children.
- *Ang moh*   Red-haired person or Caucasian.
- *Angkoo*   A type of Nyonya *kueh*.
- **Attap**   Thatched roof that used to be seen on Malay-style wooden houses.
- **Baba**   Male descendant of Chinese traders who settled in South East Asia with local women.
- **Baju panjang**   Long tunic, usually worn with a sarong.
- *Barlay*   A raised wooden platform popular in older Chinese homes for sitting on or sleeping.
- *Batek*   Beautifully patterned cloth that is traditionally dyed manually.
- *Belukar*   Cleared land which has reverted to jungle.

- Betel nut   Seed of the areca palm. A stimulant, it is chewed and traditionally offered to guests.
- *Bidan*   Malay midwife.
- Brinjal   Aubergine or eggplant.
- Catty (s), catties (p)   Traditional Chinese measure of weight equal to 604 grams.
- *Champor-champor*   A mixed bag.
- *Chapalang*   Slang with negative connotations for a person of mixed race.
- *Chiak pa boey?*   Literally 'Have you eaten?' (Hokkien). Traditional Chinese greeting meaning 'How are you?'
- Chiao-Ling   Jiaoling.
- *Chiki*   Nyonya game. Similar to mah-jong but uses cards.
- *Chiku*   Sapodilla fruit.
- *Chin-chuoh*   Marriage in which the bridegroom moves in with the bride's family.
- Curry Kapitan   A thick chicken curry with plenty of chillies and coconut.
- Dying person's head   Chinese curse phrase.
- *Ee*   Maternal aunt.
- Erhu   Southern fiddle; also known as the Chinese violin.
- *Fatt shi*   Taoist priest.
- Five-foot way   Open verandah in front of shophouses. Usually five feet wide.

- Good heart   Exclamation equivalent to 'Good gracious!'
- Green pea   Mung beans.
- *Gula melaka*   Palm sugar, often in syrup form, made by boiling the sap of the palm tree.
- *Gunong*   Mountain (Malay).
- Hokkien   The dialect of Chinese from the Fukien Province in South China.
- Ice *kachang*   Dessert of beans, jelly, syrup, peanuts and condensed milk on crushed ice.
- *Kachang*   Peanuts.
- Kampong   Malay village.
- *Kamsia*   'Thank you' (Hokkien).
- *Kangkong*   Water spinach or convolvulus.
- *Keris*   A curved dagger used by Malay warriors.
- Kling   Person of Indian descent. The term is considered pejorative and no longer used.
- *Kong-kong*   Maternal grandfather.
- Kuan Yin   The Goddess of Mercy.
- *Kuay-teow*   Flat rice noodles.
- *Kueh*   Cake.
- Kwangtong   Guangdong.
- Laksa   A noodle dish in a spicy soup base with prawns or chicken.
- *Lalang*   A type of weed.
- Mah-jong   Game traditionally played by four players for money using tiles.
- *Makche*   Aunt (Malay).
- Menangkabau   Matrilineal culture in Western Sumatra famous for its fierce women.

- *Nasi lemak*   Malay dish comprising coconut rice, sambal, cucumber, egg and peanuts.
- *Ngi ho?*   'How are you?' (Hakka).
- *Ngi cho ma kai?*   'What are you doing?' (Hakka).
- Night soil   Human excrement.
- Nyonya   Female descendant of Chinese traders who settled in South East Asia with local women.
- Orang Asli   Generic term for the indigenous aboriginal peoples of Malaysia.
- *Otak-otak*   Nyonya dish of parcels of fish in a creamy paste, wrapped in banana leaves and steamed.
- *Padang*   Playing field.
- *Pak*   Maternal uncle (Cantonese) or uncle (Malay).
- Pekalongan   City on the northern coast of central Java, Indonesia, famous for its *batek*.
- *Petai*   A bean with a distinctive taste and smell, popular in South East Asia.
- Picul   Unit of weight in South East Asia equal to one hundred catties, or approximately 60.4 kilograms.
- *Pinang*   The Malay word for the betel nut or areca nut palm tree.
- *Po-po*   Maternal grandmother.
- *Puan*   Malay for 'Mrs'.
- *Pulut*   Glutinous rice (Malay).
- *Rempah udang*   Type of savoury Nyonya *kueh* featuring prawns in a spicy paste.

- Rickshaw   A vehicle with a hood capable of seating two, pulled by a running coolie.
- *Sah Kim*   Third maternal aunt (Hokkien).
- *Sah Koo*   Third maternal uncle (Hokkien).
- Sambal   Spicy paste made of dried shrimp used as condiment or cooking base.
- Samfoo   A blouse and pair of loose trousers worn by Chinese women.
- Sampan   A small passenger boat made of wood.
- Sarong   Large tube of fabric worn around the waist by men and women.
- Sarong kebaya   Intricate top worn by Malay women, usually of sheer material, with sarong.
- *Sau*   Hakka for 'Mrs'.
- *Sayang*   'Love' (Malay).
- *Selamat pagi*   'Good morning' (Malay).
- *Seri muka*   Type of Nyonya *kueh* with an olive-green top and glutinous rice base.
- *Sinkeh*   A newly arrived Chinese immigrant.
- *Siow-chia*   'Miss' (Hokkien or Hakka).
- *Sireh* set   Set that contained all paraphernalia required for betel nut chewing.
- *Soh*   Cantonese or Hokkien for 'Mrs'.
- *Sui-hak*   An agent who recruited labour in South China.
- Swatow   Shantou.
- *Tai Fatt Shi*   Head priest.
- *Tai-tai*   'Madam' or 'mistress'.
- *Tau foo*   Tofu.

Selina Siak Chin Yoke

- *Toa Pek*   Eldest paternal uncle (Hokkien).
- *Toa Mm*   Eldest paternal aunt (Hokkien).
- Towkay   Chinese word for 'boss', taken to mean a rich tycoon.
- *Tsin-sang*   Cantonese or Hakka for 'Mr'.
- *Tuan*   'Sir' or 'master' (Malay).

ABOUT THE AUTHOR

Photo © 2014 AM London

Of Malaysian-Chinese heritage, Selina Siak Chin Yoke grew up listening to family stories and ancient legends, always knowing that one day she would write. After an eclectic life as a theoretical physicist, investment banker and trader in London, the heavens intervened. In 2009, Chin Yoke was diagnosed with cancer, the second major illness she had to battle. While recovering, she decided not to delay her dream of writing any longer. She is currently working on her second book and also writes a blog about Malaysia at www.chinyoke.wordpress.com.